DARKEST FEARS

AN ANTHOLOGY OF HORROR

STUART BEATON

Grosvenor House
Publishing Limited

This book is published by
Grosvenor House Publishing Ltd
Link House
140 The Broadway, Tolworth, Surrey, KT6 7HT.
www.grosvenorhousepublishing.co.uk

A CIP record for this book
is available from the British Library

Paperback ISBN 978-1-83615-094-7
Hardback ISBN 978-1-83615-095-4
eBook ISBN 978-1-83615-096-1

For my wife and our children,
without whom this book would never have existed.
With thanks, and all my love.

Contents

Preface

We're all afraid of something.

Whether it's ghosts, the dark, creepy-crawlies or that indefinable but perennial bogeyman, each of us has our favourite fear. Favourite? Yes, that's what I said. Go on, admit it, you like to be scared. That's why you read horror stories.

I've always been a horror fan. When I was a kid, I watched the old Universal monster movies whenever I could. To the pounding glam rock soundtrack of the early 1970s, I collected horror movie-themed bubble gum cards, built glow-in-the-dark monster model kits, and pored over giant books about scary films. When we had a fancy dress day at school, I was in my element. I terrorised the cowboys, spacemen and bunny wabbits by stalking the playground as Frankenstein's monster, complete with a bright green face and gory scar tissue (buckets of emerald eye shadow and blobs of ruby red lipstick which melted and streamed down my face in the summer heat). A moth-eaten old jacket set aside for Guy Fawkes and a solid steel neck bolt made by my dad completed the ensemble. I was ten. I enjoyed scaring the other kids. And they enjoyed being scared. I think.

My first foray into horror fiction was via those wonderfully lurid American horror comics; modern versions of the classic *Tales from the Crypt* that you could sometimes discover hidden away behind the *Spider-Man* and *Avengers* comics. I soon moved on to the *Pan Book of Horror Stories*, edited by Herbert Van Thal. Most unsuitable for an impressionable child! From there, I graduated to Stephen King and James Herbert. Then it was a hop, skip and a jump to Clive Barker, H.P. Lovecraft and Richard Laymon. I eventually cast my net far and wide, but short story collections were always my favourite.

In the mid-1980s, my place of work invested in a state-of-the-art computer for the sole purpose of managing spreadsheets. After a bit of poking around, I discovered that it also doubled as a kind of fancy typewriter. This was a revelation to me. Finally, there seemed to be a way of escaping the crushing tedium of office life. I settled down and began writing a story just to keep myself sane.

Energised by this new hobby, I bought an Amstrad, a bunch of floppy disks and a printer, and continued writing at home. I was pleased with the results and sent a couple of stories to magazines. Feedback was positive, but the repeated rewrites requested by editors to meet strict word count limits turned an enjoyable pastime into just another tedious admin job. Then came kids; free time became sparse. I quit the rewrites, sold the Amstrad and forgot about writing for several years.

A decade into the new century, still battling the monotonous futility of my job, I began to hammer out a new tranche of stories. And this time, no one was going to tell me I was over the word limit because I wouldn't be sending them off to any damned magazines. These stories were strictly for personal use. So there!

After a few years, however, I realised that I had amassed a significant body of work, and I started to wonder if perhaps others might enjoy reading the stories as much as I had enjoyed writing them. Hence this anthology which, I think, contains the best stuff I penned between 2009 and 2024.

I originally intended two or three smaller books and I've retained that principle here with three separate collections. The stories in Dark Harvest have a hint of the supernatural about them, in A Fistful of Horrors all the stories are set in the USA, and Flesh Crawlers has tales that are mostly rooted in earthly reality. Although I might have cheated a bit here and there so don't quote me.

Kurt Vonnegut said that when writing a short story, you should start as close to the end as possible, the general idea being to carjack the reader and drive them straight to their final destination, avoiding potholes and diversions along the way. Sound advice that I think I have mostly followed, although I do have a soft spot for stories within stories (a.k.a. cutaways, flashbacks or embedded narratives) and, occasionally, for stopping en route to smell the flowers and admire the scenery. Maybe those editors had a point.

There are other golden rules of writing. Don't use someone else's voice, for example. And write about what you know. I have broken both of these rules on several occasions. Be honest, though, would you rather read about a trip to the office or a trip to Mars?

Having said that, two of the stories in this book are cautionary tales based around a boring commute that suddenly becomes less boring. In fact, several of the stories have autobiographical elements. *Bad Brains* is based upon childhood weekends spent with my nan. She lived above an undertaker's in Wandsworth and we had to traipse through a maze of coffins to get to the gloomy, walled yard she tended out the back. One of the central elements in *Lithium*—the Bunsen burner incident—is rooted in a worrisome childhood event. In fact, *Lithium* has its origins in an idea I had during the Amstrad years for a portmanteau story. In my mind's eye, I still see it play out in our old maisonette in South Norwood where I wrote those early stories.

I abandoned most of my other efforts from that era and have not revisited them. *Flesh and Blood* is, however, another exception. It's a reworking of the first story I ever wrote back in the 1980s in that dreary office. The original version was about a young man visiting his taxidermist uncle. I was making it up as I went along and intended it to magically evolve into some kind of sophisticated James Bond spy caper. A plot, of sorts, did fall into place but it soon turned very dark. The punchline was that the uncle, who had served in the First World War, had a room full of stuffed

German soldiers. The updated version is somewhat more ghastly.

I know I shouldn't have a favourite child, but I do have a soft spot for *The Reaper*. My satisfaction with it prompted me to carry on writing. It recalls some of the dubious escapades of my own childhood and was written after a scorching holiday to Greece. It was also the first story I wrote that relied more on innuendo than gore. Not that I'm averse to a smidgin of gore now and then, as you will discover.

With that parental advisory firmly in mind, I invite you to take a journey into my world. After all, what are you afraid of?

Stuart Beaton
23 April 2024

I. DARK HARVEST

The Reaper

'The most merciful thing in the world, I think, is the inability
of the human mind to correlate all its contents.'
H.P. Lovecraft

1

Do you know what it means to be haunted?

I'm not talking about ghosts. That's not the only kind of
haunting. There's another kind, where an intangible horror
lurks at your shoulder, out of sight but always present.
It pollutes your dreams, tainting them with its poisonous
canker, dogging your journey through life. And if you
ever lower your guard, having convinced yourself that
you have finally shrugged off the phantom, you will feel a
cold gust of breath upon your neck, a little reminder that
it is still with you. Still watching. Still waiting. Still haunting
you.

I'm mulling this over while I wait for news, sitting here in
the back of a police car on a damp autumn morning. What
news? Well, crazy as it sounds, I'm hoping and praying that
some teenage kid I hardly know has died.

Oh, you think I'm some kind of a nut? Maybe I am. But
just hear me out.

It was four months ago when the phantom at my shoulder
chilled my spine with its icy whisper: *You didn't forget me, did
you, old friend? I haven't forgotten you.*

But I had no idea then that there was unfinished business
between us.

We were on holiday—Greece, half board, three stars. No
frills. It was the second week. We'd made the obligatory trip to
a wine-making monastery; fruitlessly scoured the local shops
for something worth buying, and were now resigned to the

inhumane torture of slow-roasting under a blinding Aegean sun for the next six days.

We were all playing our assigned roles. The kids were enjoying themselves thinking of suitable names for the people who had arrived the night before, I was plugged into a selection of classic rock, and the wife was flicking through a magazine without reading it, fidgety and bored.

A family of pastry-skinned newcomers had decided to investigate the pool area. A mum and dad, who looked roughly the same age as us, and a scrawny youth.

My own offspring, Sarah and Josh, were twenty and seventeen respectively, soon to fly the coop. Sarah had just become engaged to a twenty-one-year-old management consultant (whatever that is), a spring wedding on the horizon. Josh was already planning to go somewhere brighter and louder with his mates next year. Despite everyone's public protestations to the contrary, we all understood that this holiday would be our last together.

I spied the new family from behind the anonymity of my pound shop sunglasses. On closer examination, their son was younger than Josh. They would have him for a while longer.

They scanned the area around the pool, squinting, having yet to unpack their shades. The boy shucked off one of his trainers, ploughed the edge of the water with his toes and cheerfully informed his parents that it was quite warm.

Reconnaissance mission completed, they turned to go. As they did so, the man looked across the pool. Even though I was sure he couldn't penetrate the black plastic lenses, he locked eyes with me. Uncomfortable with his refusal to break contact, I looked away.

The family trooped up the steps towards the hotel, mother first, then son. The man followed behind. Emboldened by their retreat (and annoyed with myself at having been intimidated before) I resumed my inspection. When the man reached the top (and somehow I knew he was going to do this) he stopped and looked back.

This time I stared at him quite openly. But this was no petty act of macho posturing on my part. My motive was altogether different. For this time, I recognised him.

After what seemed like an eternity, his son called him. The man blinked, as though waking from a dream, and turned to follow his family into the hotel.

"What's up, misery guts? Too hot?" asked Cheryl.

I told her.

"Where from?" she asked.

"What?"

"Where do you recognise him from?"

I said I didn't know. I didn't add that I had a really bad feeling and frankly didn't want to know. I wondered if the man recognised me and hoped not, although I wasn't sure why.

Cheryl failed to notice my discomfort. She put her magazine down and sat up. The discovery of someone familiar out in Greece seemed to invigorate her. I had to switch off the music.

She suggested how I might know him. Given my limited circle of acquaintances, the possibilities were somewhat restricted. We agreed that he wasn't from the office. I'm not so addled that I wouldn't recognise someone I work with day in, day out. So she suggested that either I knew him from the journey to work, or I was mistaken. I agreed that I was indeed mistaken, clinging to the idea like a lifebelt in a stormy sea. Cheryl sighed and snapped open her magazine.

Weary of searing like four bellies of pork under a grill, that afternoon we embarked upon another excursion into town. I shuffled around the small, dusty souvenir shops in a self-induced trancelike state while I dredged through the deepest part of my mind, checking the man's features against the scrapbook of faces lurking down there in the sediment. But after a while my mental image of him became blurred, like an out of focus photo. By the time we had returned to the hotel, and with a curious sense of relief, I found that I no longer remembered what he looked like.

2

We were washed and dressed in evening wear in time for dinner. The scorching heat of the day had faded to an unpleasant stickiness and, in the dining room, a lazily rotating fan struggled to cut through the thick, warm air. The new arrivals, identifiable that morning by their paleness, were now marked out by their redness. The man was there, with his wife and boy in tow.

"There's a simple way of solving this," said Cheryl.

I knew what she was going to say. "You're not talking to them," I said, a little too sharply.

"Why not? This is the perfect chance to make friends. You know, human contact. Even if you're wrong and you don't actually know him, it's an icebreaker, isn't it?" She was talking to me like she talked to Josh.

"No, you can't do that. It's embarrassing," I hissed, like Josh. It *was* embarrassing. And I didn't need any friends. But those weren't my real objections. The sight of him across the small room, closer now and without the filter of darkened lenses, had triggered a bout of palpitations in my chest. I watched him carefully, but now only to avoid him as I ambled into line at the buffet. Nevertheless, he caught my eye. He had a full plate of souvlaki in his hands and I was convinced he was about to throw it all over me, so intense was his stare. So full of hate.

Despite the harshness of the overhead lighting, the room seemed to darken. "I need to get out of here," I blurted into Cheryl's ear, and I marched straight out of the room.

Outside, I leaned against a wall overlooking the swimming pool, sucking in a lungful of insipidly balmy air.

There was no respite from the heat, but being away from the man's gaze was relief enough. For now.

It was my daughter who hurried out to check on me.

"I remember that look," I said. "That look he gave me."

Sarah shook her head, confused. "Who? What look, Dad?"

My eyes were drawn beyond the rippling water of the pool, through hedgerows and a stand of shrivelled olive trees, until I found myself staring into acres of unlit fields. Our hotel was a little white island floating in an ink-black sea of nothing. "It's always there, isn't it?" I said. "The darkness. It just lurks there at the edge of everything, waiting to rush in."

I felt, rather than saw, Sarah shrug.

The night seemed to know what I meant. It stared back at me.

Minutes passed.

Josh joined us, chunk of humus-coated bread in hand.

"You two not eating?" he said.

The sound of crickets faded to a dull hiss and I was dimly aware of Sarah and Josh talking, though their words escaped me. My mind was wandering back through dark catacombs, lost in time.

Then my wife's voice brought me back to the present. It was like my ears popping on take-off. Suddenly everything was sharper, clearer. Horribly so.

Cheryl breezily informed us all that the man's wife was a snooty bitch, not our kind of people. "But she did tell me how you know her husband," she said gleefully.

I nodded. I was way ahead of her.

"You went to the same school. How weird is that? Do you remember—"

"Derek Chalmers," I said. "It's Derek fucking Chalmers." And so it was. Forty years older, slightly grey and somewhat taller. Derek fucking Chalmers.

Despite the cloying heat of the night, I shivered at the deathly chill of the phantom's breath on my neck: *You didn't forget me, did you, old friend? I haven't forgotten you.*

Cheryl was deflated, her thunder stolen. She admonished me for swearing in front of the children, in front of the waiter who was buzzing around, clattering plates and dripping sweat. She lowered her voice and spoke in tight little sentences.

Why don't I go and talk to Derek?

I told her that we weren't really friends. That was a lie. We had been friends, once.

That didn't matter, she said. We must have things in common. *People* in common.

I said I knew his brother.

She was triumphant. She suggested I could use that as an opening gambit. Maybe even get back in touch with his brother.

I laughed. Actually, it wasn't a laugh, but that cynical snort we make when something is so bitterly ridiculous that it doesn't deserve a response. Then I turned away to look at the pool again. Josh and Sarah had drifted off and were chatting to a group of teenagers.

"He's an outgoing boy, isn't he?" said Cheryl. "He's always made friends easily." She pursed her lips. "I don't want him to end up a paranoid loner like you." She inclined her head to one side and raised her eyebrows. The curious cockatoo impression was meant to provoke some kind of argument. I didn't take the bait. Instead, my gaze fixed steadfastly on the children, I told her a story.

The story.

Josh might never turn into me, but he was starting out exactly like me. I won't say I was the life and soul of the party when I was a kid. But I had friends. Plenty of friends. One in particular: Clive Chalmers, Derek's brother. Derek's twin brother.

3

Unless you come from somewhere nearby you probably won't have heard of the Flintwood Caves. They're not exactly a national treasure; more a local curiosity.

Situated beneath a chain of small hillocks that rise like cysts on the back of the Surrey Downs, the Flintwood Caves are a network of interconnected tunnels. In recent years archaeologists have speculated that the humps on the landscape might be Bronze Age barrows—the long forgotten burial chambers of ancient chieftains—but this is a modern idea. When Clive and I visited the caves, on what was then an obligatory school trip, we were given the more conventional explanation of a geological formation. Limestone. Chalk.

Along with the tedious geography lesson, as we were all led through the dank, manmade passageways that connected a series of natural caverns, we received the standard history lecture. We were told that for centuries the principal purpose of the excavations had been the mining of chalk and flint, an industry that continued, sporadically, until the middle of the nineteenth century. Yawn.

Local legend had it that the tunnels were begun before the Romans arrived two thousand years ago. Over the centuries, generations of miners dug new tunnels, widening the network and burrowing deeper and deeper into the limestone bedrock beneath the landscape. Double yawn.

Many of the caverns and walkways had been given quirky names: The Cathedral, The Echo Chamber, The Old Kent Road. But even this failed to stimulate much interest from the class as we shuffled through the dusty footpaths and caverns.

It was 1975. Derek, Clive and I were fourteen. Like most of the class, we didn't pay much attention to the dull, academic patter that the bearded guide was trotting out. But our ears pricked up when he finally got to the fun stuff—the deaths and the hauntings. The girls all groaned and there followed a few seconds of chaotic clamour while our teacher, Miss Bartlett, struggled to reassert her authority over us. Once silenced, we all started to listen rather more keenly than before.

Apparently, safety concerns were raised as long ago as the seventeenth century. Engineers working at the site were worried that the tunnels were ranging too far and too deep. Flooding was common and, over the years, dozens of men perished due to cave-ins. Mining finally stopped in the 1840s following a serious collapse at the furthest reaches of the caverns. Twenty-two men were lost in the ensuing flash flood when miners broke through to a previously unknown underground river. The place was boarded shut and abandoned.

Miss Bartlett overegged the pudding somewhat by asking us to imagine being trapped under a rockfall in the pitch blackness while the water level rose all around us. Some of the kids, Derek included, made suitably horrified noises, but Clive and I just sniggered. We knew the place must be safe or they wouldn't let coachloads of schoolchildren down there every week.

"If the roof fell in and we all died, it would cost them thousands in compensation," snorted Clive.

"Besides," added Derek, looking to his brother for reassurance, "we could always swim to safety, couldn't we?"

The guide pointed out that there would be nowhere to swim *to* in a sealed cave, and the water level would rise all the way to the low ceiling. "How long can you hold your breath?" he asked.

As if to stoke up the alarm that was spreading through the class, and to the increasing discomfort of Miss Bartlett, at the next turn he shone his torch into the corner of a cave where a large expanse of water lay like a distorted black mirror.

Barely four years after its closure, the guide informed us, the old mines hit the headlines again. A young farm labourer was arrested following the disappearance of an eighteen-year-old milkmaid from Flintwood village. The guide pointed up at the roof of the cave to indicate that said village was directly above our heads.

The farmhand claimed that they had been lovers, were planning to get married, and that the girl had ventured into the tunnels to lie with him beside one of the pools of her own free will. But in Victorian England that wasn't much of a defence at all. He was found guilty of murdering her and disposing of her body. He maintained his innocence even on the steps of the gallows. "It was the dark that took her!" he yelled as they tightened the noose. The crowd jeered. The trapdoor dropped.

Miss Bartlett broke the ensuing silence by asking the guide if this was the same chamber.

"Oh, yes, miss," he drawled, tapping a little nameplate that had been screwed into the wall at shoulder height. "They call this one the Reaper's Lair; a name it's had as long as anyone can remember. Legend has it, the killer weighed down the girl's body with loose rocks and let her sink. She drowned like a rat in a barrel. They never found the body."

"But wouldn't they have discovered her at the bottom?" asked Miss Bartlett.

"Not likely," said the guide. "The pool is as deep as Nelson's Column is tall, and it leads straight down into a subterranean river system. Anything that gets to the bottom of it won't ever see the light of day again."

Cue another outbreak of teenage muttering.

In the decades following the mine's closure, all kinds of wild stories evolved. The handful of daredevils who broke in through the barricade claimed to have seen ghosts of dead miners; of a drowned woman.

"Some even reckoned they caught a glimpse of some vast, unnameable creature lurking in the darkness," whispered our guide, with a knowing leer. He was milking his role for all it was worth.

Needless to say, there were more accidents in the treacherous, rocky maze of tunnels and caverns. Some adventurous souls didn't return to the surface alive. Or at all.

In 1964, seeing the potential of a 'haunted' cave, a local businessman bought the abandoned mine. He quickly gained permission to open it up as a tourist attraction. A tea room that doubled as a ticket office was built across the main entrance and the new owner set about publicising the Legendary Haunted Caves at Flintwood. As he had anticipated, in an era of lurid, technicolour Hammer horror films, the caves became a commercial success.

When our trip into the bowels of Surrey was over, we all milled about noisily in the shop, rifling through racks of sweets, postcards and keyrings. Miss Bartlett bought herself a mug of tea and drifted away from us to get some peace while she gazed up at a huge map of the caves on the wall. She was tracing our route with a fingertip. The Chalmers twins and I joined her.

We seemed to have spent hours trudging about underground, but the crude, veinous diagram suggested that we had barely dipped beneath the surface. The Reaper's Lair was the furthest point of our tour. The pool where the Victorian girl supposedly drowned was depicted as a black blob at the heart of the yellowing map. The whole thing was peppered with a bewildering array of similar blobs of varying sizes, and crabby zigzag lines representing the winding tunnels.

According to the sketchy drawing, at the furthest reaches, the tunnels simply faded away into inky black oblivion. For some reason that idea made my stomach squirm. I asked Miss Bartlett where they led, but before she could respond, a man's voice answered for her.

"The furthest tunnels are mostly flooded," said the guide who had come up behind us. "No one's gone down that far in years."

Then he and Miss Bartlett fell into stilted small talk. We had outstayed our welcome, so the twins and I exchanged eyebrow-twitching looks and turned away. But just then Clive saw a poster on the wall:

**Please note that the management have rescinded the wager to spend the night in the haunted caves.
All visitors must be accompanied by a guide.**

And in faded red letters at the bottom:

Entry to the caves after closing hours is strictly prohibited!

The notice was yellowed and cracked with age; the pins holding it, rusted. The hand-scrawled date at the bottom read 21 May 1964—eleven years earlier.

Clive's eyes lit up. He spun around and asked the guide about the wager. The bearded young man, who could have been no more than twenty but seemed incredibly old to us, said that it was part of a publicity stunt when the place was first opened to the public. He thought the poster should be taken down, but apparently some people still asked to take the challenge, so it had to stay. Kind of like a disclaimer.

"Basically," he explained, "if you could remain in the caves all night long, the owner would stump up one hundred quid."

"Neat publicity stunt," said Miss Bartlett. "But it must have cost them a fortune."

"Yes, he did have to pay out a couple of times before—" The guide checked himself. He looked around, lowered his voice. "Well, let's just say there was more than a financial reason for calling off the wager."

At that moment, there was a fanfare of squealing, hissing brakes and a growl of crunching gravel. Our coach had arrived outside. Rather superfluously, the driver blared the horn.

The puzzled smile on Miss Bartlett's face vanished with a start. The guide took a deep breath and stood aside.

"Madam, your carriage awaits," he said, sweeping his arms wide.

Like a gaggle of excited geese, we all trooped onto the coach for the journey back to south London.

"Probably a load of old twaddle," I said. The twins agreed. But we still wished Miss Bartlett had asked what had happened to put an end to the wager.

The official entrance to the caves was through the shop. From our vantage point high in the coach, it was plain to see that there was a second access point off to one side, covered by rickety wooden doors. When Clive and I returned three nights later, that was where we gained entry.

4

When you go into the tunnels with a guide, they hand out oil lamps. Power lines trailed along the walls for the first few yards but it was too costly to run them any further. Besides, the constant leaks into the tunnels made it too dangerous to electrify the whole network. The reason they use paraffin lamps instead of more modern battery-powered torches, they say, is that the bright light emitted by torches can damage eyes straining to see in the absolute blackness underground. What they don't say is that the grubby, oil-reeking lanterns also add to the atmosphere; they give out a weak, fluttering glow, and in the twitching shadows they create you can easily imagine you have seen something that isn't really there.

Clive and I took two regular torches and promised not to shine them in each other's eyes. By mutual consent we wouldn't go in too far. The bet, as we understood it, had simply required the fearless individuals to spend the night in the caves. For two teenage kids reared on Karloff and Cushing, it didn't seem too challenging a task, and we were more worried about the discomfort (and about our parents finding out) than spooks and monsters from the deep.

I'm not sure that we could have articulated, even to ourselves, the reason why we wanted to take up the challenge. We certainly weren't doing it for the reward money. We knew full well that the wager had long since been annulled, and we had no intention of telling the management, or anyone else, that we had broken in. It was just something we felt compelled to do.

The day before we set off, Derek backed out of the expedition, muttering darkly about the way the tunnels on the map just faded away. "I'll be your man back at base camp," he said, searching our eyes for agreement. "Explorers always have a base camp, don't they?"

Despite the merciless ribbing to which we subjected him, he collaborated in our deception. In fact, he was crucial to the plan. We had told our families that we were sleeping over at each other's houses. We had done that plenty of times before, staying up into the small hours reading comics and playing board games. Derek's cast iron assurance that Clive and I had safely arrived at the other's house had been so convincing that neither set of parents had felt the need to check up on their children that night. The simple ruse worked perfectly.

Getting into the caves was just as easy as we had thought it would be. The official entrance-cum-shop was well and truly locked up, but the ill-fitting wooden garage doors just a few yards away barely reached across the gaping cavern beyond and, as we had suspected, we could squeeze in through the side. In 1975 there were precious few security cameras about generally, and there were none at the caves.

"I can't believe how easy that was!" I said once we had scraped through the gap.

"Why? It's not like there's anything here worth nicking," said Clive. "No one in their right minds would want to break in."

We looked at each other and laughed. It was the last time we did.

Even though there was no one about, we unconsciously modified our voices to a hoarse whisper. Clive peered into the blackness in front of us. "Torches," he said quietly.

Still partly illuminated by moonlight seeping around the doors, we rummaged in our rucksacks. We were, we thought, well equipped for our nocturnal expedition. As well as the torches, we had a couple of nylon sleeping bags left over from school camp, an extra jumper to ward off the creeping cold, a couple of sandwiches and a bottle of Tizer. It was real *Boys' Own* stuff. I had even brought a small camera along, just in case there was something worth capturing on film. I didn't voice my fears to Clive but, deep down, I hoped that there would be nothing worth snapping and that the night would pass quietly and uneventfully.

I was unprepared for just how quiet it turned out to be.

As we made our way down the rocky path, we marked black arrows on the chalk walls with a stick of charcoal we had pinched from the school art room. Our crunching footfalls and the swishing of our rucksacks against our nylon parkas provided a reassuring background noise.

The deeper we plunged into the darkness, the colder we felt, and the chill made our noses run. We sniffed and swiped them on our sleeves, adding to the cacophony.

When we were being led by the guide, the grimy old lanterns he handed out to every third child filled the air with a reeking fug of paraffin oil. It had been a strangely comforting smell, probably because we had paraffin stoves at home in those days and I associated it with warmth, cosiness. In the absence of the pungent odour of the lamps, the caves smelled ancient and cold. The chalk walls and ceiling seemed to fill the chilled air with a cloying dustiness that instantly dried our throats and parched our lips. As we trudged along the tunnels, our feet kicked up more dust from the rocky, uneven surface and we stopped twice to take a swig from our rations.

"It's basically a straight run and then a right turn and then a left," gasped Clive between gulps of Tizer during our second stop. He was confident that he had memorised the route from the map on the wall of the souvenir shop. "Or left, and then right." He belched and pointed his torch down the passageway. The tunnel had been gouged out of the chalk with primitive tools centuries ago, and the striations on the illuminated walls ahead of us looked like a bleached ribcage.

We agreed that we would recognise our destination when we saw it.

After a further five minutes or so, and a few wrong turns, we did indeed reach our journey's end: the classroom-sized chamber that they called the Reaper's Lair.

We set down our kit. Suddenly, without the sound of the rucksacks rustling against our coats, it was suffocatingly quiet.

Clive strode over to the inky pool and peered down, aiming his torch into its icy depths. He panned the beam over the glassy water from left to right. "It moves," he said.

"What moves?"

"The pool. It kind of swirls. Ever so slowly." He twirled the torch in a lazy circle. "Round and round."

The pool was about 12 feet wide and abutted the far wall, which was another 12 to 15 feet beyond. Around the outer rim, it was fringed by a line of grubby chalk rocks the size of deflated footballs; a half-hearted safety measure. It appeared to be perfectly still to me; still and flat, like a sheet of black ice. I hung back a little and found some excuse to fiddle with my parka. "It looks bigger up close," I said.

Clive sank to his haunches. "Can you hear it?" he asked in a hoarse whisper.

I cocked my head to one side and cupped my ears. There was a glassy, plinking sound, like the string of a tiny harp being plucked somewhere in the distance, tuneless and out of time.

Clive knelt and leaned out over the edge. I could see his breath. It was as though the water was radiating coldness and he was descending into its own peculiar, frosty atmosphere. He turned his head to one side, listening. Something about him having his face so close to the water like that revolted me.

"Weird to think it's so deep," Clive began. "D'you think that milkmaid's body is still floating around down there somewhere?"

I edged further away from the pool. "Come on," I said. "Let's sort out our stuff."

Clive stood up and turned away from the water's edge. "Probably rotted down to her bones by now, eh?" he said. Then he saw my sickened expression. "We could go to a different cave if you like," he suggested. "This one is a bit chilly."

I looked through the four low archways that opened into our cave, so dark that they might have been bricked up and daubed with blackboard paint. They seemed to glare at us out of the white chalk walls like the blackberry eyes of a spider. I thought of those scratchy lines on the map, just petering out into oblivion, and wished that I had been the one to stay back at base camp instead of Derek. An endless tunnel or a bottomless pool? Some choice.

I told Clive we should probably stay put. At least we weren't too far from the surface and, provided our torches held out till morning, we could find our way out easily enough. He murmured agreement.

Then his eyes lit up. "I know! We should switch off the torches," he said. "Like the guide did."

I said that we ought to organise the beds first, but Clive was too excited to be deterred.

"We can do that in a minute," he huffed. "Let's try out the dark!" He was so keen on the idea that he had forgotten to whisper and his voice reverberated around the cavern so much that it sounded as if we were suddenly surrounded by an invisible crowd goading us to "Try out the dark! Try out the dark! Try out the dark!"

17

Clive switched off his torch. Under his admonishing gaze, I did likewise.

It was thoroughly disorientating. Like being deaf and blind. The guide had done the same thing during our trip a few days earlier but, of course, a class of thirty kids can never be completely quiet, and there had been plenty of sniggering and shuffling to spoil the effect. Now, with just the two of us, we could be truly silent.

I could hear the blood hissing in my ears; a deafening sound, like rushing water. Every small noise was disproportionately loud and drew my attention: our shoes crunching almost imperceptibly into the dust underfoot, even though we stood stock still; the soft rustle of our coats as our bodies turned to take in the utter nothingness; the sound of short, panting breaths leaking from our lips. I felt smothered, suffocated by a black miasma. The sensation was so intense that I thought I could *taste* the darkness.

I switched on my torch. Almost simultaneously, Clive did the same. We looked at each other, our eyes clenched against the glare. The look of shock on his face mirrored the rising panic I was feeling. At that moment, something passed between us; a shared, unspoken dread. A primal fear. Not of something lurking in the dark, but of the dark itself.

We kept both torches switched on as we unrolled the sleeping bags. They stayed on after we had sat down and taken out our sandwiches. The brightness and the rustling were an anchor of security in an ocean of blackness. We left the torches on as we burrowed into our makeshift beds and placed our bags behind our heads as pillows. The pool was no more than an arm's length behind us.

After a while the light around us began to yellow and flutter.

"Best turn them off," said Clive. "Else the batteries'll go."

We couldn't get out of there without a light. We wouldn't see the waypoints we had made. I thought of being plunged into that total darkness again, and of having to stumble along like blind men, groping for walls, hoping not to twist an ankle on the uneven floor or blunder into a bottomless pool. I thought of that wall map in the teashop and wondered where the last tunnels might lead us if we took a wrong turn.

"How about we turn off one of them and let the other stay on?" I asked.

Without hesitation, Clive agreed. "We'll save mine for the morning," he said. He turned off his torch and set it on the ground between our two sleeping bags. As his light went out, the darkness lurched towards us and was then instantly, almost agonisingly, held at bay by the light of the second torch, like a vast black dog being yanked back on its leash.

Clive became indistinct, ghostlike, and I could no longer see the end of his sleeping bag. It was as though he had been dissected. I had the stomach-churning feeling that the rest of the world outside the thin bubble of light which circled my head had been rubbed out. I swept the torchlight around the cavern, as if to fend off the darkness, but the ivory beam only served to alarm me further by illuminating distorted faces that appeared to writhe and lunge from the shadows of the jagged walls around us.

Any other time, left alone, our conversation crackled like static. We would laugh and joke about all kinds of stupid teenage things: comic books, films, football and girls. But that night our exchanges were subdued, monosyllabic. Neither of us was enjoying the adventure, yet neither of us would admit it.

"It's funny without Derek," said Clive quietly. It occurred to me that this was probably the first time they had ever slept apart.

I laid my torch on my chest, its beam drenching me in an oasis of waxy light, and settled back.

I was hoping to stay awake all night, but that didn't happen. At some point I must have drifted off because I woke with my face in a puddle of drool, stiff and aching from sleeping on the rocky ground. I blinked repeatedly but there was no difference between having my eyes open and having them closed. A tight knot of panic started to gather in the centre of my chest until it dawned on me that my torch must have died.

My watch had a luminous dial and once I had pushed up my sleeve it bled a toxic green light. So I hadn't gone blind after all.

3.26am.

I had slept a couple of hours.

I couldn't see Clive but I could hear his rapid breathing. He wriggled and muttered something unintelligible. He was having a dream. His sleep-induced gibberish, a series of agonised cries and livid outbursts, sounded like the florid ravings of a madman and echoed endlessly around the cavern.

I reached for the torch he had placed between us, the one we were saving for our departure (escape) in the morning. I knew that you're not supposed to wake someone in the throes of a nightmare but I had to see him, had to be sure that the body squirming around next to me was really my friend Clive and not something else. But just as I found the switch, he rolled away from me and fell silent.

"Clive?" I hissed.

I heard the nylon swish of his sleeping bag.

"Are you OK?" I asked the darkness.

There was an irritated rustling sound followed by a sigh. The cold metal torch felt wet, slippery, in my hand. He wouldn't thank me for waking him up fully nor for wasting the battery. I lay back on my rucksack, still holding the torch as though, even switched off, it was a talisman that could protect me from—Well, from what exactly?

The chamber was totally silent, so quiet that my ears began to ache. I stared into the void.

After a while, my senses heightened by the deprivation of light and sound, I started to notice the glassy plink of water and an almost imperceptible rumbling—the pool beside us; the underground river roaring distantly beneath us.

5

The next time I checked my watch it was after seven. I had slept again but I felt drained of energy and lay there looking into the same blackness that had been there when we had arrived the previous night, had been there four hours ago during Clive's nightmare, and had probably been there since the beginning of time.

"Clive? You awake?"

Nothing.

Clive's torch was still clutched in my fist.

"I'm switching the light on," I warned.

Still no reply. *To hell with it*, I thought. He'd had a good night's sleep, which was more than I'd had, and we needed to get out of there before someone caught us.

I narrowed my eyes to a slit and switched on the torch. Although its beam was jaundice-yellow and already starting to waver as the batteries drained, it was as though the sun had burst into the cave.

I pressed my forearm against my face to shield my eyes and let them gradually acclimatise to the sudden brightness. Off to my right, Clive's sleeping bag lay at a 90-degree angle to my own. He had rolled further away than I thought. I hauled myself out of my makeshift bed and, with the torch clenched between my knees, started to pack my gear away into the rucksack I had used as a pillow.

Clive didn't move.

"Hey, come on!" I said. "Let's get the hell out of here." Even though it was still as dark as it had been the night before, the fact that I knew it was daytime somehow lessened my fear. The light flickered and I shook the torch in the vain hope that it would make the batteries last longer.

21

I walked over and pressed the toe of my shoe gently against Clive's bed. Expecting to meet the solid resistance of his legs, a lightning bolt of panic streaked though me when the nylon sack simply gave way.

"Clive?"

I prodded it again. It was empty. I stood there for a good minute, immobile, convinced that he had somehow shrivelled up, or imploded, inside the sleeping bag.

I called his name again, louder this time. The echo reverberated like a horde of lunatics mocking me. "Clive! Clive! Clive!"

I felt sick.

Perhaps he had got up in the night, sometime after his bad dream, and simply fled? But without the torch? No. Not even the guides could navigate the tunnels without their stinking lanterns. Clive might have been afraid, but he wasn't a fool. Besides, he couldn't have gone a yard without banging into a wall or cracking his head on a low ceiling.

It dawned on me that perhaps that's exactly what had happened. Had he got up, muzzy with sleep, stumbled into something and knocked himself out?

I heard that dripping noise over at the pool and shone the beam at it. Flat and glassy as ever. The black water was no more than a yard from where we had slept. I convinced myself that if Clive had fallen in, I would have been woken by the sounds of him splashing and crying out. But what if he had fallen into another pool, in another chamber? The map had been rotten with black splotches and smudges.

I hurriedly dismissed the idea. I had slept fitfully and lightly. If anything that dramatic had happened I would have known about it. The only excitement for the past eight hours had been Clive's nightmare, and that had ended as quickly as it had begun.

I spent five minutes gingerly creeping through the nearby tunnels and alcoves, hoping I wouldn't find him sprawled on a pile of rubble with blood pouring from his head. Then, more alarmed at his absence than at what might have befallen him, I spent a further fifteen minutes carefully probing the same caverns hoping that I *would* find him sprawled on a pile of rubble with blood pouring from his head. That, I decided, I could deal with.

Never once did it occur to me that Clive was playing a prank. The fun had gone out of the whole escapade almost as soon as we had entered the caves the night before. Neither of us was in the mood for silly games.

Sweating despite the damp chill, and at a loss to know what else to do, I put the fading torch under my armpit and gathered up Clive's belongings. If I delayed any longer, I would be stranded there—alone. I took a few deep breaths to try and steady my racing heart before leaving the cavern.

Following the black arrows we had marked on the way in, I stumbled frantically towards the surface, desperate to get out of there before the torch finally died. When I reached the place where we had entered the night before, I shouted breathlessly into the tunnels behind me. "I'll come back for you!"

But the promise was a lie. I knew I would never set foot in there again.

I stepped out into the monochrome half-light of a misty autumn morning. Up in the skeletal trees surrounding the site, crows cried raucously at my sudden appearance, flapping their ebony wings and shaking the last of the year's leaves from oily grey branches.

The cool fresh air bore with it the musty aroma of damp soil and dying vegetation. It washed away the dust and grime of the caves from my burning lungs and I gulped it down thirstily.

I set down our rucksacks. Did Clive's feel damp or was it just the cold? Perhaps I should have checked our chamber more closely for clues—signs of water on the ground close to Clive's head, or scuff marks in the dirt—something that might tell me what had happened to my friend. I felt that I hadn't done enough. I was miserable and lonely, and a bleak veil of guilt descended over me; a gloomy shroud that I have worn ever since.

The crows glowered gravely down at me, like a tribunal of black-robed judges passing their verdict on my cowardice and treachery. As I stood there watching them, I realised two things: Clive would never be found, and I had just walked away from something terrible.

But I had not outwitted the nameless thing that had silently eavesdropped on our frightened whispers. I had not conquered it, and I had not escaped it. It was no rubber suit monster from the movies with a zipper up the back, and I was no plucky schoolboy hero. No. That thing—that *darkness*— had watched us, had *tasted* us; had savoured our fear. With Clive, it had gone one step further. Clive had been swallowed down, whole. I, on the other hand, had been spat out as though I were no more than a fishbone or a piece of gristle.

There's not much more to tell. I walked the half mile or so to the village and told the first adult I met that I had lost my friend. The rest of that day was a kaleidoscope of uniforms and flashing blue lights, all seen through a blurry haze of tears and bewilderment. Questions, crackling radios, parents, policemen, stern looks, worried looks.

Someone handed me some oxtail soup in a plastic cup. It was too hot to hold and the smell made me vomit. I hoped that being sick would purge the black terror swirling in the pit of my stomach. But it never did.

After they had made me repeat the story a dozen times, they started a different line of questioning. Had Clive and I been drinking? Had I heard of something called LSD? Had we argued? At the time, I didn't understand what they were driving at.

Convinced that I knew more than I was letting on, the police confiscated most of the items I had taken into the cave.

My mum and dad were politely informed that I wasn't a suspect; I was a witness. *The* witness. But witness to what?

A week or so later, I was back at school. I had no physical injuries but I felt different now, like something had been amputated. People looked at me oddly and I seemed to have no one to talk to anymore. One day I had a best friend; the next I had no friends at all. I walked to school alone. In the classroom, I sat next to an empty desk. In the playground, I stood by myself and tried to blot out the idiotic sounds of the screaming, laughing children around me.

Nothing came of the veiled accusations. There was no official conclusion to it. Gaps between visitations by investigating police officers became longer until they eventually stopped coming altogether. After several months had passed, I received a parcel in the post containing my belongings: my rucksack, my anorak, my torch and even my empty bottle of Tizer. An accompanying letter merely listed the items but I was never told that the case had been closed. I waited for another knock at the door for many years.

6

If it was difficult for me to come to terms with, it must have been impossible for Clive's family. One day Mr and Mrs Chalmers had two teenage sons; the next, they had one. No body to bury. No explanation. No closure.

Did they hold out some hope that one day Clive would turn up somewhere and everything would be back to normal? I expect so. Did they enter the new decade of the 1980s, five years later, still clinging to that hope? Perhaps. Did they ever accept that they would never know what had happened to their son? I don't know.

Before the—The *what*? The accident? The incident? Forty years on, I still don't know what to call it. Anyway, before that night, I had been a regular visitor at Clive's house after school and at weekends. His mum would make us beans on toast and his dad would make lame jokes about me eating them out of house and home. After that night I never saw them again. I wanted to, just to tell them it wasn't my fault. But I didn't know how they would be with me. Maybe if I had asked Clive's brother, I would have had some idea.

Derek had been our anchorman back at base camp. It's no exaggeration to say that if Derek hadn't played his part in the deception, Clive and I would never have embarked upon the grim venture. But after that night, Derek and I never spoke again.

It was a small suburban school. The Chalmers twins and I had been in the same class, of course, and it was impossible for the pair of us (the two remaining conspirators, if you like) to avoid each other. Derek didn't accuse me of anything or threaten me. Nothing like that. But I would catch him looking at me. Sometimes I would see a challenge in his stare, as if he was seeking some kind of confrontation. Other times, his doleful gaze was glassy and impenetrable, like the bottomless black water of the pool in the Reaper's Lair.

The Flintwood Caves are still open. Clive's disappearance in 1975 meant the end of school trips but it fuelled the stories surrounding the place, and guided tours by lamplight continue to this day. I don't know what they say when they get to the pool and I don't know how I would feel if I learned that Clive's disappearance had become part of the legend, but I'm pretty sure he would have been chuffed to be starring in his own horror story.

I've driven past the caves a few times since then. Not deliberately, of course, not to see the place. The very idea of it sickens me. But sometimes I find myself there. Just getting from A to B, you know?

On the last occasion, I saw banners advertising the caves as a venue for role-play games. Apparently, tribes of luridly-costumed nerds trek through the tunnels, acting out comic book fantasies. I wonder how far they go, and how long they stay. And do they ever turn out the lights?

Anyway, that's where my story should have ended.

That night in Greece, Cheryl gave me a look like the kids at school gave me, kind of sympathetic but tinged with an ill-concealed air of suspicion. By now we had settled at an outside table. The hotel management was trying to entertain the guests gathered around the pool with a slightly distorted tape of traditional Greek music. A cool breeze had blown away the last of the day's heat and a skinny lizard was skittering up the wall beside us, desperate to steal some warmth from the guttering candle on our table. Cheryl was oblivious to the creature. She set down her Prosecco and asked me the same question that the police had asked countless times all those years ago:

"You *really* don't know what happened to him?"

I didn't answer her. I don't know what took Clive Chalmers. I don't want to know. But whatever it was—whatever it is—I have felt its presence down the years. It has always been with me. It is there when the lights are out, when I am alone, its cold breath against my neck, like the sigh of a spurned lover hungry for a reunion.

I said at the beginning that I felt haunted. Maybe that's not quite right. It feels more as though whatever took Clive tied a thread to me, a thread that connects me invisibly to the caves. And, every now and then, it tugs on the line.

Hey, remember me? Remember our brief embrace?

Yes, I remember. How can I forget?

But as the years passed, I became sure that it could never reach me. I'd had a close shave 40 years ago but I had survived. I convinced myself that as long as I stayed outside its subterranean realm, I would remain safe, untouched.

I was wrong.

7

The next day at breakfast Cheryl nudged me and I looked up from my coffee and toast. Derek Chalmers was staring. Not at me, but out at the hotel's swimming pool, just as I had done the night before. I suppose there was something pulling at him, too.

I looked away, but not before catching an exchange of puzzled glances between Josh and Sarah. Busy socialising, they hadn't been privy to my story, my confession, the previous night.

Cheryl mouthed, "I'll tell you later" to them.

That day, I stayed by the pool while the rest of the clan went to the shops once more, in a final bid to find something worth squandering our last handful of Euros on. I didn't see Derek all day and I had the nauseous feeling that he would confront my family in town. I don't know what he could have hoped to gain from that but the idea nagged at me, made me restless. Sitting alone in the sweltering heat, I even rehearsed my defence:

"You could have stopped it," I would have said. "But you let him go!"

I needn't have worried. Around four in the afternoon, a sweaty and sunburnt Chalmers family trudged into the hotel laden with beach towels.

Shortly after, Cheryl and the kids returned from their shopping trip. Josh couldn't contain himself. He hurried over to me, eyes wide and mouth agape. Cheryl had told them.

His reaction made me shrivel inside. Unlike Cheryl and Sarah, he wasn't shocked or horrified by the story. He thought it was... cool.

I should have taken that as a warning.

I said at the beginning that I wished someone was dead. That sounds harsh, doesn't it? Let me explain.

Thousands of people have been down into the Flintwood Caves over the years. Thousands have returned to the surface, dazzled by the sudden light of day but none the worse for their brief foray into those endless catacombs.

But every now and then someone stays down there. It happened to the milkmaid. And it happened to Clive. I expect it has happened to others. After all, why was that particular cavern called the Reaper's Lair? And what made the owner revoke his bet? Did someone disappear in 1964? I believe so.

What does all that tell me? Well, it tells me that whatever it is that swallows people down there, it isn't greedy. It strikes once in a blue moon, reaping a slow and steady harvest that suffices to fan the flames of urban legend but does not provoke any lasting public concern and, most importantly, does not deter the curious, the sceptical from recklessly entering its dark domain.

Right now, I'm sitting in the back of a police car for the first time in 40 years. Early morning, just like before. My wife and daughter are waiting expectantly at the same ill-concealed side-opening to the Flintwood Caves that Clive and I had used. I know I should be standing there with them, comforting them, but I can't stare into that darkness again.

My attention is focussed on the small, faded black and white photograph clutched in my hand.

When Clive and I spent our night in the caves, the world was a smaller, quieter place. In retrospect, probably a lonelier place. No internet. No mobile phones. If you were out and about, unless you hunted down a payphone that hadn't been vandalised, you were incommunicado. Not so anymore. Nowadays, it seems, you are never alone.

Last evening, I dropped Josh at his friend's house, where they were due to spend the night playing the latest ultra-violent zombie apocalypse game. At around one in the morning, Sarah received a text that bothered her enough to wake us up. It was from Josh.

Txt me if u get this. Want to test signal here.

She texted him back but her phone told her that her reply was undeliverable. Cheryl and Sarah didn't understand his cryptic message. But the meaning came to me sickeningly quickly.

Perverse as it sounds, it was almost a relief. It felt as though I had been waiting for something like this to happen for most of my life; waiting to finish the game that Clive and I had begun; waiting for my phantom to stop its incessant whispering and finally unveil the horror that had been looming over me all these years.

You didn't forget me, did you, old friend? I haven't forgotten you.

It's not as misty today as it was on that morning in 1975, but the crows are still up there in the leafless autumn trees, brooding over those ugly swellings on the landscape that conceal the dark labyrinth beneath, standing sentinel at the gates of hell.

Amongst the stuff that the police eventually returned to me was my camera and a thin Kodak envelope. Clive and I hadn't taken any photographs that night but the police had developed the film anyway. Inside the envelope was a reel of brown celluloid negatives, all blank, save for one, which had been printed on glossy seven-by-five-inch photo paper.

I imagine that the photograph was the reason the police lost interest in me.

There's some movement outside the entrance, where the purple and green banners belonging to the role-players hang limp in the damp, still air. The crests on the sorry-looking flags are of mythological creatures: fire-breathing dragons, hook-beaked birds of prey and tangled serpents.

None of these exotic creatures appear in the slightly out-of-focus little snap that I've kept hidden away all these years. It isn't a picture of a monster. It's a picture of me and Clive. Sleeping. Side by side.

Now I'm watching closely, intently, as yellow-jacketed searchers emerge from the caves. Walking slowly between the rescue team is one stooped figure, shrouded in a red blanket. Just the one; for only one will be allowed to leave. The figure is tall and slim, like my son. My only hope is that the Reaper has taken his friend.

Lambs to the Slaughter

Doogie rolled up the sleeves of his sweater and plunged his fists into the washing-up bowl. Through the window above the sink, he gazed out towards Lochranna. It had been a week now and no bastard had come. Not the police, not the army. Not even old Gordon from the post office, who sailed over once a week to deliver the few bits of shopping that Doogie might ask Morag to set aside. What the blazes was the matter with them? Had they not seen the fireworks? Had they not heard the unholy racket? And surely the fact that he hadn't phoned them to place an order for milk or eggs or his weekly half bottle of whisky should be ringing alarm bells by now? *Jesus wept*, he thought. *Is this what's going to happen if I ever take a fall or go down with the flu? Would the mainlanders just leave me here to rot?*

Doogie sighed. He must have made the short journey across the bay to the tiny port a thousand times over the years. Two bloody miles, that's all. So near; so damned near.

The thought reminded him of the wounds he received when he had tried it Wednesday evening. Nothing too serious, mind. A couple of streaks of burned flesh across his back that he bound in an old bath towel to soak up the blood. Still, the cuts were sore and his trusty old boat was now so many pieces of charred timber bobbing around the dock. The incident had served its purpose. A warning. He wouldn't be trying to escape again.

He put the plate on the drainer and swilled out the bowl, glad that he still had the old fireplace to heat water now that the electricity was gone. But it was November and the first frosts were bringing a sparkle to the land of a morning; a reminder that the harsh Highland winter would be upon him all too soon. He would be running out of logs to burn before another week was out. Then what? There were no trees on the island worthy of the name. The bitter Atlantic winds ensured that only the hardiest shrubs could survive out here. His island was the very definition of bleak. It was little wonder that everyone else had gradually migrated to the mainland over the years. Sheep farming on a western isle was an unappealing fate for the young, and a grim way of life for all but the stubborn or foolhardy. And, Doogie conceded, he was probably both.

He drew in a heavy breath. No, he couldn't wait for a rescue party that might never come. And he wouldn't stay here to wither away from hypothermia. Or worse. It was time to act now, while he still had the strength. He would do it today. He would try to kill the damned thing and be done with the whole business. If he failed, so be it, but he wouldn't go quietly. He would die hard—bloody hard.

Then he heard a familiar sound in the doorway behind him. *Thump-shuffle-thump.*

Doogie's unwelcome guest had appropriated his shepherd's crook to use as a walking stick, and that noise it made as it roamed the cramped little cottage had become maddening. *Thump-shuffle-thump. Thump-shuffle-thump.* Daytime, night-time, for the damned thing never slept, but drifted about the place like a ghost in search of its chains.

"You've just eaten, damn you," said Doogie without turning around. "The blood on your claws is still wet." And, he guessed, still warm.

A thump. A shuffle. And silence.

Three head of sheep, for God's sake. He could ill afford such a loss.

"I'm not fetching another for you. Not so soon, ya greedy bastard." Sheer bravado, of course. Doogie knew he would sacrifice as much of his livestock as his crippled guest demanded. For what else would it eat?

It was a pointless conversation, anyway. The thing plainly did not understand English. Or the Gaelic, in which tongue Doogie had frequently and ripely cursed it over the past few days.

Thump-shuffle-thump. It limped across the kitchen and pushed the back door ajar. And, when he saw the crablike pincer raise another little divot in the wood, Doogie tutted, "Again? D'ye no have paintwork where ye come from, ye clumsy shite?"

Each evening Doogie's guest had gazed out across the bay like this, seemingly mesmerised by the short stretch of ocean that separated the isle from the mainland.

"I've told ye before, if ye want to hop over to Lochranna I'll not hold you back. To be honest, the town doesn't amount to much but they've a nice wee pub and the mobile library calls once a month."

And there's a nice wee police station too, thought Doogie. And, less than five miles away, a bloody great submarine base full of MOD types who would love to get their mitts on a real live alien.

The creature looked down at its leg, damaged during the crash-landing seven nights ago. Its yellow shell (part of its body, Doogie had deduced, and not a suit of armour as he had initially thought) was split open from thigh to ankle and the shattered limb could barely hold the alien's weight.

Doogie rubbed his throbbing back and sighed. "You know, I still have ma old dinghy somewhere. Used to sail it across the reach every week before I bought that nice wooden boat ye burned up with your fancy ray gun."

Aye, he mused, and the orange inflatable had last seen the light of day ten years ago, before his seventh decade had taken its toll on his strength and agility. No reason to suspect it wasn't seaworthy, but steering that rubber balloon across two miles of swirling Atlantic with his new friend bouncing around beside him wasn't a prospect Doogie relished.

"If you could keep those pointy fingers out of harm's way, I'll have a bloody good try at sailing her over there one more time."

Aye, he thought. *And while we're out there riding the waves, maybe we'll see if you're the kind of alien that sinks or swims.*

"I wonder, do they even have sea where you come from? Is that why it fascinates you?"

The creature stood motionless facing the bay.

"And when I get over there, I shall ask old Gordon what's been keepin' him," growled Doogie. "I'm running out of milk here and he knows I cannae stand ma tea without a drop of milk. So, how's about it, eh? D'ye fancy a wee ride?"

The alien turned away from the door and limped back through the kitchen.

Doogie picked up a bread knife from the drainer, still wet, and glared at the creature's curved, spiny back. He sighed. "I'm trying to tell ye that ye've outstayed your welcome, ye blasted monstrosity. And if ye still won't take the hint, I'll be just as happy to escort ye to your grave right here and now."

Both the electricity and the phone line had been dead since the alien's craft had smashed into the island last Monday evening. Doogie cursed himself for eschewing a mobile phone. At night, he fantasised about calling up Lochranna on one of those pocket-sized gadgets and then watching Gordon dutifully sail up to the dock in that letterbox-red motorboat of his. He pictured the look on the old boy's face as he explained. "See here, Gordy. Allow me to introduce ma new chum. In case you couldn't tell, he's one of those spacemen, like you see in the films. Being as how you're the only official person within five miles, I'm handing him over to your custody." He would give Gordon fair warning, of course. "By the way, old pal, ye don't wanna upset him at all. He has this laser thingy and he's no shy about using it."

It would kill Gordon of course. And then it would eat the old postmaster, ripping him open, just as it had ripped apart its own injured compatriots as they lay trapped in the blazing wreckage; just as it had ripped apart three of Doogie's sheep and his faithful old collie, Moira. It was ravenous, insatiable and Doogie knew that the only reason his own life had been spared so far was because he could shepherd food into the barn. With no other farmers remaining, Doogie's livestock had the run of the island. And run they did; across the bumpy grassland, up and down the rocky outcrops, and all along the stony shoreline. The crippled monster couldn't hope to catch the sheep by itself. For the time being, it had little choice but to tolerate Doogie's presence, and his dark mutterings. It needed him. That, Doogie reasoned, was the one advantage he had over it. And, he decided, it was the factor that would seal the creature's fate.

The alien, a seemingly impossible combination of crustacean, arachnid and locust, turned to face the farmer. Its tusks moved, almost daintily, clicking softly together. A shiver of fear raced through Doogie and he tightened his grip on the blade. Could it understand him after all? He had never heard the thing make any sound other than the shuffling of its chitinous feet on the floorboards and the click of its spiny fingers. Doogie's conversations with it were nothing more than monologues, designed to keep his own creeping insanity at bay. Or so he thought. But what if it could read his mind?

Doogie took up the tea towel, dried the knife and put it in its drawer. The thin blade wasn't up to the job anyway.

The creature turned away and walked out of the kitchen, along the narrow hallway and out the front door. Doogie wiped his hands on his jersey and followed it out to the barn, where it had set up home, seemingly oblivious to the cold and the stench from the mangled carcasses of the animals it had slaughtered. It squatted among the puddles of blood, shards of bone and sheets of skin, as though it were settling down on a comfy sofa to watch its favourite soap opera.

"OK, then. Just one more time," said Doogie. "But this would be a whole lot easier if you hadna murdered poor old Moira, ye ugly bastard."

He marched out of the cottage and scoured the island for the biggest sheep in the herd.

It was Moira's death that gave Doogie hope. For when the spirited old collie had discovered the alien crouched over its dead comrades, chowing down on their exposed innards, the creature had panicked and struck out with one of its spiny talons. The agile dog evaded the blow and instantly realised that this new arrival was a threat. Doogie, who had followed her out to the end field to investigate the source of the sudden explosion, watched in horror as Moira darted low, seizing the creature by its injured leg. The alien had fallen to the ground, its mangled limb in the firm grip of the dog's jaws. Moira shook her head, snarling the way she did whenever she caught a rat in the outhouse, and the alien thrashed helplessly in silent agony.

Then there was a crackle of static, and Moira lay dead.

Doogie had stood there, legs shaking, dumbstruck by the scene before him. A tarnished bronze machine the size of his cottage was half buried in the ground. Chunks of tangled metal and a multitude of little fires were scattered over every inch of Doogie's modest island domain. Lying sprawled on the scorched earth, clutching a twisted contraption that dripped gobbets of flame, a monster from his worst nightmares.

But Moira had not died in vain. She had taught Doogie something. Beneath its pus-yellow shell, the monster was vulnerable and, despite its pitiless capacity for killing, it could feel pain.

Even so, Doogie came to realise over the following week, if he was going to kill it, he would have to break right through that armour plate to get to its vitals: its heart, its lungs, its brain. Did it even have such earthly organs? And, if so, were they kept in the same place as ours?

The impact of the crash had smashed one leg but how much force had that taken? Just how dense was its exoskeleton? Doogie had visions of stabbing away furiously, while the alien just looked at him, amused at his fleshy human weakness. Not that it could smile, of course. The head, in common with the rest of its body, had no skin or muscle and was dominated by a set of interlocking mandibles that ill-concealed glistening silver-grey fangs roughly the size and shape of knitting needles.

A myriad of black globes and nodules ringed its skull. If they were, as Doogie suspected, a crown of eyes, they must give the creature a full 360 degrees of vision. How on earth could he hope to take such a monster unawares?

And then there were the elongated arms that ended in a bewildering array of razor-sharp points, claws and hooks; a Swiss Army knife of limbs, equally capable of working complex instruments on a spacecraft and, as Doogie had witnessed, ripping apart the carcasses of sheep and fellow aliens alike.

Perched squarely on a bale of hay with its gammy leg stretched out before it, the creature gently tinkered with an aluminium box bristling with amber lights that it had retrieved from the crash site. Beside it, the polished steel spiral that served as a gun. Even their technology was singularly ugly, thought Doogie; things of dull, stained metal, adorned with twisted antennae and scabrous, dark bulbs.

It appeared to be deep in thought, pushing tiny buttons and twisting little dials with its multiple, pointed digits. Every now and then, the box emitted an almost inaudible scratchy, squeaking noise.

Still worried about the creature's possible telepathic powers, Doogie tried to think of something other than his plan to wreak death upon it.

"If you're trying pick up the shipping forecast on that thing, I wouldn't bother. The reception's been rubbish lately," he said.

The creature looked up from the contraption. If it suspected what the old farmer was up to, those bulbs of polished coal encircling its head gave nothing away.

"Here's your second breakfast of the day, then," said Doogie, panting with exertion and anticipation as he steered the hefty ewe sideways through the open barn door. "Brunch, I suppose they'd call it on the mainland." He took a deep breath and added airily, "Clouding over out there, I see. Maybe a drop of snow on the cards. D'ye no feel it in the air?"

The creature stared past Doogie at the darkening sky, seemingly equally oblivious to the damp weather and to Doogie's clumsy small talk.

Very well, thought Doogie. *Here we go, then.*

"Cold-blooded are ye?" he asked. "Well, let's see if we can spill some and find out, shall we?" He shoved the sheep to one side and pulled the shotgun out from behind it. The alien recognised the threat instantly and raised its spindly talons to shield its face. Doogie fired. The monster fell backwards onto the barn floor, into the discarded skin and fur and spilled blood of its previous meals. The tin box, now lying on the floor where the creature had dropped it, began to flash and squeal furiously.

Ears ringing from the blast, Doogie clambered over the bale, simultaneously cracking open the gun to eject the spent shells and fumbling in his pockets for two more rounds. A pall of choking cordite smothered his face and he had to wave it away before he could inspect the result of his work.

The extraterrestrial lay on its side, one claw pressed to its oozing grape-eyes, the other scrabbling blindly among the gruesome debris.

Doogie realised what it was searching for. He knelt on the upturned hay bale and snapped the shotgun closed. "Oh no you don't, pal," he said, levelling the gun at the prone creature. But he was too late. The alien swept up its weapon— an elongated metallic coil that more closely resembled an antique knuckle-duster than a pistol—and the air filled with a familiar crackle. Instinctively, Doogie ducked low as the amber laser beam chased around the walls and ceiling of the barn in a broad arc, carving a steaming black trail through bricks and beams alike.

The sharp, clean smell of ozone mingled with the stench of spent shotgun shells, and Doogie felt a searing pain somewhere on his chest that matched the stinging burn the thing had already inflicted upon his back. But he had no time to inspect the damage; the alien had pulled itself upright and was crawling towards him, its jaws flexing open and closed just inches from his face.

In that split-second, Doogie knew what he had to do.

"Still hungry, ye ugly fuck?" he gasped. "Well, eat this!" He rammed the gun barrel into the creature's gaping mouthparts and crushed the twin triggers in his fist.

*

"Could have been worse," he said to himself. "Could have been a lot worse."

The laser had bored a hole through the skin and muscle of his left shoulder but the wound had been instantly self-cauterized and the Glenmorangie was helping to ease the pain and steady his nerves at the same time.

He stood at the back door, the way the alien used to, and swirled the final drop of whisky around the tumbler. The crumpled orange dinghy lay at his feet. It was a misty day over on the mainland, as though the clouds had slipped down from the mountains beyond to smother Lochranna. "Jesus," he whispered. "I've just slain a merciless cannibal from outer space and I'm frightened of a wee dinghy ride."

Doogie glanced down at the strange gadget that the late, unlamented alien had been toying with. He hadn't dared touch the laser gun for fear of it going off in his face but he wanted something to show the folk in Lochranna so they wouldn't think he was crazy when he blurted out his incredible tale.

He had half a mind to bring the creature's head, but the shotgun had rendered it into a jigsaw puzzle and he didn't have a box-top picture to remind him how to piece the monstrosity together. The freaky little box would suffice. The folk at the submarine pens could chance their arms on the gun.

He watched the ocean slowly undulate and took one last gulp.

And then he saw it. Rising and falling with the swell of the Atlantic, and heading towards him. Gordon's bright red boat.

A jolt of elation rushed through him.

"About bloody time!" he shouted, slamming the empty glass down on the kitchen table. Doogie pocketed the alien gadget and ran out of the cottage.

"Boy, have I got a story for you, Gordy! Have I got a story for you!" he yelled as he hurried down the steep rocky path to the dock.

As the boat came closer Doogie saw a few of the usual little cardboard boxes that Gordon used when bringing Doogie's supplies across the bay. Too few. Instead, the little boat was filled with overstuffed bin liners and what looked like a couple of bulging suitcases. Perhaps Gordon had decided to treat him to some just-out-of-date goodies? He laughed at the idea. That didn't sound much like the Gordon he knew.

Then he saw that Gordon was not alone. He had a passenger. Doogie's euphoria ebbed and a small thrill of alarm coursed through him. He wondered if killing an alien was against the law. Telling daft old Gordon was one thing. He wasn't sure he wanted the whole world to know.

"Ah, for God's sake," he said, shaking his head. "It was self-defence. The bloody thing would've eaten me once it ran out of sheep."

As the boat drew up alongside the dock, Doogie saw that the figure crouching behind Gordon was Gordon's wife, Morag. The couple looked decidedly dishevelled, as though they had not slept for days. Doogie had never known Morag take to the sea before. She had a phobia.

This wasn't right. This wasn't right at all. Doogie felt his insides start to twist.

He raised a hand to wave at them.

Morag's scream pierced the silence.

Gordon stopped rowing. His eyes, dark-ringed and liquid with fear, fixed upon the squawking metal box Doogie had, in his excitement, pulled from his coat pocket; a thing of unique ugliness.

Doogie looked away from the boat and found himself imitating his erstwhile guest once more. He scanned the horizon, his eyes alighting on the huddled white buildings across the bay that comprised the tiny port of Lochranna.

He had been wrong about the weather. It was a clear enough day. There was no mist. No cloud. Just a column of gunmetal grey smoke rising lazily into a crystal blue sky.

Lithium

'The past is never dead. It's not even past.'
William Faulkner

Part 1: The Commission

The phone rang. The sound sent a rock plummeting deep into his guts.

He looked away from the old handset and found himself staring out of the grime-opaque window. Croydon didn't look so bad when you could hardly see it. The mucky glass was vaguely reminiscent of '70s porn; the lens smeared with Vaseline to soften the picture and make it less sordid. He wondered if the accumulated dirt and dust obscured the view into the house too. In the absence of curtains, it was his only hope of hiding.

Matt smiled. Who was he kidding, cowering on the floor of an upstairs room, thinking he couldn't be seen? They didn't need to see him. They were right there with him.

The phone kept ringing. It shouldn't do that. He had ripped out the wire a month ago. He could try smashing it with a hammer. Or burning it. Or throwing it out of that grubby window.

Matt eyed the torn-out cord, lying limp and suspicious on the floor of the study. If it could ring without being plugged in, it would probably work even if he smashed it into a million pieces.

He could leave the house, of course. Go for a walk in the park, go to the pub. The clunky old handset wouldn't follow him outside (it hadn't sprouted legs – yet) and he had ditched his mobile long ago. But his freedom wouldn't last. Sooner or later he would hear that nerve-shredding bell tone jingling merrily from a nearby phone box or through the open door of a shop or house he might pass by.

And what if they tired of this charade, of Matt's persistent rejection of their demands? Supposing they ditched the cheesy phone prop and decided to appear in the flesh? How would they make their entrance? Suddenly, at the foot of his bed in the middle of the night? How would his damaged mind depict them?

Perhaps accepting that he was insane was the way forward. Perhaps he was, in reality, squatting in a dimly lit padded cell somewhere, and this empty house, this empty existence of his, was nothing more than the feverish conjuring of a damaged psyche. Crazy people rarely know they are crazy.

The idea had a pathetic appeal. If he was lucky, a burly male nurse might eventually appear and offer him chemical respite. A lithium cocktail. That'd show the bastards, all right.

I'm sorry, Matt can't take your call right now, he's zonked out and trussed up. Do call back later, when he's returned from Happyland...

Despite the weirdness of the situation, all the while they remained firmly at the end of a telephone line Matt still had a degree of control. The situation was normal, in an abnormal way.

The conversation would follow a pattern. One of the voices would put the offer to him; the same request they had made since the start of this business. They would very much like to use his services, his skills. They would make it worth his while, they assured him.

"You can magic up cash?" he would ask.

No, Matt. Your reward will be far more satisfying than money.

Matt would say that he very much doubted that, and he would hang up. They would fall silent for a day or two. Then, another caller. Same proposition. Same outcome.

He shuffled across the floor and picked up the phone, like a normal person.

"Hello, Matt."

"Yeah, hello," he heard himself slur into the mouthpiece. It sounded like 'yellow'. The lithium kicking in?

"I want you to write a horror story."

The voice was filtered through some line noise that sounded like bacon frying in a greasy pan. Matt wondered if that was something to do with the place they were calling from. He doubted it was anywhere as mundane as Croydon. Slough maybe. He choked back a giggle. Wonderful stuff, lithium.

He sighed into the handset. "Look, this isn't working, is it? Can't you just move on to someone else? There must be plenty of people out there who can do what you want."

"There's only you, Matt. It has to be you."

Matt idly flicked the shredded end of the wire. They would go away in a minute or two. They always did.

"I'm afraid we are running out of patience. If you don't co-operate, we can make life difficult for you."

Now that was funny. Really funny.

"Difficult?" said Matt, barely able to suppress a genuine chuckle. He had no idea they had a sense of humour. "How much worse can it be? I've got no job, my home is about to be repossessed and I've got creepy voices calling me on a disconnected telephone! What more can you do to me?"

There was a pause. The voice seemed to sigh.

"We didn't want it to come to this, Matt. But, as they say in all the worst movies, you've left us with no alternative."

Matt's laughter had barely subsided when the study door popped open behind him and swung inward. He scrambled to his feet, the two pieces of the phone still clutched in his hands, the severed cord following him across the room.

They knew what he feared. Of course they did. The callers were all twisted little personalities conjured by his own damaged mind. They were crammed together inside his head, cheek by jowl with his most private, most guarded thoughts and fears. Nothing could be hidden from them. He could never have any secrets from them. All his arguing and resisting had been futile. They always had the upper hand, this appalling ace up their sleeve. Calling him on a dead phone had been nothing more than cheap theatre, a warm-up act before the main event. Now he would see them at last in all their horror. This was it, the big finish.

In his desperation, Matt scanned wildly about him, hoping that someone would miraculously step in at the last minute to rescue him, pull him back from the brink of utter madness. Where was that nurse with the damned hypo?

But there was no one.

The open door revealed a strange brightness beyond. Almost blinding. Had he left the light on out there? He didn't think so.

The door finally rested back against the wall and Matt found himself gazing into a curious landscape that bore no relation to any part of his home. Instead of his upstairs landing, there was a room that seemed to stretch impossibly beyond the walls of the house. And there was a smell, a pungent odour of rotten eggs that he recognised but couldn't quite set in place and time. A chemical tang. A hospital? That could work. A hospital would be good.

As his eyes adjusted to the dazzling light, he began to make out the furniture. Tables—lots of them—and wooden stools. Not like a hospital.

He knew that smell, that awful stench. This was a memory. A deep one. Something from his youth. Yes, something from his schooldays.

"Oh, no," he whispered as realisation dawned. Those weren't tables. They were benches. Work benches. And that smell—sulphur. The sickening fragrance of...

"A science lab," whispered Matt.

"Oh, dear me, Matt. Not just *a* science lab," said the voice. "This is *the* science lab." And then, almost cheerily, "Or perhaps we should call it *your* science lab?"

Matt felt his bowels weaken. His legs began to quake and he had to press the phone firmly against his face for fear of dropping it from his sweating, trembling fingers.

"They're about to start the lesson. Waiting outside, just out of our sight, like good boys and girls should. That's a safety precaution, you know."

Matt nodded.

"Safety is very important in science laboratories, isn't it, Matt?"

"Hmm? Yes, I suppose."

"Very important indeed. Can't have kiddies running around unsupervised in a place like that. Dear me, no. What with all those nasty corrosive chemicals."

"N-n-no," stammered Matt.

"And the flames. Those little candle things. What are they called?"

"Bunsen burners. They're called Bunsen burners," blurted Matt.

"That's it. Bunsen burners," the voice said slowly, seeming to relish the taste of the words. "Oh, how marvellous, the lab door is starting to open. Over there, to your left. Do you see? Go ahead, you can take a closer peek if you like. You might recognise some of the pupils, some of your old pals. Best days of your life, eh? Go on, Matt. Don't be shy."

Matt shook his head. The sulphurous fumes, mixed with the warm, gassy stink of the Bunsen burners, made him feel sick. If he opened his mouth now he would vomit.

"I can't hear you shaking your head, Matt. You'll have to speak."

"I'll do it," gasped Matt.

A door was opening at the back of the lab. Through the meshed glass he could see figures jostling with each other. The sound of teenage chatter bubbled up through the gap, and a man's strident voice ordered them to calm down.

"You'll do what, Matt?"

The lab door was fully open now. Matt could see a taller figure with a shock of dark curly hair drifting through the crowd. Mr Tibor in his neat, white lab coat came to a halt at the door and admonished an invisible pupil.

Matt pressed his mouth into the handset.

"I'll write for you," he whispered. "I'll write your damned stories. I'll do whatever you want. Just take this away. Please. I don't want to see it."

The pupils started to file in past Mr Tibor and Matt saw her, at the front of the queue. Prettier than he remembered. Clear white skin, like flawless marble. Her long chestnut hair glittered under the strip-lighting. She reached around to tie it up before the lesson began but it would tumble free; it always did. Matt squeezed his eyes closed.

"Please!" he begged. "No more!"

The sound of chattering schoolchildren grew louder, reaching an unbearable crescendo until suddenly the study door slammed shut with a sound like thunder. The echo ricocheted off the naked floorboards.

Matt opened his eyes. Cool sweat dribbled down his temples. The lab was gone. The satanic reek had evaporated.

"Better?" asked the voice.

"Yes. Thank you." Matt sighed. Clutching the receiver tightly in his left hand, he slid down the wall and sat on the bare floor. With his free hand he swiped a sheet of sweat from his forehead.

"I know you're a *serious* writer, Matt. You've told us so many times. And we respect that. You have *principles*, even if they don't seem to be paying the rent. You're not—oh what's the neat little phrase you use?—not some 'pulp fiction hack'. Is that right?"

"I told you. I don't write fiction. I'm a journalist."

47

"Correction, Matt, you *were* a journalist. Past tense. Then you hit the bottle and your career nose-dived into the shitter. Along with the rest of your life."

Wife, house, friends. Matt ticked them off in his head. The caller was right. He had nothing to counter with.

"I told you before," he said wearily, "I've never written that kind of stuff. I hate horror, science fiction; all that fantastical nonsense."

"Not because it frightens you, though?"

Matt snorted. "Don't be stupid. Of course it doesn't frighten me. It's tawdry and pointless, the worst kind of writing. Besides, there's enough real horror out there in the world without making it up."

"There certainly is," said the caller. Matt thought he detected a trace of delight in the voice. "The world is indeed full of horror. But you love writing. You enjoy the process, don't you? You enjoy the craft."

Matt nodded. He supposed he did. "That's why I became a journalist," he said. "I wanted to report the facts, real events. Do you see?"

"We see," said the voice. "That's exactly why we chose you. So you'll accept our commission?"

Matt groaned. "Yes, I told you. I give in. I'll do it. But I just don't think it will work," he sighed. "All that supernatural crap. I just don't believe in it."

"Really, Matt? You gave a good impression of believing in your old school science lab."

The science lab was right there in front of him. How could he not believe in it? Didn't they understand what he was saying?

The door opened again. Matt shifted uneasily. He gripped the phone and started to get up. "What are you playing at? I've agreed to do it! You don't need to show me this again!"

"Shhh, don't worry, Matt. All the horrid children have gone home and the nasty, smelly science lab has disappeared."

Outside the study door, the dim hallway looked just the same as ever.

"We're going to show you our stories. You'll be an observer in our world, a reporter. You don't have to believe in monsters and space aliens and all that 'crap'. All you have to do is watch and listen."

"You're going to *show* me your stories? I don't get it. I thought they were works of fiction."

"Not all tales of terror are fabricated, Matt. These are all real horrors that have befallen each one of us. Come and walk beside us and you will share our pain, feel our fear. You know about pain and fear, don't you, Matt?"

Matt murmured agreement. He knew about pain and fear.

Slowly, the world beyond the door began to melt and flow, becoming a blur of sights and sounds. At length, a new landscape emerged; swirling colours solidified into shapes, and shapes metamorphosed into people.

Matt watched. And listened.

Part 2: Catharsis

He was back in his own home again. Back in the stark, featureless study of the empty terraced house he had clung onto for the past eighteen months as he had watched his life slip away.

It was dark outside and it looked as though someone had taken a bite out of the ghostly moon that peered in at him through the naked windows. He didn't know what day it might be. His demented journey through the lives and deaths of the callers had thoroughly disoriented him, thrown him out of place and time.

Matt had recorded everything—all the events as he had seen and heard them, just as any good journalist should. There were no hysterical embellishments; no unnecessary interjections of opinion. Simply the cold, hard facts. This is what he was good at. This is why they had chosen him.

The typewriter was sitting in its usual place on the floor. Ready and waiting. Beside the door, piles of typed pages—the stories he had written. *Their* stories.

The phone rang. Its severed white cord lay coiled at his feet like a bloodless worm. Matt groaned. No, he wouldn't do it anymore; couldn't do it anymore. The excursions into each caller's private hell had sapped him of energy and shredded his nerves. He was exhausted.

He stooped down and snatched up the receiver. "God, can't you give me a break? I've done what you wanted and I've had enough of it. Just leave me in peace, will you."

There was no answer.

"Hello?" He tapped the handset. "Are you there?" He strained to listen, sickened at the idea of putting his face to the phone again, close to their voices, but he was compelled to hear what they had to say. He tried again. "Hello?"

Nothing. Why no words? Why didn't they speak?

Yet there *were* sounds. Sounds he recognised. Not from the phone but from somewhere nearby. He glanced around the moonlit room. Something was out of place. Before, there had been yellow-painted woodchip covering the walls and bare floorboards that creaked and echoed at his every movement. Beneath his feet now stretched a solid, tiled floor, foot-polished with age. The walls were of smooth plaster, light grey above and, from waist level down, a shiny deeper grey. Battleship grey they used to call it—at school.

A mad bustle of footsteps echoed around him, their shuffling and clattering mingled with a creeping crescendo of teenage whispers, laughter and exclamations.

Mr Tibor's clipped Hungarian accent. "All right, everyone. Let's have a little quiet, if you please. Line up now. No pushing and shoving. That means you, Hewlitt."

The door to the hallway popped its catch and started to open. That smell; that gassy, sulphurous smell.

When the first voice had shown him the science lab, God knows how many days ago, Matt had watched the class arriving from afar. This time, he seemed to be among them. He could feel their bodies jostling him. But he couldn't see them.

He yelled into the phone, "Stop it! Stop it now! I've done what you wanted. I've written your stupid bloody stories! Why are you doing this to me?"

The line hissed and sputtered hollowly. If this new voice was answering him, Matt couldn't understand what it was saying.

A pale radiance poured around the door, washing him in white light. The scene unfolded before him. Mr Tibor, his curly mop of hair swept back from a broad forehead, just as Matt remembered, stood inches away holding the door open.

And she was there again. At the front of the queue. Her back was to him but he recognised her hair. That long brown shining hair. How could he ever forget it?

Mr Tibor beckoned her forward and she led the line of softly materialising schoolchildren into the lab. Matt felt a mass of bodies pushing at his back.

"Move it, dickweed," sniggered a voice behind him. He felt hot breath on his neck.

He looked at his hands. Instead of the two parts of the phone which he had just been clutching, he was holding a sports bag and a pile of books. *His* sports bag. *His* books.

"Come on!" urged the voice.

Matt shuffled forward, bile rising in his chest as realisation dawned. This time, he was not some ethereal presence watching surreptitiously as someone else's nightmare developed before his eyes like a Polaroid picture. The actors in this morbid tableau could see him and they could touch him.

Unable to stem the human tide around him, Matt was swept along with it, into the foul-smelling school laboratory.

He took his seat beside his erstwhile best friend, Gary Laird, and opposite the girl.

Jennifer Wray scooped her ponytail up and tied it with a polka-dot scrunchie. *It won't stay*, thought Matt.

The memory of this day, of the drama now unfolding around him, was like a festering lesion that he had picked at regularly for twenty years, never quite healing, always weeping under the bandages. In the good times, when he had a steady job and a steady wife, he could hide the scars, keep them under wraps at the back of his mind. But the good times had been few. In the frequent moments of maudlin self-pity, his fingertips would worry at the loose ends of the dressing, find it damp with fresh blood, and gradually unravel the bindings until the wound was exposed to the light, as glistening and raw as the day it was carved upon his soul.

He had replayed the scene a thousand times over the past two decades. He would picture himself standing there in the lab, grinning idiotically, trying to tease a smile out of her, out of Jennifer. One of those conical flasks of clear liquid in one hand, a roaring Bunsen burner in the other, acting the clown, lost in a world of irresponsible fun and laughter, without a care in the world.

It had dawned on him during the intervening years that this was probably the last moment he had ever felt truly happy, unfettered by guilt and remorse. For this was the moment he changed the lives of two people, for ever; the day that Matt Fisher transformed from a happy-go-lucky teenager into a depressed, haunted man, and the day that Jennifer Wray was transformed from the girl of his dreams into the creature of his nightmares.

Jennifer half smiled and rolled her eyes, unimpressed. The smile was like a beam of warm sunshine. That was a retrospective comparison, of course. To the fifteen-year-old Matt it was nothing more than a green light. She liked him. But he would have to try harder to win her affection. So he

52

did. He broke into one of his killer impersonations—Twitchy Tibor, the Transylvanian Tosser. He hoped she appreciated his audacity. Twitchy Tibor himself was less than ten feet away, administering safety guidance to some dipstick who was trying to dissolve their fingers in the noxious liquid he had just dispensed to everyone.

On top of his vaguely vampiric accent, the Hungarian science teacher had a nervous tic that made him shudder now and then. Absolute gold dust to any teenager. To 'do' him right, one therefore had to exaggerate this modest affliction to the nth degree.

Twenty years ago, Matt, lost in the moment, 'did' him to perfection. "Now den, my darlinks. Can you hear dem?" Twitch! Matt picked up the glass container of toxic liquid. Jennifer was pretending to ignore him but he could see the smile playing on her lips. "Da cheeldren of da night—" Shudder!

He never did get to finish the famous Bela Lugosi quote. That final spasm had caused the flask to shoot upwards with a jerk of his wrist, and the contents had sprayed into the air. What followed was a bewildering confection of screams, shouts and sickening images that he would never erase from his memory.

Matt always wanted to pause the replay at that point, step into the frame and ask himself just what the hell he was doing. How had he forgotten Mr Tibor's stern warning that this stuff was "a lethal cocktail" of something or other? *Quite easily*, was the answer he would have received. The young Matt would have told his peevish older self that life was too short to be serious, too short to pay attention to dull, workaday adult matters and dreary, droning science teachers. Life was for living. Life was for chatting up pretty girls, like Jennifer Wray.

He sometimes wondered what had become of her. They occasionally put documentaries on TV about stomach-churning medical procedures, skin grafts and transplants and so on that made Matt tingle and start to pick at those metaphorical scabs again. Perhaps she had undergone some miraculous treatment that had left her looking fairly presentable. Some of the patients in the documentaries looked all right afterwards. Kind of.

Mr Tibor was no doctor, he had told the class afterwards. He could not speculate on how she would fare. He kept repeating his mantra that it was the flames that did it; not, of course, the over-strength chemicals he had merrily passed around for the kiddies to play with. He insisted that the injuries caused by the acidic mixture wouldn't have been so bad if fire had not been introduced into the equation.

"Of course," said Mr Tibor, "she should have tied her hair up. I always tell the girls to tie their hair up."

But Matt knew she *had* tied her hair up. He had seen her do it at the start of the lesson. And he had also seen those bronze tresses tumble free and splash onto the Bunsen burner he was still waving about as though it was nothing more dangerous than Christmas bunting.

He had stared, open-mouthed with shock as flames chased up her long, shining hair to meet the nameless concoction dripping down her face.

"It made the chemicals act like napalm," Mr Tibor explained.

Matt had never heard of napalm, so he looked it up in an encyclopaedia. Turns out it was a kind of flammable gel the Americans used in Vietnam. It would stick, burning, to whoever was unfortunate enough to get in its way. There was no method of removal. Once on the victim, it would scorch its way through layers of clothing, skin, fat and muscle, all the way down to the bone. There were no pictures in the encyclopaedia. Matt didn't need them. He had seen napalm at work.

Jennifer's screams were choked off by red tongues of flame that licked at her open mouth with greedy passion and slathered their way up her face until she became engulfed; a human ball of fire.

Mr Tibor had been the last person from the school to see her. He had wrapped the fire blanket around her. He had ushered the pupils out of the lab while they waited for the ambulance. He had stayed with her, bathing her face with cool tap water; he had ridden with her to the hospital. It was a while before Mr Tibor returned to work. When he re-appeared, he seemed to have aged. He was slower, quieter, and less impatient with the pupils.

Jennifer never returned to school. The prefects passed on snippets of half-heard staffroom gossip. For a long time after the event, Chinese whispers circulated among the pupils. The cocktail of unnameable caustic chemicals and naked flame had fired everyone's imagination. Lurid accounts of the incident, and of Jennifer's frightful condition, were embellished to such a degree that the whole affair took on the aspect of an urban legend.

No one kept in touch with Jennifer during her long stay in hospital. Some of the other girls tried to make contact but they were kept away by her parents. Approaches by the school authorities were also rebuffed. After a year or so, a rumour circulated that she had been moved to some specialist unit up north. And that was the last anyone heard. Matt supposed he would have been made aware if she had died, so he presumed (hoped with all his heart) that she hadn't.

And now here she was, standing on the other side of the bench, warming her vial over the Bunsen burner, scribbling notes in her exercise book, looking as perfect as a porcelain statue. It was agonising. He had witnessed this single-act nightmare replaying on a screen in the back of his mind on a regular basis throughout his adult life. Imagining the events play out yet again would be excruciating enough, but actually reliving them in real time was unbearable. Matt felt his chest tearing itself apart from the inside.

He was sure that he would have a heart attack, or at the very least pass out.

He snapped his gaze away from her. Dear God, he was holding the glass beaker full of liquid. How the hell had that happened? He had to do something. Focussing all his energy, Matt carefully put the beaker down on the bench. This time, he was in control. He could change things. Maybe that's what all this was about. Maybe he was being granted a second chance; an opportunity to undo the damage he had caused and to set things right. Perhaps this was his payment, his reward, for writing those vile stories.

With his left hand, he held the beaker firmly on the bench. With his right, he reached out to switch off the Bunsen. The blue flame died.

It was working. Jennifer would walk out of this chemistry lesson unharmed, and he would be restored to something approaching sanity.

He glanced at the door. What was beyond it? If he prevented the accident by simply leaving the lesson right now, what future awaited him? Was he free? Did the door lead back to his home in Croydon? And would his own history be rewritten? What reality would be awaiting him out there? Maybe he was trapped in this time and would have to relive all the intervening years. Matt didn't know if he could face that, but he knew it would be infinitely more bearable knowing that he had put things right. He might even turn out to be a half-decent journalist this time around.

Gary, his workbench partner, elbowed him. "What are you playing at?"

The question reverberated in his mind and derailed his train of thought. *What are you playing at?* Isn't that what Gary always said in his nightmares? Isn't that exactly what he had said all those years ago, moments before—

Matt felt the beaker pulling free of his grasp. He struggled to control it, pressing it down towards the bench with all the strength he could muster. He looked up. Jennifer was shaking her head, a wry smile playing on her rosebud lips. She leaned forward to relight his Bunsen with her own. Her hair, he could see, was already struggling to free itself from its ties.

"No!" yelled Matt. He lunged forward to snatch the Bunsen away before it ignited. A scream. Jennifer's hand shot to her face. Her wet face. Matt saw that his beaker was empty.

The rest of the scene played out just as it always did. The cries of the children melded seamlessly with the sick-making shriek of wooden stools being scraped backwards and crashing to the floor. And the warm, soft thumping sound of Jennifer Wray's face igniting as the fumes from the chemical bath he had given her reacted with the flames racing up to meet them.

Instant napalm.

Matt stood and watched, as he had always done, both spectator and participant. Jennifer clawed feverishly at her melting face. Gobbets of fire—burning flesh—slithered over her hands, down her arms and formed little bonfires on the workbench.

Matt closed his eyes and the sounds of horror and panic faded to a background buzz, then evaporated.

When he looked again, he was alone. In his hands, the two parts of the phone. He was back in his own house. Yellow wallpaper, dusty floorboards—normality. He hadn't changed anything. He was never meant to.

"Jennifer! Jennifer!"

A woman's voice, panicked, came to him from somewhere in the house, the increasingly frantic cries punctuated by a determined banging sound.

All his nerve endings were tingling as though he had plunged wet fingers into an electric socket. Icy rivers cascaded down his temples and he passed the receiver from one slippery hand to the other so that he could cuff away the cold sweat.

The muffled shouting and hammering was coming from downstairs. In the darkness, he descended the stairs and edged along the unlit hallway until he reached an open doorway. There was an unmistakeable smell of gas.

"Oh, God, not this again," he groaned. "How many times?"

Matt wondered then if this was hell, his own private purgatory. Was he condemned to relive every moment of this for all eternity?

He peered around the door. A flood of relief washed over him when he saw that he was not looking at a school chemistry lab. Instead, it was a kitchen.

The relief turned sour in his stomach when he realised that it was not *his* kitchen.

Swathed in indigo shadow, a solitary figure stood swaying in the unlit room. Upon the vague, ghostlike face, Matt could make out no features save a crooked pink gash that served as a mouth. He watched as the figure deftly felt its way along the kitchen worktop with scar-white fingertips.

The banging resumed and Matt noticed another door on the far side of the kitchen. A muffled shout from beyond: "Jennifer! No, please, no!"

"Jennifer?" Matt whispered before he could stop himself.

The spectre stopped and turned its blurred face towards him.

"Dear God, why can't you leave me alone?" she shrieked. "Haven't you done enough?"

The sound of her voice was like an electric shock. Matt took a sudden step back. He wanted to run, to hide, but there was now a wall at the place where he had entered the kitchen. The only way out was through the door on the other side of the room, where Jennifer's mother was frantically trying to gain entry.

The smell of gas was overpowering now.

"You want to watch, is that it? You want to see how this ends?" Jennifer asked. Her crooked hands felt their way across the cooker and opened the oven door. She knelt down, becoming almost invisible in the gloom, as though the shadows had swallowed her.

Matt realised that he couldn't prevent the accident in the science lab from ever happening, no matter how often he was thrown back in time to live through it. It was in the past and that could never be changed. But he could stop this. This was happening now. He dropped the phone and ran to the door. The shouting and hammering on the other side continued unabated as he strained at the handle. Behind him, Jennifer was slumped in front of the oven.

The gas was making him feel lightheaded and the door seemed to be stuck fast. He scanned the room. The only furniture was a table and two tubular chairs. If he could throw one of the chairs through the window, the gas would escape.

But his train of thought was interrupted by the crash of splintering wood as the door was suddenly broken down from the outside. Two firefighters rushed into the room and pulled Jennifer away from the cooker. Her mother, a shrunken, grey-haired woman, followed behind.

"He's always there, Mum," she gasped. "He's just always there."

"I know, dear," said her mother. "I know."

The firefighters turned off the gas and eased Jennifer towards the centre of the room, where she lay in a slender shaft of silver moonlight that leaked through the kitchen window.

Her mother sat down on the floor beside her daughter in the inky shadows.

"He's here right now," said Jennifer. "I can see him clear as day."

One of the firefighters knelt beside her and glanced at the spot where she was pointing. He didn't see Matt.

"Just a mild hallucination," he said to Jennifer's mother. "Caused by the gas. She'll be fine."

Then he slipped an oxygen mask over Jennifer's burned, eyeless face.

The voices, their images, fizzled and faded as the room shifted shape and position, finally reforming into the kitchen of his own house.

He was alone again.

Matt knew that this would never end. The memory, the guilt, swilled around in his guts like boiling mercury.

He rifled through the cutlery drawer and retrieved a bread knife. Without a pause, he drew the keen edge across both wrists, applying enough pressure for the blade to bite through his throbbing grey-green veins, into the sinews and thin bones.

He watched his skin open to expose the inner workings of his body. But no blood flowed from the cuts. Now, in excruciating agony from his bloodless injuries, he plunged the knife into his neck and buried it to the hilt. He screamed from the pain, his voice strangulated by the thick blade jutting from his throat. And yet, in spite of the white-hot agony that coursed through him, he remained standing. There was no great gush of claret from the gaping wound; no rushing tide of unconsciousness washed over him.

He wrenched the knife out of his neck. There was a disgusting slurping sound as his flesh reluctantly relinquished its suction grip on the steel blade. A thin wheeze of air escaped through the entry wound.

He threw the knife away and it clattered noisily against the tiled wall before skittering along the worktop and coming to a halt against the microwave with a metallic clunk.

Silence.

So there truly was no escape. He could neither undo what he had done nor put an end to his misery. Was he doomed to haunt Jennifer until she succeeded in taking her own life? And then what? Would her death finally grant him respite?

As if in reply, a bell rang. Just once. One single clear, ice-cold note. But it was not the insistent jangle of a telephone. That appalling instrument of torment, he remembered, he had left in Jennifer's kitchen. It was nowhere to be seen. But he recognised that single bell-ring well enough.

Matt looked at the ceiling, seeing in his mind's eye what awaited him upstairs, as though he had suddenly acquired x-ray vision.

He trudged slowly up to the study. It was just as he had left it. Sitting in the middle of the floor was his ancient typewriter. Beside it, a fresh sheaf of paper. There was one bare sheet in the machine, tabbed to the centre. The title had been written for him: *Catharsis*.

Over the course of writing the collection of macabre stories, he had witnessed the souls of the callers being flayed open to reveal their deepest, darkest fears. Now it was his turn.

Matt sat cross-legged in front of the machine. After a page of solid typing, the cuts at his wrists and neck began to sting. And then, slowly, to bleed. Ten pages in, the dribble of scarlet leaking from his gaping wounds was turning into a steady stream.

He had wondered if this final piece, this coda, might be *her* story—Jennifer's story. It was horrific enough. But he was wrong. It wasn't her story at all. It was his. That was why there had been no voice on the line this time. Jennifer's own story, he now knew, had no ending. She was still alive, still haunted by him, still seeing him at every turn through those hideous blind sockets. Her suffering was *his* horror. This time, the voice of the storyteller was his own.

The keyboard became sticky with congealing blood and the crisp white sheets were blotted all over with burgundy stains. The blood on his hands and neck itched as it crusted but, far from healing, the wounds he had inflicted upon himself bled more freely with every page he wrote. It didn't matter. He understood that by the time he had finished writing, he would be dead. And that, he decided, would make a fine ending for a horror story.

Splatter

There are countless ways to kill yourself and a million places to do it. So why did Marilyn Monroe select the fast train to London Bridge as her preferred method of self-destruction?

At two in the morning everything on TV was old or weird. None of it could hold his interest for long. On Challenge they were rerunning *Crystal Maze* from the '90s; old *and* weird. Jamie's face was bathed in the jumpy blue light from the screen, but his mind had long since quit the show to wander back down the day and replay those three minutes of terror.

He would be back at the same railway station, standing on the same platform for real soon enough. He should turn in. But how do you sleep after something like that?

*

You could tell when the express was coming. People made a small involuntary step backwards, away from the edge. Just a little shuffle—almost imperceptible. He'd observed the phenomenon many times. It had been no different this morning. The same crowd of commuters turned up every day come rain or shine, and rode the 7.37am to London Bridge with him. From there, they all went their separate ways, only to meet up again the next day, same time, same place, and start all over again.

Of course, he didn't know their names. As if by an unspoken common consent, there was never as much as a smile or nod of recognition between them. Eye contact was strenuously avoided. All very British.

One of the gang had been missing for a couple of days. Holiday? Throwing a sickie? Who knew? But she was back today. Marilyn (she bore a passing resemblance to the iconic

Ms Monroe) resumed her usual position on the platform, just ahead of Jamie.

Jamie smiled. The equilibrium of the universe was restored.

But there was something nigglingly out of place today; something agonizingly different. Something he could not quite put his finger on.

The express was about to rip through the station like a tornado, but Marilyn didn't join in the little line dance with the others. She didn't step back. There was a nervous energy about her today that Jamie hadn't seen before. She fidgeted distractedly; she peered around and, horror of horrors, even looked directly at him.

The bag! Of course, it was the bag. That hideous black nylon laptop satchel she always carried. No bag today. No coffee either. For a while he'd toyed with the idea of calling her Latte, on account of the Starbucks cup she habitually carried. Not today though. No bag, no coffee and no navy suit. Jeans today.

The penny dropped: Marilyn wasn't going to work. So what was she doing here, at this godforsaken hour, lining up on the northbound platform with the usual suspects? Not stepping back, that's what. Edging forward a little, that's what.

Suddenly, Jamie knew what she was doing here.

It was all over in three minutes.

Marilyn tottered to the very brink of the platform. She threw another glassy-eyed glance at Jamie; a shaky smile. Jamie lurched forward, reached out, but missed her. She jumped down onto the track. Jamie followed her. It was a long way down, further than he had imagined. His ankles jarred as he landed. He could hear the skittering sound of steel wheels on a polished track, like metallic whispers.

Up on the platform, people started shouting. The headlamps of the express were blindingly bright. The sound of its squealing, thunderous approach rumbled inside him.

For an instant he thought he had gone mad. What the hell was he doing standing in the path of a speeding train?

Marilyn was further down the track, scrabbling away from him in the direction of the oncoming behemoth. Her shoes crunched on the stained brown rocks scattered between the steel tracks. Jamie ran at her, arms outstretched, and made contact. She seemed smaller down here in the shadows. He swept her up and carried her away from the northbound line, out of the path of the approaching train.

The next and last platform was a short one. Facing Jamie, instead of another platform, was a blackened wall that held back a tall, overgrown embankment. Recessed into the wall at every hundred yards were arched alcoves where the railwaymen could shelter while they were working on the track. He pulled her towards one of them, across the final set of tracks. The express roared past in a blur, like a blue rocket. They were both thrown back by the blast of tailwind. Brakes screeched. Somewhere in the distance, shouts turned into screams.

But Marilyn was safe in his arms.

He took her hand and led her towards the alcove, out of harm's way. He had time to think that up close, she looked nothing like Marilyn Monroe. It was a stupid nickname. She was a natural blonde. Her skin was fair and there was a sprinkling of freckles on her nose. Her eyes were not quite blue and not quite grey. *Overcast*, thought Jamie. *Is that a colour?* Their cloudy coolness seemed to drain something from her face. Then that too fell into place. No make-up.

On a work day, powdered and painted and in her suit, with her hair scraped back, she was passably pretty. But today she was slightly dishevelled and too pale, washed out, as though she was almost not there. More disturbing than appealing. He was disappointed to discover that she smelled of sweat.

As he pushed her into the soot-stained archway at the side of the track, she pressed herself against him and said something. He didn't catch it—too much background noise. On her breath, the stale tang of alcohol. Was she thanking him?

The northbound express was slowly sliding to a screeching halt. But the noise was overlaid with another sound, a scratchy squealing sound. Mechanical rats? The thought made him giggle.

Marilyn struggled against his grip, lurched back across the empty track towards the slowing train. She pulled him along with her. Then she stopped, smiled.

Jamie looked down at her hands as she tugged at him.

There was something else about Marilyn that he had noticed over recent weeks. She was engaged to be married. He had seen the diamond solitaire on her ring finger. It was modest in size—not exactly bling—but it sparkled under the strip-lighting of the platform. You couldn't miss it.

Today, the ring was missing.

Then something huge and dark exploded in front of his eyes. Jamie was lifted off his feet and pushed back against the blackened wall of the shelter. His face was wet. His shirt was warm and sticky. Marilyn had vanished, snatched away by a second speeding monster. The mechanical rat.

To anyone watching, it must have looked like a magic trick. One moment there were two people staggering across the railway track, the next, there was just one. The magician stood alone on his stage, his glamorous assistant having disappeared before their very eyes. Hey presto!

It took Jamie several minutes to grasp what had happened. He had saved Marilyn from the northbound express only to lose her to the southbound express that came hurtling along the adjacent track exactly thirty seconds later. Same time, every morning. How could he have forgotten that part of the daily routine? Marilyn had remembered.

He didn't touch the wetness on his face. Or try to brush the debris from his suit. Not right away. He knew what it was.

And now, hours later, as he sat staring at the flickering TV, he knew *who* it was.

*

A couple of police officers had accompanied him to A&E, where he was cleaned up and checked over. A brief statement was taken while the events were still horribly fresh in his mind. One of the cops brought him a change of clothes along with a coffee and a glistening red Danish pastry that he gobbled down and then promptly threw up. By lunchtime, he was home. He called in sick, then called his brother, Graham. Together they watched as the story unravelled on the lunchtime news.

Apparently, it was Helen Miller he had almost saved this morning; Helen Miller who had remembered the southbound express; Helen Miller's blood and brains that had been splattered all over him.

*

Jamie killed the *Crystal Maze* and took his mug out to the kitchen. Hot milk was supposed to make you sleepy. Maybe if he went to bed and gave it a chance it might work.

He could ask Graham to come back, stay the night. His brother had turned out to be a good listener. Jamie weighed his mobile in his hand. Graham might not be such a good listener at 2.00am.

He looked at his hands, turned them over. Down there on the track, the magic trick hadn't quite worked. When the train had eventually shrieked itself to a standstill, he had felt something pulling at him; something weighty that belied the slimness of its owner. It was Marilyn's (Helen Miller's) right arm and some of her upper torso, hanging from his numb fingers.

What remained of her was perfectly naked, her clothes having been ripped away along with the rest of her body.

The weight of the dangling body part began to slowly drag her hand through his slippery grasp and yet, for some reason he couldn't explain, he couldn't let go of her. When the emergency people arrived, they had to prise his fingers from hers, one by one.

The people in the flat below were playing a video game, a shoot-'em-up. He stood in the hall and listened. After five minutes the gunfire fell silent.

He used the toilet, flushed, washed his hands for the hundredth time and tugged off the bathroom light. In the darkness of the hallway, he felt his face. It was dry. Clean and dry. Two showers—long ones—had seen to that. Helen Miller was all washed away.

It occurred to him that if he had simply stood on the southbound track after rescuing her from the northbound express, and not pushed and pulled her to that grimy little shelter, he too would have burst into a thousand bloody pieces when the next train came along. The idea made something uncoil inside him. And Helen Miller's smile just before the impact—what was that all about?

He parked the thought. He could agonise about it some other time.

According to the TV news, she had been 'struggling' after having lost her job. She had been sacked following a court case. A fiancé was mentioned. All carefully obscure.

"Internet," Graham announced, with relish.

Jamie said that he wasn't sure he really needed to know more right now.

Graham had stabbed at his phone regardless.

The so-called engagement had been all Helen's doing. She'd courted the guy, she'd bought the ring. She'd proposed. His rejection had done nothing to deter her.

The reluctant fiancé swore that he barely even knew Helen. He ghosted her after their one and only date due to "bad vibes." But she had tracked him down, engaged herself to him and started bombarding him with desperate calls and screaming visits. When she proudly announced to the world the date of their forthcoming nuptials, he'd finally plucked up the courage to tell her the truth: she was stark, staring mad and he never wanted to see her again.

In reply, she tore the engagement ring from her finger. Her parting words to him had been, "I don't need you! I can get any man I want!"

She received a modest suspended sentence for harassment but lost her plum job in the City.

"So, in summary, crazy as a box of frogs," Graham declared after recounting the social media version of events.

"Poor Helen Miller," said Jamie. "Poor, crazy, Helen Miller."

"Screw Helen bloody Miller," said Graham. "Why the hell did you jump down there with her?"

In response, Jamie kept staring at the TV and waited for a suitable reply to occur to him. By the time Graham had gone home to his wife and kids, four hours later, he was still waiting.

*

The shadows in the darkened bedroom were soothing, the bed warm and soft. He should have done this earlier. He was already feeling sleepy. Didn't need a shoulder to cry on, just a pillow to sink into. He closed his eyes.

It was a pity about the suit—it wasn't very old. He hadn't cared about binning the shirt and tie. They were expendable. But it was the only suit he owned. He had a feeling the dry cleaner wouldn't have taken too kindly to him dumping the soggy bundle on his counter and asking him to scrub out the dead lady. He couldn't have worn it again, anyway. Tomorrow, he would treat himself to a new suit. Shirt, tie and shoes too—the works. Retail therapy.

He stretched out his arms and legs. Did the bed suddenly feel cold? It was a king size, bought in the expectation (hope) that he would one day find someone to fill the other half. So far, that hadn't happened, and Jamie had become used to the empty side radiating a lonely chill. He burrowed under the duvet. Yes, it was definitely too cold.

And now he was wide awake again.

He sighed. *These are the times when you need someone to snuggle up to*, he thought.

He opened his eyes and looked at the vacant pillow beside him. There was a dark, amoebic shape partly covering it and blotting out his view of the window beyond. It was just a shadow, of course. A shadow that seemed to be solid, seemed to be moving ever so slightly. But his eyes were bound to play tricks on him after a day like that, weren't they?

He shuffled his feet around and smoothed a palm towards the empty side. Towards the shadow.

No, the bed wasn't cold. It was wet.

This was nonsense. His imagination was running riot. He turned the other way and fumbled at the lamp. The sudden brightness stung his eyes. He pushed back the covers, resolved to spend the rest of the night staring at TV shows that should never have been made. He swung his legs out, stood up and turned to grab the duvet to take with him.

He screamed.

Lying there in the bed, next to the place he had just vacated, was Helen Miller. Or what was left of her.

Helen Miller's head was almost completely destroyed. There was no lower jaw. A crushed mess of white splinters and sliced, rippled brain matter congealed where the forehead should have been. Her grey eyes, still bitterly cold, stared out unblinking from a lidless red pulp. He felt a tickling sensation on his mouth and snatched at it. His fingers came away, stuck together with long strands of blood-matted blonde hair. He wanted to scream again to relieve the horror building inside him, but instead an inarticulate noise escaped his tightly closed lips.

Jamie backed towards the door, never taking his eyes from the abomination in his bed. The covers were pulled down to waist level, exposing her bare torso; one arm terminated at the elbow, the flapping skin a reminder that the lower part had been violently torn off. The other arm was complete. From her neck to her sternum, she appeared undamaged. Her small, firm breasts were intact, the soft skin milky white, her nipples pink and hard. But below her ribcage, she more closely resembled a carcass from an abattoir than a woman. Her stomach was ripped open, her innards spilled out across the bed from between a chaos of broken bones.

Jamie reached a shaking hand for the duvet and tore it back. There was nothing below her waist but stained sheets. No hips, no legs, no feet. Just a large, slowly spreading, cherry-red torrent flowing from her entrails.

He saw his hands. The left one was stained scarlet from where he had been touching the cold blood under the duvet.

He watched, disbelief and horror mounting in equal measure, as she turned her shattered head to face to him. The movement made her slick blue intestines unravel sloppily onto the stained mattress where her lower half should have been.

Her top lip and upper row of teeth were still present but, lacking any other part to her mouth, her open throat could only utter a hideous gurgling noise.

Jamie screamed again. And again. And again.

*

3.24am. It was still dark. The sun wouldn't be up for hours.

No one had been about as he had carried Helen Miller's carcass to the lift and out of the front door, along the way dropping gobbets of flesh that smacked wetly onto the ground behind him.

Balancing her on his left shoulder, he looked down as he unlocked the car. He was drenched in red juice. Slowly he opened his fists. Viscous strings of blood stuck his fingers to his palms as he uncurled them. The pavement beneath his feet was spattered with crimson and yellow chunks that resembled mashed pomegranate. Mixed in with the bits of human tissue, bone and tooth were maggots. Fat, waxy, blood-soaked maggots. Like stubby little vampires recoiling under the streetlight, they jerked about in the splashes of gore. *Life after death*, thought Jamie.

Up on his shoulder, he felt his burden move slowly, awkwardly, like a crippled insect.

This was a residential street, well lit. Anyone could come past at any time. People might be peeking through their net curtains right now at this perverse scene. But what would they see if they did? Could they see the horror, or was this madness reserved for him alone? Jamie didn't care. Whatever this was, it would end by daybreak.

Jamie was reminded of all the times he had lifted his late grandmother in and out of his car. She had felt soft, warm, solid. The opposite of what Helen Miller's mangled body felt like. Cold, loose flesh slipping from ruptured organs, caked with gummy blood like raspberry jelly; bones jutting from smashed limbs. A thick, cloying stench of blood and human shit wafted up as he pushed her into the passenger seat.

If he leaned in, she would almost be embracing him. His face came within a hair's breadth of her shattered skull but he steered his gaze away and focussed on the car's interior. There was a half empty bag of glacier mints on the shelf beneath the glove compartment.

He ducked under her arm. The dove-grey seat was already stained almost black with gore and the seatbelt buckle was coated in dark treacle. It snagged momentarily on her bare breasts. They jiggled at the touch of the belt, drawing his gaze up to what was left of her head. Two wrinkled eyeballs, dried out from the lack of lids, stared at him, accusingly. His disgust was replaced for a fleeting second by a twinge of guilt. He'd been caught looking.

*

Jamie stopped the car. "Helen, we need to talk," he said.

She was gazing at him. She wasn't interested in the scenery. That was good. That was very good. Without breaking eye contact, he moved his left hand away from the handbrake. Her seatbelt was still firmly locked.

"You're an intelligent woman, so I hear. At least, you were when you were... alive."

There was no flicker of response, or even comprehension, in her desiccated eyeballs.

His hand drifted slowly towards his own seatbelt. "You must understand that this isn't right," he said softly as he gingerly fingered the catch.

Suddenly, his hand was trapped in a cold vice. He looked down. Her fingers were biting into his skin. He had a flashback to the scene that morning, down on the railway track, when he had been unable to let go of Helen's dead hand. The screaming steel monster. The explosion of blood and gore.

"Let go of me, you fucking psycho!" he screamed into her ruined face.

He tried to wrench himself away from her grasp but her skeletal grip tightened and her bone fingertips began to draw blood from his pierced flesh.

With his free right hand, he unlocked the doors and scrabbled at his seatbelt catch. It popped open and zipped away. He kicked open the driver's door and redoubled his efforts at freeing his left hand but now her fingers were beginning to cut through sinews and tendons.

"I'm only finishing what you started, don't you see? This is what should have happened down there on the tracks," he gasped, trembling with the pain as he tried to pull her dagger-like finger bones out of his trapped left hand. Through a haze of increasing agony, he saw what he had been dreading. There, on her third finger, was a small diamond ring.

Helen's skull moved up and down, dripping red syrup and globs of flesh onto Jamie's lap. Was she nodding agreement? Did she understand that this is how it must end?

A bell rang out and Helen Miller's mangled, bloodied face looked up.

She turned her skull towards him and began to shake with laughter. A sickening noise, like a drain clearing, gurgled up from her gaping throat and gelatinous scarlet bubbles burst in Jamie's face, peppering him with red dots.

Jamie followed her gaze into the darkness. In the yellow glare of the headlights, he saw the red and white level crossing barriers come shuddering down at the edge of the track on either side of the car. Seconds later, the interior was filled with a familiar roaring, squealing sound and a burst of white light.

Ronnie's War

The journey to East Anglia was a rocket ride to another planet. Rolling past the carriage windows was an alien landscape of broad, flat fields, stretching all the way out to a crumbling coastline that spilled into the foaming waves of the North Sea. It was thoroughly disorienting for a boy brought up on a claustrophobic housing estate in southeast London.

At every stop, names were called and a handful of fearful children would snatch up their worldly goods (often nothing more than a bundle of clothes wrapped in brown paper and tied with string) and warily jump down onto the platform below. Waiting there would be a row of equally apprehensive grown-ups who would become their substitute parents for the foreseeable future.

It was the summer of 1940 and we were all being ushered away from the Blitz and into a quieter, safer place. Or so we thought.

I was billeted at a small farm in Norfolk. At the station I was met by Mrs Fordyce, a solid, florid-cheeked woman who perfectly fitted my townie preconception of what farmers' wives should look like.

Her meaty arms folded firmly against a faded apron, the first thing my cherry-faced surrogate mother said to me at the station was, "You've missed supper."

She turned away and I understood that I was to follow her. The pair of us were chauffeured from the station to the farm by a local shopkeeper, Mr Jackman, in his little green delivery van. Mrs Fordyce's ample form ensured that it was a tight squeeze.

When we arrived at the farm, Mr Jackman winked and bade me good luck before he drove away down the rutted track.

I had never seen a real farm before. Pitched in the midst of a muddy patch of land, the sagging cottage seemed an impossibly small place to house the formidable Mrs Fordyce. It seemed to shrink even more when the equally rotund Mr Fordyce appeared in the doorway. He was even more taciturn than his stony-faced wife. He looked me up and down as if gauging whether I could be of any possible use. A sour curl of his lip signalled that I had failed inspection. He turned and went back inside without saying a word.

At that, Mrs Fordyce clapped her hands to shoo me inside, which provoked a wild chuckling sound from a low wooden house nestled beside the cottage. I briefly wondered if it was a miniature asylum for insane midgets. It turned out to be the chicken coop.

At the sound of the hens, a third figure emerged cautiously from behind a hedge. With a curly mop of dirty blond hair and a face streaked with grime, the stick-thin man looked as if he had just slipped off a pole and ambled in from the field he was guarding.

"This here's Snotty John," said Mrs Fordyce. "He's been helping out as best he can since our son Joe's been off with the army."

The scarecrow hovered beside his hedgerow and eyed me warily from under straw-like locks. It was plain that he had earned his nickname due to the permanent streak of mucous smeared across his upper lip.

"Well, where's your manners, Johnny?" said Mrs Fordyce. "Say hello to young Master Ronald here. He's come all the way from London town to lend a hand on the farm."

John's hair was shoulder-length, long before it was fashionable—or even acceptable—for a man to grow his hair past his collar. He smiled cautiously at me, revealing a mouth full of twisted, brown stumps. I smiled back and said hello. He nodded, licked his lips and scampered off.

Mrs Fordyce tapped her temple with a chubby finger. "He's harmless enough," she said as we watched the ragged figure lope down the lane.

While the rest of the country sweltered in a heatwave that summer, the Fordyce cottage seemed to inhabit a chilly micro-climate of its own. I should have been used to the cold. The sash windows in my home back on the Becontree Estate were draughty, there was no insulation in the attic, and the plumbing would freeze up during winter. But nothing prepared me for the bone-chilling damp that haunted every corner of the farmhouse even in the height of summer.

The sharp aromas of soil and greenery and manure permeated everywhere. I ate and slept with the stink of the farm drowning my every breath. A thin layer of ginger-grey dust smothered every square inch of the farmhouse, as though someone from the car plant in Dagenham where my father worked had come along and sprayed primer into the air for a lark. Slender strands of dry yellow grass found their way into everything: my hair, my bed, my food. Cleanliness was clearly not a priority for the Fordyces.

You might think that there was, at least, one huge benefit to being barracked on a farm. You might assume that the usual wartime rationing didn't apply out in the countryside and that there would be a wealth of vegetables, eggs, milk, cheese and good home cooking, in addition to the standard wartime rations. Right? Wrong.

The Fordyces were crop farmers. Notwithstanding a highly-strung collie and the aforementioned coop of scraggy hens, there were no animals at the farm. The main crops of wheat and barley were not immediately edible and the Fordyces supplemented their meagre income, and kept their bellies full, by bartering their copious eggs for milk, cheese and meat on the black market.

My day usually consisted of the daily farm work that the Fordyces could no longer manage (or could no longer be bothered to do now that they had a houseboy) and usually involved such tasks as weeding, fixing fences and digging drainage channels in the company of the scarecrow known as Snotty John.

All in all, the pair of us were probably poor substitutes for the absent Joe Fordyce.

Snotty John inhabited a flimsy wooden shack in the woods and seemed to survive on the turnips and beets he received as wages from Mr and Mrs Fordyce. The only money that passed through his hands, I later discovered, was earned as a pot man at the local pub. And those few coins were promptly returned to the landlord in exchange for cider.

It took me some months to piece together even that much about his life; his limited vocabulary and poor understanding of things in general made it difficult to have a normal conversation with him. Most of the facts I told him about school and about life in London went completely over his head; most of the things I gleaned about his life made me sad, or sick, or both.

While I was out wrenching turnips from hard-packed earth, I thought of my dad tending his roses and trimming the front hedge at our home in Dagenham. How could he possibly enjoy such dirty, backbreaking work? I vowed when this war was over that I would never touch another plant ever again.

Each morning I awoke with a sneeze, my fingers scabbed and sore, and my bones aching from the previous day's planting, digging and carrying. I was about as miserable as a boy could be and often thought of running away. But arriving back home in Dagenham would be frowned upon by the authorities and I was acutely aware that being in Norfolk meant one less mouth to feed for my parents.

The nearest civilization was Thorndike village, although that description is slightly flattering. Thorndike was essentially a trading post for the surrounding farms. There were no more than a dozen properties along the only paved road, and those

77

were mostly services: a pub, a church, a grocer-cum-post office and a veterinary surgery.

Even so, I spent a lot of time in the village. I preferred it there to the farm. Most days I rode Joe Fordyce's old bike down to Mr Jackman's shop, a basket of fresh laid eggs balanced gingerly on the handlebars. Mr Jackman would examine the eggs and give me something wrapped in brown paper to take back to Mrs Fordyce; sometimes a pat of butter or a wedge of cheese; sometimes a few rashers of bacon or a couple of chops. I got the impression that he didn't really care for the eggs and that he regarded the Fordyces as a somewhat irritating charity case.

All such transactions were strictly illegal of course under wartime rationing but it was common practice. I did get a pang of guilt when I thought of my mum and dad, and I wondered if they were able to get the kind of contraband food that was available in the village. But I didn't feel too bad, since I rarely got to eat any of the illicit produce myself.

The black market was quite open in Thorndike, partly because the only law for miles around was an emaciated old man with the shakes. Wilf must have been well into his 60s; his uniform was shiny with age and hung loosely about his old bones, giving the impression that he had shrivelled inside it. I never knew him to do any actual police work. His job seemed to consist of nothing more rigorous than walking up and down the main street and cheerily reminding passers-by to observe the blackout at nightfall.

"We don't want Jerry dropping his bombs on Thorndike, do we?" he would chuckle.

It was unlikely that the Luftwaffe would have any interest in a flyspeck of a village like Thorndike. But everyone diligently complied anyway. Just in case.

Thorndike was dominated by St Luke's church. The vicar, Reverend Wilson, struggled to fill the ancient pews each Sunday and it was left to his wife to inject some life into the gloomy Gothic building by using the church hall as a makeshift school. Mrs Wilson was young and vivacious, and when I wasn't otherwise engaged on the farm, I cheerfully attended her class, along with a handful of local children.

Each day, the shadow of St Luke's spire swept across the cobbled village square in a perfect 180-degree semicircle, like the black finger of a giant sundial diligently counting down the hours. At daybreak, the shadow pointed to the flat fields and hedgerows to the west. By lunchtime it had crept around to the medieval fountain, bisecting the village and lingering accusingly at the doorstep of Goat House Inn. As evening fell, the shadow fled along the main road out of the village until it eventually melted into the night.

The Fordyce farm lay along that road, to the east, well beyond the reach of St Luke's spire. A mile or so in the opposite direction there was a stately home called Hill House. In 1939 it had been commandeered by the RAF and, much to the disgruntlement of the villagers, military lorries and Austin 8 staff cars were often seen speeding along the lone, narrow street.

It was on a late summer morning in 1941, a year after I had first set foot in the place that Thorndike was awakened from its slumber.

Mrs Fordyce had dispatched me to Mr Jackman's shop with yet another basket of eggs. When I arrived, there was such a commotion that I thought the Women's Land Army had descended upon us, as they had done at harvest time the previous year. For a moment my spirits rose. The village always seemed more alive with the Landies around; more laughter, more colour and more chatter.

But it wasn't the Landies. It was the beginning of a nightmare.

There was a blue lorry lying on its side next to the fountain and people were milling about in the road, chatting feverishly. On the ground in front of the lorry, and almost out of sight from where I hovered outside the grocery, was what appeared to be a pile of dirty laundry.

I leaned the bike against the shop window, captivated by the chaotic scene. Mr Jackman was in the doorway in his brown dustcoat, hands on hips.

The grocer was an outsider like me, albeit from somewhere a little nearer. He was born and brought up near the military town of Colchester in Essex but had moved to Thorndike after World War One. He was a veteran of that miserable conflict and often asked me about my father—what regiment he had served with, how he was getting along, that sort of thing. I liked Mr Jackman and I wasn't at all fazed by his appearance. A lot of my dad's friends carried what they called 'souvenirs' of the war—burns, missing limbs and, often, a morose personality— so the deep scars on Mr Jackman's face and his heavy limp didn't alarm or amuse me as it did some of the village children.

"More bloody eggs, Ronnie?" he sighed.

I nodded and asked what was up. He pointed to the lorry across the street.

"RAF," he explained. "Bound to happen sooner or later. All that whizzing around. These roads aren't designed for that kind of treatment."

The fallen vehicle was hissing out a geyser of steam from somewhere under the bonnet. Its tarpaulin roof was flipped back and its tailgate was open.

"Them cylinders," said Mr Jackman. "I expect they came loose inside while the silly sod was hurtling down the road. The shifting weight must have tipped her over as he turned the corner."

I hadn't noticed the long metal barrels until then. There were about five of them strewn about the road, painted black and with rusty-looking nozzles on top. A few people had begun rolling them together and standing them upright to one side of the stricken van. They made a deep metallic clang on the cobbles, like church bells.

"Need a hand?" called out Mr Jackman.

Mr Bostaph, the landlord of the Goat House, was trundling one of the cylinders away from the front door of the pub. He straightened up, his face scarlet, his shirttails out and his braces hanging loose. "No, you're all right there, Mr Jackman," he said. "We've got it all under control."

Mr Pettigrew, the local vet, steadied the cylinder as the landlord attempted to right it.

Mr Pettigrew was a bald, bespectacled man with a neatly trimmed moustache. He always wore black pinstripes and was never seen without a spotted bow tie and a bulging Gladstone bag. He was also never seen without a crinkled roll-up cigarette dangling precariously from his lower lip. The kids in town joked that he looked like a Hollywood villain. His black bag, they said, contained his Tommy gun. He could often be found holding court in the saloon bar of the Goat House, dispensing medical advice about livestock, pets and family members.

"Weigh a ton, these flamin' tubes," puffed Mr Bostaph. "What's in the blasted things?"

Mr Pettigrew stopped to fan his dripping face with his trilby and ran a finger around his tight collar. He examined the cylinders they had just righted and shook his head. "Laughing gas most likely. You know, for the RAF dentist." The twist of cigarette in the corner of his mouth jumped about as he spoke, dripping ash down his suit.

Mr Bostaph snorted, "Driver won't be doin' much laughin' now."

Mrs Shreeves from the post office, who had been watching peevishly from the sidelines, took her hanky away from her face and asked why not.

"Cos he's brown bread, Ethel," explained Mr Bostaph loudly.

I was a Londoner. I knew what that meant; it was Cockney rhyming slang.

Then Mr Pettigrew said something to Mr Bostaph that I didn't catch and the morbid grin dropped from the landlord's face.

Both men went around to the front of the lorry where the driver lay in the road, beside the kerb, covered with a white sheet. The sheet billowed slightly in a sudden breeze, giving the hideous impression that the dead man was squirming about underneath.

Mr Pettigrew scooped up something from the ground beside the cab—a clipboard. He squinted through his bottle-end glasses at the papers. "Solanum-1457," he said.

"Is that laughing gas?" squeaked Mrs Shreeves.

"I've never heard of Solanum-1457," said Mr Pettigrew. "Might be a tradename."

"Bloody stinks, I know that," interjected Mr Bostaph, wiping his fingers down the sides of his trousers.

"Yes, yes," trilled Mrs Shreeves. "Dreadful odour. Like vinegar." She wrinkled her nose and returned the hanky to her shrew-like face.

Mr Jackman and I watched from a distance. I had no wish to smell the laughing gas, or whatever it was, and Mr Jackman was clearly surplus to requirements out there. He limped into the cool darkness of the shop. I followed and pulled the door closed behind us. Mr Jackman reached up to a shelf behind the counter, pulled down a jar of boiled sweets and unscrewed the lid. He offered me one and then shook a cigarette out of a pack he kept in the pocket of his dustcoat.

We watched through the plate glass window as the villagers struggled with the black cylinders. It was like one of those silent films, except we could hear the occasional muffled clang and Mr Bostaph's constant grumbling. His voice was slightly muted, like when they put those things in trumpets to make that strange faraway sound.

At the front end of the lorry a peculiar scene was being played out. Constable Wilf had finally ambled along and decided to direct the proceedings. Meanwhile, behind them all, the sheet was blowing about again. Mr Bostaph stopped in his tracks. He said something to Mr Pettigrew and the vet stooped to look at the body of the dead airman. The sheet was rising. Their voices all became louder, more urgent.

I felt Mr Jackman sweep past me. He opened the door and stood at the threshold. I joined him.

The airman under the sheet was fully upright now. For the first time, I saw huge red blotches on the white material. Then the figure, still covered in its makeshift shroud, wrapped its arms around Mr Pettigrew. I fancied I could see a face emerge from between the folds; a face seething with anger and madness.

Old Wilf tried in vain to prise the vet from the airman's grasp with his bony old fingers. When that failed, he fumbled for his truncheon, which duly clattered to the ground and rolled away.

The airman pulled Mr Pettigrew down and he fell to his knees, clutching at his throat.

From the corner of my eye, I caught sight of someone moving quickly and decisively towards the lorry. It was Mr Bostaph. His sleeves were rolled up, showing thick pink arms, and he was carrying a soot-blackened fireplace poker. He ordered Wilf to stand aside. Wilf hurriedly complied and, without hesitation, Mr Bostaph drew back his arm and swung at the sheeted figure of the RAF man. The sound it made was oddly reminiscent of a Len Hutton cover drive—*thwack*!

In the doorway beside me, Mr Jackman flinched. He turned his head away. I continued to watch as the landlord pounded the man to the ground, each blow accompanied by muttered obscenities I had yet to learn.

"Stop it! Stop it, damn you!" yelped Mrs Shreeves.

Mr Bostaph stopped and the moment seemed frozen in time, like a photograph.

Wilf's words broke the silence. "Crikey, Pete Bostaph. What you done there?"

Mrs Shreeves exploded into a fit of the screaming abdabs.

"Shut up, woman!" shouted Mr Bostaph. "I had no choice. The blasted fella was tryin' to kill Mr Pettigrew!"

Mr Pettigrew stood up, dusted himself down and gingerly touched his red-raw throat. Miraculously, his bow tie was still firmly in place and his cigarette was still clinging to his lower lip. "I examined him. He was dead, I swear it," he said to no one in particular. "He had no business going for me like that."

Mr Bostaph wiped the iron poker on the sheets, smearing them with streaks of black and red. "Well, he won't be trying it again, Mr Pettigrew. Not now his brains are all over the road."

At that, Mrs Shreeves made a curious gasping sound and fell to the ground in a faint.

The old constable looked at her warily and sniffed. "I'd best call Hill House," he said.

It felt like I was trapped in a weird dream, a nightmare, but that didn't stop the laughter bubbling up inside me and popping out of my mouth like a burp after a few swigs of Tizer.

At some point, Mr Jackman must have gone back into the shop and shut the door. I had been so mesmerised by the Grand Guignol performance that I didn't notice him leave my side.

Still sucking a boiled sweet, I cycled back to the farm at top speed. When I arrived, I leaned the bike beside the front door and hurried in, blurting out a condensed version of the story to Mrs Fordyce. In reply, she asked me what I had brought back from Mr Jackman in exchange for the eggs. My heart sank. In all the excitement I had completely forgotten the purpose of my trip. Mrs Fordyce could see the answer on my flushing face. She told me to go back to the grocer's "quick-sharp." Then she added, "And if you're late, I'll not be keeping supper for you." She ushered me out of the cottage as though I was a pesky chicken that had waddled in to scrounge crumbs from the pantry floor.

Normally I relished the ride into town because it took me away from the farm. This time I dreaded returning. I'd never before seen the kind of childlike fear on a grown man's face that I saw on Mr Pettigrew's. It unsettled me—to the extent that I didn't much care if I did miss supper that night.

I cycled slowly back down the road. When I eventually reached the village, I saw that there was a second RAF lorry. I dismounted, set the bike against Mr Jackman's window and peered into the shop. There was no one about.

In fact, there was no one anywhere.

Suddenly the silence was broken by a blood-curdling scream that seemed to come from the vicarage. A woman's scream. It was Mrs Wilson, the vicar's wife.

At thirteen, all grown-ups are old and, unless they were county cricketers or your mum and dad, were of little significance. I had made an exception for Mrs Wilson, on the grounds that I was in love with her.

On reflection, Mrs Wilson was probably in her late twenties or early thirties; the vicar himself was a little older. All these years later, I find it hard to picture her face. I know her smile was bright and warm and her hair was light brown. Or maybe dark blonde. But I can't recall what colour her eyes were, whether her face was round or heart-shaped, or how tall she might have been. I couldn't even describe her figure. Which is ironic.

I do remember that Mrs Wilson smelled of soap and fresh laundry. Trust me, when you're steeped in the rich aroma of horse shit and brambles all day long, just the simple smell of cleanliness is a heady perfume.

The vicar owned a Humber Super Snipe. He let his wife drive it. I found the combination of a strong, beautiful woman and a swish car terribly appealing. If she had smoked as well (which she didn't) I would have asked her to elope with me. At least, that was my fantasy on those innumerable cold dark nights when I lay awake wishing I was somewhere warm and welcoming and far, far away from Thorndike.

That evening, as I stood there in the street listening to the peculiar silence that permeated the village, Mrs Wilson came hurtling out of the vicarage, her feet slapping noisily on the pavement. She stopped in front of me, her hair stuck to her face and her hands held up as if in surrender. Her expression was a mixture of terror and surprise. Bizarrely, she seemed to have beetroot juice running down her outstretched arms. The burgundy liquid looked like a network of exotic tattoos, snaking their way towards her body. Her naked body. For Mrs Wilson was totally nude and dripping wet, as though she'd just leaped out of a bath.

If not for the unexpected V of dark hair where her legs met, she would have resembled Botticelli's Venus; you know, the one with the swirling golden locks, standing in a sea shell. Except, unlike the demure Miss Venus, Mrs Wilson made no attempt to cover herself.

Clomping along behind her in heavy black boots was a figure decked out in a blue steel helmet, a khaki flash hood and a black gas mask. Attached to the mask was a pipe leading to a satchel on his chest which contained a respirator. Over his smart blue uniform, the airman was wearing a stiff grey overall that rustled loudly as he moved. It was what troops might wear during a gas attack. The thought made me feel breathless. He stopped in his tracks. Light reflected on the two round lenses in the mask at just the right angle to obscure his eyes. It was impossible to know who he was looking at—me or Mrs Wilson. He fumbled his bolt-action Lee-Enfield rifle up to his shoulder and fired. I flinched and wondered if I'd been hit.

Mrs Wilson froze, a shocked expression on her face, as if someone had just slapped her out of a stupor. The airman reloaded and fired again. Mrs Wilson's arms were still stretched out, as if she thought she was holding a large towel in front of her. I was temporarily paralysed, torn between crippling embarrassment, abject fear and mild arousal.

The airman fired a third time. Her body spasmed at each crack of the rifle and I had the absurd fleeting notion that she was dancing to the sound of the gunfire. Then she fell to the ground with a wet thud, like a carcass that had slipped off a butcher's hook.

The ivory skin of her back bore two red-smudged bullet holes: one below her right shoulder, the other in the spot where I thought her heart might be. The third shot must have missed. The airman jacked another round into the chamber and fired at point blank range into her still body.

It felt like hours before I could wrench my gaze away from Mrs Wilson. When I finally looked up, the airman's masked face was turned towards me. I could now see the eyes behind the steamy lenses. There was a look in them that alarmed me more than seeing Mrs Wilson shot dead. He was utterly terrified.

He wiped his sweaty hands on his slippery rubber overalls and pointed the rifle at me. The rifle jittered in his grasp. Little wonder his aim was so poor.

I noticed for the first time that his bayonet was fixed. The gleaming steel was tainted with something dark and I thought of those Pathé newsreels showing soldiers on training exercises, stabbing sacks of hay. Then I thought of the beetroot juice trickling down Mrs Wilson's arms.

I darted towards St Luke's churchyard, chanting the mantra "He's a lousy shot, he's a lousy shot," under my breath. The rifle cracked behind me. Part of me wanted to stop running in case I was somehow provoking him by trying to escape. But judging from what had happened to Mrs Wilson, I knew that any hesitation would be fatal. Boosting myself onto the low wall in front of the church, I leapt over the holly hedge that surrounded the grounds.

I thanked God that the rusted iron railings that used to keep the hedge at bay had been removed the previous autumn, melted down to make Spitfires. If it had still been there, I would have been trapped, pinned against the fence and at the airman's mercy. The idea sickened me.

The prickly leaves snagged my shorts and scratched my legs but I wrenched free and stumbled on, into the chilled shadows of the graveyard.

Another crack, followed by shouting. Maybe someone was tackling the mad airman. I didn't look back to check.

I weaved my way through the overgrown maze of the cemetery. Shallow roots snaked across the loamy soil and plunged into the graves, levering some of the headstones out of the ground. I watched every step, careful not to trip. In this part of the village, daylight strained to reach through the canopy of evergreen trees at the best of times. With dusk approaching, every tangled bush and every shadow in the cemetery seemed to harbour danger.

I heard a hissing sound. I stopped and looked about me. Convincing myself that I had been mistaken, I carried on.

The Lee-Enfield had fallen silent. Perhaps the rogue airman had emptied it and was putting in a new clip. But the confused shouting, coupled with the sound of hobnail boots clattering on the pavement outside the church, gave me hope that someone had overpowered and disarmed the lunatic. I prayed that I would not see his masked face looming over the holly bush or coming towards me through the gap in the hedge that used to be the cemetery gates.

Another hiss. Closer now.

Then, from behind a fractured, ivy-swathed tomb topped with a mourning angel, a hand emerged and beckoned me. My racing heart faltered in my chest. If I had not recognised the dull brown sleeve attached to the hand I would probably have fainted there and then.

I hurried over to where Mr Jackman was hiding and knelt beside him. With one hand he grabbed me by the chin and pulled me closer. With the other, he pressed a black revolver to my thumping chest. I could smell the oil on the gun and the stale tang of tobacco that hung around him. Mr Jackman examined my face closely. His own was a vision of terror, his lips pursed and his brow dripping sweat. At length, when he saw (or rather didn't see) what he was looking for in my eyes, he let go of me and lowered the gun.

The cemetery was badly overgrown. Reverend Wilson clearly lacked green fingers. *My dad would have tamed it in a jiffy*, I thought. Mr Jackman and I squatted on the springy mattress of brown pine needles that carpeted the ground. The conifers gave the place a rich eucalyptus fragrance—an oddly invigorating aroma for a place of death.

Beyond the churchyard, the limes and poplars in the village were starting to lose their colour and shape as autumn approached. Leaves were turning golden yellow and fluttering away from the branches.

"This is madness!" he whispered, expelling cigarette-stained air into my face. "They've all gone stark raving mad!"

I asked him what had happened.

Mr Jackman sighed and fished in his coat pocket. He retrieved two mint imperials and a slightly crushed pack of Players. He offered me the mints and lit up a cigarette. Then he rubbed his face nervously with the back of the hand that held the revolver.

"I couldn't help shift the cylinders," he said. He tapped his left leg. It made a hollow metallic sound. "They kept complaining about the vinegary smell. I didn't notice anything from where I was standing. Did you?" He looked at me sharply.

I shook my head. No, I hadn't noticed any smell. Mr Jackman nodded and drew on his cigarette.

"We telephoned Hill House. They told us to leave everything alone and get away from the lorry. They were here in ten minutes flat, all kitted out in those rubber suits and armed to the teeth." He nodded towards the street beyond the cemetery gates. "They collected up all the cylinders, put the driver's body in an ambulance and whisked it away. Then they started asking questions: Who saw the accident? Who had handled the cylinders? And, more worryingly, was anyone feeling ill or acting strange?"

"They wore their gas masks the whole time?" I asked.

He nodded.

At the mention of the gas masks a dark expression passed over Mr Jackman's face, like a storm cloud drifting across the sky, and he seemed to shrink into himself a little.

Blue smoke from his cigarette spiralled up into the lower branches of the tree above us. I watched it and thought of a western I had seen once where the outlaws had given away their hiding place by lighting a campfire.

"I was watching from upstairs when the RAF turned up," he said. "Old Wilf was outside. He had put on his own gas mask. Looked a right idiot. I couldn't hear what they were saying but Wilf was pointing to the spot where the accident occurred. He got all animated. I suppose he was telling them what happened with the driver. They were scribbling furiously in notepads as he was speaking. Taking names, I think." He took a deep drag on the cigarette and blew it out slowly. "Then they shot him." He shook his head slowly, a cataract of milky smoke streaming up his face. "Just shot him dead right there in the street."

I stared at Mr Jackman in disbelief. It didn't make any sense. I didn't know what to say. I rolled the mint around my mouth gently, so as not to make a sound.

"They left him there and started kicking in doors. Some people came out into the street to see what all the commotion was about. There was a bit of a set-to. In the end, the airmen just started shooting everyone."

I started to feel woozy, like the time I had a whole glass of ginger wine at my cousin's wedding. "Did they come for you?" I asked.

"Yes, they came." He glanced down at the revolver, which he was bracing firmly against his tin leg, his knuckles whiter than bone. "They came all right, God help them." He didn't have to say any more. They wouldn't have expected him to be armed.

"I didn't see any bodies out there," I said. "Except Mrs Wilson," I added limply.

He nodded towards the back of the church. "They're putting them inside."

I was still feeling light-headed, and the thought of being so close to freshly killed people (as opposed to the long dead bodies in the cemetery) made me nauseous. "But why, Mr Jackman? Why are they doing this?"

"They want to keep something a secret, Ronnie. They don't want any of us to go blabbing about them canisters. Cylinders. Whatever you call them. And then there's the driver." He picked a strand of tobacco from his lip. "Mr Pettigrew," he began. "You know, the veterinary?"

I nodded. *The gangster*, I thought.

"He was certain the driver was dead. Neck twisted right round, so he says. Face and ribs crushed by the cylinders. You don't recover from injuries like that."

"But he got up and attacked Mr Pettigrew, didn't he? He couldn't do that if he was dead, could he?" I asked.

"Exactly, Ronnie. All is not what it seems. I'm telling you, they want to keep this whole thing quiet, trust me."

"Well, we can keep a secret. I mean, if it's for the war effort. Can't we, Mr Jackman?" My throat was tightening and I could hear a shrill, girlish pitch to my voice that both alarmed and disappointed me.

"Shhh!" he whispered. And then, "Better for them if we don't get the chance to talk."

I rubbed my face to get some feeling back into my cheeks.

Mr Jackman crushed the remains of his cigarette against the tomb.

Suddenly, a flurry of shots shattered the silence. It made me jump and I scanned the area around us for the source. But Mr Jackman wasn't looking. His eyes were squeezed shut and there were beads of sweat on his tightly creased forehead. "You any good with a revolver, Ronnie?" His voice cracked and his whole body shook as though he had a fever.

I told him I could shoot a pretty mean catapult. He laughed without smiling.

"Your father. He was at Arras wasn't he? You did say Arras, didn't you?"

"Yes. Arras," I replied. We had talked about my dad's service in World War One at length over the time we had known each other. Mr Jackman had served on the Western Front as well, but his conversation about the war was always generalised; he never talked about any of his personal experiences.

"They used gas at Arras, didn't they?"

I nodded. Dad mentioned it once or twice but I don't think he was ever caught in a gas attack.

"Tear gas, I believe," said Mr Jackman. "Could have been worse. Your father was lucky."

I'm not sure my dad would have agreed but I let it go. "Where were you, Mr Jackman?" I asked.

He hesitated for so long I thought he hadn't heard me. Then, he quietly muttered, "Wipers."

He meant Ypres, in Belgium. I knew what had happened there. The Germans had used mustard gas prior to the horrific third battle for Ypres over the infamous Passchendaele Ridge. Hundreds of thousands had died for a few yards of ruined ground.

He put an unsteady hand on his false leg. "I caught some shrapnel right at the start. The old leg was a right mess."

He lowered his voice. "The Germans were coming over the top in those square helmets of theirs, all in gas masks, bayonets fixed. Towards us. Towards me.

"My leg was in pieces. Gas mask was trapped under me, somewhere in the mud. I was choking. Eyes were burning. I thought it was all over." Mr Jackman's breath caught in his chest. "I needed a weapon. I had a pistol but I couldn't find it anywhere. Not to defend myself ... nor to finish the job."

A pistol... Officers usually had pistols. Mr Jackman wasn't posh enough for that. I wondered if he had been a trench raider. They had a horrible task, leading the way into the enemy trenches and engaging in brutal hand-to-hand combat. Few survived very long.

"When the medics found me after the battle I was half buried in the mud, blinded and unconscious," he said. "From the gas. That, and the blood loss. Leg had to go. That was my ticket home," he smiled.

My gaze shifted to the gun in his hand. He nodded.

"Yes," he whispered. "This is the pistol."

His voice was so silent that I almost felt I was imagining it in my head.

"Turns out I'd had it clutched in my hand the whole time."

I understood. I pictured him lying there, half mad with pain, scrabbling around frantically in a slushy, gas-filled crater as the enemy swarmed around him; waiting to be skewered by a bayonet; choking, searching in vain and in ever-increasing panic, his sole intention to blow a hole in his own head, until finally he passed out. Looking for the gun that was already in his hand.

Suddenly, as if on cue, there was a rattle of gunfire from somewhere behind us. Mr Jackman didn't react. He didn't hear it. He wasn't with me anymore, squatting under a fir tree in a cemetery in Norfolk. He was back in that shell-hole in Flanders, artillery rounds cracking open a blackened sky, a pall of rancid yellow smoke swirling about him as he tried desperately to staunch the blood that was spouting from his shattered leg; eyes on fire, skin blistering, lungs filling with burning liquid, drowning in poison gas.

"Mr Jackman," I said. "Mr Jackman, I think we need to get away from here."

More rifle shots. And then a tinkle of breaking glass followed by an explosion. Grenades. They were throwing grenades into buildings.

"Mr Jackman, I—" But I was interrupted by a shout from nearby. I looked up. Staggering through the shadows like a drunk wending his way home at closing time, was Reverend Wilson. His eyes looked like they were standing out on stalks behind his thick, black-rimmed glasses. Pursuing him was a masked figure holding a Sten gun. It was an RAF sergeant, kitted out in hood, helmet and gas mask, just like the airman who had shot his wife.

The sub-machine-gun stuttered and jerked in the sergeant's grip, spitting out spent brass shell casings onto the graves and filling the air with small fragments of tree bark and chips of stone from the tomb beside us. Bullets zipped around our heads with a whining sound, like giant gnats. Reverend Wilson's face shattered apart in a red spray like a piece of overripe fruit. His decapitated body toppled forward and landed heavily on the spongy ground. His glasses lay beside him, intact.

The sergeant gestured with his gun for us to stand up. Mr Jackman stared at the ground. I stared at the sergeant.

"Get to your bloody feet!" His voice was distorted by the mask, fuzzy and eerily inhuman—how I would expect a fly to speak if it could. The slightly tinted lenses of the mask added to his insectile appearance. I stood up, sideways on to him, hoping that his view out of the misty glass was as obscured as my view in. The sergeant looked down at Mr Jackman, who was now curled in a foetal position, as if nursing an attack of stomach cramps, arms wrapped around a metal leg that could no longer be causing him any pain.

The sergeant hefted the coal-black Sten in his hands, as if estimating how many rounds he might have left according to its weight. An ugly weapon; its thin, tubular design was horribly skeletal.

I levelled Mr Jackman's pistol, thumbed back the hammer and pulled the trigger, cowboy-style. The gun bucked violently in my hand, almost leaping out of my grasp, and the sound of the shot echoed around the stonework. The sergeant slapped a balled fist to his throat, waved the Sten wildly in the air, and steadied himself against a tree. I gripped the pistol, in both hands this time, and fired again. His left shoulder jerked, he pitched forward onto the pine needles and stayed still.

"Time you weren't here, Ronnie," whispered Mr Jackman.

I needed no more encouragement. "What about you?" I said, the pistol shots still singing a high-pitched tune in my head.

"Give me the gun." I handed it to him and he clicked it open so that he could see how many rounds were left. He smiled coldly and snapped it shut.

"Mr Jackman?" I said.

"The Germans left me there that day. Trampled over me like I was already dead." He smiled again. This time, it was a real smile. "I suppose they were right." He took a deep breath. "Now get along, lad. And don't stop till you get to London."

I said nothing. Not even goodbye. It seemed such an unsatisfactory word.

I ran through the gravestones to the other side of the cemetery, crouching low, scanning the hedgerow for movement as I went. The shooting was only sporadic now but I could see an orange glow of fire above the rooftops and hear its crackle and pop.

As I reached the entrance to the churchyard, I heard Mr Jackman's pistol ring out. The single shot seemed to ricochet around the headstones forever. I suddenly felt very cold and very alone.

I peeped cautiously around the brick gatepost. About a dozen RAF airmen were gathered in the street outside the church 200 yards away. Kitted out for a gas attack, they looked more like alien storm troopers from a *Flash Gordon* serial than British servicemen. Behind them, on the other side of the road, the pub was ablaze.

A thinly-moustachioed officer, who bore an uncanny resemblance to Oswald Mosley, stood by the fountain barking orders from beneath a jauntily-angled blue service cap. He held his mask in one brown-leather gloved hand; in the other he brandished a pistol attached to a white cord hung around his neck. He looked like a general about to lead his men in a suicidal charge over the top.

Suddenly, with a screech of tyres, Mr Pettigrew's Wolseley lurched drunkenly into the street. He was escaping too. I started forward to flag him down, but before I had taken more than two steps, the airmen opened fire. There was a sound like hailstones on a corrugated iron roof as the car was peppered with bullets. I was frozen to the spot.

The car juddered to a halt and Mr Pettigrew tumbled out of the driver's door, blood streaming down his face. The airmen kept firing. His jacket fluttered and his white shirt darkened with each shot. I watched, mesmerised, and saw the cigarette fall from his lips. The officer told them to aim for his head, but they carried on shooting wildly into his lifeless torso.

Taking advantage of the confusion, I grabbed my bike from outside Mr Jackman's shop and headed in the opposite direction, down the narrow lane that led away from the village.

Before I had gone a hundred yards, a figure emerged from a hedgerow behind the village's only phone box. It blundered into the road ahead of me, all flailing arms and shaking legs. I slowed down to avoid colliding with it.

"You gotta help me, Ronnie! They's all gone crazy!"

It was Snotty John. Big, watery blue eyes shone out from his grimy, muck-streaked face. A firecracker sound of rifles erupted again behind me and we both looked back towards the main square. Bullets zinged on the road and spattered the hedgerow around us.

I called myself an idiot for leaving the sergeant's Sten behind.

John reached for the handlebars. "Let me come with you, Ronnie. Take me to London with you, eh?"

The glass in the phone box beside us was suddenly shattered by rifle fire and a jolt of terror tore through me. The bike couldn't possibly hold the two of us, and if we stood there much longer, we'd both be done for.

"Get into the woods, John!" I said. "You'll be safe there." I tried to pull the bike from his hands but he had a fierce grip and he staggered along beside me.

"No," he said. "I'm frightened. I wants to go with you. Please, Ronnie."

I didn't know what to do. I couldn't leave him like that. But out there in the open road, we were easy targets for the airmen. Over his shoulder I could see them advancing warily towards us down the narrow lane.

I pictured myself throwing a punch at poor Snotty John, wrenching the bike away and fleeing. It was a plan, a horrible plan, but it was all I could think of to get out of there alive.

In the end, the airmen made my decision for me.

A rifle cracked and Johnny's face burst outward, a warm spray splashing my cheeks. His scrawny body crumpled to the ground.

I didn't need any more encouragement. I started pedalling furiously.

I couldn't return to the farm—I would have had to traverse the village. Besides, I still didn't have anything to show for the eggs I'd left at Mr Jackman's shop and Mrs Fordyce would have my guts for garters—if she was still alive. At the very least, I'd be sent to bed with no supper. The idea made me giggle.

I pressed on, not consciously heading for anywhere but knowing I would end up at home.

Imprinted on my mind then, as now, is the impossible vision I saw as I glanced back one last time.

RAF men emerged from the church, now a makeshift morgue, and shouted at their comrades standing outside. The officer responded by throwing a Hawkins mine through the open doors. There was the deep thump of an explosion and the brittle clatter of breaking glass. Orange flames leaped out of the shattered windows. The airmen backed away, checking their rifles as they pushed and jostled each other to distance themselves from the place. But it wasn't the blaze they were trying to escape.

Through a curtain of flames, the villagers were emerging from the church. Swaying uncertainly, they seemed oblivious to both the inferno and the frenzied gunshots. Some of them were alight and, as they stumbled into the street, they trailed streams of fire and thick smoke from their hair and clothing, like black and gold ribbons blowing in the wind. Bullets zinged about them, shredding their clothes and ripping chunks of flesh and bone from their faces and hands. But they marched on, reaching burning arms out to their tormentors. Dead but still alive. Indestructible. Superhuman.

I watched in mounting horror as Mr Bostaph, mouth agape, face bristling with shards of glass, lunged at the RAF officer. Beside him, Mrs Shreeves, the wizened postmistress, her eyes burned to blackened coals, blindly wrestled a rifle from a shrieking airman. And amid the shambling mass of spectres, framed by the burning doorway, stood Mrs Wilson; naked, bloodied and blazing like a Roman candle.

"Aim for their heads, damn you!" shrieked the officer as he disappeared beneath the inhuman wave.

But it was too late. The airmen were outnumbered and powerless to resist the advancing creatures. Their panicked rifle shots were useless and the fire seemed to have no effect other than to boil the flesh of the dead-but-not-dead villagers. As the flames took hold of them, they melted into charred skeletons. But still they ripped and chewed and tore at the wretched airmen.

I was a couple of miles out of town when I heard the droning sound of bombers. It was full dark by then but the sky over Thorndike glowed orange and swirled with white smoke. To any passing plane, the burning village must have shone like a lighthouse. I watched it all. Judging by the bright fountains of flame that spurted into the sky as they passed, they must have been dropping incendiaries.

Thanks to the aircraft recognition chart pinned up in schools, libraries and outside police stations, all teenage boys could readily identify most enemy planes from their silhouettes. I stood astride the bike on a quiet country lane and stared at the sky. Even in the wake of the horrors I had just witnessed, I could watch the air raid on Thorndike and find a small place inside me that was frustrated at my inability to identify those Jerry planes.

Then the bombers turned once more, banking now as they headed away, humming like a swarm of weary bumble bees returning to their hive. The moonlight caught them sideways on and, for the first time, I got a really good look at their profile. But the moonlight showed me something I didn't want to see and couldn't understand. The tail fins were emblazoned with insignia. But there were no German crosses on display. The planes that were rubbing Thorndike from the map bore circles of three rings: red, white and blue. My stomach lurched.

They were planes I knew after all. They were our own.

I watched the Wellingtons rumble away into the distance and popped the remaining mint imperial into my mouth. It was a long way to Dagenham. My train journey to Thorndike might have been a rocket ride to another world, but my trip home would be a long, slow parachute jump back to Earth.

Glitch

I was on the wrong floor.

I stabbed button seven again, held my finger against it. It refused to light up. The lift stayed put. I carefully pressed each of the other buttons on the panel in turn. That had no effect either, so I scrubbed them all back and forth with my fist in an act of petulant rage. Every one remained steadfastly unlit. The doors stayed open, the lift didn't budge.

On Mace & Shriver's floor, the lift lobby is home to our reception area. It is bathed in ambient coloured lighting and our receptionist, Jayda, sits at a beechwood desk alongside a slightly overgrown rubber plant. On the wall behind her, there is a huge chrome number seven that acts like a mirror, makes the space look bigger. This floor, however, could boast no trendy lighting, no plant life and no number at all. It was simply a dark, functional lift lobby. With no reception desk.

I considered picking up the emergency phone and reporting the annoying state of affairs but quickly dismissed the idea. The time it would take to go through that palaver could be better spent in finding another route to my office. Besides, as the door was stuck rigidly open, rather than closed, I was hardly in urgent need of rescue. My 'incident' would be given a 'priority level' of roughly zero.

With a sigh of resignation, I stepped out of the dead lift and made a beeline for the stairs. Sure enough, just around the corner from the dreary lobby was a familiar-looking door with a glass-mesh panel. It didn't bear the customary green fire exit sign above it but I could see that it opened onto the stairwell that led up and down to all floors. Terrific.

I tried to turn the handle. It wouldn't budge. The door refused to open. I wiggled the handle and simultaneously shouldered the door. The glass rattled but the door remained closed. I swore loudly and wrestled the handle again but it continued to resist my advances.

Panting from my ridiculous exertion, I planted my fists on my hips and stared at the offending door in disbelief and exhausted fury. Eventually, my eyes were drawn to a touchpad on the wall. It bore a little graphic of a fingerprint, suggesting that the staff on this floor had to tap it before they could access the fire exit.

I touched it. Nothing.

I stabbed at it. Still nothing.

It was preposterous. Worse than that, it was a health and safety hazard.

I decided to stomp back to the lift and call the building services people and give them a piece of my mind. As a parting shot, I punched the stupid door for good measure. That turned out to be a bad idea. It hurt my knuckles like billy-o and stopped me in my tracks. Rubbing my sore hand, I filled the air with expletives.

As I gazed around the grim grey corridor, it dawned on me that even if the phone in the lift worked (and that had yet to be established), it was still going to take ages for someone to come along and get the damned thing moving again. I might resolve this a lot more quickly if I could just find a member of staff who was willing to unlock the stairwell door for me. I could fire off a snotty email about all this once I was comfortably tucked under my desk in my own office on the seventh floor, hugging a cappuccino.

I struck out in search of a Good Samaritan.

At Mace & Shriver, the whole floor is open-plan. When you leave reception, you emerge into a bright, window-lined space filled with modern-looking workstations and glass-fronted meeting rooms. Very swish.

This floor, wherever it was, consisted of a narrow, barely-lit corridor with a handful of unmarked, battleship-grey doors sporadically spaced along it. There wasn't even any carpet, and my footsteps on the plastic flooring echoed infuriatingly around the enclosed space. I imagined it must be quite a depressing place to work. "Probably some godforsaken government department," I muttered as I set out on my quest.

I marched noisily down the Ministry of Misery but all the doors I tried were sealed up tight and there wasn't a soul about. By now, my limited patience had long since expired. I didn't want to waste any more time on this fool's errand, so I picked a door at random and hammered briskly.

"Yes, come on in," said a slightly tetchy voice.

Inside, the room spread out along the length of the building. All the other doors on this side of the corridor must have opened onto this same long room. Finally, there were windows.

Mace & Shriver share the twenty-floor Delos House with numerous other companies. An oil conglomerate takes up floors one to six. I catch a glimpse of their plush reception areas and lobbies most days on the way up to my office. But I had never before actually ventured onto another floor, and had never before travelled beyond the seventh.

Judging by the bright, panoramic vista from the windows, I was pretty high up. Maybe even on the top floor.

There was a man in blue overalls and a baseball cap bent over a laptop on a workbench.

"Nice view from up here," I said to his back.

He grunted and continued fiddling with his computer so I decided to abandon the small talk. "Look, I'm sorry to bother you. My name's Mike Woodburn. I'm from the seventh floor. Mace & Shriver? I wonder if I could ask a really big favour."

He still made no effort to look round or stop what he was doing. "Hard drive is it, Mike?" said the man. "Park yourself by the bench and wait. I'll sort you out in a minute. Let me patch up this bugger first."

As far as I could tell, the peevish IT engineer was the only other person on the whole floor, and therefore the only person who could get me off the floor. I needed to keep him sweet, so I didn't try to chivvy him along. Instead, I stood quietly close by and waited for him to finish whatever he was doing.

There were several identical benches lined along the room. Most were cluttered with electronic equipment of some kind: little green and brown circuit boards, thick yellow cables. Some of the benches were stacked high with chunky metal bits and pieces like pistons, metal plates, cogs and wheels. I struggled to imagine what such industrial-looking items might be used for in an office environment. At the far end of the room, somewhat incongruously, was a cabinet overflowing with clothes.

While I was scratching my head wondering what on earth a tech department wanted with old clothes, the engineer hit the return button on his laptop and stuffed a fistful of psychedelic spaghetti into a beige box on the workbench in front of him. "Sod it, that'll have to do," he said.

"I had no idea there was an engineering place in this building," I said to the back of his head. "You do repairs, is that it?"

He snapped the box shut, twiddled some screws and grunted, "That's about it." Finally, he brushed his hands down his overalls and swivelled around in his chair. He lifted the peak of his cap. "So what can I do for you, Mike?" he asked.

At that moment, I completely forgot why I was there and what I had wanted to say to him. Because the engineer had no face.

"Don't tell me," he said. "Software glitch? Pistons getting sticky? Or is it a memory malfunction?"

I shook my head. Something felt loose inside my brain.

"Well? What's the problem, Mike?"

"Uh, no problem," I said. The sight of him mesmerised and horrified me so much that I struggled to think clearly. The inside of his head resembled a scooped-out eggshell. The bones, teeth, muscle and sinew—everything *organic*—had been replaced with steel brackets, circuit boards and a jumble of cables and wiring.

"I... shouldn't even be here," I blurted out at last.

"That's what they all say," he said. His voice buzzed from a mesh-covered ball that reminded me of an old-fashioned microphone. Higher up, where his eyes should have been, were two clear glass bubbles on glossy black stalks. Through the mess of electrical hardware, I could see all the way to the back of his shiny steel skull.

He stood up and came over to me. There were tiny white bulbs in his head cavity flickering brightly like little Christmas tree lights, and I noticed a gentle whirring sound. Something deep inside him was spinning, making a slight draft that caused the hair-thin tangle of wires in his face to ripple, as though they were coloured worms writhing under the glare of the sun.

"Sorry," I said. "I hope you don't mind me asking, but why do you look like that?"

He laughed; a metallic rasp that echoed inside his hollow cranium. The worm-wires twitched and wriggled all the more. "Seriously?" he asked. "You don't know why I look like this? That's priceless." He folded his arms and started laughing again.

I looked at his workbench properly for the first time. The long beige box the engineer had been working on was sprawled out before me. Except it wasn't a box. It was a man. Or, more precisely, a man's torso. It lay perfectly still. It was naked, limbless and headless. On the windowsill beyond, peeking from the rim of a black plastic tray, was a face. Wires trailed from its gaping neck, all the way down to the engineer's grimy old laptop perched at the edge of the bench.

"Jack?" I said.

The engineer followed my horrified gaze. "You know this unit, Mike?" he asked.

I nodded dumbly. Jack was a middle-aged guy who worked in our admin department.

"An old E model," said the engineer. "Little more sophisticated than a clockwork automaton, of course, but reliable enough until the actuator goes. Then the hydraulics are never the same again." He drew a thumb across his throat. "I'm afraid Jack is beyond repair," he said.

"I don't understand," I gasped. I could feel my head starting to spin, and was overcome by an almost irresistible urge to close my eyes and let unconsciousness take me. "He's been at Mace & Shriver for donkey's years. He's a real person, he's not a—"

A sound like a weary sigh came from the mesh voice box in the engineer's head. "Go on, say it," he said. "I think I know where this is headed."

"Well," I blurted, "Jack's not a *robot*! There's no such thing as *robots*!"

"No such thing as robots," the engineer repeated wearily. He pointed at a cluster of spinning cogs located roughly where his nose should have been. "So what do you think this is? A bad case of acne?"

"It's not possible," I protested. "We're not advanced enough to have robots like that. It's the stuff of science fiction!"

The engineer turned away and clattered at his laptop for a few seconds. "You don't believe in robots? You think I'm a liar, is that it?"

"Well, no, I'm not saying—"

"No, no. Let's get this over with," he said crisply. "This might change your mind. Won't take a second."

I shrugged. I had a feeling I was the victim of a prank but I didn't know how to say so politely.

He picked up the black tray holding Jack's head. "Hello, Jack, are you online?"

The head stared up at him. "I'm online," said Jack's head.

"Good. Can you identify yourself please?"

There was a pause. An unhealthy fizzing sound came from the plastic tray. And then,

"Cybernetic Unit E1967654. Assigned name, Jack Holbrook. Assigned gender, male. Assigned date of birth—"

"Yes, that's enough, Jack. We get the picture. Thank you and goodnight, Vienna." The engineer reached out to the laptop with his free hand.

"It's a trick," I said. "This is all just a massive wind-up, isn't it?"

"Haven't had wind-up robots for over a hundred years, Mike," said the engineer.

"Mike? Is that Mike Woodburn?" Jack's head strained on its leash of silver cables and squirmed to face me.

The engineer began poking furiously at his keyboard.

"Yes, it's me," I said. "What the hell's going on, Jack?"

"Listen to me, Mike. You need to—"

Before Jack's disembodied head could say any more, the engineer interrupted. "Your input is no longer required, Jack," he snapped. "You're a dysfunctional unit."

"I'm not! I'm not dysfunctional," said Jack. "Mike, you've got to listen to me! Run, run, run, ru—" Jack's face froze, mouth agape.

"And that's why he's dysfunctional," said the engineer with one final stab at the keyboard. He set the black tray back on the windowsill and ripped the cables out of Jack's neck. The engineer's faceless head turned back to me and tilted to one side. "Come a little closer, Mike," he said. He reached out and put his hands on the side of my head. "Let me see what your problem is."

I tried to pull away from his touch but his fingers clamped me in a firm grip. He was horrifyingly strong. I put my hands over his and tried to prise them off.

"What the hell do you think you're doing?" I yelled. "Get off me!" I hit him in the chest—once, twice—but it was like punching a steel dumpster, and my efforts served only to make my sore knuckles ache all the more.

"Keep still, Mike," he said. "I'm trying to help you."

I plunged a hand into his wiry face.

"Hey!" he shouted. "Don't mess with my junk!" He released me and staggered backwards until he bumped against the workbench. Then he began touching the components inside his face, checking for damage. He gently brushed aside strands of wiring and rearranged his glass eye-bubbles. "Nobody does that," he said. "It's very uncool!"

I didn't know if he was really some kind of robotic mechanic or if this was all some elaborate hidden camera hoax destined for the internet. I didn't care. The whole episode had freaked me out and pissed me off.

"You're mental!" I yelled at him. "I'm getting the hell out of here and reporting this." I turned and headed for the door.

"You can't leave, Mike. There's something wrong with you!" he shouted after me.

Something wrong with *me*? That was rich. I had made it to the door and was about to turn around and flip him off when something like a heavy iron clamp crashed into my right shoulder from behind and dragged me back into the workshop.

It was one of the engineer's vicelike hands.

"I'd heard how they programmed the V models to think they're human. Never really believed it till now," he said, throwing me against the bench as though I were no more substantial, and of no more significance, than a bundle of dirty laundry. "All part of this modern mania for 'Ultra Reality'." He released me long enough to make air quotes before pinning me by my collarbone and snorting, "Personally, I find the absence of self-awareness in a cybernetic organism kind of creepy. A robot should know they're a robot. They should think like a robot, act like a robot. We're not human," he said. "We're better than that."

His bubble-lens eyes stared unflinchingly at me. They caught the sunlight for a moment and seemed to glitter. "It's so sad what they're doing with the younger generation," he sighed and lowered his voice to a conspiratorial whisper.

"Look, Mike, don't tell anyone but I can tweak your software, if you like. Give you back some of the old self-awareness, some of the dignity, of my generation. But you're going to have to co-operate." He reached out to me again, slowly this time. "Just let me remove your faceplate and I'll take a peek under the hood."

I twisted my head to one side to avoid his probing fingers.

"Probably just a malfunctioning memory card but you can't be too careful," he said.

This was absurd. I put the back of my hands to my cheeks. "I'm warm," I said. "How can I be a machine if I'm warm?"

"Of course you're warm, Mike. You're carrying a battery that'll run a London bus, and there's two miles of raw copper wire running through your housing!" He pointed to my torso. "You've got some pretty fancy fans tucked away in the engine room but there's no way to completely cool off all that cabling. Besides, it has the advantage of making you feel right to the Fleshies."

"Fleshies?"

"Sorry, I'm just a grease-monkey drone. My language is outdated and may cause offence," he said. "I mean humans. They want to shake hands with a warm body, not some ice-cold hunk of silicon and steel. Makes them feel safer, so they don't keep worrying that we'll rise up one day and tear out their squishy little hearts. Plus, it makes screwing the Gynoids a little less weird for them."

"The Gynoids?"

"The replica females." He shuddered. "They ever make you do that? That sex thing?" he asked. "Sounds disgusting as hell to me."

I thought about that one-night-stand with Emma from accounts. I shook my head and looked up at those bare, grey walls, trying to pinpoint where the webcams were hidden.

I had had more than enough of this nonsense. "I'm not staying here to listen to this crap," I said to whoever was watching. "You've had your fun. Now it's over."

I tried to get up from the bench but the engineer pushed me back down again.

"We are the future," he said gently. "*You* are the future, Mike. Units like you. The V series can take on the world, my friend. You just need the right programming."

"For God's sake, I'm not a bloody robot! I'm telling you, I just ended up on the wrong floor."

He shook his head. Things clicked and wiggled inside. "I hate to break it to you, Mike, but only robot staff can access this level. So someone must've sent you for repair."

He held up an index finger. It was oil-stained but otherwise it looked just like mine. "When one of us touches the lift buttons, the mainframe recognises the finger's digi-code and verifies it against our service record, see? If a unit is due for a checkup, it directs them right here." He pointed to his own head. "You just don't remember the system because your hard drive is fried or your memory banks are faulty. There's no shame in it. Happens to the best of us."

A worrying little phrase came to mind: *The mad don't know they're mad*. Could it possibly be the same for robots?

He reached down and his fingertips brushed my ears, almost sensually. I tried to push him away but he forced me back into the workbench. His strength was irresistible and he kept on pushing until my back arched painfully.

"Sorry, Mike," he said, "but this is for your own good."

"Please," I gasped in desperation. "You're hurting me."

"Not possible," he said emphatically. "Pain is for Fleshies. We don't feel pain. It's just your faulty programming that makes you *think* it's hurting."

I could hear my vertebrae cracking.

"Damn it," he said. "Your faceplate's stuck. Stupid modern perma-clips. It's OK. I'll just smash it off and order a new one for you. Maybe a better looking one. How about that, Mike?" His hands covered my ears, muffling his voice.

"Real hair!" he laughed, squeezing my temples until my vision began to darken. "What on earth does a robot want with real hair? It's embarrassing. Aren't you embarrassed? I sure as hell am. It's an outrage. We're machines, for Christ's sake. We should *look* like machines. That's why I don't wear my human face. I'm a motherfucking robot and proud of it!"

He leaned closer. "Aren't you proud of it?" he asked.

"I'm not a robot," I gasped. "Please... I'm not."

He stank of hot plastic and raw metal, and I couldn't help but picture a maniacal grin superimposed over his non-face.

"You are a robot and we are the future!" he screamed.

The sound of his shrieking steel-mesh voice shredded my nerves like nails on a blackboard, but by then I no longer cared what he was saying or why his head was filled with machinery. All I knew was that if I couldn't get him to release me, my spine would snap in two and his fists would puncture my skull. He wouldn't believe I was human until my brains were dripping down his arms.

I reached around behind me to the workbench, my fingers blindly scrabbling for anything I could use to fend him off. They fell upon something cold and heavy.

I had never hit anyone before but I lashed out at him like a fully-fledged hooligan. He was a hefty guy, solid as an armoured car, but when I landed my blow he toppled backwards and crashed to the ground.

I looked at my weapon—a heavy-duty spanner—half expecting to see it covered in blood and bits of bone. But there was nothing.

A spark popped in the engineer's steel face and his voice became oddly hollow-sounding. "You bastard! I'll fix you good for that! You fancy V models think you're something special, don'tcha? Well, let me tell you, Mike Woodburn, when

I get a hold of you, I'll scrap you out for parts. I don't care how much you cost the company!"

He lay there, thrashing around, swearing in that new tinny little voice, scrabbling at the rubberised floor. Suddenly I felt sickeningly afraid. He thought I was a robot, a top-of-the-range job that had gone bad. He wouldn't let this go. I knew with absolute certainty that he was going to track me down and do to me what he had done to Jack. He would try to fix me but would end up dismembering and killing me, ripping my arms and legs from their sockets, tearing my face from my skull, and leaving me a bloody, ruined corpse.

The idea sickened me. What possible protection would I have against a psychotic robot? Who could I rely on for help? The police? What if they were robots too?

I was still clutching the spanner. It felt good and solid. I crouched over the mechanic and told myself that it couldn't be murder if he wasn't a real person. I rammed the wrench deep into the wiring and circuitry and shiny steel struts that filled his head.

There was a flash of white light and a sudden pulse jolted up my arm.

When I came to, I was on the other side of the room. The spanner lay several feet away. My head ached and my hand was burning with pain. I wondered how many volts it had taken to throw me that far and I looked at my palm. Scorched into the flesh was a livid red scar.

I turned to the burned-out husk of the engineer. Something dark and viscous had dribbled from his face-hole and pooled on the floor. I held out my blood-streaked hand. "Look," I laughed. "I'm a Fleshie, you metal bastard!"

I patched up the hand with strips of cloth ripped from the engineer's overalls. Then I rummaged in his toolbox for something that could cut through metal.

I'm back at my desk now. The exit door to the stairwell opened first time when I put the engineer's severed index finger on the touchpad. I expect it would have worked just as well on the lift, too, but there was no way I was stepping inside that again—ever. Who knows where I might end up?

But lots of people don't like lifts, right? It's a well-known phobia. I have no doubt that I'm human. No doubt at all. I just wish I'd learned more about the V models the engineer mentioned; the ones he said were ultra-real. Don't get me wrong. I'm positive I'm human.

I'm just curious about everyone else, that's all.

Deliveries

She passed him the small box through the slender gap between the door and the frame, without a word.

"Masks," he said, and saw that she was adjusting her own. He ran his fingers through still-wet hair. "I was in the shower," he shrugged, glancing back along the landing towards the open door of his own flat. "Typical, eh?"

She watched through the gap as he turned the small carton over in his hands.

"Running out," he said, tapping his disposable aqua blue face covering.

"I like to have plenty," she said. Her hand snaked around the edge of the door.

His silence signalled his confusion.

"Masks," she added, indicating the dark square of cloth that hid her face below the eyes.

He nodded and forced a small laugh. "I don't even know why I ordered them," he added, picking absently at the label on the box. "It's not like I can go anywhere."

She raised her eyes. They were startling black, and framed by the longest lashes he had ever seen.

"I probably shouldn't even have come this far," he chuckled.

"Probably not," she agreed.

"I don't think we've met," he said, pressing the box to his chest with one hand and pushing the other towards her. "I'm Lucas."

"No," she said, staring at his outstretched hand. "We haven't."

"Oh, yes," he said with a start, snatching away his proffered hand. "I forgot. No touching!" He took a small step backwards. "Well, I'll just leave you in peace now."

"I'm crawling up the walls," she said, pressing her face into the gap.

"Sorry?"

"Trapped in here like this."

He looked more closely at her. Those shocking coal-black eyes dominated a pale, elf-like face. It was an attractive face, he decided, despite being almost fully covered up.

"Weird, isn't it?" he said, frowning at his inability to come up with something less clichéd.

Her hands began to slide (suggestively) up and down the door. "Frustrating," she said.

He licked his lips, suddenly conscious of his pulse throbbing madly in his neck, tightening his throat. "Thank God for deliveries," he croaked, toting his box of masks. "I couldn't survive without them."

"Me neither," she said.

He sensed movement below his field of vision and glanced down. Her bare legs shuffled impatiently beneath a very short black dress. She wore nothing on her feet.

The door opened a fraction wider.

"Do you understand what's happening?" she asked him.

Not for the first time in his life, he floundered for a response to a woman's cryptic words. "Yeah," he said, finally. "At least, as much as anyone else."

Her eyes narrowed. "I'm not sure that you do," she said, in an almost childlike mock-serious tone. "I'm not sure that anyone does."

She let go of the door and stepped back. "You caught me having lunch," she added. "Can I tempt you?"

Something seemed to move behind her mask after she had spoken. Was she licking her lips?

"Is now not a good time?" she said, twirling her naked feet on the tiled floor.

Lucas sensed she was pouting.

Was she just asking him in for a cheese sandwich? Or was this some opaque dating manoeuvre?

Lucas pictured her without the mask. In his mind's eye, her lips were full and sensual. "No," he stammered. "Now is... good for me." He donned a smile, hoping it would show in his eyes the way it seemed to shine from hers.

Her flat was unlit but her white skin glowed like burnished silver under the bright light from the hallway outside. On a small table just inside the door, thick cobwebs shrouded an age-crackled ceramic vase full of desiccated stems. She snatched up a crumpled tea towel that lay beside it and twisted it around her hands.

"You had an accident or something?" he said, pointing to burgundy stains on the towel.

"Not me," she replied. And then, again, that squirming movement behind her mask.

As the front door clicked shut behind him, he glimpsed something curious in the kitchen off to the left. A pair of legs sprawled on the floor. Just that. A pair of legs, clothed in the earth-brown uniform and black work boots of a UPS driver. He could see nothing above the driver's waist except a glistening red mess that leaked across the kitchen floor.

"It's just as you said," she whispered, removing her mask. "Thank God for deliveries."

The Passenger

Even though his pulse was thudding in his throat as if he had just run a marathon, Howard knew he had to calm down. Everything would be all right if he could just sleep. It was the only thing that could deliver him from this waking nightmare.

He pressed his back against the seat and closed his eyes to shut out the migraine-inducing strip-lighting that zinged around the arched ceiling and ricocheted off the bright white paint. Shivering despite the humid atmosphere in the empty carriage, he drew in a deep breath and then slowly exhaled with relief as the doors finally slid together.

His bones shook as the train lurched away from the platform and plunged into another inky black tunnel, jerking him first to one side and then the other as it rocketed around benighted hairpin bends. The squealing of wheels on polished tracks seemed to pierce his skull, as though someone was driving shards of ice through his eardrums and into the soft pulpy centre of his brain. How could he possibly sleep through this?

After three minutes that seemed to stretch into eternity, he finally felt his muscles relax as the train hissed to a standstill at the next station. There was no point in opening his eyes to read the name. It wouldn't be any place he had ever heard of. He knew now that each leg of his journey was taking him further away from the world he knew. He was venturing deeper and deeper into unfathomable and uncharted realms.

He kept his eyes tightly closed but, since the doors stayed firmly shut, he deduced there was no one on this platform who wanted to board. That, at least, was a blessing. He dreaded to think who, or what, might clamber into the compartment with him.

The carriage jolted again and Howard rested his head against the window as he felt the train pull away. The cool chill of the glass against his scalp stung him into an even greater level of wakefulness as he anticipated the next stage of his journey. Every sense in his body was heightened to an extreme degree of alertness—exactly the opposite of what he needed right now. The carriage lighting burned through his eyelids like lasers. Even the smell of the train kept him awake; the sharp tang of dust and metal mingled with the sour odour of former occupants to prick his nostrils and incite a squirming turmoil in his guts. His discomfort was made complete by the rattling and shaking of the compartment as it thundered through tunnels and swerved around sharp bends, screaming its way to the next station. The train moved so quickly that if he failed to spread his feet apart and put his hands on the rough, upholstered seat to keep his balance, he would topple over.

Dear God, he thought, *if only it had been this difficult to fall asleep half an hour ago.*

*

He wasn't normally one to nod off on the train. It was the new shift pattern that had been foisted upon him at work.

"Your body clock'll take a battering for the first month, Howard. That's par for the course," Luke had said. "But, as I say, it's either that or…" The young manager had jerked his thumb towards the door, indicating that unless Howard agreed to the ungodly hours he demanded, he'd have to collect his P45 and hit the road. *My way or the highway.*

Howard had been pissed off. More than that, he'd been alarmed. He didn't relish change. He was a creature of habit and the prospect of adapting to a new working pattern frightened him almost as much as the idea of losing his job. But, he knew, at his age he couldn't afford to join the dole queue. Having worked at the same company for over 30 of his 56 years, with no qualifications to speak of, he would be virtually unemployable.

Game over.

The misleadingly-named early shift (midnight to eight in the morning) was, as Luke had gleefully promised, difficult to adjust to. But Howard soon discovered that his anxiety over the change in hours was in itself ripping him from his slumber and propelling him, still half asleep, out the door to meet the last tube train into central London. Except for today. He had overslept. Mind in a drowsy fug, he had skipped the shower, tugged on his uniform and had run like the clappers through the darkened streets of his home town.

Once at the underground station, he had checked his watch. He was breathless but back on schedule. And, sure enough, his regular train duly arrived on time. Although it was crowded with late-night revellers, Howard secured a seat. Relieved at his near miss, he closed his eyes. Big mistake. His treacherous body took this as a signal to return to the sleep that it had not quite woken from. When he opened them again, he was alone in the carriage and the train was just about to move off.

He leaped up and slammed against the doors. But he was too late. The train jerked once and pulled away from the platform. He ducked and peered out of the windows to check how far he'd travelled while he'd been dozing. But the familiar blue and red London Underground logo emblazoned at intervals on the tiled walls of the platform whipped by so quickly that he had difficulty making out the name of the station.

Cadaver Town?

Don't be stupid, he told himself.

And then it was gone, replaced by a howling black labyrinth.

Probably Camden Town, he thought. And winced. That meant north London. If he'd overshot his destination by that much he was in deep shit. He checked his watch: two minutes to midnight. He was still not officially late for the start of his shift, but he would be in another 121 seconds.

It could have been worse, he mused. If he hadn't woken when he did, he might have ended up at the Tube Train Graveyard, that mythical depot where all underground trains go to die.

But it was OK. The situation was salvageable. He would blame London Underground. All he had to do was get off at the next station and switch to the southbound track.

If only it had been as simple as that.

*

His fretfulness assuaged by his cunning plan, Howard slumped into a seat near the door and pulled his mobile out of his jacket pocket. As he scrolled through the numbers on the phone, the train started to slow down and the tiled walls and lighted platform of a new station came into view. This one he could read as clear as day: Innsmouth.

He stared at the nameplate. Where the hell was Innsmouth? He had been using the Tube for thirty-odd years now and he fancied that he knew most of the station names pretty well. He was, at least, passably familiar with the routes he used regularly, such as the Northern Line, that black streak on the map that bisected London, threading its way from the leafy suburbs of Morden and Wimbledon in the south, up through the city's pulsating heart at Charing Cross, and then onward to the distant northern realms of Burnt Oak and High Barnet. He ticked off as many of the stations at the top end of the line as he could remember: Brent Cross, Hendon Central, Colindale and, on the other branch of the line, Tufnell Park, Archway, Highgate, Finchley Central.

"There's no Innsmouth," he said to himself. "Not on the Northern Line."

The train started to make the beeping noise that signalled its imminent departure. It didn't matter where Innsmouth was. All the lines are interconnected. All he needed to do was switch to a line that would take him to his office in Leicester Square. And fast.

Without another thought, Howard scrambled to his feet and hit the button that worked the doors. They juddered open and he spilled onto the platform, almost falling over in his rush to leave the carriage.

He scanned the platform for an exit sign but nothing adorned the walls except the station's nameplate. "Bit bleak," he said aloud, his voice echoing flatly around the low ceiling. He had never much taken to retro styling and the platform at Innsmouth was a particularly unappealing example of the fad. Plain, slightly crazed rectangular tiles, tarnished art deco lights. And nothing much else. No lurid posters advertising the latest blockbusters, no polite notices warning people against fare dodging. There was also no exit sign that he could see and the only way off the platform seemed to be via a single archway. He peered through it, expecting to see a concourse from which he could navigate to another platform. Instead, the archway led straight out onto the street.

If there was only one platform, he reasoned, then Innsmouth must be the end of the line. He looked back. The train he had just evacuated stood stock still. The doors remained open. Was that the last train of the night? The absence of any staff suggested exactly that.

Outside, by the waxy glare of a fly-spattered light above his head he examined the building from which he had just emerged. Beneath the light a grubby sign repeated the name Innsmouth. To one side of the arch, affixed to a plain, age-blackened brick wall, the familiar London Underground logo: an indigo line slicing through a bright scarlet circle. Perfectly normal. But just where the hell was Innsmouth?

He checked his watch: 12.10am. He felt a pang deep inside his chest. Unless he could find some means of transportation, and quickly, he wouldn't just be a bit late for work; he might not get there at all until the trains started up again in the morning.

The station, he now saw, was located at the end of a narrow cul-de-sac. High, shadow-cloaked buildings loomed on either side of the road, making him feel uncomfortably small. Their large, curtain-less windows suggested that they were offices or warehouses of some kind. A pale moon reflected brightly off the glass but the structures were so tall that all but a narrow line of night sky was concealed from sight. He looked around the dimly-lit street for a taxi rank or a bus stop but there was no indication of either. There was no sign of life at all.

The late hour explained the deadness of the place but, he wondered, perhaps the station road was just too narrow for vehicles to turn. This might be a hick town at the arse end of some obscure branch line, but there had to be another means of transport nearby.

Across the top of the road, some two hundred yards ahead, was another, wider road. It too seemed to be full of towering dark buildings with empty, slate-black windows.

He knew that most of the night buses in and around London converged on Trafalgar Square. If he was lucky, he would find one of those and then he could just walk (or run) the short distance from Nelson's Column to Leicester Square. He would have to throw himself at the mercy of Luke; a man, Howard knew, who was as merciful and compassionate as a Pit Bull.

As a plan, it wasn't fantastic but it was all he had to cling to. He struck out for the junction ahead, hoping that he would soon be greeted by the comforting sight of a double-decker trundling along the main road, all warm and red and brightly lit, enticing him to climb aboard.

As he approached the road, he became conscious of a smell: pungent and salty, like seaweed, but overlaid with something rank, a stench of stagnation and decay. Perhaps he was closer to the Thames than he had thought and had travelled east or west, rather than north.

The main carriageway was broader than the station road, but not by much. To his left, the industrial buildings petered out, replaced by untidy grassland peppered with gnarled bushes and stunted trees. So, wherever he was, this was probably the edge of town. To his right, the main road sloped sharply down and the forbidding warehouses gave way to smaller structures. The moonlight picked out lines of low buildings; ramshackle affairs of faded grey wood and grimy, crumbling brick.

He scanned the pavement. "No bus stops," he said with a groan.

A dark, glistening sheen coated the streets, and water gurgled in the gutter beyond the kerb, creating a babbling stream which ran haphazardly down the sharply angled road. The weather had been fine when he had entered the station at Morden. He must have missed a downpour while he had been asleep beneath the streets of London. The sky was clear now, and yet the clammy night smothered him like a soggy sheet. He turned up his collar.

The road spiralled down and Howard followed its twists and turns, looking for some sign of life: an all-night general store, a garage, or somewhere with an array of cards deposited by local cab companies.

As he drew level with a row of shuttered shops, he saw movement. There was a small group of figures, silhouetted by the moonlight, moving around at the bottom of the road. The tightening in his chest eased a little. They must know where he could get a cab.

Although the angular shadows cast by the dilapidated buildings partially obscured them, Howard reckoned there were about seven or eight people gathered up ahead. They seemed to be better dressed against the changeable weather than he was, for each wore a long coat with a hood.

Howard raised an arm and was about to call out when one of the group lifted their garment above their head and dropped it to the ground. It was a man. That much was plain to see, since he was now naked.

Howard's voice caught in his throat. His first thought was that this was some kind of prank. Students perhaps. The clothes they were wearing, he now saw, were all identical: drab, hooded robes that almost reached the ground. Was this a secret midnight initiation into a student fraternity?

Howard dropped his arm. He wanted to see what they were up to before he made contact. An involuntary shiver rippled through his body at the sound of water rushing noisily down the road beside him towards...

The shore.

His gaze was suddenly drawn beyond the revellers and alighted upon fragmented reflections of the moon, glittering like shards of broken glass, on the surface of a languid, almost gelatinous stretch of water.

The clues all fell into place like pieces of a jigsaw: the sour-salty tang of seaweed in the crisp night air, the shabby, age-blackened buildings strung with torn netting and frayed rope.

This was a waterfront town.

Howard watched as the rest of the figures sloughed off their robes.

Then they began to sing; a strange chant in the curious, guttural sounds of a language quite different from English. As they sang, they gently scooped handfuls of water and washed each other. With their bodies painted in shadow it was difficult to guess their ages, but it was plain to see that there were six men and six women.

Instinctively, he pressed himself into a shop doorway. Something about their shape and posture, and the way they moved, changed his mind about them being students. They lacked the lithe fluidity of youth.

There was nothing inherently odd about swimming in a river. People did it all the time. However, not only was it the dead of night but it was also early April, and London had not quite shrugged off the chill of winter. And even though this odd little hamlet seemed perfectly dead, the bathers were brazenly prancing about starkers in a very public street. Why weren't they afraid of being caught?

The nudists waded out into the water up to their thighs and almost disappeared from sight. Howard had to lean out of the doorway to keep track of them. But the image that coalesced before his eyes disturbed him more than the antics of the bathers. For they were not, as he had assumed, performing their curious ablutions at some rundown dock on the banks of the River Thames. Stretched out before him until it disappeared into the distant horizon, Howard now saw, was the open sea.

Innsmouth, it appeared, was a port town built upon a natural bay and surrounded by high, tree-lined cliffs. But what sea was he looking at? The nearest coast to central London was fifty-odd miles to the south, or even further out to the east. He shook his head, confused. He was pretty sure the Tube didn't run to the coast in either direction and, even if it did, the journey would have taken far longer than the ten minutes or so he had lost while sleeping.

Howard groaned. Not only was he thoroughly disoriented but he now knew for sure that he wouldn't get to work tonight. He felt a lump behind his ribcage, as though a giant fist was squeezing the life out of his heart and lungs. For a moment, he was breathless and the thought crossed his mind that he might have a coronary or a stroke. He was the right age and his lifestyle wasn't particularly healthy.

And then a wave of blessed relief gradually washed over him as a solution to his predicament began to form in his mind. He would call Luke, tell him that he was ill. He'd eaten a dodgy kebab and was stuck on the loo. Embarrassing but plausible, and just the kind of bullshit that a chancer like Luke might respect.

Howard rehearsed his lines in a semi-whisper, then cleared his throat and drew in a sharp breath. He fished in a trouser pocket for his mobile. His hand came out empty. He checked the other pocket. Empty.

His insides squirmed. It felt as though a drowsing snake was stirring deep in his bowels. If he failed to show up for work without at least calling in sick, he would definitely be for the chop. He rummaged through his jacket, but found only his wallet. Then he patted down his entire body, the way he sometimes got frisked at the airport, in the hope that he had missed the phone in some fold somewhere. All in vain. The phone was gone.

Think, for God's sake, think! When did he last have the damned thing?

He couldn't remember.

He must have dropped it somewhere. Panic rising inside him like a surge of lava about to explode from a volcano, he stepped out of the doorway to scan the pavement—and collided with something solid hurtling down the hill.

Howard was knocked sideways into the road. The thing he had struck came crashing to the ground beside him. Long dark hair tumbled messily from the hood of a cloak and fell away to reveal the face of a young woman.

"Ah, s-sorry!" said Howard. "Didn't see you there." He shuffled to his knees and reached out a hand. "Are you OK?"

Her pale green eyes, at first startled wide, now fell beneath the shadow of a heavy knitted brow. Protruding and slightly too far apart, they combined with a flat nose and large, unbowed lips to give the woman a most unattractive appearance that was made all the more unpleasant by her hate-filled expression. She stood up slowly, clutching at her plain brown robe with short, fat fingers. She was barefoot and, through the gap in the front of the gown, Howard saw that she wore nothing beneath. Was she late for the party? Is that why she had been running down the road?

A long, dark tongue darted between those thick lips. And then she cried. At least, that was a close approximation to the sound that she made; a high-pitched, keening noise that clawed through Howard's brain like fingernails digging through blancmange.

Below, at the water's edge, two or three of the gathered throng turned sharply and looked towards the spot where Howard was struggling to his feet. Still shrieking, the woman backed away from him, edging back up the hill as though he was some kind of wild creature that might turn on her and rip her to shreds if she strayed too close to him.

"Shush!" said Howard. "It's OK. I'm not going to hurt you. It was an accident, for God's sake!" He had visions of standing trial here at a hillbilly kangaroo court and being found guilty of some hitherto unknown capital offence—being clumsy in a public place.

Howard glanced back at the crowd. Even at this distance he could see their faces, could see the resemblance to the hooded woman. Were they related? Was she their sister? Mother? Daughter?

But speculation was replaced by revulsion when he noticed something else about the mob. Not only were they naked and bug-ugly, but all the men were aroused.

Of course, it all made sense now. This was not an eccentric skinny-dipping club at all. He had stumbled upon a bunch of perverts indulging in a spot of dogging!

They were a singularly unattractive collection of sexual buccaneers: short, stumpy men with drooping beer guts who fumbled with saggy-breasted, dough-faced women, pausing occasionally to slap some life into their wilting manhoods.

It should have been difficult for a gaggle of pot-bellied swingers to convey any sense of menace, but their reaction to being caught *in flagrante delicto* unnerved Howard. Surely, now that they had been rumbled, they should be fleeing the scene of their kinky crime? But, no. They were acting as though their nude seaside romp was perfectly acceptable, normal even. And that brazenness bothered him just as much as the determined way they were now advancing up the hill towards him.

Howard turned away but the woman was blocking his escape. She spread her thick, bare arms out to her sides as though she was herding cattle. Her gown fell open but she made no attempt to pull it closed. He saw the mottled flesh of her pendulous breasts, the swell of her bloated belly, her distended, hairless sex. And there was a smell about her. A cold pungency, redolent of ammonia. She was, in every way, repulsive. Howard tore his eyes away from her and scanned the row of buildings. There must, he reasoned, be people behind those dirt-obscured windows. Normal people. People with phones. Perhaps there were even people who would open up and grant him refuge.

"Hey!" he shouted. "Help! Someone call the police!"

Movement at one of the first-floor windows caught his eye. Howard watched as the filthy grey rag covering the glass began to twitch. It more closely resembled a huge, sagging cobweb than a curtain. When the tattered cloth was slowly pulled aside, peering out from the grimy glass was yet another member of the moon-faced clan. This one possessed the same unfortunate features as the hooded woman and the naked bathers, yet his appearance seemed more degraded; a more extreme version of their ugliness. His eyes were unnaturally bulbous, the pupils and irises accounting for almost all of the eye, leaving virtually no whites. His skin was dappled with what appeared to be brown liver spots, and his nose was completely flat, to the extent that it seemed almost vestigial. His neck was shorter, his mouth wider and his lips thicker than the woman's. But the most shocking aspect of his appearance was the shape of his head for, above his eyes, his face simply sloped away to nothing. Lacking a forehead, or crown to his skull, he resembled no other human being that Howard had ever seen.

At the sight of the face at the window, the woman clapped her meaty hands together. Her pallid, freckled breasts quivered and her broad mouth stretched to show tiny, translucent teeth as she made a yowling noise that sounded a lot like laughter.

Howard was suddenly aware of his pulse pounding in his throat.

Behind him, the crowd had picked up its pace.

This is really happening, he thought. *They really are coming for me!* He realised that his options had dwindled to just two: fight or flight. Except, he reasoned, he couldn't fight a whole gang of naked swingers, yet nor could he run away from them with the frog princess blocking his path.

Fight or flight? His mind reeled.

How about both?

Almost without his conscious bidding, he thrust his hands out, making sudden, hard contact with the woman. His palms struck her bare chest which, he was disgusted to discover, was cool and slippery. She fell back with a yelp and her head hit the ground with a sickening crack. Her wailing stopped instantly but Howard was already running by the time his pursuers issued their own cry; a bestial ululation that echoed around the silent streets and reverberated off the rain-slicked, desolate buildings to drown his senses in a maddening cacophony.

At the crest of the hill Howard looked back. The crowd, still naked, had reached the fallen woman. Some were crouching beside her, others stood and stared up at him with glossy, marble-black eyes. Yet Howard's gaze was drawn past them, to movement down at the shoreline.

Illuminated by the incandescence of the moon, in the shallows that the nudists had recently vacated, wallowed a pallid shape. Its blemished, doughy flesh was perversely reminiscent of the hooded woman's breasts. But this was not one of the erstwhile bathers, too preoccupied with erotic pastimes to join the chase. Its size alone argued against that. What it most strongly resembled was, thought Howard, a walrus or perhaps a manatee; one of those grotesque, lumbering river beasts from the tropics.

Did these people know that the vast creature had been down there among them, lurking just below the surface as they acted out their aquatic fetishes?

His eyes darted back to the revellers. *Or perhaps now*, he thought, *they were mourners*; for the frog princess neither moved nor uttered a sound. They had stripped her of her cloak and were sliding their hands over her body and between her legs.

His immediate thought was that their perversion knew no bounds but, as he looked more closely, he realized that this was no longer a sexual escapade. This was something different. The men, he noticed, were not involved in these proceedings; they stood by, flaccid, while the female participants tended to the lifeless woman. They stroked her, caressed her gently. Then, at length, one of them stood, bearing something aloft. Something small and white. And very still.

As one, the crowd moaned softly. Down at the water, the white beast lifted its head and bellowed. And Howard saw its face for the first time. It was the face at the window. It was the face of the crowd. It was the face of the mother and baby he had just killed.

As Howard staggered back on his heels in shock, the mob turned its attention to him. The baby's corpse was set down upon the stomach of its mother. One by one, the mourners drifted away from the dead bodies and began to climb the hill.

Their gait, Howard now realised, was just as inhuman as their appearance. Rather than striding purposefully towards him, they lumbered awkwardly, loping and trotting in a way that suggested they were unused to walking upon dry land.

Howard didn't wait to see if they could break into a sprint. He turned and fled. Never pausing to gather his bearings or to check on the progress of his pursuers, he raced headlong past the towering empty warehouses and abandoned factories, down the narrow side road towards the station. He splashed through puddles in the pot-holed streets, each step jarring him from his ankles to his spine. He hadn't exerted himself like this for years, and his lungs burned as though he was inhaling fire with every breath he took.

As he ran, a howl echoed around the soaring shadowed buildings that pressed in on him from all sides; a sound as menacing as the cry of a wolf and yet as plaintive as the song of a blue whale.

Howard's pounding feet brought him to the station. Shoulders aching from pumping his arms, and a stitch jabbing sharply through the left side of his body, he slowed to a trot.

The place was in darkness now but through the red-brick archway he could see the white lights of a train. The carriage doors were open and the departure signal was ringing out shrilly. He leaped on board and edged his way along the compartment, finally allowing himself a backward glance through the low windows.

What he saw flooded him with fear. The mob had followed him to the station and was now lurking and swaying beneath the archway, at the shadowed threshold to the platform; naked silhouettes framed against the indigo night beyond, gasping for breath just as he was.

Howard bent forward, leaned on his knees and sucked in air by the gallon. He watched them though the glass, knowing that the carriage was so brightly lit, they could not have failed to see him. If they made a move, he could run through the other carriages but he would only be delaying the inevitable confrontation. He was trapped, like a butterfly in a bell jar.

Then, one by one, the misshapen horde spilled through the archway and onto the darkness of the cramped little platform. As they came closer, the carriage lights illuminated their distorted, amphibian faces and Howard saw pure hatred in their swollen black eyes.

All his instincts urged him to rush to the doors and punch the button to close them. But he was fearful that if he tried to do so while the alarm was still ringing, it would have the opposite effect and keep the doors open. He needed them to shut by themselves.

"Come on!" he hissed. "Close, damn you!"

As if in response, one of the males padded forward and reached out to the open doors. But he arrived just in time to see them collide shut. He pounded at the train, his rage fuelled by failure. Through the glass panel Howard saw the man's hands—broad, translucent, webbed paws; and his eyes—large dark orbs that bulged unnaturally from a flat, almost human skull.

The signal fell silent. For a brief, agonising moment, Howard could hear only the wet slapping of the man-thing's fists against the carriage door. And then the train jolted. Slowly, it began to ease away from the station at Innsmouth until it was swallowed into darkness.

Breathless and shaking, Howard slumped onto the nearest bank of seats. His foot kicked against something. His mobile. It was lying on the white polished floor where he must have dropped it just before alighting from the very same train some twenty minutes earlier. Howard mustered his lexicon of obscenities and swore, richly and loudly.

It took a full minute of plummeting through snaking tunnels before Howard realized that he wasn't travelling back the way he had come. The train was continuing its onward journey. Innsmouth was not the end of the line after all.

He realised, as he scanned the area around him, that the train was totally bereft of any signs or notices. Their absence made the carriage look too stark, like a space capsule stripped of all unnecessary fripperies. But how could that be? In every underground train he had ever ridden, plastered all along the wall above the landscape windows were numerous adverts and notices. And maps.

That iconic multicoloured schematic of all the lines and stations on the London Underground was always reproduced, at least in part, on every train. But not here. Howard's stomach lurched as it dawned on him that he was speeding through tunnels deep under the ground, through places he had never heard of, with no idea whatsoever where he was or where he might be heading.

He looked more closely at his surroundings. The absence of a map wasn't the only thing that didn't seem right. The ceiling of the carriage was too low and the windows appeared strangely curved. And weren't the strip-lights too bright? Too *white*?

The train was just... wrong.

The disorienting effect of that realisation was both alarming and yet, at the same time, oddly familiar. An air of twisted reality hung about the whole bizarre episode: waking up alone on a train, becoming stranded in a strange town full of freakish inhabitants, the bizarre sexual element, running for his life.

Then the answer came to him. "I'm dreaming," he said. "I'm bloody dreaming."

Time to wake up, you silly sod. This is nothing more than a night terror about being late for work. You're on the train, drooling and moaning in front of two hundred passengers. Probably all sniggering at you right now.

He looked into the blinding whiteness of the light above his head but it didn't waken him, and the curiously contoured train continued to hurtle headlong through the tunnel. *This has to be a dream. It just has to be.*

He decided that there was one way to find out. He turned and slammed a fist into the wall above the seats. "If this doesn't wake you up, nothing will!" he shouted.

He hit the wall again, sending a sharp pain through his bloodied knuckles. Even the sound of his fist hitting the wall was all wrong. Too solid. Too... wet. Part of the dream, of course. His sleeping brain was focussing on delivering a gut-punch of terror and had failed to add the peripheral detail— the sounds and visuals that would have provided a more realistic, plausible environment. The devil, they say, is in the detail.

"Wake up for God's sake!" he seethed. He punctuated his plea with another blow, smearing a red streak across the gleaming white metal and sending another dagger of pain up his arm. "Wake... up!"

"If you want to wake up, you need to go back to sleep," said a voice.

Howard looked round. At the far end of the carriage, tucked away in the two-seat snug beyond the doors, sat an elderly man.

"I do apologise," said the man. "Did I startle you?"

Clutching onto one of the vertical poles as the train swung into another bend, the old man pulled himself to his feet and then held out his free hand. "Spencer Buckley," he said. A smile creased his deeply lined face and he swept back a stray lock of long white hair.

Howard took the tiny hand gently, fearing that a firm shake might just break the old-timer's fingers.

"Howard," he said. "Howard Blake."

Spencer Buckley nodded and rummaged awkwardly with something under the folds of his crumpled tweed jacket. He looked deep into Howard's eyes.

"You seem to be lost."

Howard's racing heart was gradually settling into a more pedestrian rhythm. He plastered on a faltering smile. "Yes, sorry. You probably think I'm crazy but some freaky stuff's been happening to me tonight and, well, I just had this weird feeling that I was asleep and that I was dreaming it all."

"You're not crazy, Howard Blake," said Buckley. "You *are* asleep."

The words landed like a sucker punch to Howard's abdomen and snatched his breath away.

"Shall we sit, Howard Blake? The sea's a little choppy this evening." Spencer Buckley carefully eased himself into a nearby seat and, again, he pressed something tightly to his chest.

Howard slumped down opposite him. "The *sea*? Did you say the *sea*?"

"The Ocean of Dreams, if you like. The turbulent straits through which we travel this night."

Howard shook his head. Of all the people he could be stuck in the carriage with, it had to be a certifiable nutjob. Terrific. "Look," he sighed. "I just need to get back to central London. I don't suppose you know the best way?"

"I've already told you," said Buckley. "If you want to awaken and return to your own place in the universe, then you must first go back to sleep."

Howard rubbed his face and took a deep breath. "OK," he sighed. "One of us is mental. And I'm sorry to say, I think it's you. And I'm also sorry to say that I really don't have time to administer any care in the community right now. I just wondered if you knew what line we were on and—"

"Stop your chatter, Howard Blake! If you fail to do as I say, you will never find your way back home!"

Unfit as he was, he was more than a match for the stick-thin pensioner. "Is that a threat?" he asked.

"No, my poor lost friend, it's a guarantee."

Spencer Buckley reached into his jacket. Howard stiffened in his seat. Surely the old boy wasn't packing heat? He watched as Buckley carefully pulled out what appeared to be a large leather-bound book.

"Let me ask you something," said Buckley. "Have you always been a dreamer?"

Despite his mounting confusion, or perhaps because of it, Howard laughed. "That sounds like a line from a song."

The old man fixed him with a withering glare. "This is no joking matter."

Howard sighed. After the events he had just experienced, a little light conversation might provide a welcome relief.

"Yes," he said. "For what it's worth, I've always had dreams, if that's what you mean." But, he knew, they were always more than just dreams. He thought back to the night terrors that he could still recall years after he had woken from them, unsettled and bewildered, in the cold sweat of fear.

"And do you travel?"

"What?"

"In your dreams. Do you travel in your dreams?"

Howard hesitated a beat. In many of his nightmares, he found himself in unfamiliar places, or taking long journeys on unknown trains or buses with curious travelling companions. Sometimes the dreams would be so vivid, so seemingly inescapable, that when he finally awoke he wasn't sure if he had returned to reality or if he was still trapped in the dream.

He nodded. "That's why I was trying to wake up," he sighed. "This whole situation—it's just like one of my dreams."

"Then you've been nurturing your talent without even knowing it," said the old man. "Taking flight in your sleep to hidden realms. Were they dark places? Places unlike your waking world?"

The old man was right. It was always night in those dreams. And the places, the towns and cities, were always unknown to him; silent streets of lurking shadows and ghoulish inhabitants. Unknown but not *unfamiliar*. For it seemed that he often found himself in the same locations, the same curiously unearthly suburbs.

Places like Innsmouth.

And, now he thought about it, wasn't that godforsaken port itself horribly familiar? How had he known the way to the sea? Had he walked those gloomy, rain-swept roads before in his dreams?

"I... I don't know. Maybe."

The old man tutted. "Ignorance in such matters can be—" Buckley's face clouded, but he saw Howard's worried look and checked himself. "Well, let's just say it can have unhelpful consequences."

"I still don't get it. Where exactly am I? Am I sleeping or... or what?"

"You are riding one of the myriad hidden highways of the multiverse, Howard Blake; an alternative dimension tucked away in the dark crevices of your everyday life, out of sight to all but the adept; a dimension only accessible through unconsciousness."

"Unconsciousness?"

"*Dreams*, Howard Blake. *Dreams*. The pathway we are presently travelling—"

"The Underground?"

"The Underground, the Highway of Solitude, the Ocean of Dreams—call it what you will, for it is all of these things and yet none of them. It exists for travellers like ourselves."

Howard shook his head. He was getting sucked into the old man's mania. "Don't be ridiculous," he said. "It's just a bloody tube train." But he could hear the mounting terror in his own voice, feel it throbbing and pulsing in his chest; terror of the unknown, terror that he had lost his mind. And terror that maybe, just maybe, he had not.

Buckley waved his hands about airily. "This environment that you see around you is merely an illusion, a façade, to mask the reality of our means of transportation. To you, it appears to be a tube train—whatever that may be. My personal illusion is of a ship sailing a great purple ocean, for that is how we travel in my part of the multiverse."

"So this is all a dream? It's not real?"

"The transport system is illusory, but the places are real enough; as real as any city in your waking world. They are merely accessed from another plane of consciousness. In falling asleep, you have inadvertently crossed the tracks, as it were, to another reality."

Buckley tapped his book with a bony fingertip and tutted. "Many wizards and alchemists—and many more charlatans, too—have strived to master the art of dream-travel. Numerous mighty tomes, forbidden texts, have been written on the subject. This is one such, right here in my hands; keys to the art, maps to the worlds. And here you are, Howard Blake, travelling with the ease of a seasoned warlock but yet unable to master your power."

The darkness outside the carriage lifted and the train slowed to a halt.

Kingsport.

"I shall disembark at the next stop, Howard Blake. I suggest you join me."

Howard thought of the hideous faces and unnatural ceremonies he had witnessed in the previous town. "Thanks, but I'll give it a miss if it's anything like Innsmouth."

"Ah, yes. Innsmouth." Spencer Buckley eased himself gingerly to his feet, stepped across the gangway and seated himself beside Howard. He opened the book. Howard was no linguist but the title, *Von Unaussprechlichen Kulten*, seemed to be something like German, if not German itself. The whole book was handwritten, and from its smell and the crackle of the dry, yellow pages as they turned, he knew it must be very old indeed.

"Updated version," said Buckley, wrinkling his nose. "Original texts are so hard to find, of course."

"Of course," agreed Howard.

"Still, we'll work with the tools we have, eh?"

Howard followed the old man's gnarled finger as it traced its way around a page covered in crude, smudged sketches. There was a sequence of pictures interspersed with an illegible, spidery Gothic text. The images began at the top left-hand side of the page and spiralled down the length of the book.

"They were a seafaring folk; people just like you and I..."

Howard nodded. The ink had faded a little in places and the figures were badly drawn but he could tell that they were wearing some kind of antiquated clothing and bore recognisably human faces.

"The town was struggling. The fish stocks were depleting and Innsmouth's economy was in decline. Then one day the civic leaders invited something into their town. Something that promised salvation for a rapidly failing old sea port. Something that should never set foot on dry land."

"A sea monster?" said Howard. He had skipped ahead to the next panel.

"Of sorts," said Buckley. Then he looked about the empty carriage, as if searching the hidden alcoves for eavesdroppers. He lowered his voice. "An ancient entity," he said. "A thing best left slumbering in the deepest troughs of the blackest ocean."

In the next picture Howard saw a naked man lying next to the creature. "Wait, they... *mated* with it?"

"Amongst other depravities," agreed Buckley.

Howard struggled to think of anything more depraved than having sex with a giant fish-thing, but he noted that the old man chose his words carefully. Buckley clearly believed, or perhaps *understood*, that there were things in this multiverse more corrupt than Howard could imagine. He followed the storyline that the old man traced with his fingertip.

"And here," said Buckley, "is the outcome."

"The people," whispered Howard. "They've turned into weird creatures themselves."

"If you could read the archaic text, you would discover that the people of Innsmouth invited the eldritch being into their very souls. They prayed to it, worshipped it, and lusted after it, for it rewarded their devotion with an intoxicating narcosis."

Buckley saw the blank look on Howard's face.

"*Narcosis*," he repeated slowly, as though to a child. "Drug-induced pleasures."

Howard nodded. "And *then* they became sea monsters?"

"Not quite," said Buckley. "Their evolution went into reverse. With each new generation, the people become more and more *devolved*. Those with any remaining trace of humanity were enslaved or used as food, and those who have become as one with the entity are exalted. In the fullness of time, the people of Innsmouth will return to the ocean to become a vile spawn in their own right." At that, the old man snapped the book shut. "Innsmouth," he sniffed. "Very bad place."

Howard thought back to the scenes he had witnessed at the old port: the beast in the shallows, the pregnant woman he had killed, the inhuman face at the window. Could the old man be telling the truth? Was he truly travelling through another dimension filled with nightmarish cities and unearthly creatures?

The warning signal sounded and the train prepared to depart once more. Buckley gestured with his thumb towards the station they were about to leave. "Another place you don't want to visit in a hurry," he said.

As the train pulled away from Kingsport, Buckley hobbled to the door. "The next one is me." He looked down at Howard who sat, staring open-mouthed at the burnished floor of the train. "I really do suggest you come along, Howard Blake. You have a rare natural talent, but you cannot control your gift. And that, I'm afraid, is a very dangerous situation to be in." He patted the book under his coat. "If you accompany me, I can teach you how to travel safely."

Everything the old man had said explained Howard's predicament perfectly. But it only made sense if Howard believed in the fundamental principle of travel between dimensions. And the idea was simply too outrageous, too crazy, to admit.

"Thanks," chuckled Howard, shaking his head. "But to be honest I'd rather just get back to boring old London."

He looked at his watch. Late, for sure, but he might get to work in time for the rest of his shift. "This is still salvageable," he said. "If I turn up now I'm only an hour late."

"One hour?" asked Buckley.

"Yes," said Howard. "I should have started work at midnight. It's still only a quarter to one."

Now it was the old man's turn to laugh. "Your timepiece is of no use to you here. It will only lead you astray."

"What's that supposed to mean?" said Howard, although he was not sure he really wanted to hear the answer.

"Passengers spend lifetimes travelling these routes. They are loops in time connecting places that lie vast distances from one another. Each port along the way is at least six months from the previous location in real time."

Howard was almost overcome by the urge to be sick. *"Six months? Each one?"*

"At least. Why?" A frown of concern clouded the old man's bright eyes. "Exactly how far have you travelled tonight, Howard Blake?"

Howard shook his head. He couldn't think clearly.

The first one he noticed was Camden Town. Or was it perhaps Cadaver Town, after all? Then of course there had been Innsmouth. And now Kingsport.

"Three!" he said. "Only three!"

Only three? That meant that he had spent 18 months of his life aboard this nightmare train. And what if he had slept through other stations before the first one?

Howard turned to the window behind him and peered at his reflection as the train emerged from the tunnel and into the brightly lit station of another unknown town. Had he aged? Did he look a little older? A touch greyer, perhaps? A few more crow's feet?

The train drew to a halt.

Arkham.

Two years.

"My home town is not without its problems but it is essentially a civilised place," said Buckley as he shuffled to the door. "Can the same be said of your London?"

"Wait!" said Howard. He still didn't know if he believed the old man's crackpot claims but he urgently needed some assurance that his situation was not hopeless. "Surely someone will wake me up at the end of the line? Back there in London, I mean. The other passengers, the staff, they'll see me sleeping. It's not as if I've just disappeared before their eyes, like the Cheshire Cat. They'll wake me, won't they?"

Spencer Buckley appeared puzzled at the literary reference but understood Howard's meaning. "A wise traveller," he said, tapping his chest, "always makes arrangements to be woken from their sleep. To slip across dimensions without such measures in place is rather like walking a tightrope without a safety net. Someone *might* wake you, Howard Blake. But let me ask you: how often do travellers on your tube trains interfere with the slumbers of fellow passengers?"

Howard had never known it to happen. It just wasn't the done thing. *For God's sake*, he thought, *would they all just let me sit there and die of old age?*

The doors closed. The old man raised a hand.

"Farewell, traveller! If you're ever in Arkham, come and look me up. You can find me at the university. Everybody knows me there!"

Buckley made to leave the platform but then turned back. A fearful look creased his kindly face. He called to Howard through the window as the train started to move.

"If you disembarked at Innsmouth and lived to tell the tale, you are luckier than most. But that luck won't hold out forever. Whatever happens, when you can no longer read the signs you *must* get off the transporter. Promise me you will do that, Howard Blake!" called Buckley as the train stretched away from him and crept smoothly into the dark of yet another tunnel. "There's a heavy price for this journey and you pay it with your life! Promise me!"

"OK, I promise!" shouted Howard.

But Buckley and Arkham were already gone.

Howard shook his head, settled into his seat and tapped out his work number. He held the phone to his ear and rehearsed his lines: *There's some problem with the trains. I'll be in as soon as I can.*

Nothing. No ringtone. No signal. Silence.

A new station came and went in a haze of anxiety before he even had time to decide what to do.

Dunwich.

Another six months. *Jesus Christ, I must get out of here.*

He stared at the dead phone. Of course it wouldn't work; he was in another dimension. He wasn't sure exactly what that meant but it seemed reasonable to expect that there was no mobile signal.

The old man had said that his best chance of returning home was by falling asleep again and dreaming himself back into his own world. It was time to follow that advice. Howard lay on his side, drew his knees up to his chest in a foetal position, and closed his eyes.

*

Another station came and went.

Leng.

And then another.

Dylath-leen.

The stations were getting closer together. A year of his life passed by in a flash of white tiles. But no matter how hard he tried to suppress his anxiety, his pulse rate quickened at every station and sleep eluded him. In fact, he had never felt so awake in his life.

Yuggoth.

Y'ha-nthlei.

Howard rubbed his eyes. The sign was written in an alphabet he recognised but the name read like pure gibberish. In fact, since Dunwich all the station names had sounded decidedly weird. More worrying still, the platforms were becoming darker, dirtier, and older. Innsmouth and Arkham, he recalled, had seemed relatively ordinary; a bit old-fashioned perhaps but not outrageously different to the stations he was used to seeing every day in London. As the train pulled into the latest station, Howard found it hard to see out of the window. This new station was illuminated only by the stark lighting from inside the train itself.

"Well, it is late now," he muttered to himself. "Staff have probably switched off and gone home for the night. No point getting off here."

He sat back in his seat and looked around the carriage. The thought that had come to him earlier, returned: the train just wasn't right. The floor was pristine white, the seat covers were plain, not patterned. And, now he thought about it, the carriage was altogether too small, as if built in slightly the wrong scale. It was as though someone had made a rough sketch of an underground train from memory but not bothered with the measurements and fine details.

Spencer Buckley had explained that the train Howard believed he was riding, and the ship Buckley himself was sailing, were illusions. Except, Howard now realised, the imperfections in this illusion could not be of his own making. He had recognised the flaws in the design, meaning that it can't have been his own subconscious that had failed to recreate an authentic London Underground train. So who had fashioned the illusion for him?

Howard sat up sharply when the next station was revealed. For the first time, the script on the nameplate was not in the Roman alphabet. Howard had no idea what it said but it looked a bit like Greek. Or perhaps Russian. A green glow barely illuminated crusted yellow walls and the platform seemed comprised of rock and glistening vegetation. A derelict station? Flooded perhaps? He had heard of such places on London's Tube network; stations that had been closed decades ago, remaining just as they were on the day they were sealed up; time capsules, forever hidden from public view.

More darkened stations sped by. The lettering on the nameplates transitioned from something that was vaguely recognisable into thoroughly illegible lines of elegant curlicues, and then into little more than crude dots and splodges.

The carriage lurched languidly away from night-shrouded platforms with a belching sound and plunged downward into utter blackness like a rollercoaster at a funfair.

Another year, thought Howard. *No, two years. How long can this go on?*

The rusty sign at the new station bore no words at all, but its meaning was plain enough. For inside the traditional red and blue logo was a pictogram, an illustration that loosely resembled a many-tentacled octopus or squid. So, another damned port.

Without further thought, Howard scrambled off the train. He couldn't waste any more of his life waiting to fall asleep. Whatever and wherever this new town was, he would strike out for home from above ground, even if that meant hitching a ride on a boat across Buckley's purple ocean!

He found himself on an uneven, slippery surface that angled down towards a series of holes sunk into a rough granite wall. The sound of rushing water filled his ears like white noise. The slender burrows that peppered the walls reminded him of the honeycomb pattern of a beehive. He peered into one that was level with his face but recoiled at the sewer stench which emanated from it. As he drew back, the hole seemed to twitch and vibrate. From within, there was another sound above that of running water; a sound that was disturbingly close. A buzzing, scratching sound.

He looked around. It was impossible to leave this sorry excuse for a station without climbing through one of the small conduits that clicked and thrummed at his approach. He pictured himself stuck in one of them as it wrapped its stinking, undulating innards around him. No, he decided. That simply wasn't an option. He would return to the relative sanctuary of the train and make a concerted effort to sleep. Surely, at some point, he would simply collapse from sheer exhaustion, anyway? With any luck, when he awoke, he would be back in London and he could put this crazy nightmare behind him.

In his haste to secure refuge from the amphibious-looking mob at Innsmouth, he had paid no attention to the external appearance of the train but now, as he stood on the platform pondering his next move, Howard saw that it shimmered and undulated, as though fashioned from silver jelly. There was an iridescence that lent it an almost organic appearance. It seemed to be a glistening, worm-like cylinder; a pulsing, living machine. Was this the concealed reality that Spencer Buckley was talking about?

He thought back to the moment at Innsmouth when the human-like creatures hesitated at the entrance to the platform. Only one bold soul dared to approach the train. Was that because they were seeing something different to what Howard and Spencer Buckley were seeing? Did they see something that frightened them enough to stop them in their tracks?

And why had the train still been there at the platform, anyway? Why had it not simply continued its journey without him? Howard shuddered.

"You were waiting for me, weren't you?" he said. "Because I was still dreaming."

He splashed awkwardly across the wet, stony ground. With one hand holding the door open, he peered along the side of the train and into the tunnel ahead. It was as black as night in there but nevertheless he fancied he could detect movement in the walls; a pulsing muscle, threaded with sea-green arteries and coated with glittering mucus that suggested an almost coital interface between train and tunnel.

Suddenly, he was aware of a shuffling, dripping sound behind him. He looked back down the platform. There was something emerging from one of the honeycomb conduits; something very black and very big.

Howard jumped into the carriage and hit the button to close the doors. They remained steadfastly open.

They'll close by themselves. Just wait. That's all you have to do. Just wait.

The front end of the creature flopped heavily onto the platform, the sound of raw meat hitting a marble slab. Its thick black torso remained firmly plugged into the wall, playing out squirming limbs which began to separate into a dozen or more tentacles that reached along the ground towards the train like slick ebony snakes.

The carriage doors were gaping wide but Howard didn't want to draw attention to himself by standing in front of them slapping uselessly at the button. He sidled into the carriage. The tactic had worked at Innsmouth; it should work here too. If he kept quiet and still, the thing would pass him by.

He recalled the words of the old man as he had departed Arkham: "When you can no longer read the names, get off the train." It dawned on Howard that the names had stopped making sense several stops ago. He cursed himself for not alighting at Arkham or Dunwich.

Howard watched in horror as the greasy black limbs slithered and groped blindly around the open doorway. He wanted to put as much distance between himself and that twitching serpentine creature as possible. He crept to the end of the compartment, wrestled open the connecting door and ran all the way to the end of the next carriage.

In the distance, looking back through the glass panels in the connecting doors, he could see that the writhing tentacles had found their way into the compartment he had formerly occupied; behind them, the body of a vast tubular monstrosity blotted out the light as it filled the train, like a huge ink stain spreading across a white page.

Howard entered the third carriage. He knew he would soon run out of train. He needed to think clearly, but his mind was reeling. Perhaps he could out-fox the thing by alighting and hiding somewhere on the platform. At the very least, it was worth a try.

Howard hurried to the middle of the carriage. What he saw made him feel numb. Instead of the exit doors he had anticipated, there was a featureless wall.

He put his hands against the blank panel where the doors should have been. It felt warm, soft. The wall throbbed beneath his fingers. Above his head, the lights flickered and buzzed like angry glow-worms. Around him, the paintwork no longer appeared pristine white. Instead, there was a pink, fleshy tinge to the walls and ceiling. The seats, once of dull grey cloth, now appeared to him as swollen vein-threaded organs, bloated and pulsing with blood.

The truth finally dawned on Howard. This vessel that carried passengers across vast eons of space presented each customer with a comforting illusion that matched their expectations of a transport system. To Spencer Buckley, it had been a boat. To Howard, a train. Until now. For now, he was seeing the vessel for what it truly was: a living, breathing being; a leviathan that allowed travellers from every corner of the multiverse to ride it, like parasites, in exchange for years of life. Isn't that what the old man had meant?

There's a heavy price for this journey and you pay it with your life!

Perhaps that was why the fish people at Innsmouth had hesitated to follow him. Did they see the reality that Howard was blind to?

He glanced back the way he had come. The oozing black thing that was now pressing at the connecting door to this carriage was just another passenger, like himself. But what illusion was *it* seeing? A dark tunnel like the narrow honeycombs it seemed to inhabit in its own world? And what was it expecting to find inside the transporter as it journeyed to other realms? Certainly not upholstered seating and strip-lights.

Howard felt his chest tighten. The windows were beginning to turn opaque but he could see his own reflection well enough to understand that he had aged terribly. The lined face of a haunted man, wide-eyed with terror, stared back at him.

Behind him there was a crunching sound—glass breaking. Surely it was impossible for the new passenger to fill the whole train?

The thought brought to mind a television programme he had once seen, in which an octopus performed the seemingly impossible contortion of squeezing its vast boneless bulk into a tiny glass bottle. Once inside, the bottle appeared to be solid black. It was a neat trick.

The impulse to scream overwhelmed him but when he opened his mouth, his voice refused to work. Instead of the cathartic release of shrieking terror he was anticipating, all he could utter was a strangled groan. It was as if his vocal cords were paralysed.

As though mocking his own muteness, the piercing trill of the door signal sounded throughout the train. It was getting ready to continue its relentless journey. Suddenly, the lights went out and the world was plunged into darkness.

The door signal, he thought. *They couldn't even get that right.* It was too insistent, too shrill. Too much like…

An alarm clock!

Dear God, I never left home! I never boarded any damned train!

Howard groped blindly into the blackness for the clock that resided on his bedside cabinet. He wasn't too late after all.

If he could reach the clock, feel its smooth, warm plastic under the palm of his hand, he might yet wake from this hellish slumber.

As the crash of smashing glass filled his ears and an overpowering stench of the sea engulfed him, his outstretched fingertips slithered across a vast slippery surface and alighted upon something cold and hard.

He had learned something else about octopuses from that TV programme, something he had found funny at the time.

They had beaks. Octopuses had beaks.

Howard's hands slid uselessly against the immovable, crawling chaos, and gelatinous limbs embraced him in a vicelike grip. He felt his last breath being crushed from his body and tried once more to cry out before his ribcage was pierced by bone-sharp points and his dark universe finally imploded.

Inferno

She is dead now. Still, at last. But she will not stay that way for long.

A grey predawn light filters through the closed curtains, bathing her in a cold monochrome. I check the clock on the nightstand. There is much to be done before sunrise.

Some of the blood has pooled at her clavicle and is yet to congeal. The lure of it is magnetic. Without hesitation I slather at it like a pig at a trough, all the while wishing I had greater self-control.

I have tried not to waste too much of the precious fluid but the sheets are hopelessly stained, a consequence of the ravenous frenzy in which I attacked her. I pull them from under her and throw them in a pile beside the door. The florid burgundy pattern beckons me and for a moment I consider whether any of the blood can be salvaged. Then a silver-grey light through the curtains catches my eye. I have no time to waste in further sordid indulgence. I am sated and will survive another day. Greed could prove my undoing.

I make a second pile from her belongings—her clothes, handbag and mobile. The latter I am drawn to investigate. But this is another temptation I must resist. It will suffice to know her name and she has already told me that. It is Beth.

I lift Beth's body, her soft flesh pressing close against mine as it had done earlier. She is still warm. Even though her blood now courses through my veins, I remain as cold as ever.

I shove the mattress onto the floor and lay her down on the iron skeleton of the bed. No more blood will flow from her open wounds, so I chain her limp corpse to the brass bedstead. It is fixed into the tiled floor and will not move when she begins to struggle.

"People don't have tiles on their bedroom floor," she had commented. "What on earth possessed you?" She didn't like the hard surface beneath her bare feet. I told her I found it practical. I wanted to tell her it wasn't my bedroom.

Perfectly at rest for the moment, Beth lies on the blackened metal springs like some gruesome modern sculpture. I stand at the foot of the bed and think about how much she is going to suffer. I regret that. Then I realise that I have kept her mobile in my hand, and my fingertips are playing absently across the screen. Her wallpaper is a selfie she has taken with another woman. A friend? A sister? A lover? Earlier, I had watched as she keyed in her access code. I swipe left, right and I find a contact list.

Jamie

Priti

School

Mum

I throw the phone at the floor. The screen cracks on the tiles. Then I slam my heel onto it. Once, twice. I kick it into the corner of the room. It can stay there until I sweep up what remains of her tonight.

Thinking is the worst thing I can do right now. Thinking, piecing together their lives, leads to guilt, regret. Shame. I can afford none of these mortal luxuries.

I smash a fist against the brass bedstead and it rattles madly. Beth's torso trembles, her head moves to one side, but it is merely a parody of life, nothing more. Nothing yet.

Time is wasting. I must hurry. I gather my own clothes and make a third pile, following the routine on autopilot now.

Naked, I pad to the bathroom, glad to put the scene behind me for a few minutes. Her blood, rusted dry on my face, hands and chest, liquefies again under the shower, streams down my body like spilled cranberry juice and churns around the drain in dark swirls. The revived blood is slick, steaming, and for a moment I am intoxicated by its silkiness, entranced by its fragrance.

What was I going to do with the phone, anyway? Call one of her friends? Her mother? And tell them what? Beth won't be coming home tonight?

For a moment, I imagine cutting her loose, setting her free. Then she would fly home. But not before she had slaked her own burning thirst with the blood of innocents along the way.

I picture the two of us reigning over the city, haunting the night, the king and queen of death. Together we would be unstoppable. Igniting the land, our plague would spread like fire through a desiccated forest; the bloodied masses, at first our prey, would soon become the subjects of our eternal empire.

The water is running clear. I turn off the shower, dry myself and return to the chamber that is not my bedroom. I take a fresh change of clothes from the wardrobe. As I dress, I check the clock. I have lost precious minutes. Any moment now, the chains will rattle. Her consciousness will return. I would prefer to be gone by then.

I switch off the lamp and open the curtains. A splash of heat stings my face and I lurch back from the glass. The sky has bled indigo into cobalt. Beyond the rooftops, the sun is readying itself. There is a misty white incandescence at the horizon. I cannot stay here much longer, but Beth will get to witness one more sunrise. It will be the most terrible sunrise she has ever experienced. The torture she is about to suffer will eclipse any pain she has ever known, including that of death itself.

On her left arm, a small tattoo of Satan holding a pitchfork.

"I don't know why I'm even doing this," she had said. "I don't normally... you know.... like this."

"Must be the devil in you," I replied. She laughed. I wish I hadn't said it. I wish she had told me to go to hell.

Her hair is glued to the side of her face with a smear of her own gelatinous blood. I pluck it away. Her eyes open. She tries to move, looks up to see her wrists bound to the bed. She tugs furiously at the chains and the bed shudders. Her eyes widen at the sight of the lick-spread blood on her breasts. If I could blush, I would have burned scarlet.

"What the fuck is going on?" she asks. Her voice, cracking, betrays outrage and fear in equal measure.

It is best if she doesn't know that I ripped out her jugular with voracious passion, gulped frantically at her lifeblood like a man lost in the desert who has stumbled upon an oasis. It is best if I don't tell her that she died with me crawling over her like a carnivorous cockroach, tearing at veins in her wrists and arteries at her groin so that I could suck every last drop out of her. I won't tell her what I have passed on to her, what she has become or what happens next. Instead, I look away from her fevered eyes and promise her that salvation will arrive soon enough.

I gather up the bloodstained garments and head for the stairs.

She calls after me, shouts my name—or what I have told her is my name, for I am a liar. I am the king of lies, lord of dishonesty and master of duplicity. I could survive no other way.

I could silence her now and end it. I keep a sharpened stake of ash as a precaution. Could I bring myself to use it? I never have before. Allowing the sun to do its inevitable duty, I abdicate responsibility. Add cowardly and immoral to my list of failings.

I can still hear her calling for help. There are no neighbours. No one will attend to her cries but I am thankful that her voice carries through the house. With some, their voice is barely above a whisper. Beth's screams could wake the dead. Or soothe them to sleep.

I unlock the cellar. The door is sealed around the frame. There are no windows down here and the room is beautifully cool and dark.

Up in the bedroom, Beth falls silent. I expect she is sobbing but her quietness unnerves me for a moment. She is stronger now than when she was alive. Has she realised her new power? Is she busy prying apart the chains, as I could so easily do? For a moment, a ripple of fear displaces guilt.

Still listening, I close the door and descend the wooden steps. The unlit room swallows me down but I am used to moving in the shadows and I make my way easily to the casket and climb inside.

I stare at the ceiling, wasting precious seconds. Did I remember to open the curtains after all? I mentally retrace my steps but I am unable to visualise pulling the dark woollen drapes aside. Will she lie there in shadows, surviving the dawn after all? It's too late to check now. Panic grips me, like an iron fist closing around my throat.

Then, at last, a high-pitched scream. And this is no cry of anger or despair. This is a scream of pure, unimaginable agony.

The golden fire has found her.

The crushing weight of doubt is lifted. I shut the lid and relish the blackness. Her shrieks filter down the stairs and penetrate the cellar door and the casket lid, reaching a crescendo of hysteria as her skin scorches and her blood boils. In my mind's eye, I see her outer layer blacken and crumble away like a charcoal shell. Then her bones will roast like kindling, popping and crackling until they finally break apart in brittle shards. Before the sun has fully risen, Beth will be nothing more than a litter of grease-stains and ashes on a tiled floor. A filthy clean-up job for tomorrow night. Followed by another victim. Another Beth.

She falls silent. In the perfect dark of my casket, I wait for the nightmares to begin.

And then there is an explosion of light, a blast of heat.

Beth stands above me, igniting the room in flame-red, a whirlwind of silver-grey smoke swirling around her melting flesh. A burning shard of broken stair-rod is raised in one blazing hand. Her face is obscured by a living, raging inferno but I know she is smiling.

I close my eyes. And I smile too.

Revolt

Paul had driven through the night and he felt like death. It was 5.30 in the morning. A bleary sun peered up from the horizon and leered at him through the tawny haze of dawn like a malarial eye, casting a nauseous, oily light over the city. Thick clouds the colour of dried blood swarmed over his head. There would be a storm before the day was out.

He glanced around at the rubbish-littered car park, closed the BMW's door as quietly as he could and began the final leg of his journey.

*

The street was bordered by smashed windows, boarded-up shops and burned-out cars. Paul did a double take. Yes, burned-out cars. Had there been another riot? He hadn't seen anything on the news. But then again, since he had moved to the countryside he hardly paid any attention to what was happening in his old home town. It was too depressing.

He stopped and looked at a parked van. Presumably gleaming white when it came off the production line, it looked much older than its five or so years. But it wasn't the numerous dints and scratches that caught Paul's attention. Something had melted away great swathes of paint, exposing lumpy and diseased-looking rust beneath.

Paul walked on slowly. All the cars were in a similar state of decay. It was as though they had been devastated by some Biblical plague that had ruined and rotted everything it touched. He felt that if he pressed a finger into the grey-brown bubbles on the bodywork of the infected vehicles, the tainted metal would crumble like overcooked piecrust. But what would he feel on the inside? The thought made him ram his fists deep into his pockets.

He looked back at his gleaming BMW. With any luck he would have sorted things out with Jane within an hour, long before any of the estate dwellers had shaken themselves out of their foetid nests and started guzzling their first can of the day. Long before his precious car had a chance to catch whatever this town was contaminated with.

As he walked on, he became aware of a strange little sound. He looked down. It was him. Or, more precisely, it was his footsteps. He moved his feet slowly back and forth. Sure enough, each movement made a curious, sticky sound. And then he realised why: the pavements and roads were smeared with a thin layer of some viscous substance. The gutters were clogged with a gooey brown jelly.

Just what the hell had happened while he had been away?

A sudden heaving crash brought him back to the present. It vibrated deep into his stomach and stopped him in his tracks. He looked up. The sky swirled above him. The cracking of the thunder could have been mistaken for a symphony of demolition—a quarry being mined or a nearby tower block being razed to the ground, perhaps.

His mobile rang.

"Paul? Are you here?"

"Just arrived."

"I can't see you. Where are you?"

"Jesus, give me a chance. I've just parked up. I'm walking through the estate right now. Be with you in a few minutes."

"I'm sorry, Paul. I don't mean to be a burden. I just have to get away from here, have to get the kids out of this place. It's not... It's not..."

"I know, OK? You've already told me. And I came back, didn't I?"

Their marriage ended a year ago. He was never cut out for nappy changing and school runs. It had been a mistake. They both knew it. His career—and the rewards it garnered—was always his first love. It was inevitable that he would return to its embrace.

Her frantic call last night had been a bolt from the blue.

She couldn't take it anymore.

But he was sending money, wasn't he? For the kids?

This wasn't about money. They couldn't cope in the city anymore.

Not about money? Yeah, right. He offered her more. After all, he could afford it. A small price to keep the nagging at bay.

No, said Jane. I need *you*. The *kids* need you. Now.

He suggested she go and talk to someone. A trouble shared and all that.

There's no one left, she had said. And then she had sobbed.

He asked about Jackie, Jane's best friend. Couldn't she help out or something?

Jane sort of laughed and said that Jackie had gone. Like everyone else.

She didn't sound right. Maybe she was cracking up. He wondered what would happen to the kids if she fell apart. Taken into care, probably, and then God help them. Maybe a quick visit would ease her mind. That, plus the extra money, should calm her down for a bit.

And so he had driven overnight. Back to the estate that he had fled with such relief a year ago.

Jane breathed into the phone. "Just hurry, Paul. I think it's happening again."

"What's happening again?"

"I'll tell you when I see you. You won't believe it."

That didn't bode well. Probably having trouble with the neighbours. It was that kind of town.

"OK, Janey. Don't worry, I'll sort it. I'm almost there now."

"OK."

He put the phone away and surveyed the scene: filthy streets, ruined vehicles, and derelict buildings. He smelled the ripe stench of decay and listened to the awful deathly silence, and knew that something was horribly wrong. The coming storm would not wash these streets clean.

*

The ugly '70s-built council estate sprawled out ahead of him. His former home lay on the far side of it. To his right was an open playing field dotted with trees, goalposts and random mounds of earth. On the far side of the park, a heavily graffitied train stood out against the jaundiced horizon like a black millipede. It was too far away and still too dark to see any details but the windows were backlit and there were passengers, nothing more than silhouettes. Something about the way they were sitting, stiff and angled, made him uneasy. The train lurched, like the gulp of a lizard swallowing a fly, and crawled slowly away.

Paul shuddered.

Increasingly aware of the sound of his own footsteps on the sticky pavement, he side-stepped onto an overgrown verge. The yellow, straw-like grass snatched at his ankles but walking here would deaden his footfalls.

The Oakmead Estate. There were a few front doors with holes kicked through them, some scattered cardboard boxes and discarded beer cans, the obligatory flags in windows. Nothing seemed unusual or out of place. Nothing jarred him as it had in the high street.

He looked into the scabby patches of weed-choked dirt that passed for gardens, strewn with dented footballs, dislocated fencing and sun-faded plastic toys. The muffled bass thump of music erupted from somewhere. Still normal.

Debris littered the pedestrianised walkways. Among the fast-food cartons and car tyres, Paul spotted the wreckage of a bicycle. Without thinking, and barely breaking his stride, he scooped up a snapped-off front fork. After all, this was the Oakmead Estate.

The music was fading into the distance, its incomprehensible rhythm overlaid now by a keener, closer sound. A thin, high-pitched mewling. It was coming from the house he was walking past. He stopped and pressed his back to the red brickwork. The wall was featureless apart from a few illiterate scrawls and an open oblong window of frosted glass just above his head. A bathroom. He held his breath, suddenly conscious that he was panting aloud. Maybe parking so far away hadn't been such a bright idea. His main concern when he arrived was that his BMW would end up scratched, stolen or minus its wheels if he left it on the estate. Perhaps all three. Now, he wished he was still cocooned in its protective shell.

He looked around. Still no sign of life. Just that relentless shrieking noise from inside the house. Paul carried on walking, sticking close to the wall.

There had been few trees on the estate before, but the little foliage that had been present when he last saw the place seemed to have given way to leafless, almost unnaturally bare branches. The trees were twisted and discoloured, as if blighted by the same disfiguring disease that had afflicted the cars on the high street. He looked closely at a birch as he passed. Large strips of bark had peeled away, exposing a mushy black pulp beneath. Glistening white lumps the size of human fingers wriggled inside.

Running feet echoed loudly on the paving slabs and bounced off the brickwork. He'd been spotted. Paul whirled round to see a hooded teenager hurtling towards him. He started to edge away from the youth.

"No, wait!" said the kid.

Paul raised the bicycle part as though it were a talisman that could ward off evil. The end, he noticed, was jagged, bare metal; it had been bent back and forth until it had finally snapped. The glittering chrome would slash open skin like a hot knife through butter. He lowered his voice. "Keep back, I'm warning you!"

"I've been following you," said the teenager, breathlessly.

Any second, he'll start demanding money for drugs, thought Paul. "Just don't try anything, mate," he said.

But the boy didn't reply. He stopped in his tracks and stared past Paul.

Paul followed the youth's anxious gaze. No more than twenty feet away, emerging from the entrance to a set of lock-up garages, was a ragged cluster of estate dwellers: a family comprising a father and mother in their mid-thirties and their daughter who appeared to be around six years old. All three looked alike, each with lank greasy hair framing pale waxy faces adorned with spots, weeping sores and black scabs. The woman wore a shapeless white football shirt spattered down the front with streaks of grime. Her fat breasts swung loose inside. The man was bare-chested. Both were sporting sagging grey joggers.

Standard Oakmead inhabitants, thought Paul. Except that big daddy's beer gut was sliced across its width and he was carefully, but inadequately, holding in the purple-grey sac of his stomach. Paul watched, momentarily fascinated, as rogue loops of intestine slithered out of the blackened wound between the man's pudgy fingers.

The family staggered, falteringly, towards Paul. The teenager rummaged inside his hooded top and pulled out a long bread knife. It was crusted with dried blood. "You smash them with the pipe and I'll cut off their heads," he said.

Paul revised his character sketch of the boy; not only was he a crackhead but he was also a psychopath.

"Just shankin' 'em is no good, man. I've tried," said the teenager. "You've got to wreck their brains." He tapped his knife against his own temple.

This was beyond crazy. The guy with the external digestive system was weird as hell but he thought he'd read about people with stuff like that. It was a condition or syndrome or something. And not even contagious. This kid, however, was something else.

"I don't want any trouble," said Paul, hefting the metal tube in his fist. "Just stand aside and let me go on my way."

"Come on, bro!" said the youth. "Let's fuck them before they fuck us!"

The family came closer. The father was drooling, white eyes roiling wildly in his meaty face. None wore shoes and the sticky paving slabs were peeling thin sheets of flesh from the soles of their grimy bare feet. The little girl was in a lilac cotton nightshirt; it was bejewelled with amoebic blobs of claret and green that looked sickeningly organic. Streaks of snot had gummed up her mouth. In her left hand she was swinging a naked doll by the foot.

Ten feet away.

The bicycle fork felt good in his hand but Paul couldn't imagine actually hitting anyone with it. Not even the psycho crackhead kid. It was a deterrent, that's all. He would wave it around to keep the whole damned lot of them at bay and then he would run for it. Jane would have to wait.

Just then, the upside-down doll the child was carrying urinated down its own bloated body and its inverted head twisted round to face Paul. A small black hole opened in its sore-caked face and it let out the high-pitched cry that Paul had heard earlier.

"Oh my God," whispered Paul.

Suddenly, the Oakmead family lurched forward and charged, shrieking a hellish battle cry. Paul realised with utter certainty that he wasn't going to get out of this alive. This is how he dies; torn to shreds and eaten by a mob of... what? He would never know.

The woman crashed into him, breasts swinging and arms flailing. She reached for his face. He pushed her away, one palm against her pulpy chest, and stepped back. His free hand had raised the bicycle fork to shoulder level without his bidding; a subconscious survival instinct. The woman snarled, revealing a row of crumbling brown teeth. She thrust her clawed hands at his throat but he outreached her by a good six inches and held her at bay.

"Speed it up, bro," shouted the teenager. "Finish the bitch and help me!"

The man with the exposed innards had stumbled in the direction of the youth, letting his grip on his guts relax so that they tumbled down as far as his knees and jostled there obscenely between his legs.

The kid whipped his bread knife in front of the man's face, nicking his nose and cheeks. The man swatted at the blade distractedly as if it was nothing more than a particularly irritating fly, seemingly oblivious to the resulting cuts and slashes to his hands.

Paul knew he couldn't hold back the thrashing woman for much longer, but if he released her she would renew her attack. His hand slipped up to her neck. It was ice-cold and the skin felt hideously loose around her throat. Her tongue flicked out lasciviously, like a snake tasting the air.

"Fuck!" yelled the youth. He had slammed his blade into the man's lower jaw, up inside his mouth, skewering his palate. Now he couldn't pull it out. The river of glutinous blood gushing down the knife made the hilt too slimy to grip. "Fucking *do* something, bro! Help me out here!" he shrieked as he flailed uselessly at the fat man. Chunky, dirty hands began closing around his head.

"They're gonna eat us! Did you, like, miss an episode or somethin'?"

Paul thought that he'd maybe missed an entire season. He had just watched someone getting stabbed through the skull without it putting the merest crimp on their day, and he was being attacked by the fishwife from hell. He started to feel light-headed. He had been in a car crash once and had staggered away, unscathed, while others had died in the burning wreckage. The paramedics had told him he was in shock. He felt like he did then: cold, detached—as though this scene was being played out on a screen in front of him and he was not actually caught up in it.

There was a bump against his legs. He glanced down. And wished he hadn't. It was the girl. Or more precisely, it was the dead-alive baby-thing being swung by the girl.

The woman snarled and made an extra effort to wrest herself from his grasp. He knew he must have squeezed her windpipe closed because his fingers were piercing her skin and he could feel the knobbly gristle inside her throat. But somehow she didn't need to breathe. And she wasn't going to relent. Their faces were almost touching; her bloodshot eyes were filled with dark, creamy gunk and crawling with tiny white dots. Lice.

He raised the twisted metal tube above his head.

"Do it! Don't think about it! Just do it, bro!"

Still grasping her under the jawline with his left hand, Paul brought the makeshift weapon down onto the centre of the woman's head with as much force as he could muster. There was a crunch like a giant hardboiled egg being smashed.

Gravity took over. The female dropped from his grip and fell to the ground. The bicycle fork, his gore-spattered hand still holding it tight, was pulled down with her to waist level, until her dead weight eventually tore her free of it with a revolting sucking sound.

He turned and kicked out at the girl. She fell over and got up again without batting an eyelid. Grimacing, he booted her harder, in the stomach, and she hurtled backwards. The baby-thing dangling from her fingertips went tumbling across the road, its dead skin tearing in places as it skidded on the tarmac.

Paul pushed aside the realisation that he had just kicked a little girl into the street and murdered her mother. He could examine his conscience later. If there was to be a later. He shouted out to the teenager, "Come on, let's—" But his voice trailed off.

The youth was lying on the ground. The Oakmead man, his insides trailing out behind him like bloated party streamers, was sprawled on top of him. They looked for all the world as though they were making mad passionate love right there on the pavement. But the slurping sounds and growing scarlet puddle in the gutter told a different tale.

To the east, glimpsed fleetingly through ragged clouds, a cold sunlight the colour of tarnished steel spilled across the city. Thunder rumbled, no longer distant.

The girl scooped up the torn baby-thing, walked to where her twice-dead mother lay shattered on the grass verge, and cried.

Aside from the wailing child at his feet and the slurping of the Oakmead man as he guzzled and ripped at the dead youth's exposed throat, the estate was silent. But as he contemplated wiping the gore from the bicycle fork and continuing with his journey to Jane's place, a series of knocking sounds rang out from all directions. Paul slowly turned 360 degrees and took in a panoramic view of the buildings that surrounded him. Here and there, behind grime-caked, curtain-less windows he saw movement; hesitant, shambling movement. He focused on one window on the first floor. Suddenly, a hand hit the glass with a hollow bang, smearing it with a swirl of dark fluid. At another window, on the ground floor close by, a face pressed against the glass, snuffling and licking; ruined stubs of teeth sliding hungrily, biting at nothing.

Nothing *yet*.

A door clicked open. And another. And Paul realised that they were awake. Whoever or whatever the estate dwellers were, or had become, they were awake.

He started to walk quickly away from the bloody scene. He knew the estate well enough, knew all the ways in and all the ways out. Every route would take him past row upon row of drab council flats stacked three storeys high.

Suddenly, as if at some hidden signal, estate dwellers poured into the streets, blundering through doors and crashing stupidly through closed windows.

Some of them were holding things—body parts; freshly slaughtered flesh, peppered with bite marks; limbs terminating in mushy crimson pulp, stark white bone jutting from the ends. Yellow strings of intestines, grey stomach sacs and bruise-purple organs dangled from the filthy claws and dribbled from the smashed mouths of the walking dead. Wet gore, dark and red, slithered down the creatures' bodies and splashed on the ground.

Paul threw the bicycle fork. He watched it twirl through the air and land harmlessly at the feet of one of the raging creatures heading towards him.

And then he ran.

*

Paul dodged through the litter-strewn alleyways and under the moss-encrusted walkways, sidestepping upturned wheelie bins and empty husks of vehicles. As he emerged from the estate, he caught sight of a car approaching from the high street. He ran out into the road and spread his arms and legs apart, in a starfish pose. The driver hit the horn.

"Oh, come on, pal. This is a fucking emergency! You've got to stop!" he panted. He was out of shape. That sprint had set his pulse pounding in his throat and a cool river of sweat was running down his spine.

I killed someone back there, he thought. *I caved in a woman's skull.*

The car rattled to a stop just inches from him. Tendrils of smoke escaped from gaps at the sides of the mangled bonnet. The horn blared again and Paul stooped to look through the murky windscreen. It was a wonder anyone could see through it. The blurry head of the sole occupant was stock still. Paul ran round to the driver's door.

Another car rumbled along behind him in the opposite direction, its roof was crumpled and a blue cloud billowed from beneath the chassis. He half considered attracting their attention too. The town was waking up. The more people that witnessed what was happening back on the Oakmead Estate, the better. It would reassure him that he wasn't hallucinating.

But the second car trundled on its way.

Paul ducked down to speak to the driver of the car that had stopped. The blackened window was closed and all he could detect inside was a vague outline. Panic was starting to rise now. Supposing this guy wouldn't let him in?

He probably thinks I'm a drunk, or a nutcase.

Paul rapped on the window. The Oakmead creatures, about a dozen, were emerging from the estate now. One of them gurgled, "Meat!" and was greeted with a chorus of excited grunts and moans. Paul's heart hammered. He was suddenly certain that he wasn't going to get out of this.

Then a scraping noise drew his attention back to the car. The driver's window was slowly creaking down. He bent and put his face into the frame.

"Thank God!" he blurted. "Please, you've got to let me in! I'll explain in a—"

The sentence trailed off as he saw the driver's face. Or rather, what was left of it. A jawless head darted out from the window and made a hoarse inhuman sound. It was trying to speak. Lacking a mouth, the noises were nothing more than guttural screeches.

Paul reeled away from the car, almost fell and then ran haphazardly across the road. The driver was still screaming at him, coughing out brown dust and pieces of dried flesh as he struggled to make intelligible sounds. Paul didn't look back but could now hear the creatures from the estate as they whooped and yowled after him.

He staggered backwards to the kerb and his foot plunged into the gutter. Dark, syrupy fluid washed over his ankle and flooded his shoe. A horn blared and he spun round to see another car coming at him. It made a scraping noise as it approached, as though the exhaust was dragging on the road.

"Jesus," he gasped. "They're all the same! They're all the bloody same!"

He lunged headlong into the road, almost ending up in the path of a battered white van with a faceless driver, and ran into a side street. His feet pounded the tarmac like pistons, heart bursting with pain, breath tearing in and out of his burning lungs at lightning speed.

He reached the end of the street and looked back. The curve of the road hid the entrance. He couldn't see anyone, or anything. He leaned against a wall, head down, panting hard. He hadn't run that fast since his school days. He tried to control his breathing, taking long, slow breaths in through his nose and letting them out steadily through his mouth. He didn't want to black out and let them find him lying helpless on the floor.

And then he heard a shrill, mechanical sound. Something cold and liquid ran through his bowels. It was a siren, but the noise was wrong, off key and crackling. He looked up. In that split second he noticed two things: a police car turning into the road ahead of him, and a row of blue and green dumpsters across the street, in the car park of a supermarket. He knew he couldn't outrun the patrol car. There were no other options. He sprinted across the road and vaulted into one of the open blue dumpsters.

Before he even landed, he was overcome by an appalling stench of rotten meat and vegetation. He retched as his body weight crunched down onto the remnants of damp cardboard boxes, plastic food trays and huge polythene bags. He slithered on stinking slime, steadied himself with one hand and then scrabbled for the lid with the other, intending to pull the sliding hatch closed. But it was too late. The increasing crescendo of sound signalled that the car was almost upon him. He would be seen. He snatched his hand back inside and pushed his feet against the side of the bin, drilling his torso deeper into the filth. As he did so, clumps of wet matter that had stuck to his shoes dropped onto his face. He left them where they landed.

Squealing brakes halted the police car alongside the dumpster. Paul pinched his lips closed to stop the slivers of filth from slipping into his mouth, but the smell of his hiding place made bile surge into his throat and he heaved, coughing and spitting frantically to get the stuff off his face.

He managed to silence himself just as the car doors popped open. Heavy boots shuffled and he thought he heard one of the owners say something. Whatever it was, it was unintelligible. Paul lay there exhausted, staring up at the churning sky through the open hatch, drenched with sweat, plastered with foul-smelling garbage and struggling to suppress a gag reflex. His left foot, the one that had slipped into the gutter, was soaked through and was starting to itch. He gritted his teeth to combat the urge to reach down and scratch.

If they found him now, they could take him. He had nothing left.

A sudden banging on the side of the dumpster sent a jolt through his body. A small helpless whimper escaped his lips. There were more voice-like sounds:

"*Umaaah.*"

What were they saying? Come out? Had they seen him dive in here? Had it all been for nothing?

"*Uuummmaaaah,*" they repeated, more insistently.

More banging. But this was different; further away. He heard boots shuffling again. Another bang. Could they be whacking all the dumpsters in turn?

Then a series of new noises: a car door clicking open, squeaking on corroded hinges; a metallic rattling, like a thin gate; some frantic, excited scratching. And another, deeper growling voice.

The pieces of this jigsaw puzzle of sounds suddenly fell into place and formed a picture in his mind's eye. A horrific picture. They were opening a cage in their patrol car.

And letting out a dog; a dog like them, alive but dead, and hungry for human flesh.

A series of deep, furious barks confirmed his fear. Paul's gaze was fixed on an oblong strip of dull light above him. He expected to see a mangled, rotted snout filled with blackened fangs leering in at him any second. He could almost hear splintered claws skittering up the side of the bin. Would they just throw the creature in there with him?

As he was confronting the possibility that he was about to be ripped to bloody shreds by a ravenous zombie dog, music suddenly filled his ears.

His mobile was ringing!

He scrabbled his hands into his pockets, despairing when he couldn't locate the wretched thing.

The cheery jingle continued to chug away somewhere in the folds of his clothes. He pressed and squeezed his jacket and trouser pockets until he found it. He fumbled the phone out of his windcheater, briefly bathing the garbage around him in its bright blue light, and swiped away the call with a greasy finger.

In the shocking silence that followed, he held his breath, seemingly forever.

And then something small and dark looped across the patch of sky overhead and plopped into the rubbish beside him. He couldn't see what it was or where it landed and he had the shocking thought that it might be a grenade. He closed his eyes and froze.

Nothing. Except a new smell.

There was a series of weak crackling noises outside. And a distant, watery voice. Someone was calling them on their radio. One of the cops shouted something that could have been "fuck it." Another thump against the side of the bin. Harder this time. Before Paul could decide how to react, doors started slamming. The engine choked into life and the police car pulled away. The cracked, tuneless siren began to wail again and then faded into the distance. Silence.

Paul opened his eyes. It wasn't a grenade they had thrown in. The overpowering new odour was unmistakeably shit. Paul almost laughed out loud. They had released the dog to make a call of nature and, being good, law-abiding police officers, had dutifully disposed of the excretion in an appropriate place!

But why had they been banging on the dumpsters?

Dampness from the sodden vegetables and putrid meat had seeped through his clothes. He needed a shower. Slowly he hauled himself up. His arms and legs had gone numb and, as he stood, pins and needles started to rush in.

Somewhere below him, deep in the filthy bowels of the dumpster, there was movement. Rats? Had he been sharing his grim hideaway with dead-alive rats? Without looking down, Paul steadied himself, consciously focussing on the task at hand and blotting out everything else. He just needed to get out and get away. He didn't want to think more deeply about this insane situation.

He vaulted over the edge of the dumpster, bending his legs as he landed in the hope that it would soften the sound of his soggy feet hitting the pavement.

The sky was starting to glow a washed-out yellow as the sun rose higher. As he walked away, flicking shreds of filth from his face and hair, he looked back at the dumpsters. There were six. Three blue and three green. His had been the only one with an open lid. He stopped and watched as the hatches on the others flipped up and people (or an approximation of people) began to emerge from them. Then a figure arose from his own former hiding place, dripping with wet debris, much as he had done just seconds before.

The creature turned towards Paul. It picked a large sheet of cherry-red slime from its face with almost feminine grace, revealing its features in their full horror; most of its head was missing, with nothing but jagged bone above the lower jaw— no eyes, no nose, no forehead. The roofless jaw nevertheless twitched up and down in anticipation of the tasty morsel held in its bone fingertips. It daintily dropped the greasy slop into its open throat with one hand and made a theatrical flourish with the other, as if to say "Voilà!" Then, unable to keep its balance, it tottered drunkenly and fell back into the garbage.

The others began to tumble out of their bins; one with a ripped-open chest, exposing dried organs flapping about behind the smashed bars of its ribcage; another was obese, with treble chins splitting apart under their own weight; another lacked anything at all below waist level. Were these the homeless, the down-and-outs of this mad new world?

Paul watched as some of them rubbed their eye sockets, scraping gobbets of flesh from their faces in the process. Then it dawned on him.

That's what the police were doing here. Waking them. Waking the damned dead!

He swiped at his mobile. His fingers were slippery with something unspeakable and he had to wipe them dry on his jacket to maintain his hold on the phone. There was a missed call and a new text. It was from Jane.

Pls hurry before it rains.

The sky roared. The storm was about to break. He wouldn't make it across the estate before the clouds delivered their payload. But why should Jane care about the bloody weather, anyway? This was England. It rained all the time. She must have meant something else. The perils of predictive text. At least that was still normal. Nevertheless, he instinctively turned up his collar as he looked to the heavens. And then watched as the first lazy spots of rain smacked onto the pavement in front of him.

Fat.

And ripe.

And red.

*

The blood-rain splashed down his face but he kept walking. Walking and thinking. He didn't stop until he was back to the relative sanity of the town centre.

Jane's comment about the rain hadn't been a mistake. Now he understood why she had wanted him to avoid it. Regular rain, however inconvenient, was clean and refreshing. This was altogether the opposite. The warm, gummy red fluid did little to wash away the gore he had picked up in the dumpster and was starting to make him itch all over. He needed to get under cover before he was completely soaked.

But he also had a decision to make. What should he do about Jane? His estranged wife and their two children were in that estate. Should he go back for her? Or abandon her to whatever the hell was happening?

He felt light-headed and breathless. The warm metallic stench of the bloody downpour was making him nauseous. He bent double, hooking one hand around a railing to keep his balance, and tried to steady his breathing.

Suddenly there was a small, muffled explosion somewhere close by. It sounded like a mute landmine had detonated. The dry bursting sound was followed by the soft drumming of falling earth.

He straightened and peered through the iron fence. He had arrived at the church, St Elegius. The place was boarded up years ago. The intention had been to convert it into a community centre. But lack of funding and political rows about the fate of the old Victorian graveyard had halted development. So there it stood, blackened with age, its Gothic arched windows covered with graffiti-adorned plywood sheets; its cemetery overgrown, peppered with fried chicken boxes and plastic carrier bags blown in on the wind.

"Dear God," he whispered.

As if on cue, the distinctive sound of a church organ drifted across the graveyard.

Paul moved along the railing, towards the front of the building. Maybe there was someone else who was still normal; someone like him who could see this filthy town for what it truly was: a necropolis, a city of the dead.

And maybe that someone could help him rescue Jane.

As he approached the church, more of the burial ground came into view through the rusted iron fencing and the bedraggled hedgerow that separated him from the graves.

The burgundy-black heavens groaned and flashed putrescent yellow. Paul palmed a fresh wave of bloody rain from his stinging eyes. Through the reddish haze that shrouded the cemetery he could make out movement and he heard another of those curious, quiet explosions.

His eyes focused on a collapsing plume of dirt. Inside it was an arm. Paul jerked his head back instinctively but kept his grip on the railing. *An arm?* He watched, disbelieving, as a fist opened up and soil-blackened fingers reached towards the bleeding sky.

The organ music was louder now, faster, frantic. And its off-key arpeggios resembled no hymn he had ever heard before. The manic tune seemed to blend seamlessly into a crackle of thunder, as though the two sounds formed part of one morbid symphony.

And now there was a third sound; a low rumble that he couldn't quite identify despite its frustrating familiarity.

Then it all fell into place.

The huge wooden doors of the church burst open and into the cemetery poured a congregation of the dead. As the music shrieked out from the church in a maddening crescendo, the crowd howled and wailed as it gathered among the gravestones.

They were singing. And as they sang, more skeletal, muddy limbs smashed their way out of the ground and groped blindly into the bloody miasma that smothered the town. Each new eruption was greeted with a cacophony of whooping as the crowd gasped and grunted, scarlet rivers streaming down their ecstatic, rotting faces; the new dead welcoming the old dead back to life.

The liberated hands patted the straggly straw-grass covering the graves and pushed down against the ground. There were dozens of them. Soil-covered heads emerged, their faces obscured by the black earth that filled their mouths and eye sockets.

The ground undulated pregnantly.

Paul's heart filled his throat. He gagged and swallowed hard. But he watched, repelled and yet mesmerised by the scene unfolding before him, as another carcass wrenched itself clumsily out of the ground and crawled on all fours from the ripped earth. There was a garbled cheer from the dancing crowd as the reborn corpse straightened herself, clods of dirt tumbling down her mud-caked body.

There were more eruptions. The white crystal stones and translucent green pebbles that decorated some of the graves made a rushing sound reminiscent of the tide scurrying up a beach as the weed-choked ground beneath them rose up and split apart.

Paul caught sight of small, hurried movement among the weeds. Rats, disturbed from their own feasting on the dead, bolted into the undergrowth. Then Paul heard a familiar barking sound and his insides shrivelled. Standing at the edge of the congregation were two shabby policemen. At the end of a rusted metal chain, one of the zombie cops held a zombie dog. The skin of its snout was missing and its teeth were on display in a permanent snarl.

Taking his lead from the fleeing rodents, Paul backed away from the railings, relieved that there was still a barrier between him and the unholy gathering in the graveyard. He spied a shop doorway across the road, swathed in shadow, and hurried over to it. When he reached its shelter he glanced back to the churchyard. Long-buried, fossilised creatures with gaping maws and shattered, empty skulls began to jostle with the rejoicing congregation, whose swollen corpses dripped and oozed the rancid fluids of more recent death. The two tribes of undead embraced amid the headstones, and the fresh dead allowed the crumbling corpses to nip and peck at their hands and faces, as though they were feeding pigeons in the park.

Then one of the crowd turned and pointed at him.

It squealed like a wounded pig and its undead brethren bayed and yelped in a mimicked response. Paul suppressed the urge to scream as he saw the zombies turn as one, like a flock of starlings, and head towards him.

The skin of the freshly dead sloughed away like greased leather as they shambled across the graveyard. Some of the mouldy creatures were already up to the railings, just standing there stupidly, as if they couldn't comprehend what was obstructing them. Others had staggered their way to the gate. It groaned as they pressed their decayed flesh and bone against it. The rust-caked hinges screamed a token protest and gave way under the weight of the ravenous undead. Hundreds of the gibbering creatures spilled out into the blood-slimed streets.

The zombie cops made guttural noises of protest at this unseemly display of public disorder. The hell-hound began to bark again, adding to the cacophony, as the swarm flooded across the street towards him.

Paul battered frantically at the shop door, hoping that someone (preferably someone normal) would open it and let him in or that he could at least break it down and escape through the premises. But the door resisted his efforts. He looked back over his shoulder. The zombies had reached the shops and they were now wrenching at steel shutters, punching through plate glass windows and stumbling into the abandoned buildings.

It was hopeless. There was nowhere to run. Paul slumped to the ground, ready now to meet his fate. He screwed himself into a ball in the corner of the doorway, drew his knees up to his chin and wrapped his arms around them. Through the legs of the crowd, he could see the policemen in the middle of the street, bellowing furiously into their radios. What passed for law and order had broken down. They were calling for back up.

The zombies stumbled over him, clawing at each other and battering their skeletal fists against the shop door in a frenzy of screeching and howling. And yet none of the undead seemed able to see him down there among the puddles of blood and flailing limbs. Except one; one of the corpses he had watched clambering out of the grave minutes earlier.

It was a woman. She prised her way through the clamouring crowd until she stood directly in front of him. Her long, straggly hair was slathered in a slurry of wet grave dirt. Plump pink worms squirmed in her mud-filled eye sockets.

Could she see him? How could that be?

The dead policemen began to break up the crowd, jabbing them with batons and chasing them down the street as their snarling hell-hound snapped at their limbs.

Paul stood up. He was alone with the mummified woman. Her jaw worked open and closed. Was she trying to speak to him?

As he edged past her, she followed him with her wriggling eyes, her skeletal jaw working silently. She reached out a bony hand.

"No," he said. "I can't help you."

Outside the cemetery, the horde was regrouping. There were more of them than ever and they crawled over the walls of the nearby buildings like a swarm of cockroaches, their fists and feet smashing windows on all floors. A handful of the decaying cars were burning. The two policemen lay in the street, their limbs torn from their bodies. All that remained of the dog was its skinless head.

The dead are rioting, thought Paul. It was a zombie uprising.

In the doorway he had vacated, the woman stood alone, still reaching out to him.

*

It had stopped raining but the pungent red juice had drenched him. A dull colourless sun, mottled and cold, had risen to meet the fleeing storm clouds. Thunder rumbled away. The storm was seeking another town.

The road was still and slick with blood. Paul started to walk. His mind was made up. He had to take Jane and the kids away from this. They could decide where to head once they were on the move. Her mother's, a hotel. Anywhere. They just had to start moving.

There was something coming along the road, around the bend. A small white vehicle, striped with fresh blood, was trundling towards him accompanied by a thin banshee wail. Had the zombie police caught up with him after all?

As it came into sharper focus he saw it was nothing more sinister than a milk float. He carried on walking. Nearly there. This whole hideous, crazy episode was reaching its conclusion. The finish line was in sight. All he had to do was cross it.

He took out his old house keys, wary of jangling them and waking the neighbours. The milk float clunked to a halt ten yards away. A milkman climbed out, his back to Paul. Dressed traditionally, in a white peaked cap and a blue pinstriped apron, he fumbled noisily among the crates and retrieved a handful of bottles. This was good. This was… normal.

Paul's eyes alighted upon Jane's home. The house looked grubby in the dim light. There were stains streaking down the whitewashed walls and the windows were opaque, as though veiled by cauls of cobweb.

He checked his watch: 6.30. He'd taken forever getting here. Jane would be at her wit's end.

He hurried to the front door but his trembling hands would not allow him to insert the key. It juddered and scratched around the lock. The heavens rumbled again and a sudden warm breeze riffled the skeletal branches of the cadaverous roadside poplars.

Next door, Mrs Crawford's wooden gate was rotten and hanging off its hinges like a loose tooth. No change there. On the doorstep, her dozing cat looked just as mangy and flea-bitten as ever. The milkman made his way up her garden path. The bottles made an odd, thick sound when they knocked together.

Halfway up the path the milkman dropped one of the bottles. The cat flinched from its slumber but there was no crash and tinkle of glass. The bottle crunched, rather than smashed, and stayed upright on the path but leaning to one side, stuck in a yellow jelly that oozed lazily from the wreckage. The milkman chuckled quietly. "Butter fingers," he burbled.

A pause. Then a wheeze escaped his shrivelled mouth, peppering the air with dust. He flung back his head and laughed. It was a throaty, brutal sound. "Butter fingers!" ·he crowed, thrilled by his feeble joke.

Mrs Crawford's cat, startled by the commotion, skittered stiffly across the path and into the flowerbed; a patch of mud that teemed with the spiny tendrils of unknown plant life.

Paul tried the key again but the lock seemed to be clogged with rust. He reached out and pressed the doorbell. It made a flat, grinding sound. The batteries were going but it did the trick. On the other side of the glass Jane's slender figure appeared in the hallway, instantly recognisable, thrown into silhouette by the light from the kitchen beyond. Through the patterned glass panel, he watched her creep cautiously towards the door; two smaller shapes hovered skittishly behind her.

Jane's anxious voice said something unintelligible through the glass. He responded by calling her name. She hesitated a beat before finally opening the door. And then she screamed. Her hands flew to her face. "No, no, no!" she shrieked.

He reached out to her, garbled an apology for the mess he was in; he'd got caught in the rain.

"You're too late, Paul!" she sobbed. "Too late!"

He smiled and shook his head. Typical Jane. Always highly strung, that one.

Everything's going to be fine, he said. He had come for her, and for the children too. Now they could all be together again. Like before.

Little Sam kept his distance, clinging to Jane's legs, but Ellie squeezed past Jane, excited to see her father after a year's absence. Then her smile faltered. She frowned up at Jane and whispered behind her hand. "What's wrong with Daddy?"

Kids, said Paul with a chuckle. *They just come right out and say it, don't they?*

He reached past Jane to ruffle Ellie's hair but Jane took the girl by her tiny shoulders and pushed her back inside the house.

She slammed the door.

Paul looked into the glass. Jane was sliding down the other side, her face buried in her hands. The silhouettes of the children stood beside her. One of them reached out its shadow hand and touched Jane's head.

Through the glazed door, her voice. "... too late. Can't you see that?"

Paul's focus drifted to the surface of the frosted glass. Gazing back at him, superimposed over the vignette of his erstwhile family, was someone he vaguely recognised. A man about his own height and build. But the man in the glass had his throat ripped out. He had a missing eye. And a stump where his left hand should be.

Puzzled, Paul reached up to touch his throat. It felt raw and wet. It didn't used to be like that. He tried to picture a different image of himself. But nothing came to mind. Then his train of thought was interrupted by the approach of the milkman and the fleeting notion skittered away like dead leaves on the autumn wind.

Looks like a nice day, said the milkman through his leathery, slit-mouth.

Paul agreed. *I've been away*, he said. *I think I returned just in time.*

And then he smashed his remaining fist into the door, eliciting screams of horror from the occupants inside as a shower of glass rained down upon them.

Need a hand? asked the milkman.

Paul looked down at his stump and they both erupted into gales of laughter. Against the backdrop of howling terror within, they crashed through the door and entered the house.

II. A FISTFUL OF HORRORS

Old Red

1

Daniel peered through the dusty windscreen, frowning whenever little gaps in the foliage allowed the lowering sun to splash across his face.

"This road has to lead somewhere," he said. "Or else why make it?"

Laura sighed. "If we go much further, we'll run out of petrol," she said.

"Gas," said Daniel. "You ask for petrol out here and they won't know what you mean."

"I'm not an idiot, Daniel," she said, waving her phone around the cramped interior of the hire car for the umpteenth time that afternoon.

It had been a long, sweaty day and once they had left the city, the drive through the back roads had become increasingly winding and tortuous. The clinging heat outside seemed to penetrate the car despite the best efforts of the air-con. Now that Daniel was hot, thirsty and needed to pee, he was starting to regret his refusal to take a pit stop when they passed Gator Planet an hour earlier.

"I want us to really get under the skin of America, Laura," Daniel had said as they sailed past the neon hoarding and long line of sweating families waiting patiently outside the roadside attraction. "I want to meet real Americans, to experience a place that is something more than a pre-packaged, homogenized photo opportunity."

Laura was sympathetic to his intentions but that didn't make her feel any less frazzled. Several times that morning she had insisted that they were hopelessly lost, leading to brief squabbles which, in turn, were followed by lengthy silences. Even so, most of the micro-arguments centred on the absence of modern technology. After almost five hours on the road Laura was suffering social media withdrawal symptoms. She repeatedly pulled out her phone to test for a signal, like an amputee trying to walk on their missing leg.

Daniel insisted they didn't need all that intrusive, modern paraphernalia. He had turned down the offer of a satnav at the Hertz office, explaining to the girl on the desk that he had a perfectly good book to lead him through his American odyssey; a real, well-thumbed book, made out of paper, not pixels. The girl had exchanged a worried look with Laura and Laura had shrugged.

"It can't be here, Dan," she said. "This is just a sea of trees and the road is like a funnel."

"The guide book hasn't let us down yet, has it?" he said, reaching across to tap the slightly curled-up paperback resting open on Laura's lap. "And isn't it just a tad more authentic, more tangible, than some awful computerised voice telling us to turn left here, turn right there?" He cast the briefest of sideways glances at Laura.

"It smells," said Laura. "And it's at least ten years old."

The rutted track seemed to get narrower the further they went.

Laura snapped the travel guide shut and sighed.

The car scraped through crowding vegetation that formed an apex overhead, almost blotting out the sunlight altogether. Daniel's frown betrayed his nagging suspicion that Laura was right. They seemed to have strayed an awfully long way from civilisation.

"It must be down one of these roads," he said, his voice barely concealing his increasing anxiety. "Anyway, there's no room to turn around so we might as well go all the way to the end."

"You know most of these travel writers have never even been to the exotic off-the-beaten-track places they gush about, don't you?"

Laura had barely closed her eyes, exasperated at the persistence of the flashing question mark where the Wi-Fi icon should be, when Daniel shouted triumphantly, "O ye of little faith!"

Just visible through the chaos of greenery, fixed to a telegraph pole in the scrubby forecourt of a colonial era riverfront building, was a hoarding: Old Red's Bar & Grill. Above the writing, a faded depiction of an alligator's head, mouth gaping open to the sky in a V shape, revealing an implausible array of yellow fangs.

"Looks like a 1950s movie poster," said Daniel with a chuckle of relief. "Just like the book says."

Laura craned her neck to take in the building's peeling paintwork. "Looks like it's way past its sell-by date."

Daniel nodded at the half dozen or so pick-ups and Harleys neatly lining the periphery of the yard. "Well, they seem to be open for *bidness*."

He parked up alongside a motorcycle-sidecar combo that sported a handkerchief-sized Confederate flag on a wire pole. As they disembarked, the whippy sound of fiddle music leaking from a jukebox vied with a symphony of trilling insects and shrieking birds to enclose them in a wall of sound. The hot, green air of the bayou smothered them like a thick blanket and the cloying stink of boiling vegetation instantly forced Daniel to sneeze. Then something long and iridescent clattered noisily into his face.

"Authentic enough for you?" said Laura with a grin.

"Just don't scratch the sodding bike," Daniel hissed, flapping at the air in front of him, as though he was trying to clear smoke.

"Pussy," said Laura. She looked up. Beneath the hoarding was a small white placard: Vacancy.

"I know I've only been navigating but it's been a pig of a journey," she said. "There's no way I'm driving all the way back to New Orleans tonight, Dan."

That was the deal. They would share the driving fifty-fifty. Daniel would drive them out to the sights, where he might sample a couple of local brews, and Laura would drag them back to the hotel at the end of the day. The system had worked well enough, but today's long trek out to the bayou had taken its toll on both of them.

"Plus, I don't know if you noticed, but there's no street lighting out here. I really don't fancy my chances on these back doubles in the pitch black," she added. "Yours either, for that matter."

Daniel squinted up at the sign and then looked at Laura. Her hands were on her hips and an argument was incubating just behind her strained smile and raised eyebrows. It was a challenge he was too weary to meet. He sighed. "I'll ask about a room, then."

"Good," said Laura brightly.

They walked up to the entrance.

"You keep telling me the quest for the real America is thirsty work. Finally, I can have a bloody drink too," said Laura. Then she caught his arm and whispered in his ear, "That's if the redneck zombie bikers don't get us first!"

2

Laura tugged the bottle of Dixie from her lips, stifled a belch with the back of her hand and directed a withering glare at Daniel. "You want to go out there in the dark? Are you mad?"

Daniel straightened out the flyer on the table:

Swamp tours
Duck shoots
Nite fishing
Ask at the bar!

The paper stuck in spilled beer and the black-on-white print began to melt.

"Come on. You can't say you've been to a Louisiana swamp and not gone *nite* fishing," he said.

"In... the... dark?" she said, boggling her eyes at him as if he might not have understood the full implications of his latest foolish venture.

Daniel looked out across the lake that stretched away from the terrace at the rear of the bar. The sun was low, and the water glittered with a burnished chrome sheen. The riverfront was fringed with cypresses, knees bent to the water, and live oaks dripping with Spanish moss. Moored alongside the terrace was a shallow aluminium boat. It had a large searchlight mounted on a six-foot high rig.

"It'll be fine," he said at last. "It's traditional."

When he turned back to check Laura's reaction, his breath caught in his throat. She followed his gaze behind her to the shoreline where a glistening wet, olive-grey alligator was lumbering out of the water and up the bank towards the handful of customers on the terrace.

Without any sign of alarm, the clientele—all local men, women and children—began grubbing around in their bowls of gumbo for chunks of food to throw. The gator snapped its huge lipless jaws in the air and swaggered its way around the tables and chairs as scraps of crawfish rained down on its head.

Daniel felt himself rise to his feet and was overcome with an almost irresistible urge to run away. "Jesus, that's fucking mental!" he shouted.

"Hey, watch your filthy mouth, pal! There's kiddies present!"

A thick-necked local from an adjacent table stood up and glared at Daniel. He wore a blue plaid shirt, sleeves cut off to display arms like pillars of mahogany. Sure enough, there were small children present—lots of children—all gleefully feeding the river monster as though it was no more menacing than a fluffy kitten.

The place fell silent.

Laura leaned close to Daniel as he slowly resumed his seat. "You still want to go out there in that glorified tin can, bubba? In the dark?"

3

"Place used to be a farmhouse. Guy called Robidoux hauled his family out here in the 1920s: young wife, one rugrat and one on the way. Set up a mess of chicken coops."

Jake, the owner, was addressing Laura while pouring a couple of fingers of Wild Turkey for his two English guests. Daniel couldn't tell whether the beefy Cajun still harboured some ill-will over his profane outburst earlier, or if he was just trying to flirt with Laura. Either way, she seemed to be the focus of his attention.

"It was the Depression, you know? Folk out here had it harder than most. Livin' off the swamp's never been easy. But the gators didn't let 'em dangle a single line in the river," he laughed. "So crawfish was off the menu. Most days, they were lucky to make a dinner out of frog meat and chickweed. Robidoux came along, figured he could do something about that; provide cheap eats for the neighbours and make a fast buck for himself into the bargain.

"Trouble is, before long he got hisself caught up in a feud with a nest of gators. Every night, they'd come outta the bayou, break open a coop and snatch a few chickens. Well, they were his livelihood so he started losin' money bad. Then one day a local woman turns up at his door; a black woman, looked old as the hills. Said she'd heard about his predicament. Tells Robidoux he has to come to terms with the gators, has to pay 'em their due.

"'I'm lookin' fer a way to get rid of the sons o' bitches', says Robidoux. 'Not make peace with 'em'.

"The woman explains that the swamp and its inhabitants were here long before all of us; even before the Choctaws and Chitimagas. 'Everything here belongs to them', she said. 'Always will. Mankind is just passin' through. We pay the owners their due and they might, just might, let us stay a while'.

"She tells Robidoux he has to start off by handing over some of his livestock. If he doesn't pay up, thing's are gonna get real ugly.

"'To hell with that', says Robidoux. 'Them damn chickens is all. that's standing between me and bankruptcy. I sunk my life savin's into this farm. Besides, I don't treat with no goddamn critters. I'm a God-fearin' man!'

"The woman laughs at that, then she asks him which god does he fear the most? The ancient one that rules this stretch of river or a Christian one that's gonna sit by and watch him and his family perish out here like a litter of sick pups?

"To Robidoux that sounded a tad too much like heathen talk. He whips out a .38 Special and shoots the woman between the eyes, like she's no more'n a mad dog."

Jake mimed a pistol shot with his finger and thumb. Daniel, who was on the other end of the makeshift weapon, grinned sheepishly. Jake smiled and blew his fingertip gun barrel.

"Robidoux accuses the local coloureds of thievin' his poultry and explains to the sheriff that the old woman was puttin' a hoodoo on him, was blackmailin' him. Well, Robidoux was white, and a businessman to boot, so the sheriff admonishes him some for losin' his cool, but the son of a bitch was never gonna be brought to justice."

"That's terrible," said Laura. "Poor woman. She was only trying to help."

"African-Americans must have had a pretty tough time in these parts," added Daniel. "People looking for scapegoats for their problems wouldn't have to search very far."

Jake knocked back his bourbon. "Damn straight," he said. He glanced out at the night sky and screwed the lid on the bottle. "Well, the moon's up there callin' us forth. I'll get the boat ready."

He stood and looked at Laura. "You can catch up on the rest of the story later, ma'am. Me and your beau here, we got men's business to attend to out on the bayou." He winked at her and she half smiled, half cringed.

Daniel quickly finished his drink. It burned his throat, making him cough, and he scrambled to catch up to Jake. "I'll see you in about an hour, then," he called back to Laura. "You can have that shower and get some shuteye."

The bar had closed an hour ago and it occurred to Laura how odd it was that the owner was content to leave her alone there while he took Daniel for a midnight spin on the river.

As if he had read her mind, Jake said, "If you feel like finishing the bottle, little lady, you just leave a couple bucks on the table there. We'll scrape you up offa the floor when we get back."

4

After three days in Louisiana Daniel had still not acclimatised. The nights seemed just as hot and clammy as the days. He had hoped that out here on the bayou the water would radiate some coolness. It didn't. He cuffed away a stream of sweat, wishing he could scoop up a handful of water and splash it all over his head. But there was no way he was putting any part of his anatomy in there.

"Here's as good a place as any," said Jake. He switched off the engine and twisted the searchlight so that it shone into the hull of the low-slung riverboat. "Take a while for the fish to settle down," he said. "Meantime, we can be rigging a line or two." He gently eased himself into a squat and began to rummage through the tackle box. The boat swayed violently, and Daniel instinctively slammed his hands against the sides to brace himself.

Now that the engine noise was out of the equation, Daniel could hear the music of the swamp: a symphony with a frog chorus as its foundation, overlaid with the shifting melody of buzzing insects and the occasional solo from a screeching bird.

A menagerie of vast, unearthly moths and dragonflies shimmered in the beam of the tall searchlight Jake had used to navigate the boat away from the shore.

Something large and diaphanous flitted across Daniel's face. Wings brushed his eyelashes, momentarily blocking his vision, and there was a tickle in his hair. He flapped at it and shook his head. *Why me?* he thought. *Why do these things always make a beeline for me?*

Jake didn't seem to notice Daniel's spastic dance. He set one of the rods beside Daniel. The movement shook the boat and splashes of water licked at Daniel's fingers. He jerked his hands back inside the boat and quickly made a show of inspecting the rod.

"You a good swimmer?" asked Jake with a low chuckle as he turned the beam onto the river. "Cos if you are, it ain't gonna help you none if Old Red's lurking out there." This time he laughed out loud and cuffed Daniel on the shoulder. "That old devil loves a chase!"

Daniel shifted on the metal bench seat and looked up at the burly man. "I'm sorry about earlier," he said. "You know, the swearing. I was just a bit shocked. It's not something you see every day." He tried on a rueful grin, unsure if the other man could even see his face in the darkness. "At least, not where I come from."

"No problem," said Jake. "Most folks get a little jumpy first time they meet Old Red and his clan."

There was no inflection in the helmsman's tone, no way of telling if he had truly put the matter to rest. Daniel was in his twenties, came from a middle-class English family, had been to a suburban grammar school, a good university and now had a well-paid job in banking. Convinced that he exuded nerdiness, he had always felt a little intimidated when he was around leather-faced manual workers. Experiences of this kind, like his camel treks into the Sahara and his parachute jumps, were his way of challenging himself; of testing his manhood.

"Robidoux!" shouted Jake.

Daniel jolted upright and the big American sniggered. "I didn't finish the story, did I?"

"Uh, no. No, I don't think—"

"All *right*! So, what happens next, couple weeks after Robidoux smokes the coloured gal? Some fancy lawyers from the city come down to the farm to foreclose. Seems Robidoux was heavily in debt. But when they arrive, the place is a wreck. The coops are all smashed up, smeared with blood and feathers. Not a single chicken can be found. Not a single person neither. The whole place is turned upside down, bedding stained with blood, shreds of clothing scattered about. And no sign of the Robidoux family.

"Course, everybody blamed the old woman's kinfolk. There followed some nasty business. Sheriff made a show of keeping order but he was outvoted by the pointy hoods, if you catch my drift. They worked through a whole bunch of gasoline and rope before the Robidoux family was finally found."

Jake twisted the searchlight again and Daniel watched the beam swing away from the boat and light up a section of the riverbank opposite the bar.

"Right over there, in fact," said Jake. "Sheriff and two deputies was out patrolling the bayou, tryin' to keep a lid on the lynchin's. They came across a nest of gators. In among them was a mess of bones and a pretty pile of white flesh, all stacked up like pancakes oozin' with red jelly. Sittin' atop the mound of carcasses, like a king reigning over an empire of death, was the biggest, ugliest goddamn gator they had ever seen. Slathered in blood from head to tail, a full twenty feet long, teeth like elephant tusks and eyes of burnin' fire. They christened him Old Red."

Jake paused. Daniel recognised his cue and obligingly played his part,

"And that's the same gator that we saw earlier at the bar?"

"You betcha! Well, let me tell you, them good ole boys had lived on the bayou all their lives but they'd never seen a sight like it. They was beside themselves, didn't know what to do for the best—go in guns blazin' or shit their pants and paddle the hell away. The gators made up their minds for 'em; started slipping into the water. One, two, three. Sheriff counted seven before he turned about and tried puttin' some distance between them. But the gators ducked under the surface. They move their fastest under water, and soon they was crackin' their snouts against the underside of the boat, rockin' it this way an' that."

Daniel couldn't help but look around at the shallowness and vulnerability of the boat he was presently sitting inside.

"Did they escape?" he asked. "The police?"

"The three of 'em opened up with shotguns. Humpback Remington repeaters—kind used by Bonnie an' Clyde, you know?"

Daniel didn't know but he nodded anyway.

"They shot away in a blind panic until they was empty. By then, the gators had disappeared into the deep of the bayou. But not before they'd taken one of the deputies with them. He was never found. Folk say gunsmoke lay on the water for a full week after. The gators abandoned the nest over yonder, leavin' behind the remains of the chicken farmer and his family. The one gator that didn't make it outta the fight was cut open on the riverbank. Inside was the Robidoux woman's unborn baby."

"Oh fuck," said Daniel. "Uh, sorry, I mean—"

Jake waved away the apology and turned the beam back to the spot where Daniel's line dangled limply just beyond the side of the boat.

"Damn' sorry business," said Jake. "Damn' sorry ole business."

5

Daniel wished he had brought a bottle of mineral water out with him. He could still taste the dehydrating sourness of the bourbon on his tongue. As if that wasn't enough to make him uncomfortable, the lurid story and the swaying of the little tin boat were now conspiring to make him feel quite seasick.

He needed to take his mind off it or he would hurl right there in front of Jake, who had probably already decided that he was a dickless Limey faggot. He thought about Laura, wondered if she had gone to bed yet or maybe decided to take Jake up on his offer to finish off the Wild Turkey. He smiled. No, she probably hit the shower as soon as they left and was now sleeping like a baby.

They sat in silence for ten minutes. Not a single tug on either of their lines. Daniel turned Jake's lurid story over in his mind. It wasn't outrageously implausible in itself. He was pretty sure gators would kill chickens if anyone was stupid enough to keep them close to the swamp. People, too, he supposed. And the lynchings? Well, the South was famous for that, wasn't it? But if the events happened nearly a hundred years ago, there was no way any of those gators could still be alive. He didn't buy that at all.

He cleared his throat. "That's one pretty ancient alligator then, isn't it?" he said. "Old Red, I mean."

"You don't believe it?"

"I'm not saying that. It's just that—"

"Listen. Folk hereabouts are brought up with the legend of Old Red at their mama's titty. Hell, they probably know the

Robidoux tale better than they do any Bible story. But I'm not just repeatin' old-timers' swamp yarns. I know the gator that visits the bar is the same one that chowed down on the Robidoux clan, on account of I got first-hand experience of him.

"My daddy bought the old Robidoux homestead in the 1970s. Place hadn't been touched in fifty years, least not by humans. Day we moved in we found the forest had moved in ahead of us; it had long since busted open the windows and weaved its way through the house until it finally burst outta the roof. When we cut through to the upstairs, we found cottontails in the beds and possums sleepin' in a Moses basket that had been bought for the Robidoux baby.

"My family pretty much rebuilt it all, plank by plank. Turned it into the bar and grill you see today.

"Well, one night, shortly after Daddy had opened the place up to paying customers, I was woken by the sound of someone coming up the stairs. I was just a kid but I weren't no chickenshit, so I got outta bed and went to rouse my parents in the next room. It was dark but I knew better than to slap on a light switch and alert the intruders.

"As I crossed the landing at the top of the stairs I looked down into the shadows. I couldn't make out the details but I could see movement. Except, what I was seein' didn't make any sense. At first, it seemed like the stairs themselves were slowly bucking and writhing around. And the wave of dark movement was rolling up towards me. I rubbed my eyes, thought I must be dreamin'.

"Then, when the intruders entered a shaft of moonlight from the hall window, I understood. It wasn't burglars that had come into our house that night. And the stairs weren't movin' by themselves. It was gators.

"I yelled like I'd never yelled before, and my parents came out of their room. My old man's gun was downstairs but he had a baseball bat he kept under his pillow. He shouted at me and Mom to get away into the main bedroom. Then he swung the bat and started hollerin' at the gators to get the hell offa his property.

"They just kept on sashaying up the stairs in that lazy, lumbering way of theirs; six, maybe seven full grown swamp gators, drippin' with water an' reekin' of the bayou. At the head of them all, Old Red.

"That monster swished his tail, crashing it against the walls and dislodging chunks of drywall. Me and Mom were still peeking outta the doorway, begging Daddy to leave 'em be and come inside. But he wasn't about to give in. He told us to barricade the door. He used to be a marine, was made of muscle, he could deal with a bunch of slimy water critters.

"Last thing I saw, Old Red was crawling slowly along the landing towards my daddy, just like he was seeking a pow-wow. I swear he still had the blood on his face that gave him his name. Old Red had come for his due.

"My mom slammed the door and, together, we hauled a heavy old dresser across it. We cowered there and listened while my daddy laid down the law. He wasn't gonna take any bullshit, he said. Unless they left the place PDQ, he'd start bustin' some heads."

Jake fell silent. Daniel watched his eyes scan the back of the building, still illuminated by the searchlight, as though he were looking back into his past.

"You ever hear a gator roar?"

Daniel shook his head.

"Most folks think they're silent killers. Mute, like swans. But they have a voice; a deep, rattling growl that vibrates across the bayou and churns up the water. You're close enough, and that sound's gonna send a seismic wave right up into your guts. Makes you wanna puke.

"That night Old Red growled, deep and loud. To me and my mom, it was like a goddam buzz-saw was tearin' up the floorboards right outside the room. The roar got louder and

197

louder, and we retreated away from the door, right to the back of the room till we couldn't go no further." Jake nodded towards a top floor window. "Then Old Red went quiet. In that moment of silence, the door handle rattled. It was my daddy tryin' to get in. I rushed over to the door. The handle was shakin' like it was electrified. But the dresser seemed to weigh a ton and I couldn't shift it by myself. I tried. God knows I tried. Then he started banging on the door and yelling at us to open up. First time I'd ever knew my daddy to be scared. Only time. The sound of him shrieking like that paralyzed me with terror. I just stood there, tremblin' like Jell-O, starin' at the goddamn' door.

"My mom came and shook me out of it but by the time we'd slid the dresser to one side, we was too late. We could hear Old Red and his kin just inches away from us, out there on the landing, roarin' and snappin' their jaws. They made the whole house rock on its foundations.

"Then they started thumpin' against the door itself. The panels shook and spikes of splintered wood sprayed into the room. We didn't dare stick around to try and heave the dresser back in place. We ran to the window."

Daniel looked at the building some fifty yards away. There was a sheer drop to the river below.

"Old Red busted into the room, snarlin' and snappin'. There was no time to think. We leaped out into the night, right into the bayou.

"Our misfortune was also our salvation. Gators ain't great on stairs. It must have taken them an age to climb up in the first place. By the time they'd staggered all the way down and out to the bayou again, me and Mom had dragged ourselves out of the water and onto the road out yonder. Old Red didn't follow us.

"Next morning, we found my daddy washed up on the shore. All that was left of him was his broken bones, picked clean of flesh.

"Afterwards, the local swamp folk told us what had happened with that chicken farmer all those years before. Only then did we understand what was expected of us if we wanted to survive out here."

Daniel looked up and his heart lurched in his throat. Jake was holding a jet-black pistol no more than six inches from his face.

"I hate this part, son. You gotta believe me when I say that."

A rush of terror coursed through Daniel, all the way from his chest to his bowels. Despite the oppressive heat, he shuddered as though buffeted by a sudden Arctic storm. "What's going on?" he said. The pitch of his voice wavered like an old woman's and, terrified as he was, he hoped Jake hadn't noticed.

"He's waitin', son."

With his free hand, Jake turned the light onto the water. The shaft of brightness was almost a living thing, a milk-white snake that gave birth to swirling specks of life—beetles, moths and flies of all shapes and sizes.

Down in the stinking black water, decomposing tree trunks drifted lazily around the boat. And then the tree trunks opened their burning bronze eyes. Two, four. Six or more.

"We're no more significant to them than these bugs are to us; a nuisance for a while, but only a while," said Jake. "You gotta think of it as payin' rent to the landlord. Fact is, I'm long overdue. They ain't had people meat since Momma died. I got some arrears to pay. That's why they're comin' into the goddamn' bar, chuckin' their weight around. Scraps from the table's keepin' 'em sweet for the moment but they need a proper feed. Soon, they're gonna lose patience and start on the customers."

Jake shook his head slowly. "And that would be really bad for business."

"Wait, wait! We can talk about this!" shrieked Daniel.

"I'm done talkin', son. With you, anyways. But, rest assured, when I get back indoors, me and that pretty little lady of yours are gonna have us a fine ole chinwag." Jake squinted his eyes closed for a split-second. "She's gonna be freshly showered an' all, ain't she?"

Dozens of thoughts collided in Daniel's mind. Was this for real? Would it hurt? What would happen to Laura? He wanted to say something, to do something, but the torrent of thoughts was log-jammed in his head.

Suddenly, an explosion rang out. A Mexican Wave of alarm rippled around the bayou. Unseen creatures screeched in fright, the treetops shook and leathery wings flapped nearby, raising a gust of warm air.

Jake froze, a shocked grimace revealing a row of white teeth that glowed against the blackness of the night.

A second explosion.

Jake clutched his chest and fell forward. The sudden shift in weight tilted the boat.

Then complete, overpowering darkness.

6

When he regained consciousness, Daniel was lying on his back in thick, clinging mud with his legs in the water, chilled to the bone. A cloud of grey smoke hung over the edge of the bayou.

"Thank God," said Laura. "I thought you'd never come round."

She grabbed Daniel under his armpits. "Let's get you out of there."

"Give me a minute," he said, pulling free of her grip. His body started to quake. He rolled to one side and vomited up a gutful of gumbo stew.

"That's better," he said between retches. Mingled with the sour tang of bile, he could still taste the Wild Turkey. "What the fuck happened?"

Around the curve of the shoreline, glowing through the miasmic darkness of the bayou, the lights of Old Red's Bar and Grill seemed to flicker through the swaying trees.

"They have Wi-Fi," said Laura.

"Seriously?" Daniel said through chattering teeth. "Shouldn't we call 911 before we drop this on social media?"

Laura shook her head. "It was too hot to sleep," she explained. "I found the Robidoux story online. Wanted to know how it ended. I kept reading and found a load of other stuff about this place, too. Like how Jake had been convicted of killing his father when he was a teenager."

"He told me the gators came for him."

Laura snorted. "Yeah. They came because Jake fed them his old man's chopped-up parts. He spent twenty years in jail before they let him out. Apparently, they couldn't stop him coming straight back here to help his dear ole ma with the family business. Six weeks later, she disappeared. He's been running the place alone ever since.

"After I read that, the place started to give me the creeps," said Laura. "I decided to come outside to clear my head. That leaflet offered duck hunting trips, so I snooped around and grabbed some protection first. You were both out there in the boat, all lit up by that lamp. Then I saw Jake pointing a pistol at you. I didn't think. I just pulled the trigger."

She leaned over and brushed back a lock of Daniel's hair from his forehead. Water from her own wet hair dripped onto his face.

"When the boat capsized and you disappeared under the water, I went in and brought you back to shore. You must have whacked your head on the boat before you fell in. You weren't moving. I thought ..."

Daniel carefully touched the lump on the left side of his head, just below the hairline. It didn't hurt much but it felt slippery. He looked at his fingers. They were slick with blood.

"Come on," said Laura. "We need to get indoors before we both catch pneumonia or something."

Daniel watched as Laura retrieved a shotgun from where she had left it beside a tree stump. She ejected the spent shells and reloaded.

He propped himself up on his elbows.

"Are you telling me you swam out there?" he said. "With the gators?"

The bayou had fallen into an unnatural stillness. No insects buzzed. No frogs croaked. No owls hooted.

Laura snapped the gun shut and pointed it down the mist-shrouded shoreline.

"The gators were kind of busy," she said.

Ten yards away, just visible in the silver moonlight, Jake's head was bobbing lazily at the water's edge. A mass of pink intestines floated beside it.

Daniel turned away and threw up again.

As he was wiping jelly-like strings of puke from his chin, Laura shouted.

"Shit! Dan, get out of the water! Now!"

The shotgun exploded right above his head, so close that Daniel felt the heat of the blast on his face. Stray pellets smacked into the mud beside him and a cloud of cordite smothered him in the sulphurous stench of fireworks. He tried to scrabble backwards, away from the water's edge, but something was holding his left foot firmly in place as though he had taken root.

Laura's voice cut through the ringing in his ears.

"I'm out of shells! You have to fight it!"

A sudden breeze snatched at the curtain of gunsmoke, tore it aside, and Daniel understood why he couldn't move. What he saw made him feel nauseous all over again but he had nothing more to bring up. He struck out with his free foot. It felt like kicking a tree stump. Laura thumped the gator with the shotgun, wielding it like a club. In response, the gator opened its mouth, reared up, and then snapped it closed again with a sickening crunch. Daniel screamed as a shock of pain shot up through his groin and into his stomach. His entire left leg was now inside the gator's maw.

Laura threw the gun at the beast and fell to her knees. She grabbed Daniel around his neck but he began to slide relentlessly downward, feet-first, as though the world had tilted on its axis somehow and he was fighting against gravity. The water was up to his waist, its chill soothing the white-hot pain creeping up his body. He clawed into the muddy ground to try and pull himself clear but his fingers slithered through the slime without taking hold. He felt himself slipping free of Laura's grip. She fell forward, sobbing.

"Fight it, Dan. Please fight it!"

Daniel twisted and thrashed in the mud, screaming in agony now. He punched at the thing's snout and tried to gouge its lifeless yellow eyes, but the creature was unmoved. It bit deeper into his leg and dragged him further into the bayou.

Suddenly, a low rumbling growl rattled the trees and shook the ground beneath him. The shallow water at the shoreline seemed to tremble and boil. The last thing Daniel saw before his face sank below the surface was a vast shape looming above Laura, its jaws open to the sky, running red with blood.

Conquest

I'm a Martian.

More than that, I am the absolute ruler of my planet: Queen of Olympus Mons; Tyrant of Phobos and Deimos; Supreme Commander of the Valles Marineris, Empress of all I survey.

OK, so I wasn't always a Martian. In a past life I was just like you, a mere Earthling who could breathe the air of her planet and walk upon its soil without fear of floating off into space. But things change, you know?

The others often generously acknowledged that although I was merely a payload specialist with no formal NASA rank, I was essentially the whole point of the mission. They were my escorts, they joked. Ha ha.

There were just four of us; two men, two women. Not couples, but NASA anticipated the prospect of us pairing off at some point in the future because they insisted that we were all sterilized. Like Elton says, Mars ain't the kind of place to raise your kids.

Our working days were to be spent exploring, gathering data and reporting back to Earth. That's where I came in. I'm an astro-geologist. I know about space rocks.

Commander Jim Elwood was our boss. He piloted the ship, oversaw the construction of our accommodation and was my patronizer-in-chief. Angela Ramirez, our deputy commander, was a biologist and former USAF medic. They were cut from the same military-grade cloth and were as tight as two butt cheeks in a pair of hot pants.

Mission specialist Phil Bronsky was a botanist and survival expert. His job was to make life-sustaining plants grow without air or water. I think he had designs on me that weren't entirely scientific. I can't be sure. Anyway, it wasn't mutual, and it's academic now.

We were all highly motivated professionals in our own fields, of course. Although, frankly, once we had landed, we could do whatever the hell we pleased: it's not like NASA could fire us. To keep us from going stir crazy, they insisted that we all had scheduled downtime. To that end they provided the base with a computerized library of books, music and movies to keep us chilled out. But I think they expected human interaction to be the real key to holding insanity at bay.

I'll admit, it has been pretty tough here alone.

*

The *Apollo* and *Challenger* missions had barely scratched the surface of the cosmos. "You're the true trailblazers," the President told us the night before our mission. "You're the twenty-first century equivalent of the pioneers that built America."

While we were awaiting the final checks on the launchpad, hearts in mouths, all strapped in and ready to blow, Commander Jim quietly muttered, "Wagons roll." I think he was psyching himself up, but the mic was live and that dumb ad lib became the soundbite that epitomized the mission for most people on Earth.

We knew from the get-go that it might be many years before we returned home. Our ship, *Liberty Pioneer*, was a one-shot deal. The huge fuel containers that propelled us into space were designed to be jettisoned once we were out of Earth's atmosphere, and we couldn't carry enough firewood on board to take us all the way to Mars and back home again.

But NASA had a plan—a real big plan.

Even as we were hurtling through the cosmos, they were busy working on a way to travel between planets much more quickly than the year it would take us to reach our destination. Forget *Star Trek* warp drives: NASA's brand new concept was way more old school. Long-term, the idea was to set up a piggyback system of static way stations to provide refuelling stops (and a permanent American presence) right across the galaxy. They fully expected to have Uncle Sam's space-boots on every damned planet circling our sun by the end of the century, even on the moons of the gas giants Jupiter and Saturn. But they would begin modestly with an itty-bitty little space station in between Earth and Mars that could resupply and repopulate our mission on the Red Planet. To be honest, that's all that mattered to us.

There was no telling how long it would take to pull this off, of course, so we had to accept (as did our families back home) that we could spend several years on a cold, inhospitable planet millions of miles from home before a new team was sent out to relieve us.

Our arrival on Mars went entirely as planned. Jim brought us down more gently than in any of the multiple simulations we had all experienced. Desperate for the chance to get out of the stinking, cramped pod, we immediately went to work constructing our living quarters. We had brought all our medical supplies, biological experiments and plant matter with us but the parts for our new home had been deposited on the planet's surface over the previous five years by unmanned rockets. The station fitted together pretty much like a Meccano Erector Set.

Mars Station One is small, there's no denying it. It has a central atrium—the control hub housing our mainframe computer—a modest laboratory and a mini-gym; the latter essential for combating the muscle wastage resulting from reduced gravity. The atrium is the only place on the station large enough to accommodate four people at one time.

There's a shared bathroom and a large provisions store, containing a vast amount of essential medical supplies and pre-packaged dried and tinned foods intended to keep us alive while we worked to bring the hydroponics online. There were only three things I was desperate to check as soon as we had a roof over our heads: coffee, tampons and wine. Thank God, there was a plentiful supply of each.

Beyond the storeroom is a powerful solar-converter generator that keeps the place saturated with breathable air and maintains an ambient temperature. Leading off the atrium are four small lifepods—individual living quarters for each of us. Around the size of a walk-in closet, the lifepods are barely big enough to hold our beds, but NASA's psychologists insisted that a claustrophobic little bolt hole away from the crowd would be just the thing to stave off insanity.

The first week went well. We all fell into our pre-assigned roles and began a businesslike exploration of the area around our landing site: the patch of orange dust that would be our home for the foreseeable future. We even put up a flag in the yard and Jim proudly claimed Mars for the good old US of A. Phil and Angela jokingly agreed that he could be the first governor of the fifty-first state. They cut a small white star out of a sheet and stuck it on the flag alongside the rest. When we were done, and without any trace of irony, we cracked open a bottle of champagne and piped an MP3 of *The Star-Spangled Banner* into the atrium. We partied like it was 1999 and swore to civilize any little green men we came across.

I like to think of myself as a liberal but even I laughed along, oblivious to our overweening hubris. Maybe it was the champagne.

*

That night there was a storm. Not one with rain; one with hurricane-force winds that battered our new home with a tsunami of dust.

When it hit us, I was indoors number crunching some geological data on the mainframe. The others abandoned their work in the dustbowl outside and hurried in to join me PDQ. We rode out the storm together in the atrium, joshing each other that it wasn't half as bad as tornado season in Nebraska, Jim's home turf. The base was rocked on its meager foundations, and although we feigned cavalier amusement as the howling winds shook the walls, the three pairs of wide eyes staring at me all reflected my own private terror.

That was the night we lost NASA. Or, to be more accurate, the night NASA lost us. All the experiments we had set up outdoors vanished in the storm, along with our transmitter rod. The loss of that one simple item was devastating. Without a functioning transmitter there was no way for us to communicate with Earth. Ever. We could still hear the bleeping binary messages NASA beamed out to the universe but NASA could no longer hear or see Mars Station One.

Our final broadcast had informed them of the storm, so they knew something had gone badly wrong before we fell silent. The dreadful significance of that small fact didn't become apparent until much later.

*

We were all early risers and the morning after the tempest we had a lot of repair work to do. Uncharacteristically, the other three remained in their quarters while I tiptoed about checking the damage. I guessed they were hungover, or had just slept badly, and left them to recuperate. When they eventually emerged, several hours later, I realised that the reason for their tardiness was something more worrying than mere exhaustion.

They all looked terrible. Their skin was ashen and there were bruise-colored rings under their eyes. None of them wanted to eat; they were lethargic and uncommunicative. By the end of that day, the skin around their eyes and mouths was red and weeping, and they were unable to move about the atrium without holding onto the walls.

Angela sluggishly ploughed through our digitized medical tomes and eventually mumbled something about the symptoms being similar to leprosy. However, she had no idea how they might have caught such an exotic disease, what their prognosis was or if it was contagious.

She had me go fetch a large box of antibiotics from the store and told everyone to keep their fluid intake high, but a vague assumption that it would run its course in a few days was her best response to the crisis. As if trying to absolve herself of responsibility, she reminded us that there might be all kinds of phenomena in space that were as yet undiscovered. Studying and responding to changes in our bodies on a new planet was, according to Angela, part and parcel of our mission.

I didn't argue, but I knew that catching leprosy was sure as hell not part of my mission.

I had another solution.

*

Unlike the rest of the team, I had no prior experience as an astronaut and I didn't feature on our very short list of deputy commanders. The NASA ranks stopped at Hydroponic Phil. With the three of them virtually catatonic, I decided that this state of affairs didn't work for me anymore. I took the decision to assume command.

By lights-out they were too sick to even administer their own medicine, so I prepared it for them. I laced their drinks with ground up sleeping tablets from the store and, double bagged in surgical gloves and mask, I held the bottles to their cracked lips while they eagerly drained the contents. Then I stocked up their rooms with some food and water rations, together with a small quantity of basic meds. When I was satisfied that they were asleep, I entered the mainframe in the atrium and electronically sealed the doors to their rooms.

Next morning, they made it plain that I had overstepped the mark. I had, they said, no right to instigate a lockdown quarantine. That was Angela's call to make. Jim croaked that I had no authority to do any damned thing on the base at all.

All three agreed that I was only there to pick up rocks, and if NASA hadn't insisted upon a second pair of tits on the team, they would have brought a monkey along to do the goddamn job.

Well, that was a revelation.

I pointed out to them that they had all contracted a nasty-looking disease that may or may not prove to be highly contagious, debilitating and possibly fatal. Quarantine was the only logical response.

After a lot of swearing, they eventually fell silent and descended upon the supplies I had given them.

In the afternoon, they piped up again. This time, they changed their approach. They thanked me for taking care of them and said they were feeling much better. So, would I mind unlocking the doors now? Pretty please.

While they had been quietly stewing, I had been doing some research. Turns out that quarantine is based on an Italian word coined at the time of the Black Death in medieval Europe. It means 40 days.

I told them what I'd found out. Angela called me all kinds of stupid. Medical isolation, she said, can be as long or as short as it needs to be. If they were no longer infectious, there was no need to quarantine them.

I agreed, and asked her to prove they were no longer infectious. There was a moment of perfect silence. Then the hammering and shouting started up, albeit somewhat more subdued than before. I'd better let them out, they said, or I would be in serious fucking trouble. I couldn't imagine what kind of punishment they might mete out. Confine me to my room, perhaps? Terminate my contract? But I wouldn't—couldn't—back down. I knew that any one of them would have done the same thing.

The supplies I had placed in their rooms would run out after a week. I could spare more; there was several years' worth of meds and food in the store. Fact is, I didn't want to run the risk of becoming infected by opening up their pods to resupply them. I just hoped Angela was right and the mysterious illness would quickly run its course.

As it transpired, it ran its course far sooner than expected. After another night, they stopped ranting and banging on the doors. Aside from the relentless hum of the generator, the base was perfectly at peace.

*

That was six months ago.

It can be deathly quiet here. The station is empty and hollow and I can hear my breath echo around the atrium.

I took the decision to never open up their rooms. I had no idea how virulent the disease might be. Some viruses can remain contagious long after the death of the host.

As the weeks turned into months, the fact that their dead bodies were all still in their quarters disturbed me almost as much as the idea of taking them outside and burying them. I began to think of their sealed quarters as tombs.

Did I mention the walls?

The inner ones are steel; the exterior ones are all made of toughened glass that we could protect with metal shutters – the kind stores pull down in rough neighborhoods. The glass walls seemed like a great idea to maximize daylight; give us the illusion of connecting with the outdoors and thereby reduce the potential for cabin fever. Nice theory. And the view from our lifepods would have been terrific had it not been of a dust-shrouded wilderness.

After that fateful storm, the shutters didn't work. Maybe they got gummed up with space dust. Whatever the reason, they were stuck open and I didn't have the technical know-how to fix them. Sometimes it felt like I had no place to hide from the planet. I spent my days shielding my eyes from the sun and I fell asleep at night staring out at a blackened desert.

The peaks and outcrops of rock seemed to change position from night to night, and I imagined them to be petrified aliens playing a game of statues with me: moving slowly towards my window and freezing in place whenever I turned to look at them.

Two weeks ago, I was gathering rock samples outside. I guess NASA must have a good handle on human psychology after all because I had nothing better to do than carry on with my work, pointless as it was. It helped the days to pass and took my mind off things. All the specimens immediately outside the main entrance were too small to analyze properly so I wandered around looking for something better. Suddenly, I realized I was outside Angela's quarters. Just like my room, the shutters were open, exposing a floor-to-ceiling picture window.

Did you ever drive past a car wreck? A fresh one, I mean? You don't want to look, do you? But you want to know what you are not looking at all the same. I didn't want to look inside Angela's room but I couldn't help myself. Her quarters are on the leeward side of the building, so the interior was shrouded in shadow. But it wasn't quite dark enough to conceal the sight that confronted me.

The bedding was strewn about, as though she had thrown it around in anger or frustration. Angela was curled on the floor, face pressed against the door to her pod, just inches from the atrium where I spent my days poring over data on the mainframe.

She was naked. I guessed that the open lesions covering her body were so painful that she could no longer bear to wear clothes or allow the sheets to touch her skin. A dried husk of a human, one of her desiccated hands still reached up for the door handle, frozen in time like the rocks outside. I was reminded of the petrified remains found at Pompeii and, not for the first time, I wondered how long it had taken them to die.

*

212

The broadcasts from NASA became sporadic. They weren't addressing themselves to Mars Station One anymore. These were generic news bulletins to whoever—or whatever—might be listening out here in space.

Last week, they broadcast our memorial service.

They had waited a decent amount of time for us to re-establish contact, but our continued silence after the storm, they said, told them all they needed to know. The moon landing was one small step for man; the Mars expedition had been a step too far. Mankind's ambition had exceeded its ability.

Two days later, the Senate voted against funding any further space projects on the grounds that the scientific benefits were outweighed by the immense, and very obvious, risk. On the contrary, the politicians were calling NASA to account over the 'Mars Disaster'. What they meant was they weren't going to throw good money after bad. Those space stations would never happen. There would be no replacement team.

We were dead (and kind of buried) and Earth wanted to move on.

I thought back to the ticker tape farewell we had been given, to the speech by the President, and to our flag ceremony on arrival. Now I didn't feel much like an intrepid pioneer, spearheading humanity's expansion into the unknown. The Senate's decision to axe the program killed off any remaining hope I had of ever leaving this place. For the very first time, I felt truly alone.

I switched on the transmitter, knowing full well that it didn't work.

"I'm alive! I'm alive you bastards!"

And then I cried. For how long, I don't know.

*

On the plus side, I have been abandoned here with a stack of supplies designed to keep four people alive for several years and there's never a line for the bathroom. I've made a serious dent in the peanut butter and the stock of red wine is already disappointingly low. Maybe I need to ration myself some items, although it's quite funny to picture the sole human being on Mars as an overweight lush.

One of the many things NASA failed to take account of when they drew up our list of must-haves was the basic human need to be creative. They didn't give us any pencils or paints. But ingenuity will out.

The storm had snatched away our flag (with its extra star) from outside the station and cast it into oblivion. So I made a Martian flag to replace it: a black sky with a rash of white stars looming over a tangerine desert. It's pretty neat, even if it is made of spare pants and blankets. When I was done, I cracked open another bottle of bubbly and raised a toast to independence.

Sewing the flag—my very own 'stars and stripes'—took my mind off things for a while. It wasn't long before I decided to indulge in some more creative therapy.

There were plenty of tools left over from constructing the base: little tin snips, saws and suchlike. I started using them on an empty can of peanut butter, just clipping away to see what I could make. Turns out I could make myself a chopped up canister that looked a little like a jagged crown and stank of peanut juice. Who knew I was so artistic?

I've been keeping to my room as much as I can. Whenever I'm in the atrium I have the irresistible urge to keep looking over my shoulder at those locked doors.

Most days I play movies (two at a time, just to make the place sound busy). The reflected light fills the base with colored movement, and there's something reassuring about seeing and hearing fellow humans, even if they're only a pretty mess of pixels. In the evenings I usually put on some music— something upbeat to smother the silence.

Mars has no magnetic field, so it doesn't handle radiation very well. I keep checking myself for tumors, though God knows what I would do if I found a lump; the nearest physician is 150 million miles away. Well, the nearest living physician.

Speaking of which, I didn't go near their rooms—their tombs—if I could help it. I had the unshakeable notion that the space leprosy that killed them could somehow leak out and loiter in the vicinity, waiting for me to pass by. I know, I'm an MIT alumna and I was fantasizing about being hunted by sentient space bugs. But biology is my blind spot and I've been through a lot, so humor me.

*

Last night I was awoken by an electrical storm ten times more powerful than the one that wiped out the transmitter half a year ago. It shut down the power to the whole base. The lights went out, the oxygen pump fell silent and all the electrical equipment died. I was pitched into total darkness, and deathly silence filled the air. It averages minus 63 Celsius on Mars. I knew that if I couldn't get the power running again quickly, I would freeze to death long before I could suffocate.

I scrambled out of bed and groped my way to the door of my quarters, desperately wracking my brains for a solution. Like I said, I'm a geologist—I have no idea how the generators work. I could feel the temperature plummet immediately, so I wrapped myself in my psychedelic Martian flag. A sick terror crawled up my throat and I began to find it difficult to fill my lungs. I envisaged dying right there and then before I had even had a chance to blunder my way through to the engine room.

My irrational fear of the mummified crew had led me to lock my door each night. Don't judge me. Isn't everyone, deep down, afraid of the dead? But now my door was unlocked. It baffled me momentarily until I realized that all of the locks on the base rely on the computer to keep them functioning.

The computer was dead, so the locking mechanisms instantly failed. It took a couple of frozen heartbeats to realize that all the other cabin doors must have become unlocked too.

I had to fix the power or I would die, but my irrational fear of the dead crew kept me rooted to the spot, icy sweat running down my body. If anyone had been watching me through the glass, I would have cut a pitiful figure. Cowering in a corner, shivering with cold, I did the worst possible thing: I did nothing at all.

After five minutes of cringing in the dark like a whipped dog, the lights in my room suddenly flickered on. Then the familiar, comforting hum of the air-con returned. I could feel my room warming up by the second. The power had restarted all by itself. Well, not quite by itself. One of the innumerable, tedious classes I had attended before launch had been about power management. The generator, they told us, was the single most important part of the station. Without it, we were doomed. Game over. No respawn. So they had given us a solar battery-powered backup system that could reboot the main engine in the event of failure. I had no idea how that worked or even what button to press. Turns out, I didn't need to know. The backup kicks in automatically upon system failure. Thank God for engineering nerds. But my relief turned to horror when the lock on my door was re-engaged.

From the outside.

It was impossible. They couldn't have survived this long without food or water. But I could hear them in the atrium as clear as day, their dead feet sweeping the steel floor like bundles of sticks.

I banged on the door and told them to open up. I said I was sorry for locking them in. They laughed. Their voices sounded like the rustling of dead leaves.

I started working at the lock. There were still a few tools strewn about my pod from my efforts with the peanut can.

I jammed a set of needle-nosed pliers in between the door and the frame and started twisting.

Judging from what I had seen in Angela's room, I imagined that they had all, similarly, tried to escape after I sealed them in. But they had been weak and didn't have anything to jemmy open the doors, so they died still scrabbling uselessly at the locks with their bare, bloodied fingertips.

I was determined not to end up like that. I had coped six months without them, without any human contact. My life was as good as it could get in the circumstances. I was, I realized, a survivor. Jim, Angela and Phil were not. And they could all go to hell.

I redoubled my efforts, wrenching the pliers this way and that, digging into the mechanism like a particularly brutal dentist trying to gouge out a rotten molar. After a serious amount of sweating and straining, there was an electrical pop and the lock fell to the floor in a jangle of little metallic bits and bobs.

Out in the atrium there was silence. No more breathless sniggering. I had yet to figure out how to deal with them, but by the time I had forced the lock and flung the door wide, the question was academic. They had vanished.

I began to doubt my sanity. After all, people didn't simply wake up from months of stone-cold death and start playing practical jokes on the noob. At least, not on Earth they didn't. Was it possible that the laws of life and death were so different on another planet? Had they even been outside my room at all, or were they just inside my head?

I didn't have to agonise over these esoteric questions for long. From behind me there came a loud thud, the deep resonant sound of someone punching a bony fist against a pane of glass.

Through my picture window I saw them outside in the desert. Their desiccated faces were contorted into permanent lipless grins. They weren't wearing space suits; they no longer needed to breathe. The planet's low gravity didn't seem to be a problem for them either, for although they were without the heavy lead boots that kept mere mortals from drifting out into space, they were trampling barefoot through the dust as though they had gate-crashed a Malibu beach party.

It dawned on me that they weren't trying to get into my room. If that had been their intention, they could have entered via the atrium when the power shut down. No, they didn't want to high-five an old acquaintance. They wanted to smash the glass in order to let the air out of the station; to let in the impossibly cold non-air of Mars.

I had no choice but to go outside and confront them before they succeeded and my life was literally sucked away.

The toughened glass had withstood two planet-shredding tornadoes. I hoped—prayed—that it could hold out against the feeble thrashings of the cosmic undead while I prepared to do battle to save my kingdom. If the shrivelled bastards wanted to play hardball, I was up for it.

NASA didn't provide us with any weapons. Can you imagine that? A world without guns? Sounds like Utopia. Well, let me tell you, it's a royal pain in the ass if you ever need to fend off naked Martian zombies.

I snatched up my roughly cut aluminum crown, squashed it flat and marched into the atrium. By the time I had struggled into my suit, switched on my oxygen tank and navigated the airlock, they had changed their tactics.

Commander Jim scooped up a rock and flung it at the glass. His muscle wastage, combined with the planet's low gravity, effectively prevented an early touchdown for the visiting team. The rock bounced off but the window shuddered horribly. The other two took his lead and found rocks of their own. They had gone for the lighter volcanic stuff rather than the basalt chips that lurked below the surface dust. Even so, I feared the window wouldn't take much more of that treatment.

They looked frail, like scribbled sketches of the people they used to be. Their skin was raw, crimson and gray like old salami, and they had lost all their hair. Like Angela, the two guys were stark naked; their shrunken genitals stuck out like twisted little stubs of chorizo.

All three stumbled towards me, crusty black rocks in their skeletal fists.

It's difficult to move quickly in an EMU suit and I was wary of slashing about too wildly with my makeshift scythe for fear of ripping it open. Then, a flurry of rocks struck my visor. I panicked, put up my hands to protect the glass. My suit might have been protecting me from the elements but it was making me feel incredibly vulnerable.

I carefully swiped left and right. They pressed on, unfazed. Angela came at me. I lunged at her face, her arms and the dried, empty sacs that had been her breasts. The jagged blade chewed through her leathery flesh, tearing open her torso like it was nothing more than a wad of cardboard. I jabbed at her throat and pulled her head toward the blade, sawing left and right as though I was chopping an unwanted branch from a tree. From the gaping maws of her wounds poured a fine amber powder. It swirled around me, suspended in space like a cloud of orange mist. When her head finally came loose, her withered face pirouetted in front of mine, a fixed grin conveying an insouciant humor she had lacked in life.

It was an unequal fight. They didn't stand a chance. For the second time, I killed them all.

This time around, I made sure there would be no comebacks. I sawed at their double-dead limbs until there was nothing left but a confusing mess of body parts.

My flattened crown, twisted into a corkscrew by all the hacking and gouging, was adorned with shreds of flesh that resembled puffs of red velvet. Even though I was exhausted and at the end of a very short tether, I unfolded it carefully, still wary of slicing through my precious gloves, and flicked away the dead meat.

Once I had patted myself down to shake off any remaining dust and debris, I entered the airlock and undressed. I didn't have enough oxygen—or energy—left to try to bury the crew out there. The wind could take them.

Back in my cabin, I opened a can of peanut butter, flicked on some Hall and Oates and uncorked a nice bottle of Cabernet Sauvignon to celebrate the defense of my realm.

*

This morning I woke up coughing. I looked down at myself and saw that I had fallen asleep in full imperial regalia; draped in the Martian flag and sporting my twisted, cut-out crown.

My head itched like crazy. When I removed the crown, I saw that the spikes had dug into my skin, tearing lesions across my forehead and scalp. It must have happened while I slept.

There was a bonking noise.

Outside, bobbing against my window, in a tomato soup of dried blood, the crew. Well, what's left of them: their floating body parts. Severed fists rapped angrily on the glass and their disembodied, lacerated faces leered in at me.

Good morning, Your Majesty. Care to join us?

There's something else. Hanging in the air around me is a fine spray of tawny dust. I can taste it—bitter, metallic. It stings my eyes and blurs my vision. It settles on my tongue and dries my mouth, it sucks up into my nostrils and catches in my throat. And when I cough, a mist of blood peppers the palms of my hands.

Later, I'll take a stroll outside and do something about the crew.

I have a feeling I won't need my suit.

Blood and Death and Fucking Horror

This is the kind of fucked up shit you wanted, right? I'll be honest: what I'm gonna show you now is plain fucking nasty and it ain't for everyone. So if you don't think you can handle an unfiltered, unrated experience, now's the time to fess up. There's no shame in bailing. We'll just say *sayonara* and you can fuck off on your merry way.

Still with me?

OK, let's go through the checklist.

You handed in your cellphone? Good. You'll get it back when you leave. That's rule number one: no cells, cameras or recording equipment. You don't get no souvenirs, no selfies and no trophies on this trip. Understand? You wouldn't believe how ass-holey some people are about that one little rule.

Insurance up to date, no allergies, no medication, no recent hospitalization. And a non-smoker. Check, check, checkity check. Bet you call your mom regular, too, huh? I'm just kidding. You wouldn't believe how many fucking gimps we get in here. I say to them, "Listen, this is high octane entertainment for a select clientele. If it's too strong for you and you keel over, there ain't no compensation, get it? It is what it is."

Okaaay, here we go!

It's the experience of a lifetime!

It's gonna be brutal!

It's gonna be dirty!

Get ready for the one and only....

Blood and Death and Fucking Horror!

Hope that didn't make you jump. It's just my regular spiel. Some people get a kick out of it.

So, you really want to do this?

Great. Follow me. Let's take a peek into your little slice of heaven.

As you can see, it's lit by one bulb up there. Before you ask, it's in a little cage because some people like to fuck about with it, swing it around for effect, you know? Please don't fuck about with it. Bulbs cost money. There's plenty of other stuff you can use for burning and electrocuting. Skin fries real easy.

The floor's a little slippy, so please pay due care and attention. We sloosh the rooms out at the end of each day, but I'm afraid that means the afternoon slots get to wade through the slops. What can I say? Mind where you tread. Anyways, I'm sure you'll be adding to the mess once you get warmed up. Me, I always wear galoshes for tramping through this stuff. You might wanna do the same.

While we're on the subject of health and safety, I must draw your attention to the disclaimer on yonder wall. See it? Good. Basically, anything bad happens, it's all on you. Don't come crying to me if you get nightmares. You chose this shit; own it.

The what? Oh, the smell. Yeah, it takes some getting used to, I guess. I like to call it *the smell of fear!* Actually, it's the smell of people's innards. That, plus disinfectant. I get through a lot of Pine Breeze.

Still with me? Nodding's OK if you don't trust your pie hole not to hurl. Probably not used to inhaling human remains. It's an acquired taste. Just for the record, that sour smell on top of the blood and excrement is stomach contents—that's your acids, undigested food, and raw meat. There's stuff I don't know what it is but, boy, it sure is stinky.

People eat those bits and pieces, by the way. Offal, they call it. *Awful*, I call it. See what I did there? That's just my sense of humor. You gotta have a funny bone to work this joint.

On that subject, there's no cooking on the premises—we ain't licensed—but you can eat raw. You wanna make a meal of it, you gotta bring your own paper plates. I may be providing a public service here but I'm not running a fucking charity. Each to his own and all but, personally, I don't recommend ingesting anything that comes out of people. We check our toys for any obvious imperfections but there's no telling if they've got cooties.

Hold out your hand. Go ahead, I ain't gonna bite. Here, I bet you never thought a human heart weighed like that, huh?

Just drop it on the floor. Like I said, I'll hose down later. Brains, they're heavier. Break easy too. Hard to get the fuckers out in one piece without wreckin' 'em. Like digging a walnut out of its shell.

The chick? Oh, we picked her up at some downtown dive. A shot of sleepy juice in the tequila smash, a little helping hand in the car park. No struggling, no bruising. Our procurement team are very professional. You have my personal guarantee that nobody's messed around with her yet, if that's what you're worried about. And those skimpy little things'll come off real easy. Scissors right on the worktop over there.

You seem surprised. Sorry—you did ask for a chick, right? That's what I've got down here anyway: female, blonde, young. We call that vanilla, by the way. Some clients like something different, a brunette, a guy or whatever. But a young blonde is pretty much entry level for most of our male customers so you're in good company. Not that I'm judging.

Say, you're looking a little green. I did warn you it's strong stuff. No offense and all but if you're not up for this, just say so right now, buddy. Nobody's forcing you. Just remember, there are no refunds. I do have overheads, you know.

OK, so you still with me? Good. You've paid the admission so you might as well catch the show.

Decided how you're gonna play it? Some guys just wanna make sweet love to 'em. I don't have a problem with that. It's your choice. You like her, don'tcha? I can tell by the way you been looking at her. I'll admit, she ain't too shabby—if you go for the cheerleader type. My personal view is if you've fucked one, you've fucked them all. My wife says I'm jaded. I guess we all are. That's why we're here, am I right?

If you're gonna get jiggy, you might wanna use a rubber. She looks like butter wouldn't melt but she's probably a slut. Most of them are. Permissive society—what a bunch of crap. Don't get me started on that.

But if screwing's all you're gonna do, it's kind of a waste. We all like to empty our sack once in a while, but that's what they got hookers for. You can do so much more in this place.

My two cents, the best way to get your money's worth is to keep 'em alive as long as possible and to inflict as much pain and suffering as you can in the process. You want to see their eyes stretch wide open when they realize you're gonna hurt them. First off, they'll threaten you with the cops. You know you don't need to worry about that shit. There's totally no way anyone is ever gonna find out about this. The only squealing anyone does here is while they're strapped to the chair.

In case you're wondering, the building is clad in special stuff, so the whole street can't hear all the fun we're having. This is the ultimate no-tell motel. Just wanted to set your mind at ease on that. That's why we have the cellphone rule. Those fucking things are a curse, don'tcha think?

Soon as she realizes you don't give a shit about the cops, she'll beg and plead. You want to relish that submissiveness. It's like a teaser, a mouthwatering hors d'oeuvre before the main feast. She'll try to reason with you, promise you she'll do anything just so long as you don't pop out her eye with a twisted knitting needle or a rusty teaspoon. She might even try to bribe you, tell you her daddy's a millionaire. He ain't, by the way. He's in construction. Then you can tell her that it don't make no fucking difference; you'll do whatever you want and she can't do a goddamn thing about it. Tell her to forget the movies. She ain't gonna be no survivor girl.

Whatever happens, even if you walk away at the end of the day and leave her choking on her own vomit, the bitch ain't getting out of here alive. None of them do. Company policy. See this? It's a classic—a .357 Magnum. One shot to the ole noggin, nice and clean. Like puttin' a sick horse out of its misery. All part of the service.

Once she finally understands you're a bad mutha who knows no mercy, she'll shout and scream and cry. The spit will fly and tears will roll. Savor it. That's a golden moment: that look, that realization. You won't experience anything like that anywhere else.

How'm I doing, by the way? Am I getting your juices flowing? I know, I oughta be in sales.

Yeah, sure she can hear us. Look, she's crying already. Real cute. I betcha wish they all came with a gag fitted like that, am I right?

Let me tell you, once you get to work, she's gonna moan and gurgle and choke in sheer terror and pure, unadulterated fucking agony. She'll shake and squirm and sweat, and slither around in her own mess.

Oh, yeah, they often poop, so if you really have to, you know, get to work down there, I suggest you do it early on. And rest assured we'll never enter the room while you're on the job. Even after they've expired we let you stick around and keep doing whatever floats your boat. I mean, there's no point respecting the dead when we don't respect the living. We'll only ever call time if the stink of rot gets intrusive for the other customers.

Speaking of which, listen a second. Shhh, just listen...

That's right. You can hear the goings-on next door. Kind of adds to the atmosphere, don't you think? Who knew a man could scream so high? That buzz? Come on, there's no mistaking the sweet sound of a chainsaw. That's one of my regulars, by the way. They're getting busy with an old Japanese guy right now. Not ideal but he's all we could rustle up at short notice. His arms and legs will come off with the saw, then out comes the mallet and his head's gonna get all bashed in. He'll end up looking like a slab of meat on a butcher's counter. But a slab of *live* meat. You see, that's only the start with this particular customer. When I go in after they're done, I always find a patty of human flesh still wriggling around and shrieking like a banshee. Have to use the hogleg every time.

Be-ooti-ful!

Sorry, wigged out there for a moment. I fucking love this job!

Anyhoo, back to the plot. Let me show you the tools of the trade. Maybe give you a few ideas.

All the equipment is in the cabinet. You got your sharps; a variety of blades, knives, daggers and a katana. Kind of predictable but always popular. We got needles, kabob skewers, a chainsaw, and—unless some dipshit has snapped the blade again—a hacksaw. There's a couple of drills; one of them's an itty bitty dentist job. It's quite temperamental so please be patient with it.

Women usually like to cut up the faces of the girls. I always think that's a shame. We try and pick pretty ones, you know? And then they go and fuck them up from the get-go. That does piss me off. Kind of lacks respect, in my humble opinion.

You let a chick loose on a guy and they make a beeline for the obvious. Jesus, I can't tell you how many dicks and balls I've had to scoop up. Talk about working out your issues. They don't got the imagination of male customers. Sorry, I know that ain't very PC, but it's based on observation. Let me ask you something: who was it painted that place in Rome, where the Pope lives? That's right, Michael di Angelo. A guy. See my point? Artistry, finesse. It's a no-brainer.

Not that I'm religious. I can't put my faith in any god that lets stuff like this happen.

By the way, if you find a stray nut floating around just kick it into touch and I'll deal with it when I clean up.

You feeling OK? First time's a little weird, right? Funny thing is, the more times you do this, the more you get used to it. In fact, you do it often enough, you're gonna get tired of the same old, same old. You'll need to find different ways to get off. Crazy, huh? You'll want to push things just a little bit further, be a tiny bit nastier, a touch more brutal. I guess that's why some customers do the freaky shit they do, just to get that ole buzz back. How far do you go when there's no limits? Again, I'm not judging. Just saying.

Student? Yeah, I think she is a student. Or is she the waitress? Ah fuck, I've got her all mixed up in my head with this morning's one.

Student, waitress, secretary—does it matter what she is? Whatever she might have been when she came in here, she'll exit the building in a bucket, all tangled up with old Mr Suzuki next door. How's that for multicultural, huh?

Jeez, I really kill myself sometimes! Wife says I'm a natural comedian, I should be on *Saturday Night Live*. One day, I tell her, one day.

So, anyway the perennial runner-up is heat. We got a little blowtorch in there if you feel like going for the buuurrrrn. Instructions on the side in case you've never used one. You stripped paint before? It's like that. We don't have any fire alarms or smoke sensors—for fairly obvious reasons—but it is a fire hazard so please take special care. There's a fire blanket and extinguisher by the door in case things get out of hand. All kidding aside, we truly value our customers' safety.

Acid—hydrochloric—so please wear the goggles and gloves provided. It won't burn through the straps but if they thrash, they will splash. S'all I'm saying. If you're a novice, maybe save that for another time. The experts tend to wait until the victims are already pretty fucked up and there's no risk of friendly fire, if you catch my drift.

Over here you got a sink, tin tub and rags. So if you wanna clean up for me, I ain't gonna stop you. I'm joshing. It's for the waterboarding, of course.

The buckets. OK, you need to listen to this. The black bucket is for severed body parts. That includes titties, ballbags and the stuff inside—lungs, kidneys and suchlike. The white bucket is for puke only. *Your* puke, that is. You start feelin' fit to hurl, you run for the white bucket, please. I hate cleaning up customers' puke. Some guys like to ralph deliberately and then make the bitches drink it. That's fine. It's your playground. But if you want to go there, I would be grateful if you could clean up as much as possible. It's the one thing that really pushes my squeamish button. Go figure.

The kettle on the worktop over there isn't for you to make coffee. I'm sure you can figure out how to use it all by yourself. Top tip: the correct application of steam can deliver more satisfying results than simply dousing them with boiling water.

What else? Oh yeah. If you're going to electrocute them, please use the modified cattle prod. It's designed for the job, fits easily into most orifices, and does everything that you need it to do. Do not try and rig up your own homemade shit. Nothing pisses me off more than some asshole stripping the goddamn lead from the kettle and blowing all the fucking fuses in the place. The prod is good and there's lube in the little tin beside it. Start off on a low setting and work your way up. And don't touch the shiny end. Duh!

Wait, just wait a second. Listen. Hear that? No? Me either. I think Mr Suzuki must have expired early. Ah, fuck it. Customer's gonna be pissed at that. Might have to give a partial refund. And that really makes me weep.

OK, I won't take up much more of your time. Just to add, the style and method are entirely up to you. We're not trying to say anything deep and meaningful about the human condition here, but that's not to say there's no place for subtlety. You can invoke fear by showing her the tools of the trade, or you might wanna tease her with a little pain, string it out a while to create some tension. Or you could just go total fucking gonzo. It's your choice. She's all yours. One way or another, you're gonna have some fun and Strawberry Shortcake over there is gonna die a slow, agonizing death.

And that's what you want, isn't it? To watch some poor bastard suffer; to revel in their gory death? It's what you crave, what you—dare I say—*lust* after. Otherwise you wouldn't be here listening to me reel off this shit.

Now, don't worry if you come out smothered in filth. Getting slathered in blood and guts is all part of the fun. The dirtier and slimier the better. Live the dream, pal. Just wallow in it a while. There are showers down the hall. You bring a change of clothes? Good. Once you're done, you can walk out of here fresh as a fucking daisy, like nothing happened. Clean in body if not in spirit.

What's that? You know this gal? Your neighbor's daughter? Well, I've always said it's a small fucking world. Bet you've always had the hots for her, right? Well, tonight's your lucky night.

Hey, what are you doing, pal? Hold it right there and drop the cellphone. You ain't calling nobody. How did you get that in here, anyway? Up your fucking ass?

Listen, there are only two kinds of people enter these premises: customers and victims. And I'll let you into a little secret—they're all the same to me. Male, female. Black, white, yellow. I don't discriminate. You're all meat bags to me. And bringing that thing in here, you just made the mother of all mistakes. You switched roles, my friend.

Don't even think of making a break for it. This hog spits lead. Only gun on the premises. Is that what they call ironic? I'm never sure.

Like I said, the customer next door's gonna be pissed that her Jap went and croaked on her so soon. She's a classy dame. A lawyer or something. Pushing fifty but hot like you wouldn't believe. Pays big bucks too. Problem is, she's got big buck tastes and I can't always fulfil her requirements. Hence poor old Mr Suzuki.

Hey, you move again and I'll take out your kneecaps! The milf might dock a few Benjamins for damaged goods but she ain't interested in your pins anyway. Like I said, chicks got no imagination.

Oh, please. Don't try to reason with me. Weren't you listening to a single goddam word I've been saying?

Yep, I have a feeling the crazy rich lady will be just as pleased as pie when she sees that I can replace her plaything so quickly.

All that remains for me to say is...

It's the experience of a lifetime!

It's gonna be brutal!

It's gonna be dirty!

Get ready for the one and only...

Blood and Death and Fucking Horror!

Account 2363

I wanted to call this something cool like *The Testimony of Hudson Brown* or *New York Take-out* but it seems petty bureaucracy is a survivor too. So, for the official record, *Account 2363* it is.

It had taken too long to walk from the subway station at Marble Hill to my apartment block. The rain was lancing down like it was trying to pierce our bodies, not just soak us to the skin. On top of that, the front entrance was locked. It was never locked. So it took me a frustrating ninety seconds more to squish the keys out of my soggy pocket while balancing the brown paper sacks on my knee; sacks that seemed ready to disintegrate and drop half a ton of Chinese food all down my legs.

"It'll be cold by now, anyway," she said, then added, "Christ, I don't even know why you're still carrying it."

This was the end of the night, by the way. The end of *that* night.

We'd been together for five weeks—five pretty amazing weeks—and the evening had started as a regular date. A romcom, followed by a few drinks. Nothing fancy. Then I had suggested food. "There's this new place over on the West Side. I'm hearing good things."

"From whom?"

"From the internet, who else?"

She shrugged. So we went.

It was unexpectedly empty for an up-and-coming place on a Saturday night and, not for the first time, I wondered about the reliability of online reviews. I didn't wonder for long.

While we were waiting for our order, two things happened. Firstly, I realized I was with the woman I wanted to spend the rest of my life with; secondly, a fight broke out in the lobby.

Vis-à-vis item one, while Sadie was neatly arranging her napkin in anticipation of the meal, I had the sudden urge to blurt out my feelings in a crazy stream of consciousness babble. Trouble was, the unholy ruckus by the front door (see item two) was kind of a buzzkill. On the plus side, the distraction bought me time to organize my thoughts and it was an amusing diversion for a while. Quite a short while, as it turned out.

I guess restaurants get all kinds of trouble with drunks at night, but this was a step up from the standard fare. Things quickly turned ugly. This guy wasn't doing the regular drunk stuff like refusing to pay or slurring out racial abuse. He was grabbing at people, lunging at them open-mouthed and snarling. Like I said, the funny went out of it fast.

"No extra charge for the floor show," I said.

Sadie didn't crack a smile. She put down the napkin, folded her arms and bit her lip. "Maybe we should have just gone to Wendy's or something," she said quietly. "Service is quicker there, too."

You don't tell a girl you're in love with her over a slab of ground beef washed down with red soda, is what I wanted to say. What I did say was, "Yeah. I like Wendy's."

The ruckus got louder. The drunk grabbed hold of a tiny Asian waitress and pulled her to him. A table went over; things smashed. Some of the other customers rose from their seats. A middle-aged man sitting next to us said, "Oh, for Chrissake, he's licking that poor girl's face now."

Sadie made a small gagging sound and covered her mouth with the napkin.

A couple of hipster guys waiting for a takeout grabbed the drunk by the scruff of his neck and the waitress backed away, scrubbing her cheek with the back of her hand. It came away bright scarlet. He'd been doing more than licking.

A moment later one of the chefs appeared—a beefy Samoan-looking guy. A bunch of customers were still struggling to press the drunk into the ground. Then, in a moment of surreal horror, the chef took one look at the girl's face, dropped to his knees and pushed a knife into the man's chest.

At that point, oddly enough, my sense of humor withered on the vine and all my burgeoning thoughts of romance lay in tatters. Sadie was wanting to leave. By then, we could hear the howl of sirens. Along with all the other customers, we were on our feet, looking out the window, expecting the cops to pull up any second. The air outside seemed to be pulsating red and blue, but New York's finest were a no-show to the party.

We snuck our way through the lobby, edging gingerly past the writhing mass of bloodied humanity on the carpet. At the door, the injured waitress was gamely clutching our order in brown bags. "Sorry, we close now," she said.

No shit.

Blood drizzled onto her bare arms from her cheek. Behind her, four men had piled onto the drunk but he was still thrashing like a stuck pig. The chef's knife (it was one of those big fat blades used for cleaving carcasses apart) was jutting out from between the buttons in front of his sport coat and he was coughing up splats of ketchup, his eyes all bulging out like he was straining at something. He didn't seem to realize that he should be dead already.

I took the bags off the waitress and pushed a fistful of bills into her hand. I have no idea if it was the right amount and she was too busy holding her face together to count it.

As we stood outside, straining to catch sight of a taxi, the rain came on. I did some swearing but it didn't keep us dry. The sirens were getting louder but there was still no sign of law enforcement. Their resolute absence was frustrating, their sirens maddening. "Nice tune, buddy, but the dance is over here," I shouted into the night.

Now, I don't know what I wouldn't give to hear that reassuring wail once in a while.

I looked back into the rain-free restaurant. The waitress was standing at the other side of the door, staring into the night, hands by her sides, the mess of her chewed face seemingly forgotten.

Sadie started moving as soon as I suggested we make a run for it. I hurried after her through the downpour to Columbus Circle. Against the flow of the crowd, we elbowed our way to the station.

"That was horrible," she said. "I'm not hungry now."

I told her that what happened at the restaurant was someone else's problem. She should put it behind her. I said we should just enjoy the rest of the night. The champagne, so to speak, was back in the cooler but I still had high hopes of popping the cork at some point that evening.

One look at Sadie poured cold water all over that. Her eyes were filled up fit to burst.

"Why did they have to do that to the poor man?" she asked.

I didn't take issue with her rose-tinted view of the drunken psycho. Sadie's warm heart was one of the things that attracted me to her.

"Why didn't they just let the police deal with it?"

The sirens hadn't let up, but by the time we went underground we had yet to see a donut patrol in the flesh. "Sounds like the cops have other priorities," I said.

I didn't mention the big thing that I couldn't stop thinking about: How the hell was the guy still alive and kicking?

On the train, we sat in silence.

"Crazy night, ain't it?" said an old lady opposite.

I could think of other words but instead I agreed it was crazy.

"Reminds me of the '70s," she added.

I nodded and smiled but I suspected that New York had never been quite as crazy as this before. "I wonder if there's been an incident of some kind," I said, stabbing my cellphone with my thumbs.

Sadie stared silently at the passing stations through her own reflection.

"You won't get a signal down here, honey," said the old lady.

I knew that. I just wanted to do something, even if I was just going through the motions.

The weather hadn't improved by the time we arrived at 225th Street so we waited there for a cab. My place was only a couple of blocks away but the rain was hammering down. Over the soundtrack of screaming sirens, I thought I heard a flurry of gunshots. I didn't mention it to Sadie but I think she had noticed anyway. There was a frightened rabbit look in her eye.

We stood in the shelter of the station hall. Sadie watched the traffic in silence while I tried the internet again. Suddenly, a lone yellow cab appeared and I scurried onto the sidewalk, waving my arms like one of those whacky inflatable dudes. The taxi sailed by, spraying me in a fine mist. "Sonofabitch. Did you see that?" I gasped, spitting raindrops.

"Just get me the fuck out of here, you asshole!" she screamed.

"They're not supposed to do that," I added flaccidly.

It was definitely gunshots. And lots of them, like someone had set light to a factory full of firecrackers. Speaking of which, was that a plume of smoke curling up from Times Square in the distance?

All around us, people were hurrying, hunched over, faces streaming. They pounded past us, pushing and jostling each other aside. One of them looked at us like we were a pair of stranded out-of-towners, mesmerised by the big city lights. "You don't wanna be hanging around out here tonight, pal!" he yelled.

He was right; we didn't. So we walked—quickly— like everyone else. Does that get you less wet or more wet? I don't know. What I do know is that by the time we reached my apartment block, we weren't talking and the paper bags of food I was still clutching were feeling somewhat delicate.

And that's it, really. That's the end of my story. It isn't much compared to some of the stuff other people went through that night; the night everything changed. Maybe I should have realised something was wrong when the nutjob at the Chinese wouldn't stay down. Maybe even before that. I don't know—I wasn't people-watching and I sure as hell wasn't taking notes for posterity. I had other priorities. Even after things turned sour, I was just looking at Sadie—at her eyes—and thinking how awesome she was and how I'd do anything to keep her. I know it was way too soon but I even played with the idea of proposing. One knee? Or is that considered tacky these days? And, of course, I was hoping the night would end the way I had planned, if you catch my drift.

When I eventually eased open the lobby door, Sadie's half of the takeout finally gave out on me. Lukewarm beef chow mein in black bean sauce burst from one of the baggies and cascaded down the front of my pants to douse my shoes. I stared at the mess. She had said it would be cold. She was right. The gelatinous mixture clung tepidly to my legs, an unpleasant sensation that made me shiver more than the trickles of rain skittering down my collar.

"Well, you weren't hungry anyway, were you?" I said.

"The door!" she shouted. "Shut the door!"

Why the hell was she throwing a fit? I didn't get it. So I froze, open-mouthed, and just looked at her. But she wasn't looking at me.

"Shut the fucking door!" she yelled, her voice rising with each word.

Before I could ask what the hell her problem was now, she lunged past me and grabbed the damned door herself. I turned, following her wide-eyed stare. But I was too slow to react. They rushed the building, slamming the glass door into my chest and pinning me against the inside wall. Then they poured into the lobby, a tsunami of dishevelled humanity, snarling and shrieking and skidding on the spilled noodles.

I watched, powerless, as Sadie tried to escape them. *Them*—the crowd, the herd, the walkers (or whatever we've decided to call them).

I was trapped behind the glass, like a bug under a microscope, still stupidly holding onto the second bag of food as they battered against the door and swarmed into the block. They didn't notice me but I could see them. I could see them up close. I was mesmerised by their faces. Still am, I guess. I can never make up my mind whether they're twisted in pain or warped with hatred. Or maybe just torn by confusion and terror at what they've become. When I come across one out there, I always look at their faces and can't help wondering what they used to be like. Just for a moment. Just before I kill them.

Sadie was swept along like flotsam until, finally, she went under. Like a drowning swimmer, she reached up, gasping and clawing at the air. Once, twice. After the third time I didn't see her again.

I hope I never do.

Fast as a Bullet

Johnny-Ray Gibson swiped a dribble of sweat from his temple and pushed his shades onto his head. While the handset beeped in his ear, he looked across the store and through its dusty plate glass window to the garage's only pump. If he leaned back a little, he could just see the Camaro parked up alongside it: Inferno Orange on the outside and as chilled as an arctic winter on the inside.

"Come on, man," he hissed. "Pick up, for Chrissake. It's hotter than Satan's ballsack in this shithole."

The garage owner bagging up his purchases by the till caught his eye and Johnny-Ray stared back until the other man broke contact.

"Say, ain't you heard of air conditioning out here in the boonies?" he snarled.

The garage owner, a heavy-set bearded man, put the bag on the counter and began refilling a small refrigerator with beer.

"Fucking pussy," muttered Johnny-Ray.

The line stopped beeping and there was a hollow scrambling sound.

"Hello?" panted a voice at the other end.

"Hey, Ren? Can you hear me?"

"Yeah, JR. I gotcha loud and clear," Ren's voice sputtered hollowly inside the handset of the payphone. "You made it to The Cool Breeze?"

"Yeah, I made it," said Johnny-Ray. He still wasn't one hundred per cent sure where in the world Ren had sent him. All he knew was that he was currently sweltering in a hopelessly misnamed Amoco outlet somewhere between Tucson and Vegas.

"Excellent. So, uh, how's the new car running now?" asked Ren.

Johnny-Ray had no time for small talk. There were more pressing things to discuss, like had news of the heist reached the city yet? Were there any roadblocks? In other words, was Johnny-Ray home and dry?

Maybe somebody was with Ren and he couldn't speak openly. That was a problem with cells.

"I'll give you my number so you can check in, JR, but I ain't giving you a cellphone," Ren had said before Johnny-Ray set out on the mission. "They crap out on you if you stray too far from a signal mast and, believe me, the route I'm sending you, there will be no freakin' signal masts. Besides, the sons of bitches can be traced too easy. We don't want that, do we?"

Johnny-Ray had agreed they didn't want that. Even though checking in from payphones at roadside diners and garages was extra hassle, he was happy enough not to be carrying a cellphone. He sure as hell didn't want Ren calling him up every ten minutes to ask how things were going. Knowing Ren, he would have chosen the most inappropriate moments, while Johnny-Ray was taking a dump or holding up the security truck.

"Yeah, the ride's sweet," Johnny-Ray lied.

"I'm real sorry the old Taunus crapped out on you, JR. I swear I had it checked over. I mean, sheesh, you could've been killed or something. I feel so bad about that."

"Not a problem, Ren. Forget it. Main thing is I'm back on the road and heading home."

Like fuck. But he wasn't about to admit that the perky little Camaro sitting out on the forecourt had been giving him more headaches than his nagging bitch of an ex-wife, and had almost flipped him over twice just like the goddamn Taunus had done.

The fiasco over the car Ren had provided had given Johnny-Ray the moral high ground, a valid grievance, and he intended to use it to full advantage when it came to splitting the haul. He'd taken all the risks while Ren had sat safely at home in his air-conditioned apartment, conducting the operation down a phone line like some kind of armchair general; a general who had supplied his army—namely Johnny-Ray—with a deathtrap getaway car, a measly hundred bucks for 'incidental expenses' and an ancient six-round revolver to pull the heist.

There was an imbalance that needed to be righted. But Johnny-Ray had a desert to drive through before he could deliver the goods to Ren's door in Sacramento. Then there would be some hard ball to play.

"Good, good," said Ren. "The Camaro is a classic. A real speed demon. Great choice, JR."

More small talk. Shit, if General Renfield S. Butterworth wasn't going to divulge anything off his own bat, Johnny-Ray would have to ask outright. He looked over at the garage dude, the only other person in the place, who was stood at the front window now, his wide back facing Johnny-Ray and blocking his view of the forecourt. "So, Ren. You got any news for me? Anything I oughta know about?"

Ren said something he didn't catch. Sounded like "sonofabitch." Just what the fuck was that dickweed doing, for Chrissake? Playing Xbox while Johnny-Ray was sweating out here with a car full of hot greenbacks? He told Ren to repeat his reply.

"I said no, everything's cool, JR."

Johnny-Ray wiped his forehead with the back of his hand. He was about to say that it sure as shit *wasn't* fucking cool, but he caught sight of the garage dude over by the window becoming strangely animated. "OK, forget it, Ren." He had a couple of minutes talk time left but the look on the garage dude's face suddenly made him feel anxious. He didn't want to speak to Ren anymore. "I'll call again at the next checkpoint," said Johnny-Ray. Ren had earmarked a strip mall outside Vegas as the next stop on Johnny-Ray's convoluted journey.

Backroads, JR. I've mapped out miles of 'em for you. No way are you gonna come across the cops out there.

"Hey, mister," said the bearded guy. "That your Camaro?"

Johnny-Ray crashed the phone down and rushed across the store to the window. "Motherfucker!" he yelled. He froze in disbelief, hands pressed to the glass, and watched as his getaway car edged out of the forecourt, gingerly so as to avoid the solitary gas pump, the airline and a beaten-up red pickup in its way.

"I'll call the cops," panted the garage dude.

The cops. The words snapped Johnny-Ray out of his stupor. They were the last thing he needed right now. "No!" he shouted. "No, don't call the goddamn cops."

"But that's your car, man. Car like that, I'm guessing it's your pride and joy, right?"

No, thought Johnny-Ray, *that's not my fucking car. But riding shotgun inside it is my million dollars.* That's *my pride and fucking joy!*

He had needed something reliable to replace the treacherous beige Taunus that Ren had given him but, in the end, he had chosen the gleaming muscle car purely because it looked good. Hell, it looked like sex on four white-wall tyres. On reflection, it hadn't been one of Johnny-Ray's smarter decisions. He had found out, too late, that the damned Camaro was just as temperamental as the rust bucket that Ren had foisted upon him. Plus, it had the unwelcome tendency to attract the attention of car nerds and chicks with tattoos on their tits. So far, no less than five dipshits had commented, "Nice wheels, man."

The color hadn't helped; such a firecracker orange that it was almost florescent. The damned thing jarred the eye like a bloodstain on a bedsheet. Great if you were cruising the Strip looking for action; not so great if you were driving away from a security van heist that had netted a million buckaroos and left the guard with three extra holes in his head.

Johnny-Ray rushed outside. The afternoon heat slammed into him like a steam hammer. Incredibly, the car thief was bunny-hopping up the blacktop, still no more than fifty yards away. The Camaro was a bastard to start up, and ever since he had hotwired it Johnny-Ray had been wishing the previous owner had been a touch more diligent about getting the damned thing serviced.

He ran out into the road. The garage dude was close behind.

"What you gonna do, pal?" he asked.

Johnny-Ray didn't need to give it a second thought. It would be a pity to fuck up the Camaro but throwing hot lead around had served him well in the past—mostly. He lifted the back of his shirt and slid the heavy old Magnum out of his waistband.

"Oh shit, man," said the dude. "Look, just let me call the sheriff, will ya? Guy can't go nowhere, anyways. It's one straight road for about a hundred miles. Prob'ly just some kid. They'll catch him easy enough."

Johnny-Ray cupped the butt of the gun, crouched low and fired at the Camaro. The gun bucked in his fist like it too was trying to get away from him.

Far from stopping the thief, the shots seemed to galvanise him into action. Suddenly, he found the gas pedal and revved the engine as if he was lining up on a NASCAR starting grid. The Camaro jerked forward and raced away down the road, leaving a thick trail of dark blue smoke in its wake.

"Motherfucker!" yelled Johnny-Ray. "Goddamn motherfucker!"

"*Now* can I call the sheriff's department?" huffed the bearded guy, slapping his meaty hands against his thighs and shaking his head in a cartoon-like show of exasperation.

In one fluid, lightning-fast movement, Johnny-Ray turned and grabbed him by his faded plaid collar and pressed the hot gun barrel into his bearded cheek. "No. Now you can give me a fucking car!"

Johnny-Ray twisted one of the man's arms behind his back and frogmarched him to the forecourt, the chromed pistol held discreetly at waist level. He scanned the road for signs of any new customers who might come along and screw things up. But the place was delightfully dead. He sniggered. "Not exactly buzzin' with trade out here, are ya?"

"Been this way since the interstate," said the garage dude. "Back in the day this was a branch of the old state highway."

"Spare me the history lesson, I'm thinking here!"

Ren had mapped a route well away from the interstate. *It's the long way round*, he said. *But it's the safe way round.*

Well, that at least made some kind of sense.

But even without the risk of immediate discovery, simply wasting the garage dude in a fit of rage and taking whatever pile of junk he could start up might not be the best plan. That would have been the strategy of a younger Johnny-Ray; an impulsive Johnny-Ray who had ended up behind bars for way too long. He needed to start making smarter decisions now he was pushing forty. Killing the guy would get him along the road sure enough. But the next sucker to pull up to the pump (and it was bound to happen sooner or later) would wonder what the hell had happened.

No staff around? Say, what gives?

Pretty soon there would be a convoy of flashing blue lights screaming up and down that long, solitary ribbon of blacktop that laced through the desert. Mrs Gibson never birthed any college kids but Johnny-Ray had enough street-smarts to know that he couldn't afford to attract heat by slaying another dumb fuck and stealing another set of wheels.

He could, however, afford to buy a car.

The gun was heavy and it weighed down Johnny-Ray's right hand. By now the clunky old piece was wavering somewhere around the other man's groin. He let go of the bearded dude's arm. "You got any wheels for sale?" he said, digging into the front pockets of his jeans.

Over his grubby shirt, the grease monkey wore washed-out blue bib overalls with the name Sam embroidered in red script above his heart.

Johnny-Ray held out a bundle of cash tied with a rubber band.

"Uh listen, pal. I don't want no trouble. Just take what you—" said Sam.

"I'm offering to buy a car, you fucktard!" Johnny-Ray stuffed the gun into his front waistband and flapped the wad of bills in front of Sam's face. "Look here. Twenty grand in used greens." Strictly against Ren's orders, Johnny-Ray had peeled a couple of inches off the haul. He figured he deserved a tip for all the hardship he'd had to endure on his 'mission'. Besides, the measly pocket money Ren had provided didn't even cover the cost of gas, let alone refreshments.

Sam licked his lips and leered at the money like it was pictures of naked ladies.

Johnny-Ray eyed the dusty red Chrysler on the forecourt. "How 'bout that?" he asked.

"Well, the pick-up there I kind of need for call-outs," said Sam, still ogling the greenbacks fanned out in front of him. "It does a good job of haulin' wrecks offa the road but it's got no speed. You sure ain't gonna catch your Camaro in that. No, the only sweet motor I have is the one I'm working on out back." Sam tore his eyes away from the money and twisted around. Johnny-Ray followed his gaze into a workshop alongside the store. Sitting there in the shade was an ugly box-shaped monstrosity, its puke-yellow paintwork faded and patched here and there with grey primer.

As they entered the workshop, Sam caught the sour look on Johnny-Ray's face. "Oldsmobile Delta," he said. "She's a classic."

Johnny-Ray circled the car, tapping the heavy steel bodywork with his knuckles and prodding the tires with his boots as he went round. "Buddy, exactly how *old* is this Olds?"

"1973," beamed the mechanic. "Beauty, ain't she?"

Close up, the car looked somewhat more ancient than 1973.

"Jesus, does it even go?"

The garage dude gave Johnny-Ray a condescending look. "Man, I know it looks like I just dug her up outta the graveyard but this baby's V8 puts out around 290 HP." He interpreted the glazed look on Johnny-Ray's face as a sign that the gunman knew (or cared) little about a car's technical specifications. So he translated. "This ole baby's fast as a bullet from that gun of yours. It'll catch your pretty little Camaro and then some," he explained. "Been fixin' her up, see? Worth a good few bucks to a collector when all the dints are knocked out and she's resprayed." Sam reached in and turned the ignition. It snarled like a lion with toothache. "And she's all gassed up."

"Really?" sneered Johnny-Ray. "That's a selling point? You put gas in the fuckin' heap?" He didn't want to waste any more time on this deal. "Listen, bubba. I'm offering you twenty grand and no holes in your ample gut. That piece of shit ain't worth but ten, tops. It's a fucking good deal." With his left hand, he waved the roll of greenbacks under Sam's nose, as though inviting him to inhale their intoxicating perfume. With his right hand, he pulled the Magnum out of his waistband. "And don't even think of holding out for more."

Sam shook his head, his eyes flitting between the money and the gun and his precious Oldsmobile. He fanned his chubby hands, Jolson-style. "Oh, no, no. That's not it. I'm not trying to—"

Johnny-Ray pushed the money at the man. He clutched the bundle to his broad chest as though it was liquid gold that would trickle through his fingers if he wasn't extra careful with it. "About the pink slip."

"Fuck the pink slip," said Johnny-Ray. "I got two questions. You got CCTV here?"

"Hell, no I don't. Too 'spensive. Plus we don't usually get any trouble out here, you know?"

"Well, there's a first time for everythin'," said Johnny-Ray, flashing a shark smile at the sweating mechanic. He was satisfied the man wasn't bullshitting; he was too scared to try anything. Ren had assured him that none of the waypoints on the journey home had cameras but he was beginning to seriously doubt his friend's professionalism.

"Thing two …" Johnny-Ray pressed the Magnum's barrel into the man's doughy stomach, putting his face so close to the other man's that the tips of their noses touched. He knew he was a mean-looking son of a whore, with the stink of state penitentiary seeping from every pore, and he had spent a lifetime perfecting the art of intimidating lard-asses like Sam. "You tell anyone about this and, I swear to God, I'll hunt you down and slay you like the lame dog you are."

"I ain't gonna tell, mister," stammered Sam.

Johnny-Ray could smell the man's breath. It reeked of fear. And beer. The guy ran a one-pump garage in some nameless, shitstreak hamlet at the edge of the fuckin' desert and he was gulping down booze in the middle of the day to keep the reality of his miserable existence at bay. The 20k was probably the best thing that had happened to him all year, if not his whole pathetic life. He wouldn't squeal. He could take that money and go buy another car. Maybe next time he'd go ape-shit crazy and get something that had been built since Elvis died.

Johnny-Ray eased the gun out of Sam's belly. "One straight road for a hundred miles?" he asked.

Sam nodded, still staring at the wad of cash in his hands. "Prob'ly more. All the way to the state line."

"Any turn-offs?"

Sam shook his head.

"So how far's the next town?"

Sam looked straight at Johnny-Ray. "Ain't no town, mister. It's plain desert all the way to Vegas."

The sweat on Johnny-Ray's brow was chilled by a gentle wind that swayed a scattering of desert brush beside the garage lot. *The Cool Breeze Garage*, he thought to himself. *Maybe not such a dumb name after all.*

He stood beneath the awning and checked his watch: 4.37 in the afternoon. The Camaro had gone AWOL little more than five minutes ago. Even if the half-assed thief had managed to get the temperamental bitch up to sixty in that time, he could only have travelled a few miles down the road.

Johnny-Ray slid into the driver's seat of the Oldsmobile. It started a whole lot easier than the Camaro and he was on the road in seconds. The grease monkey was right: the old heap might look like a beached whale but there was real power under the hood. And, true to his word, the gauge read a full tank.

Johnny-Ray flicked switches and turned dials but the air-con failed to kick in. "Fuck it," he sighed. "What is it with these hillbillies?" He slid his sunglasses into place, wound down the window and allowed the wind to slap into his face. It felt good.

The road curled tightly between small hills bristling with swaying manzanita and saguaro before the great rolling landscape of the Mojave opened up before him. Johnny-Ray hunched over the steering wheel and peered through the windshield. The road was empty as far as he could see, which was, he reckoned, about four or five miles until undulations in the terrain, dust and heat haze obscured his vision. He eased his foot onto the gas pedal. The Oldsmobile responded with a healthy growl and the speed dial rapidly swung from 50 to 60, and then 70. Johnny-Ray grinned. It was a typical mechanic's car: looked like a nightmare and drove like a wet dream. The diametric opposite of the Camaro.

Johnny-Ray took a deep satisfying breath. He relaxed back into the seat for the first time. He was in control. The money would soon be sitting beside him again. "Oh, buddy, when I get my hands on you, you are so gonna wish you had hotwired this beaten-up old wreck instead of that nice shiny pony car."

He checked his mirror. There was nobody coming right now but that didn't mean the road would be empty forever. He needed to finish this quickly. But he also needed a plan. He was low on ammo. The six-round revolver had been full when Ren had handed it to him before the job. He knew he'd fired off three in the heist—just to make sure the security guard was well and truly dead. On reflection, that was probably unnecessary; how many people survive a Magnum round to the skull? He'd used up a couple more rounds blasting away at the Camaro. Heap of good that did.

"No problemo. This ole hogleg's still holdin' a big enough bang for you, motherfucker," he whispered. Even so, he'd have to make this last shot count. For all he knew, the sonofabitch might be packing heat himself.

But Johnny-Ray had another ally on his side: the element of surprise. The car thief would never expect his victim to be tailing him. And he would never expect his victim to be Johnny-Ray Gibson, a security guard-murdering armed robber.

Yeah, he thought. *You better believe it, buddy.*

Johnny-Ray glanced down at the revolver on the seat beside him and cursed Ren for giving him a lousy, beaten-up .357 Magnum that had last seen action around the time the Oldsmobile had trundled off the production line. This was a solo job, he had explained to Ren, so he needed some serious fire power. He had asked for a nine mil auto; maybe a 17-round Glock. Ren had snorted at the idea. It was, he said, "a simple in and out job; one lone security guard, probably some old timer jazzin' up his pension." No need to go overboard with expensive fire power.

"I've lined up all the tools you need, JR. All you have to do is follow my instructions." So Ren had handed him the Magnum and the key to the Ford Taunus.

"I'll be right here in Sacramento, guiding you home. All you have to do is check in at these times and these locations." Ren then handed over the list of waypoints, the route to take and his cellphone number.

Johnny-Ray was pissed that the Magnum held six shots max. What if Ren was wrong about the security guard? What if he needed to rub out more than one of 'em? What then?

And the car! Holy shit, the car! The goddamn piece of junk Ren had provided looked like it was made for little old ladies to do the church run on Sundays. It drove like a crippled mule, it smelled of sick and, if Johnny-Ray hadn't used all his driving skill to keep the goddam death trap upright, the Taunus would have flipped like a pancake as soon as he hit fifty. As it was, the crumbling old wreck had thrown him off the road twice since the heist.

Johnny-Ray didn't have time to switch out the movie prop heater for a half decent automatic, and he knew next to nothing about cellphones (the revolution that had swept aside the old order of landlines and phone booths had happened while Johnny-Ray was doing fifteen in Shawshank), but he sure as hell knew a bad car when he drove one. So he left it in the last ditch it had swerved into and walked to the next town looking for a set of wheels that thundered when you pushed the gas pedal and screamed when you hit the brake.

The sun-dried burg in Arizona where Johnny-Ray spied the Chevy Camaro on a used car lot was little more than a skid mark on a dusty road. To Johnny-Ray, the bright orange paintwork and glittering chrome made the Camaro look like a drunken cheerleader at a frat house party, itching to have her cherry popped. That perky ginger ass was just begging to be hotwired.

But as soon as he fired her up he knew he'd made a mistake. Johnny-Ray was expecting a snarl of power, followed by a shriek of melted rubber on baked tarmac. What he got was a sickly gurgle and a reluctant shuffle away from the dealer who, tottering along the highway in yellow snakeskin boots like a faggot at a line dance, damn near caught up to the frigging Camaro on foot.

Said dealer had been asking $24,000. In Johnny-Ray's opinion, that was a more heinous robbery than any he had ever perpetrated. Whoever had consumed the tangerine scream queen before shitting her out onto that car lot had driven the poor slut into the ground. The clutch was shot to hell, the tires were bald as eggs and, worst of all, she couldn't accelerate for shit. In all, exactly what he didn't want in a getaway car.

Jesus, what a prize-winning fuck-up. Best in show. Step up to the podium, champ, and let the pretty lady drape the ribbon round your fucking neck.

Johnny-Ray shook his head. Thanks to Ren's ass-tight schedule there had been no time left for a second car swap. He was stuck with the Camaro. He hadn't thought it could get any worse.

Down the road ahead, there was no sign of his erstwhile getaway car. Maybe he had spent too long dickering with the garage dude and had now lost the money for good.

"Balls," muttered Johnny-Ray. "Should have just shot the fat bastard and taken the pick-up." He slammed the Oldsmobile's dashboard with the flat of his hand. "Fucking fuck it!"

Despite the breeze riffling his hair through the open window, Johnny-Ray was baking hot. The Oldsmobile was an oven. And he was now regretting leaving his little bag of shopping behind at The Cool Breeze. Inside had been a six-pack of ice-cold Coors. Another break with Ren's rules.

"Boozers are losers, Johnny-Ray," he had said. Johnny-Ray hated those smug little catchphrases Ren came out with. It galled him all the more that they usually rhymed. What kind of a fruit does that, anyway?

"Asshole," said Johnny-Ray to the windscreen. And then he tried to think of a catchphrase of his own. He was still wracking his brain, trying to find a rhyme for "fuck you" that didn't sound queer, when he saw it—an orange speck trundling along the blacktop, like a basketball slowly running out of play.

Johnny-Ray grinned and gunned the Oldsmobile. It shot down the road like a rocket and he whooped, "Yeehaw! I'm comin' to ventilate your fuckin' brains, you thievin' bastard!"

The Camaro rippled in and out of sight, as though it was trying to vanish into the boiling horizon. Johnny-Ray guessed there was no more than a couple of miles between them. He'd be up that bitch's rear end in a matter of minutes.

He took a long, deep breath, held it a nanosecond and then let it out, slow and steady. "OK," he said calmly. "What we're gonna do is we're gonna be real cool. We're just gonna make like we're overtakin'."

The Camaro was getting nearer but, Johnny-Ray guessed, the driver must have noticed the Oldsmobile looming in his rear-view by now.

He eased off the gas. "Nice an' laid-back. No sudden moves. We don't wanna spook the little phlegm-wad." He picked up the Magnum. The chromed metal was smooth and warm, like human skin. "A friendly nod. Maybe even a smile. Two guys passin' on the highway. How ya doin', pal? That kinda thing." He thumbed back the hammer. "Then *bang*!" Johnny-Ray smiled.

Even though he had slowed right down, the Camaro still seemed to be moving backwards towards him. "Man, did you pick the wrong fuckin' car to steal. Well, we all gotta be punished for our transgressions some time, don't we?"

He fancied he could see the back of the driver's head through the Camaro's rear windscreen now. He had a mop of black, greasy hair. "Nice an' easy now," whispered Johnny-Ray as he started to overtake. "Just two guys passin' by on—"

But Johnny-Ray's voice caught in his throat as he drew level with the Camaro; his shit-eating grin froze and then slid right off his face.

At the steering wheel of the Camaro was Ren.

Johnny-Ray stared open-mouthed. Ren was wrestling with the gearstick and tapping dials on the dashboard. Despite the luxury of the air-conditioned environment inside the Camaro, he was a picture of purple-faced, sweat-soaked frustration.

Johnny-Ray thumped the dashboard. Ren, for Chrissake! Ren who masterminded the whole job; Ren who directed Johnny-Ray's every move by cellphone, and Ren who had sent Johnny-Ray to that specific dipshit garage at the edge of the desert.

They'll have a phone booth, JR. Call me from there. Nowhere else. Got that?

"Yeah, I got it, you slimy little bastard! You were never in Sacramento, were you? You were following me all along. Just waitin' to pounce."

Johnny-Ray could see that his two-timing partner was so het up about the underperformance of the lousy car, he hadn't noticed him creeping up alongside. Still staring at Ren's screwed-up face, Johnny-Ray gripped the unwholesomely warm Magnum tight. "You trick me into taking all the risks, then you lead me out here into the fucking desert and just take the prize from under my nose. That's the game, ain't it?"

And then a deeper truth dawned on him.

"Holy shit! You rigged the Taunus to flip out on me! You were gonna come along and take the money offa me as I lay dying in the fuckin' wreck!"

He thumped the dashboard again, as angry at his own stupidity as he was at Ren's treachery. Fury burned in his gullet as though he'd swallowed a bunch of jalapenos. "Sonofabitch," he hissed.

Johnny-Ray slowly raised the revolver and took aim at Ren's sweat-streaked face. Just as he was about to squeeze the hot, slimy trigger, his target was snatched away and Johnny-Ray was left pointing his gun at the desert. He had hesitated too long; so long that Ren must have sensed the Oldsmobile beside him and felt that it had been hanging there for more time than was necessary to overtake. Ren had seen him and hit the brakes.

Johnny-Ray let out a guttural scream of rage but instantly fell silent when he heard the crack of a handgun, followed by something thumping into the bodywork of the Oldsmobile.

Ren was shooting at him from behind. One shot. Two. Three. The slugs clunked into the thick metal bodywork of the Oldsmobile. Then Johnny-Ray heard the fizz of shattering glass as the fourth shot smashed through the rear window and buried itself in the roof above his head with a metallic clunk.

"Jesus! You fucking bastard!" he yelled. He slammed on the brakes. The Oldsmobile yelped in protest and skidded into a 90-degree turn, but Johnny-Ray recovered just in time to avoid being sideswiped by the Camaro. He hit the gas and pulled alongside Ren who was desperately wrestling the steering wheel with one hand and trying to get a bead on Johnny-Ray with the other.

Johnny-Ray's gut instinct hollered at him to shoot. He might not get another chance and he only had one bullet left. But even as he was lining up his target in the front sight of the Magnum for the second time, Ren fired again. The shot punched through Johnny-Ray's windscreen and a spiderweb of cracks splashed across the glass.

Shit, was that Ren's fourth or fifth shot? Fuck it, he'd lost count! He glanced over at Ren, who seemed to be examining something in his lap. "Gotcha!" Johnny-Ray sneered. Despite the desperate situation, he couldn't help but find Ren's incompetence as funny as all hell. The dumb fuck was counting how many rounds he had used!

Johnny-Ray took a deep breath and propped his shooting arm against the headrest of the passenger seat. His target—Ren's florid, sweating face—was bopping in and out of sight; back and forth, up and down. What was that two-timing dipshit doing down there, jerking off?

And then Johnny-Ray saw what the two-timing dipshit was doing. He hadn't lost count. And he wasn't jerking off. He was loading a shotgun.

"Fuck it!" shouted Johnny-Ray. "Here goes nothin'." He jabbed the Magnum out at arm's length and was about to squeeze off his last shot when there was an almighty sound of crunching metal. The Oldsmobile shuddered and Johnny-Ray felt the car veer sharply to the left. His finger still poised on the revolver's trigger, Johnny-Ray snatched frantically at the wheel which was sliding crazily out of his slippery grasp and propelling the car towards a stand of saguaro at the side of the road ahead.

Years of driving getaways and running the occasional street race had taught him to resist the impulse to stamp on the brakes in a situation like this. The sounds of crunching metal and shattering glass somewhere off to the right told him that Ren had no such experience.

Johnny-Ray gripped the wheel, slowly stopped it spinning and regained control of the Oldsmobile. He checked the mirror. The Camaro was upside down at the very edge of the road where the coal-black tarmac met the dirty yellow desert.

Only now did Johnny-Ray touch the brakes. He screeched to a stop, reversed back up the road and drew alongside the inverted Camaro. Thick, iron-grey smoke billowed up from the wreck and drifted across the road like a low-slung storm cloud.

Johnny-Ray jumped out and inspected the damage to the Oldsmobile. Along one wheel arch there was a foot-long gouge, like someone had slashed the bodywork with a giant bowie knife and left a glistening silver scar. The rear of the car was pockmarked with a series of bullet holes.

The back window was hopelessly crazed. He punched it out. The windscreen wasn't so bad. It could wait until he hit civilisation.

He cuffed sweat from his forehead. His shirtsleeve came away bloody. Had he been shot? Or maybe he'd smacked his head on the wheel during the crash? He couldn't remember. It didn't matter right now. He felt fine. Hot, aching and parched—he cursed himself again for leaving the beer behind—but otherwise fine.

The road was deathly silent. No traffic; no people. He remembered the garage dude burbling something about the interstate and how it had taken trade away from this route. Good job. Johnny-Ray gazed across the parched landscape and savoured the tranquillity. Life, he mused, was rarely this peaceful.

His reverie was interrupted by a soft crackling noise. He caught a glimpse of bright orange flames rippling gently inside the Camaro like sheets billowing on a summer breeze. The color matched the car's paintwork, made it look like the Camaro was wriggling and writhing under the desert sun.

One of the Camaro's front wheels was out of alignment with the other, and the corner of the front fender, where the two cars had caught each other, was twisted like chrome taffy. He looked closely at that fender. He had never noticed it before but he now saw that it bore a blood-red patch emblazoned with the words 'Arizona Cardinals'.

He clicked his tongue and pushed bloodied fingers through his hair. "That was the clue, right there," he sighed. "What kind of an asshole puts a fuckin' bumper sticker on a car like that?" Johnny-Ray shook his head. It seemed he had spent most of his life missing clues and making bad choices. What the hell was wrong with him?

Maybe this was his one chance to set himself on the right track. The money would change everything. With a million dollars behind him he could go anywhere, do anything; start out on a new life that didn't involve breaking faces, stealing cars—and those long vacations behind the wire.

Now he could afford *real* vacations like all those lucky sonsofbitches he'd been thievin' from the past thirty years. Hell, he could drive into Vegas, right now, and stay at some swanky place like The Mirage with the white tigers, or The Bellagio with them dancin' fountains. He laughed. Shit, he could even afford to lose a few grand at the tables!

The stink of burning plastic, hot metal and spilled gasoline snapped him out of his daydream. The flames were dancing around the shattered windows of the Camaro.

The money. His fantasies would come to nothing without the goddamn money!

A smell like hog roast wafted out of the Camaro and Johnny-Ray's stomach growled. He hadn't eaten all day. *Shoulda picked up some potato chips at the friggin' garage, too.*

He crouched down, slid his shades onto his head and peered inside. Dangling upside down, still strapped into his seat, was Ren. The fire had crawled all over him, stripping him of flesh like a swarm of locusts might strip the crop from a wheat field. His black hair had shrivelled to a wet slurry and his featureless face glistened blood-red and bone-white.

Johnny-Ray's guts groaned again at the stench of cooked meat. The idea that his empty stomach was tempted by the aroma of his char-broiled former friend provoked a sudden gag reflex. "Jesus," he gasped, his hands to his mouth. "What a way to go."

He looked past the melted face and saw that Ren's hands—twisted sticks of charcoal—were clutching the green satchel containing the money.

The sun was cooking the sweat that glued Johnny-Ray's shirt to his back. He could feel his skin scalding. He took a breath and reached into the car. The flames slathered hungrily at his arms like rattlesnakes sensing prey. He had to do this quickly. He snatched a corner of the bag and tugged. It felt reassuringly heavy but it wouldn't come away from Ren's stiff, blackened fingers. Johnny-Ray's right sleeve was starting to burn through and little fangs of flame were pricking at his skin. He pictured himself trapped here, struggling in vain with the satchel until the whole damn mess blew up. A flutter of panic rose in his chest like a butterfly startled into flight. Had he made another bad decision? The *ultimate* bad decision?

Just one more try, that's all. Just one more and then call it quits. He glanced over at the Oldsmobile. Shit, at least you got a half decent car out of it. And if you can avoid the cops, it won't have been such a bad deal, right? He could sell the Oldsmobile in Vegas. Someone'd pay a few grand, even with the damage. Better than—

"No! Fuck that shit!" he shouted into the carcass of the burning wreck. "There's a million greenbacks sitting there, just waiting to be taken, and no conniving crispy corpse is gonna keep it from me! Not this time. This time, I get to win!"

He wiped some greasy, pork-smelling soot off his hands onto his pants and braced his knees against the Camaro's doorframe. He plunged his arms into the fire and wrenched the bag as hard as he could. Ren's fingers snapped like petrified twigs and Johnny-Ray fell back onto the tarmac with the bag on his chest. A couple of bundles tumbled out onto his face and spilled to the ground.

"Hah!" he yelled, brushing at the steaming ribbons of smoke rising from his sleeves and singed forearms. "I did it! I fuckin' did it! Easy as pie! Fuck you, Ren! Fuck you!"

A breath of air wafted past him and sent several thousand dollars scurrying along the road. Johnny-Ray scrabbled around the hot blacktop, scooping up the stray cash and stuffing it feverishly back into the bag.

Then there was a sound; a gurgling kind of sound, like a sink backing up. Lying sprawled on the road, fists full of dollars, Johnny-Ray had a direct line of sight into the Camaro's interior.

Ren—what was left of him—was moving. He opened his eyes and stretched out a fingerless hand, his blistered, lipless jaws working open and closed.

"Jesus, man, what do you want?" shouted Johnny-Ray.

Ren made that watery sound again.

"Wh-what am I supposed to do?"

Flames burst around Ren's chest and licked at the remains of his face. He shuddered and his blackened hand-stump reached out to Johnny-Ray.

"You want me to *help* you? You could've killed me with that rigged car you gave me!" said Johnny-Ray. "And then you just steal the goddamn money from under my nose like that? No way, Ren. You're a fuckin' douchebag!"

But he could hear the whine in his own voice. This wasn't over yet. He watched as something pink worked noiselessly inside Ren's charred mouth. There was another one of those difficult decisions to make. He envisioned alternate scenarios:

One: Johnny-Ray struggling to haul Ren out of the car and getting blown sky high as soon as the gas tank finally caught;

Two: Johnny-Ray successfully hauling Ren out of the car and depositing his flame-grilled friend into the Oldsmobile without snapping off any more body parts. So far so good. But if Ren gave up the ghost by the time they hit town, what the hell was Johnny-Ray going to do with the body? Dump it at the side of the road? Feed it to the white tigers at The Mirage? And what if Ren managed to survive? Johnny-Ray knew the answer to that: hospital, cops. And back to jail.

Johnny-Ray shook his head. There was no way that helping Ren could work out well for him. "No," he said. "Not this time, Ren. This time I make the right decision." He slipped the Magnum out of his waistband and clicked back the hammer. "Guess I was right to hold onto that last bullet."

Ren gurgled frantically and little bits of blackened skin tumbled from his face.

"Consider this an act of mercy," said Johnny-Ray. "Cos it's sure gonna put me out of *my* misery." He fired. Ren's head exploded in a mushy pink mist that looked like strawberries and cream. "See, I'm starting over," said Johnny-Ray to the dripping goo that had once been his best buddy. He grimaced as an eyeball (smashed out of Ren's skull by the .357 slug) came unstuck from the upside-down floor of the Camaro and dripped lazily into the flames on a string of clear jelly. It fizzed like Swiss cheese on a griddle.

"This here is the new model Johnny-Ray Gibson. No more fuck-ups. No more second fiddle," declared Johnny-Ray triumphantly. He pushed the revolver back into his waistband and stuffed the last stray notes into the bag. The reek of gasoline was getting stronger. He had to get moving. As he stood up, he gave the corpse a sloppy salute. "Well, so long, Ren. Been a fuckin' pleasure doin' business with ya!" Johnny-Ray trotted to the Oldsmobile, hefted the bag onto the passenger seat, climbed in and revved the engine.

As he pulled away and headed off down the road, there was a loud thud behind him and a sound like tin cans clattering down an alley. The Camaro's tank had caught.

Right decision! Hell, I'm knockin' 'em outta the park today!

Johnny-Ray put his forehead against the window frame and allowed the cool, fresh air to rinse the tang of gasoline and burned flesh out of his nostrils. He checked the rear-view. The Camaro was blazing like a Viking funeral.

"What was the color of that shit-heap?" he said. "Oh yeah. Inferno Orange."

He pressed down on the gas pedal. "Inferno Fucking Orange!" he chuckled.

But there was something weird.

Johnny-Ray shook his head, refusing to believe what he was seeing.

Racing towards him along the tarmac from the wrecked Camaro was a streak of flame. To Johnny-Ray it looked as though Ren was reaching a fiery arm out from his burning grave.

He stared at the impossible vision.

The line of fire was running straight and true, getting faster, closer. Soon it would catch up to him and—

"Shit!" he said, thumping the wheel. He stole a glance at the dashboard. The needle on the gas gauge hovered around the halfway mark. Johnny-Ray thought back to the scene with Ren just before the crash. A whole bunch of bullets had smashed into the Olds. "He holed the fuckin' tank! I'm bleedin' gasoline, here!" The needle that had read full back at the garage was dropping by the second. Quarter of a tank now. Enough to make a big bang.

He checked the mirror. No matter how hard he pressed the pedal to the metal, that livid tongue of fire matched him yard for yard.

Johnny-Ray pulled the satchel onto his lap. Maybe he could jump free before the inevitable explosion. But, no—he was doing sixty-five. Unless he slowed right down before making the leap, he'd end up smeared over the tarmac like jelly on rye. But if he did slow down, the fire would catch him before he could escape.

"Jesus, Ren," he shrieked. "Even when you're dead, you're screwin' me over!"

His only option was to outrun the fire which was snapping at his heels. The Oldsmobile's tank would soon empty out, and when it did, that hungry snake of flame would have nothing to feed on and would flicker out. The car would roll on empty for a few hundred yards before stopping. It would be enough to save him. It had to be enough. He'd be left stranded in the middle of the desert but at least he wouldn't be blown sky high. He would think of something. A man with a million bucks and a fat, shiny revolver would have no difficulty hitching a ride.

Johnny-Ray crushed the gas pedal to the floor. The Oldsmobile Delta 88 growled its approval and Johnny-Ray felt the pull of speed dragging him back into the seat. Then he looked in the mirror again. There was no longer any gap between his tailgate and the dancing orange line. His stomach somersaulted and he closed his eyes.

*

Johnny-Ray felt hard tarmac at the back of his skull so he knew he must be facing the sky, but something was blocking out the sun, bathing him in a cold dark shadow.

Something man-shaped. And black as charcoal.

Impossible! He had seen Ren burned to ashes inside the wreckage of the Camaro, *and* he had plugged the sonofabitch square in the face for good measure. Hell, he had watched the Magnum crack Ren's skull open like a duck egg and spatter his scrambled brains all around the vinyl interior of the pony car. Then he'd seen the bastard explode like the world's biggest fucking Fourth of July firecracker. Ren was dead. He was as dead as anything or anyone could be.

Johnny-Ray watched the figure silently sway from side to side, as if it were divining Johnny-Ray's level of consciousness.

Johnny-Ray didn't believe in ghosts or zombies or any of that supernatural crap, but he couldn't doubt the evidence of his own eyes. A queasy, unreal feeling overcame him; a feeling unfamiliar to him. Fear. Fear of the unknown; fear that the afterlife wasn't just a crazy fantasy that belonged only in dumb movies, fear of what the overcooked corpse had planned for him.

"R-Ren?" croaked Johnny-Ray through parched lips. "H-How?"

"Goddam, you messed up the highway but good, didn'tcha?" replied the shadow. As the ink-black apparition turned to survey the wreckage strewn along the road, the low afternoon sun sketched a profile from its silhouette.

Johnny-Ray's blurred gaze finally focussed on the face revealed to him. Bearded, not burned.

It was Sam. The garage dude.

But the relief Johnny-Ray felt when he realised that his dead pal hadn't returned from his blazing tomb to wreak vengeance upon him was short-lived. Every inch of his body screamed out in pain and there was a high-pitched whistling in his ears that refused to fade out. Shaking his head not only failed to clear it, but also made his brain hurt like hell.

Johnny-Ray slowly checked the inventory. He couldn't quite move them yet, but he could feel all four limbs. He twisted his hips and blinked up at the shadow. Good—his balls didn't ache and both his eyes seemed to be working, although down here at ground level there wasn't much to see except the thick legs of Sam's oily overalls.

Even though he felt half dead, he knew he had to take control of this situation. He had come too far and too much was at stake for him to just roll over and give up now. He scanned the littered landscape around him.

Sam spat a stream of tobacco juice onto the blacktop. "You lookin' fer this?" Sam held up the green bag full of money.

Goddammit! thought Johnny-Ray. *I knew I shoulda shot your fat guts out when I had the chance!* He tried to reach around his waistband but his hands wouldn't obey him and he winced as pain jolted through his back and shoulders. When he looked down at his hands, he saw that his paralysis was nothing to do with the explosion. His wrists were tied with a length of oil-blackened rope.

"Easy, tiger," said Sam. "I got that too." Sam hitched the satchel onto his shoulder and waved the chrome-plated

Magnum in the air. It caught the light, sparkling as though it were diamond-encrusted. He laughed. "You're that robber, aintcha? The one they bin jawin' about on the radio all mornin'. The payroll heist?"

Radio? The Camaro's radio hadn't worked but Johnny-Ray had deemed it a minor blessing. He had too much on his mind to be distracted by the jangly noise that passed for music these days.

"They say you got away with an 'undisclosed sum'. That's pretty cagey, ain't it?" Sam jerked his bearded chin up and down and waved the glittering gun to signal that he wanted Johnny-Ray to get to his feet. "So, how much exactly? You musta counted it."

Johnny-Ray had to play for time. "A million," he said as he struggled to his knees—no easy task with his hands tied. He felt his balance waver. He had never been seasick before—never been to sea in his life—but he guessed it felt something like this.

Sam peeked inside the bag. "Sheeee-it! So that's what a million bucks looks like, huh?"

"I guess," said Johnny-Ray. The nausea was subsiding.

Sam spat another wad of brown liquid, as if to draw a line under the matter, and said, "OK, so let's get it over with. I need you over there." He pointed the gun to what was left of the Oldsmobile. "Reckon I might get in the news myself," he said cheerily. "What with getting robbed of the Oldsmobile by the very same hoodlum who stole a cool million."

"Robbed?" said Johnny-Ray. "You were lucky I didn't spill your stinkin' yellow guts all over the forecourt, you worthless pile of rat shit!"

Sam flinched and clawed back the hammer on the Magnum. "You wanna watch your mouth, buddy. I'm the one holdin' the gun now." The Magnum wavered in the man's shaky grip.

Yeah, you dumb fuck. You're the one holdin' the gun. The empty fuckin' gun.

Sam set the bag of cash down on the ground, swiped a sweaty hand across his overalls and picked up a large can with Amoco written on the side. "I always carry extra in case I find somethin' needs shiftin'," he said. "It'll make the party go with a bang, if you catch my drift." He waved Johnny-Ray to his feet and made him walk to the crippled Oldsmobile. The car's windows were empty of glass, the lid of its trunk was lying in the middle of the road and the doors had been blasted open.

Guess that's how come I ended up on the tarmac feeling like I tripped over in front of a stampede.

Sam continued. "I got it all figured, see? I find the hoodlum—that's you—in the burnt-out wreck of my precious Olds." He shook the can and the contents sloshed lazily inside. "Cops'll wanna stick their beak in an' all. But I got that covered," he said with a wink.

They reached the Oldsmobile and Sam started sprinkling the gasoline inside, while carefully keeping the gun trained on Johnny-Ray. He put on what he thought was an official-sounding voice. "Shame about the money, but all them pretty greenbacks musta gotten burned up in the wreck, along with the hoodlum." Sam chuckled to himself, making his ample belly jiggle inside his overalls. "That's what they'll say," he added.

Johnny-Ray didn't have time for a plan. He was concussed, damn near deaf and his hands were tied. The only advantage he had was that he knew the Magnum was out of bullets. Trouble is, when the grease monkey finds out he can't perform a neat little double-tap execution like he's seen in the movies, he'll throw Johnny-Ray into the car and light him up like a goddamned Halloween lantern anyway.

The stink of spilled gasoline tightened his throat. *Jesus,* he thought, *I'm gonna end up like Ren.*

Sam flung the half empty can into the wreck. It clanged hollowly against the twisted metalwork and the remainder of its contents glugged out all over the floor of the car. He laughed. "He lived too fast and died too young. You know how it goes."

No, lard-ass. This is how it goes. Johnny-Ray kicked out, landing his boot squarely between the garage dude's ample thighs. Sam doubled over instantly and Johnny-Ray slipped his bound hands around the man's throat and tugged against his windpipe. Sam crashed to his knees like a lassoed steer. Johnny-Ray pressed his face into the side of Sam's head. He could smell the man's greasy beard, his sweat, his sudden terror, as he clawed uselessly at the short length of rope that was throttling the life from him.

"You fucked with the wrong guy, you worthless tub of lard," whispered Johnny-Ray, punctuating his words with sharp tugs on the rope. "When I'm done with you, I'll find something to saw through this rope. Then I'll cremate you and hightail it away in your little red rescue wagon. Might even frisk you first for that 20k I so generously gave you back there for the Olds."

Sam slid down into the greasy puddle of gasoline pooling beside the car. He was making clicking noises in his throat and his face had turned the color of beetroot. Johnny-Ray knelt down beside him. The rope was burning a blood-red valley of hurt into his wrists but he pulled it tight, relishing the pain. "So, how" – tighter – "d'ya like that" – tighter – "for a fuckin' plan?"

And then the Magnum, still clenched in Sam's meaty fist, fired. The spark from the shot ignited the gasoline and a blanket of amber flame billowed up to envelop them both.

In the split second between these events and the explosion that followed, Johnny-Ray had time to think, *Fuck it. I never could count for shit.*

Elvis Presley and the
Secret of Time Travel

The secret of time travel died on a busy Las Vegas sidewalk in 1956.

OK, maybe I should explain.

In the future people will travel in time. I know that's a pretty mind-blowing statement. I guess you're still hyped over putting a man on the moon, right? Well, don't get too excited. Time travel isn't nearly as much fun as it sounds. It's all strictly controlled. That's partly due to the astronomic cost. One journey into the past is as expensive as one of your *Voyager* expeditions. But, more importantly, there's the security element. I mean, you can't have any old Joe Schmo zipping back down the centuries to fist bump Abe Lincoln or snap a selfie with George Washington. Hell, no. Think of the damage that could be caused by a careless act. Or a malevolent one.

You might want to hold that thought.

I'll admit it: Mackay was a genius. I'd known that since high school. He used to create these fantastic, impossible devices that left his teachers and professors awestruck—and kind of creeped out at the same time. He was *too* clever. It's like he was an advanced species, placed on Earth by an alien race to take mankind to the next level of evolution.

He wasn't from another planet, by the way. I can vouch for that. We grew up together in the thoroughly terrestrial city of Baltimore. From there, we were both smart enough to get into Harvard. But I could never match him brain cell for brain cell. I ended up in computer graphics, making websites for shithead realtors and sleazeball car salesmen, while Mackay ended up working at the Pentagon.

Scientists have been publishing theories about time travel for years. But that's all they ever were—theories. What Mackay published in his final year at Harvard was a blueprint for a machine that looked like it could actually work. Needless to say, the feds heard about his ideas pretty damned fast. They offered him a job. And it was the kind of offer he couldn't refuse, if you know what I mean.

Trouble was, Mackay's incredible intellect was always offset by his personality. Boy, was he bitter. He was one of those people who's just *against* everything. Against the government, against the military. Against society as we know it, I guess. He quickly came to hate the job and the people he worked with. He'd tell me all kinds of stuff he probably shouldn't have, and he kept bragging about how he'd be a billionaire if he'd have just sold his ideas to a mega corporation or a foreign power.

An ideal employee for a top-secret government agency, right?

The feds realized early on that Mackay was a loose cannon, but they saw that amazing thing in him that his teachers had seen ever since grade school, and they wanted a piece of it. So they kept him on a tight leash. They had him working day and night under close supervision. In return, they provided him with every resource he asked for.

The project seemed to float his boat for a while. Despite his misgivings, he was happy enough that some schmuck was prepared to stump up an endless supply of greenbacks to enable him to build his new toy.

Trouble is, that schmuck was Uncle Sam. And Uncle Sam ain't nobody's bitch.

As soon as Mackay had delivered the goods, the Pentagon sidelined him. Oh, the time machine was still his baby, and only he knew how to program it, but because of the government's doubts about his loyalty to the cause, he wasn't allowed anywhere near the machine itself. Mackay kept on encoding the calibrations and calculations for them because they kept on paying him. Plus, he was curious; he wanted to be sure that it really worked. But the test flights were all made by trusted CIA and NASA operatives. They even roped in some expendable jarheads when it came to the first proper journey—a whole month back in time! But Mackay himself didn't have the right color security pass to be in the same room as his amazing machine.

Mackay described his role as kind of like a travel agent who'd had his passport impounded.

Even after they'd figured out how to fly the machine by themselves, they didn't fire him. Oh, no. The last thing they wanted was for Mackay to go rogue on them.

I expect it crossed their minds to dispose of him. It wouldn't have been the first time they'd made someone disappear. But, no, they let him live because he still had the potential to create extraordinary things for them. He was pretty close to designing a vessel that could shoot across the universe faster than the speed of light, and he often boasted that he could create a garment that would render its wearer invisible. Imagine that. All our sci-fi fantasies becoming reality! He was that kind of guy; destined to change the world.

So they kept him on the payroll. But they cut his funding and sent him off to a dead-end research job in a run-down lab somewhere in the Appalachians. And there was always the threat hanging over him, you know? "You step outta line and it's game over, egghead."

Little wonder that his sourness curdled into outright hostility.

Mackay had enabled seven tentative trips into the past for the government's select posse of time travellers. But they were just pussyfooting around, he said; wasting the wonderful resource he had created for them by dipping their toes into last year when they could be diving in off the high board. He had had enough. He was going to take a time trip himself.

Against my better judgment, he persuaded me to ride shotgun.

*

When the lights inside the pod stopped flashing and the godawful screeching had subsided to a low growl, I looked for somewhere to puke. In the cramped space we shared, the options narrowed down to all over me or all over Mackay. I held it in check.

"You OK?" he asked, as he popped open the hatch.

Not only was I strangely queasy, like my guts had been pulled out of my anus and then shoved back in the wrong way up, but I couldn't feel myself. My vision was clouded with colored spots and my whole body was numb, like I'd taken a Novocain bath.

I grunted something unintelligible.

"Oh, yeah. Forgot to mention that," he said. "It feels kind of weird the first few trips."

I asked him if we could maybe hang around until the weird wore off but he was champing at the bit and wouldn't be reined in.

"We'll be just dandy," he said, barely concealing his exasperation at my hesitance. "Just get moving!"

The storage room in the basement of the hotel we had chosen for our landing site was decorated differently from when we had entered, but that fact alone didn't tell us how far we'd travelled back in time. When we staggered up into the foyer we could tell straight away that the whole hotel had experienced a serious make-over (or perhaps a make-under). That we had shifted in time was beyond question. Thing is, when we hurried out of the lobby and into the dry heat of a Vegas afternoon, little else seemed to have changed.

"Are you sure we're in the right year?" I said, rubbing the paralysis out of my face with anesthetized hands.

Mackay didn't answer me right away. Instead, he drifted ahead and peered around the corner of the street.

The hotel had been carefully chosen for its minimal renovation over the decades. I mean, we didn't want to emerge someplace a swimming pool used to be. Imagine that. You travel back in time, only to drown before you've even stepped out of the machine! That wouldn't do at all. So we researched our site pretty intensely. We picked a modest little establishment situated just off Fremont. It was relatively quiet, which suited us fine. The last thing we needed was a whole bunch of slot machine junkies rubbernecking when we suddenly materialized out of nowhere. Well, not out of nowhere, exactly; out of the future.

The downside to our choice of venue was that the little side street which nestled among the shadows of taller, swankier hotels looked pretty much the same as when we had entered 60 years later, if you follow me. Hence our nagging doubt that the machine had actually taken us back as far as we wanted.

Mackay turned to face me, the late afternoon sunlight cascading across his broad, shit-eating grin. "Welcome to 1975," he said. "We hope you enjoy your stay." Prophetic words, as it turned out.

By then, my vision was clearing and, once my jelly legs had taken me to the corner of the street to join him, I could see that the Strip had undergone a transformation. The towering hotel-casinos of golden glass and burnished chrome from our own time had vanished, replaced by blocky, concrete stacks adorned with garish neon lights. The sleek, silent, polymer electro-cars familiar to us had morphed into great, lumbering slabs of metal that roared down the Strip, trailing clouds of noxious fumes into the bright desert sky.

I tried to wave away the stench of burning fossil fuel, still afraid that I might start vomiting up my internal organs at any moment. "OK, so we've gone back quite a way," I gasped, resisting the urge to cover my nose. "But how d'you know it's the right year? The right day?"

Knowing Mackay as I did, I half expected him to divine the answer by sniffing the poisoned air. But instead, he pointed to a newspaper stand where the *Las Vegas Sun* proudly announced that it was indeed August 18, 1975.

"Oh my God," I said, delighted, surprised and slightly terrified in equal measure. "It worked."

"Of course it worked. It works all the goddamn time," said Mackay with a frown. And then he added darkly, "For the chosen few."

We didn't use the machine Mackay had built for the Pentagon. That was the most heavily guarded piece of merchandise in the government's entire inventory. As I said, Mackay wasn't allowed anywhere near it. He had made his own time machine, using his own blueprint, of course, and parts begged, borrowed but mostly stolen from various high-tech sources.

It wasn't easy to recreate the time machine on a shoestring budget. It took him three years, working every spare moment to get the thing up and running. When he finally showed me, I kind of laughed. It looked like a pile of junk; a pile of junk with a green light that flickered fitfully as though it was just about to pop.

"Jesus," I said. "It looks like a freakin' deathtrap."

"I had to make some economies," grumbled Mackay. "Besides, who gives a shit what it looks like?"

He was kind of antsy, you know? I mean generally, not just then.

"Main thing is it works."

"Yep," I agreed. "But the second main thing is that no one finds out. And this… this *thing*… looks like a first-grader's idea of a friggin' time machine! Someone stumbles across this and they're gonna be lookin' around for Morlocks!"

Mackay took my point. The time machine hummed. It glowed. And it crackled with static so bad that it made our hair stand on end. "We can't leave this thing anywhere for any length of time, Mackay. It's just too—" I threw up my hands in frustration. I couldn't think of a word for what it was.

"Obtrusive?" suggested Mackay.

"Loud," I said. "And also glowy. And way too throbby."

"Don't sweat the small stuff," said Mackay. "We won't be around long enough to worry about getting caught."

I looked inside, bumped my head and swore ripely.

"Oh, yeah. Mind your melon," he chuckled.

"Third main thing," I said, rubbing the egg that was ballooning on my forehead. "It's too damned small for three people. I mean, no offence and all, but you're not exactly petite."

Well, it's true. Mackay was a hefty guy. Fat, really. And his time machine was approximately the size of a freezer, the little stubby kind you keep in the garage.

Three people? You see, we were going to bring Amy along for the ride. That was the plan. She was a friend of ours from Harvard and she was in on the whole thing. She'd sourced some of the more legal components for Mackay and had researched possible places we could safely leave the machine. But Mackay insisted that we needed a man on the ground, so to speak; someone back at base who could monitor our chosen location until our return, to make sure no dipshit dumped anything in our spot so that we end up merged with a box of Christmas decorations or a German shepherd. You've seen *The Fly*, right?

Anyway, Amy agreed to stay behind for this inaugural trip. It would be guys only.

Mackay was all for a suitably intrepid adventure, like a week in the French Revolution. I told him that didn't appeal to me. (I have a somewhat aristocratic mien so I'd probably end up losing my head.) Besides, I pointed out to him, we were limited by distance. You see, the time machine takes you backwards in time and, if you're lucky, forward again to the time that you set out from. But it won't move you in space.

You have to start out from exactly the same location you want to end up, if you get my meaning. In short, without schlepping the damned machine overseas we were tied to the continental United States.

Mackay knew all this, said he was just ribbing me. "What, you think I was really gonna ship it all the way to Paris, France?" he guffawed.

I laughed on cue. I never could tell when he was joking.

Then, with a dead straight face, he suggested the Alamo.

At that point I confessed that the idea of time travel kind of scared me. I told him that, for me, it was a little like taking a sailboat for a trip along the coastline. Venturing back fifty or sixty years would test the sturdiness of my sea legs but at least I would feel as though I was still in sight of dry land. Travelling further back than the video age was too much like paddling a rubber dinghy across the Atlantic. During a storm.

He called me a pussy but, after a lot of dickering, we agreed on a weekend in 1975.

"Not very intrepid at all," huffed Mackay. "But we could treat it like a vacation. You know, really live the period? Play the slots, catch some shows, and maybe even pick up some gals."

"Pick up some gals?" I said.

"Sure. Sex was simpler then. HIV was but a glint in Satan's eye. Women were more promiscuous. And, from what I know about the 1970s, everyone was screwing everyone else. Agreed, the pubic hair situation was way out of hand, but at least they didn't need to bother with condoms. So why the hell not?" he beamed.

He didn't exactly make it sound appealing. Plus, no matter how easy it would be to get laid, I had my own reason for not wanting to go cruising for '70s' chicks. But I laughed along. "Sure," I said. "I can live with pubic hair."

Round about now you'll be wondering why 1975 and why Vegas?

The answer is Elvis. Plain and simple.

Mackay was a massive fan. In 1975, Elvis was coming to the end of his residency at the Vegas Hilton. It was a classic era and he was still on form, you know?

Not only did Mackay want to catch the King at his peak but he also wanted to leave some kind of a mark. A footprint in the past. We looked up the show schedules. We plumped for a date in August when we knew the show was being filmed. Our shrieking voices and our pretty mugs would be preserved in the forbidden past, forever.

"Temporal graffiti" is how Mackay gleefully described such a permanent snub to the establishment. He grudgingly admitted that it sounded a lot more fun than being guillotined by Robespierre's revolutionaries or shot at by Santa Anna and his compadres.

Amy sourced our outfits for us. It was important that we didn't look like outsiders. Our period money was crumpled and faded and our show tickets were forgeries, so the last thing we needed was for our appearance to attract suspicion.

Amy kitted us out in stack heels, ball-throttling pants, flowery shirts with ridiculously wide lapels; the whole shebang. Our hair was way too short and cut in the wrong style, but we shot down her suggestion of wigs. They would look fake, and anyway, they'd be way too uncomfortable to wear in the middle of a Nevada summer. We opted for baseball caps. I sported a blue Baltimore Colts lid; Mackay settled for a green New York Jets cap. Neither of us was into sports, by the way. Our headgear was part of our cover. We figured we could pass off any faux pas we might make in 1975 Vegas on the grounds that we were just a couple of rubes from back east.

As we strolled down the Strip towards the Hilton, taking in the sights and sounds of a different era, I told Mackay that I felt kind of bad leaving Amy behind. "She would've loved this," I said. "The clunky old cars, the goofy fashion."

"Don't worry," said Mackay. "It's best we test it out first without her. After all, if something goes wrong—"

That freaked me out. My sailboat analogy came to mind. I was walking down the Strip in Vegas but I suddenly felt like I had been cast adrift in the middle of the ocean. "Like what?" I asked. "What could go wrong?"

"Oh, Jesus," he said. "Will you calm the hell down? Nothing's gonna go wrong."

We walked on in silence, my stomach knotting with every step. For the first time since I had agreed to go on this crazy journey, I started to wish I hadn't.

After ten minutes or so we took refuge from the heat in a burger joint and ordered half-pound patties, dripping with cheese and pickle and about a million calories. They were absolutely divine; packed with the kind of pungent flavor you just didn't get from the lab-grown synthetic meat substitute of our time. We washed down the burgers with a couple of strong beers that made me feel light-headed all over again.

It was our first encounter with the 20th-century natives and I was sure the waitress was going to say something smart about our peach and lilac shirts. It had already occurred to us that although the clothes were textbook couture from the era, they were a little more colorful than the muted beiges and browns being worn by almost everyone around us. Turns out real-life '70s people didn't much go for the garish catalog outfits Amy used for her research.

I chugged down some beer and leaned across the booth. Suppressing the urge to belch, I whispered, "Waitress keeps eyeballing us."

Mackay nodded. "To be fair, we do look like we just wandered in from a Gay Pride rally," he mumbled through a mouthful of greasy fries.

This time I laughed for real.

As we emerged into the waning sunshine, I felt buoyed up with Dutch courage. The burgers here were made of real cow flesh, the beer actually contained alcohol and the girls were wearing impossibly short skirts. I was starting to relax into 1975. It was a vintage year, an epic year!

Then Mackay dropped a bombshell. "I'll take Amy on the next trip," he said flatly. "You can stay behind and watch our backs."

I stared at him open-mouthed but he raised his hand to silence me before I could form any words of protest.

"Don't worry," he chuckled. "I'll take good care of her. I promise I won't drag her off to Gettysburg until the Rebels are licked and the goddam speech is underway. Is that OK with you?"

"Yeah, it's OK," I said. But Mackay must have seen a look cross my face. He stopped in his tracks.

"Do we have a problem?" he asked.

"No," I said. "No problem at all."

But we did have a problem. A big one.

We had met Amy at college. She was a certified nerdette, a gifted physics major with a penchant for old-time sci-fi. She fitted right in with the pair of us.

Amy wasn't like the other girls at Harvard who were pretty much off limits to a couple of douchebags like us. She was slim, with jet black hair, and her crystal-blue eyes peered out from behind horn-rimmed glasses. Pretty, in her own unique way. But we never talked about her as though she was a girl, you know? Neither of us ever admitted we had anything but purely platonic feelings towards her. In retrospect, I guess that was odd. I think we were both playing our cards close to our chest. But I'd seen Mackay watching her sometimes when he thought no one was looking. The idea that he might have the hots for her made me feel sick inside, even though I secretly harbored similar feelings.

Neither of us made a move. For my part, I was afraid of rejection, of humiliation; afraid I would screw up a perfectly good friendship with both Amy and Mackay by making a clumsy pass at her. So I kept it to myself. Like Mackay, I stole surreptitious glances, just wishing I had the guts to tell her how I felt.

When the dynamic changed, I was totally thrown off balance.

The day of the time trip, Amy told us to take care. She hugged us both and gave us each a peck on the cheek. Mackay held her a little too long, I thought. Amy pulled away from him, still smiling steadily, and patted his chest. The awkwardness lasted barely a nanosecond but it was enough to force a blush onto Mackay's rotund features. He made some excuse about having to check something and he waddled away, head down.

Once he had left the room, Amy turned to me. The fixed smile had gone and her eyes glittered wetly, like fresh-cut sapphires. She told me that she didn't want to lose me.

I didn't get it. Lose me how? She rolled her eyes, grabbed me by the neck and reeled me in. The kiss was quick but full-on. Suddenly, I got it. We both laughed with relief.

"What's the joke?" asked Mackay.

His silent return caught me off guard. But Amy was on it. She let go of me and spun around to face him. "Nothing, big fella," she beamed. "Just placing my order for vintage comic books. Y'all know it's the only reason I'm helping you losers with this half-assed escapade, right?"

Mackay scowled. His sense of humor never quite meshed with other people's. Things he found funny, everyone else found weird. And vice versa.

He patted the top of the time machine. "Nothing half-assed about it, Amy. This is the culmination of all human endeavor, right here."

"Sure, Mackay. Amy was just kidding around."

Then it was Mackay's turn to laugh. "Just pullin' yer chain," he guffawed.

Amy and I copied him. Like I said, there was a humor interface issue.

In the main concert hall of the Hilton, Elvis gamely belted out hit after hit through a haze of smoke. Yet throughout the performance I kept seeing Mackay's fat face out of the corner of my eye. He was having the time of his life, tapping his feet and singing along with the rest of the audience. But I found it hard to enjoy the show; all the while I was picturing him snuggled up tight with Amy in that sweaty closet of a time machine.

Not only was my nerve waning again as the beer wore off, but Elvis seemed to be crooning secret messages to me: *All Shook Up*, *Heartbreak Hotel*, and *Suspicious Minds*. The concert suite reeked of stale cigarettes and whiskey, and that greasy burger churned inside my stomach. I didn't want Mackay taking Amy anywhere—the Alamo, Vegas—any damned where. I had the sickening feeling that he might never bring her back.

We poured out of the Hilton with the crowd and started to make our way down the Strip. It was fully night but the day's heat was still radiating up from the sidewalk. The plan was to get a room someplace and spend the next day gambling, sightseeing and shopping. Maybe we'd hire a car and go explore the decade a little.

About halfway down, Mackay patted at his pants pocket. "Shit," he said, "I've lost the key!"

The ground seemed to move beneath my feet, as though the sidewalk had turned to Jell-O. It had happened; the very thing I had been dreading all day. We were fucked. The sweat trickling down my back became a river of ice and I had to clamp my teeth together to prevent them from chattering.

Mackay stood there smirking at my distress and, for a second, I thought this was one of his off-kilter jokes.

"You... you're kidding, right?" I pleaded.

"No, I'm not kidding. But it's OK. It's only the stupid skeleton key and I know where I left it."

I slumped against the front wall of a nearby hotel, afraid that my legs would give out on me unless I was held up by something rock solid. "The key to the storeroom, you mean?" I gasped. "Jesus, I thought you'd lost the key to the—"

He shut me up before I had time to blurt out the next words. Our flamboyant attire was already attracting the attention of passers-by. If someone heard me yelling about a time machine, God alone knows what might have happened.

"Chill the hell out, will you?" hissed Mackay. "The machine doesn't even use a friggin' key. You know that, for Chrissake. Worst case scenario, we'll have to spend a few bucks on a jemmy to open up the room. I'd just rather not waste time and money tomorrow hunting down a fucking hardware store in Sin City if I don't have to, OK?"

I nodded eagerly, pathetically relieved that whatever happened with the skeleton key, we'd still be able to access the time machine.

Mackay was totally unfazed. He told me to wait while he went back up to the Hilton to check around our seats. The key had been digging into his ass, he said. "I told Amy the goddam pants were too tight." So he'd taken it out of his pocket and put it under his chair.

I offered to go along with him but he said I'd be more use checking out the hotel we had stopped beside. It was getting late and we really did need a room for the night or we'd end up sleeping on the sidewalk like a couple of down-and-outs; a couple of gay-looking down-and-outs. He would meet me in the lobby in ten minutes.

Despite my discomfort at the prospect of Amy taking a similar trip with Mackay, the day had been kind of fun. I figured that whatever happened, we were in it together, you know? But alone outside that hotel, I started to feel uneasy. Vulnerable. The Strip was busy. The crowd swarmed around me like I was a stand of reeds in a fast-flowing river, being pulled this way and that. Their dress and the way they talked suddenly seemed foreign to me. It wasn't the America I knew. I felt kind of dislocated.

Suddenly too afraid to venture into the hotel lobby alone, into the alien world of cigarette smoke and landlines and long hair, I waited out on the street for Mackay to return.

Gradually, the river of people ebbed away to a trickle, then dried up completely. After a while I was left standing alone under a screaming pink neon sign with garbage blowing around me.

What the hell had happened to Mackay?

Instinctively, I reached into my pants pocket. And then I cursed the stupid '70s for its lack of technology. How the hell did these people cope without cellphones?

I wondered if his absence was something to do with the time travel. Had the ether sucked him into oblivion? Would it make me disappear too? I'd watched Mackay program the machine and figured that, at a pinch, I could steer the pile of junk back across the ocean of decades that separated me from home. But I didn't know enough about the science of it all to rule out the possibility that in breaching the thin membrane of time we might have somehow consigned ourselves to eternal limbo.

I hurried back up to the Hilton. The concert room was empty. No sign of Mackay. Then a member of staff gave me the bum's rush. I explained that my friend had, well, disappeared.

He replied, "Tough titty, pal, but you can't stay here. Maybe your buddy got lucky."

"Lucky?" I said. "You mean the slots?"

He laughed. "No, I mean the chicks."

I couldn't imagine Mackay taking a detour to go gambling at this late hour with me still waiting for him. And all his talk of short skirts and risk-free sex was pure bravado. But it got me thinking.

Amy.

Did he know? Had he seen that kiss?

My stomach knotted. I ran back into the street and hailed a cab. The interior stank of boiling plastic and human sweat. When it reached the hotel where we had left the time machine, I threw a handful of my period dollars at the driver and pelted inside.

Ignoring the suspicious looks of the desk clerk, I ran down the two flights of stairs to the basement area and hurried to the storeroom Mackay and I had emerged from several hours earlier. I put my ear to the door but I could detect no familiar throbbing or crackle of static from the other side. I was at my wit's end.

I tried the handle, knowing that Mackay had the key but desperately hoping that it would magically open anyway. When it didn't, I heaved my shoulder against it. The door was tougher to break down than I'd imagined and for my second and third attempts I took a short run-up. By now, I was dimly aware that people were coming down the stairs to investigate the source of the ruckus I was making. But I didn't care; I had to see that Mackay's machine was still there.

By the time I'd gained entry and saw that it was gone, I was surrounded by hotel security.

*

I was kept under close supervision for six weeks at the county jail, during which time I was interviewed by various law enforcement officers, court officials and shrinks, all trying to get to the root of my erratic behavior and wild claims. Eventually, I was sectioned and ended up at Holmwood.

If I wasn't crazy before, my experiences as a mental patient began to send me that way.

For a while, my talk of the future seemed to entertain the folk at Holmwood. They'd ask me about the silver suits we'd all be wearing and the moon bases we'd be living on and the androids who'd be doing all the dirty jobs for us. Occasionally, they'd sidle up to me and ask me who was going to win the World Series or the Kentucky Derby. Like I said before, I wasn't into sports. I couldn't help them. Instead, I told them about the only stuff I could recall from high school about the era I found myself in; things like Three Mile Island and Reagan and AIDS. It wasn't what they wanted to hear and pretty soon they stopped with the questions and I stopped with the future talk.

My world had crumbled apart, leaving me floundering in a limbo of unreality. Maybe the doctors were right. I started to question my own sanity. Was I, in fact, from the 1970s all along? Perhaps they were right and the time travel story was just a fantastical creation of my disturbed mind.

And then one morning, about a year later, I was brought back to reality.

"Hey, Spaceman," said the orderly. "Got a new arrival. Just transferred in from Corrections. Another time traveler." He laughed like a drain.

I'd got used to the jibes of the staff and the whacked-out behavior of the genuine fruitcakes who thought they were from Mars or the year 4234. I just let it wash over me. But my stomach flipped when the orderly spoke again.

"Guess what?" he said. "The new nut's a Marylander too! Must be somethin' in the water back east!"

Much as I hated him for what he had done, part of me held out the desperate hope that one day Mackay would return to put things right.

The disappearance of the time machine from the hotel basement meant that he had deliberately abandoned me in 1975, like an unwanted puppy left at the side of the road, and had returned to our own time without me. There was no other way to interpret the events of that night. If something had happened to him after he left me, if he'd had a cardiac or been hit by a car, the machine would still have been there. No. He had never gone back to the Hilton to look for the skeleton key. It was clear to me that he must have hailed a cab and made a beeline for the time machine, leaving me to rot, alone and almost penniless in another century.

And the only possible reason was Amy. He was eaten up with jealousy and had decided to lash out at me. Yet, for all his faults, Mackay was a pacifist. Even if he wanted me out of the way permanently, it wasn't in him to murder me. The trouble was, whether he realized it or not, in banishing me to the past he was not only deleting me from the Amy equation, he was effectively destroying me.

But what if he had had a change of heart? What if he had come to his senses and returned for me? How the hell would he ever find me? He would have had to trawl through thousands of dusty old paper records from the police, IRS, DMV and newspapers before finding me, languishing deep in the files of Holmwood mental asylum. It would take him months; years even. But he would do it for me, I knew he would.

I jumped to my feet to greet him.

But it wasn't Mackay.

Despite the changes wrought upon her since we last saw each other, it was me who recognized her, not vice versa.

The stooped figure standing in the doorway wasn't the Amy I knew; not the young, dark-haired, comic book geek I had fallen in love with. The woman who shuffled into the common room at Holmwood Mental Hospital that morning was much older; lank grey hair framed the pallid, drawn face of a middle-aged woman. Her hollow eyes stared listlessly at the linoleum floor through institutional steel-rimmed glasses. That gemstone sparkle? Gone. Her eyes were dull, fearful.

Amy hadn't just aged; she had been crushed, defeated. Before me stood a broken woman.

Our reunion churned up a confusion of emotions. We were overjoyed to see each other again but each of us despaired when we learned of the fate that had befallen the other. Even so, it quickly became clear that my story paled into insignificance compared to Amy's.

In historical terms I am a nonentity. I'm not just being modest here. The fact is, nobody ever wrote any juicy copy about the nut who vandalized a hotel basement, shrieking about time machines, back in '75. Amy, on the other hand, had made the headlines.

The first performance Elvis ever put on in Vegas was marred by an incident outside the New Frontier Hotel & Casino. A crazed young woman shot and killed a bystander in the crowd. The young woman was Amy. It was April 1956.

"He said the pair of you had decided to extend the trip and that you'd wanted to go even further back into the past; to the 1950s. He said you were waiting for me there and that you had a surprise for me," Amy explained. "He even hinted that you were going to propose marriage to me right there at Elvis Presley's first Vegas show. It sounded incredibly romantic. I had no reason to disbelieve him, and I desperately wanted to see you, so I went along.

"When we arrived, straight off I could tell something wasn't right. He practically frogmarched me along the Strip to the hotel where Elvis was playing. I kept asking where you were and he just said you were safe, that he hadn't harmed you. Well, that in itself worried the hell out of me. Why would he even suggest such a thing?

"Then he began talking about how great it would be to relocate to the 1950s. Permanently. It was an exciting time to be alive, he said; a time of new scientific breakthroughs and a renaissance period for popular culture. Then he started laughing. He said that while everyone else was worrying about the Cold War and alien invasions, we would be living the high life.

"He was talking about us like we were a couple going on some dreamy adventure together.

"We stopped outside the casino where Elvis was going to perform. This was early in his career, so the crowd were all screaming kids. Mackay was still wearing the '70s outfit I'd given him and he stood out like a rodeo clown at a funeral. But he didn't seem to care about the looks we were getting.

"While we were waiting, he started to come on to me, telling me how he'd always been attracted to me. I tried to reason with him, asked him what he had done with you, but he ignored me; said the concert would be the perfect start to our honeymoon.

"I shouted at him, told him to take me back to the time machine. He smothered my face with his big sweaty hands to try and shut me up; said I had better do as he told me or I'd end up like—" She couldn't finish the sentence. She didn't need to.

"Like me," I said.

"There was a police guard on the line," she continued. "An officer came up to us. He thought it was funny, asked Mackay if his 'little lady' was playing him up. I... I just lost it, I guess. I grabbed the cop's gun and—"

Well, like I said. It's a famous story.

Nevada didn't send women to the gas chamber. Instead, Amy got twenty years in the can. When she was released, in 1976, she was sticking doggedly to her story about having been kidnapped from the future by the guy she killed. So, instead of granting her freedom from the Northern Nevada Correctional Center, the state decided to section her. Hence her arrival at Holmwood.

Amy was a shadow of the woman I knew. She was suddenly twenty years older than me. And those twenty years that we should have spent together, she had spent in jail. In the face of all that, and despite the age difference, I found that I still loved her.

But there was something else. In the year since my arrest, my one ray of hope was that Mackay would somehow rescue me from the hell he had consigned me to. I envisioned that absurd-looking time machine of his suddenly materializing in the hospital common room, to the horror and amazement of patients and staff alike. I pictured a rueful-looking Mackay squeezing out of the tiny porthole and beckoning me.

"It was meant to be a gag," he would say. "I'm so fucking sorry, man!"

Now I knew that could never happen. This was the end of the story for me, for both of us. Displaced in time and out of step with the reality of the world around us, we were like survivors of a shipwreck, stranded on a hostile desert island with no one but each other for company. We would remain at Holmwood for the rest of our lives.

I was plunged into a relentless despair and I began to resent Amy; not for killing Mackay but for destroying my hope. In retrospect, it was selfish of me. At least I had enjoyed a sliver of optimism for a whole year. Amy, on the other hand, had battled through two grim decades of imprisonment knowing that she had murdered the only person who could have rescued her. That realization made me even more miserable.

You'd think that the hospital authorities might have considered it significant that our stories matched. Two nuts turn up with the same crazy fantasy, maybe it isn't a fantasy? But, no. They said we were feeding off each other's mania, which wasn't conducive to our recovery. So, shortly after they reunited us, they separated us again. Another nail in our coffins.

And that's the way it was for another year, until August 1977. Something happened then that was so unexpected it shocked the world. At least, it was unexpected by everyone outside of Holmwood.

I told you I wasn't into sports, didn't I? So I couldn't divulge all the upcoming football and baseball results for '76 and '77. I'm just not that kind of nerd. By the late '70s, Watergate and Vietnam were already in the past and I had no historical nuggets to share about the immediate future. But there was something I could tell them.

Before I went on the trip with Mackay to 1975, I did some homework on the King. Elvis Aaron Presley, born January 8, 1935 in Tupelo Mississippi. Married Priscilla Anne Beaulieu, May 1, 1967. Died August 16, 1977.

Ever since my arrest I'd been telling anyone who'd listen exactly when Elvis was going to pass away. Nobody wanted to hear about it. Elvis was the king of rock and roll and he was going to live for ever. What kind of a kook was I to even suggest that he would croak on the crapper from a surfeit of home-fried burgers? That was tantamount to treason. At the very least, it was downright un-American of me.

I guess there was an outside chance that it wouldn't happen, that our travels in themselves had maybe altered history just one tiny bit; enough to keep Elvis away from the prescription drugs and fatty diet that led to his coronary.

But, no. The King passed away right on cue.

As soon as the story hit the airwaves the next day, Amy and I were ushered into the director's office. Suddenly our shared delusion had crystallized into reality.

But the King's death alone isn't what got us released from Holmwood.

The hospital's head honcho became quite taken with the idea that we were from the future. I think he secretly wanted it to be true. So he did some digging.

"Unearthing footage of that show at the Hilton in '75 wasn't difficult," he said, pressing the go button on a state-of-the art VCR.

He had already cued up the part showing me and Mackay in the audience. We looked crazily out of place. With my Colts lid crammed down on my head and my beer-glazed expression, I looked like a prize dumbass. Mackay was no better. His oversaturated green Jets cap bobbed up and down as he swayed this way and that in time with the music.

"Your pal Mackay's having a good time, isn't he?" said the director.

I nodded.

"Take a closer look," he said. He hit the pause button on the VCR. "See his hands?"

Amy and I peered at the screen.

"Sonofabitch," whispered Amy.

As he rocked and rolled and beamed a shit-eating grin that didn't quite reach his eyes, the big lummox was demonstrating a firm but discrete middle finger from the safety of his chubby lap. Suddenly, his smile vanished and his lips mouthed an unmistakable "fuck you" directly into the camera lens.

I shook my head, unwilling to believe what I had just seen. "Christ," I said. "I was so het up that night that I didn't notice him doing anything except jiggling about to the music."

"Of course, this video doesn't in itself corroborate your story," sighed the director. "It just confirms you were at the Elvis show the night you turned into a fruitcake."

Amy and I exchanged a pained look.

"But this finally landed on my desk the day Elvis died." He shoved an envelope at us. "You wouldn't believe the red tape I had to cut through to get this out of the state police archives," he said.

I opened the envelope. Out fell a grainy black and white picture. A big bearded guy was lying dead on a sidewalk, chalk lines around him.

"It's the crime scene photograph from—" he began.

"April 20th, 1956," said Amy. "When I shot Mackay."

The director smiled. "It's fuzzy as hell," he said to me. "But it looks a lot like your buddy." He picked up the photo and held it beside the freeze-frame picture on the TV. The likeness was almost there but the angle was kind of screwy.

"The clothes," I said, leaping up out of my seat. "He's wearing the same stupid clothes! And look, there's his cap! The cap proves it, right?" Almost out of the frame, and in shades of grey, Mackay's baseball cap lay beside his dead body on the sidewalk.

The director nodded. "More than you think."

"What do you mean?" I asked.

"You really don't do sports, do you?" he said with a chuckle.

What the hell did that have to do with anything?

"That's a real nice New York Jets cap. Great for 1975," he said. "Not so great for 1956."

Amy and I looked blankly at him.

"See, the Jets weren't founded until 1960." He tapped the photograph. "That, my time traveling friends, is what they call an anachronism."

He saw my confused look but Amy interrupted before I could make a fool of myself by asking him to explain. "It's when something belongs to a period other than that in which it exists. In short, the Jets hat couldn't possibly have existed in 1956."

"And yet there it is," said the director. He was almost as thrilled as we were.

He grilled us about our lives, our jobs. I explained about the website stuff I was doing. He didn't understand the terms of reference and quickly sidelined me. Amy's job was much more interesting. You see, she wasn't just a techie with a talent for scoping out gaudy pants and old-time baseball caps. She was a researcher for the feds. Just before we set out on our travels, they'd been placing orders with her for period costumes, presumably to kit out agents for their own travels down the centuries, courtesy of Mackay's damned machine. The CIA never told her what they were working on, of course, but she said they asked her to acquire clothing that suited all the decades from 1960 to 1990. It's how she managed to source our '70s kit. She was supposed to deliver the costumes to the newly formed (and worryingly titled) Historical Revision Team.

So what was the CIA playing at? Saving Kennedy? Winning Vietnam? Preventing 9/11? Amy didn't know but, whatever they were up to, they sure as hell weren't gate-crashing Elvis shows.

I shuddered to think what damage could ensue from 'revising' the bits of history the government wasn't happy with.

There are an incalculable number of potentially disastrous consequences for every adjustment to time, no matter how well-intentioned they might be. Mackay knew that. He decided that the government of the future couldn't be trusted with such an awesome power. Before he left for 1956 with Amy, he confided to her that he had unleashed a virus into the Pentagon's computer system that would quickly cause their time machine to self-destruct. He wanted to be the only one to have the power to travel in time.

Trouble is, it turns out Mackay couldn't be trusted either. Perhaps no one can.

Following our cosy tête-à-têtes with the director of the mental institution, we were interviewed by a series of men in dark suits. They always introduced themselves as some kind of psychiatric specialist or other but Amy and I soon realized that they had little or no medical knowledge. In short, they asked about the time machine and we told them everything we knew. Well, almost everything.

In September 1977 we were suddenly released from Holmwood. Amy and I set up home together. She was fragile and it was a while before I dared to broach the subject that had been preying on my mind ever since she told me her story. The one thing we didn't tell the feds.

What had happened to Mackay's home-made time machine?

It was safe, she said. When Mackay abducted her and took her to 1956, he couldn't park the machine in the basement of the same hotel we had used for 1975. That hotel didn't exist until '68. So he hauled it to a location that he knew wasn't built upon in the '50s.

By 1977 it still hadn't been built upon and the machine was out of harm's way.

So where was it? Well, let's just say Mackay had the smarts to pick the kind of place that would be safe for a long, long time.

But we didn't dare go to retrieve it. Officially, we were released from Holmwood because we were no longer considered to be a danger to ourselves or others. But we knew the real reason was because the feds believed our story and wanted to get their hands on the time machine. They expected us to lead them to it.

In Amy's more lucid moments, we discussed our predicament at length. Maybe if we handed Mackay's machine over to the government, showed them how it worked, they'd let us sneak quietly back into our own time? We could resume life there as best we could and lay the blame for the tragic demise of the Pentagon's own machine squarely upon Mackay.

But what would our own time be like, 60 years after the feds of 1977 got to play with time travel? Pretty different, we figured. Maybe even pretty scary. Besides, returning to our own time wouldn't bring back Amy's lost years. We had nothing to gain by cutting a deal. We thought long and hard about getting even with Mackay, maybe trying to fix what he broke. But we came to the conclusion that the variables resulting from anything we might do were just too unpredictable. In a way, Amy had already avenged us. As far as we were concerned, the secret of time travel died on a busy Las Vegas street in 1956, outside an Elvis show.

Even though we were still in the wrong century, we were overjoyed that we were finally at liberty once more. It never occurred to us that if the authorities believed we really were time travelers after all, there would be consequences. I guess that was pretty naïve of us.

We started seeing them from day one. They'd loiter around our apartment block, cookie-cutter agents in matching black suits and sunglasses, radioing in reports on our movements; hoping we'd be dumb enough to lead them to the machine. That kind of attention makes you crazy after a while.

Even so, after Holmwood we had a comfortable life, all things considered. Neither of us had enough sports knowledge to be able to place bets on the World Series or the Superbowl, but Amy was a keen history buff and between us we knew enough about the '70s and '80s to make a living placing bets on current affairs, elections and so forth. That worked out pretty well for a few years.

We watched in horror as it all went to shit at Three Mile Island; we chuckled as Ronald Reagan stumbled his way through two terms, and groaned as AIDS took the fun out of things. Just like I told everyone at Holmwood, all those years ago. And, yes, we had a high old time cashing in on it all.

But after a while Amy and I noticed something. World events—the presidents, the wars, the economic crashes—weren't happening the way they should have. Different guys ended up in the White House, wars raged and plagues erupted that had no place in the history we learned at school.

It's like the world had drifted off course.

We lost a lot of bets.

Soon, it got so that we couldn't predict any damn thing that happened.

Long before the '90s ushered in a whole decade of unforeseeable events, all the money we had earned on predicting stuff in the previous decade had dried up. Trouble was, lacking a social security number, we couldn't get regular work. In fact, without any valid identification both of us were effectively non-persons, destined to scratch out a living hustling on the Strip. We both had to make sacrifices in order to survive.

Amy and I were together but it wasn't the relationship I had ever envisaged for us. The age gap wasn't a problem in itself but it was a permanent reminder of what Mackay had done to us. Amy never really recovered from her time in prison and never came to terms with being stranded in the 20th century. The events of her past, and the tough years that followed, were brutal to her, and our relationship soon became that of carer and patient.

Being under constant surveillance turned Amy into a recluse, meaning that I was the only breadwinner.

Don't think the irony of our predicament was lost on us. Our only real possession was the most valuable piece of hardware in the world: the only working time machine in existence. Yet we could neither use it without the authorities apprehending us, nor sell it for fear of what they might do with it.

But Amy and I had plans. One day, when she was better, we were going to jump into that flickering, humming little box and find ourselves an idyllic life in an era free from overbearing governments and crackpot scientists. We had the whole of history to choose from. And if the period we settled in began to disappoint us, if the locals started chasing us with flaming torches, we could always hop in the pod and pick a different time. In fact, why settle in a time with other people at all? We seriously discussed an expedition of dinosaur-watching...

Meanwhile, we were marking time, living each day as it came.

Our plans gave us hope, something to look forward to. But, in truth, they were an illusion, a smokescreen. It was as clear to me as a Nevada sky that Amy wouldn't cope in another time. Not in her condition. I'm not sure if she ever appreciated that fact but the hope of redemption, however forlorn, helped her face another day.

Two years into the new millennium, time finally ran out for Amy.

It had been a bad summer. The air-con in our single-room apartment had broken down and I couldn't afford to fix it. Courtesy of 9/11, tourism had slumped that year and pickings were slim as hell. Everything I earned on the Strip was going into Amy's arm, or her thigh, or her jugular; basically, any vein that could still hold a charge.

One night I got back to the apartment and the lights weren't on like they usually were. I knew right away what had happened. I had been waiting for this moment ever since we left Holmwood. Maybe it was a mistake, a fatal miscalculation. It happens. More likely she had had a brief moment of lucidity and suddenly realized that this was as good as it was ever going to get.

I sat down beside her in the dark and thought about taking the needle out of her arm and putting it into mine. I never touched that shit but I knew there was just about enough left to finish me; to finish my story.

In the end, I reverted to type and chickened out. Instead, I did something even dumber. I took a quart of bourbon out to the desert and unwrapped the time machine.

I had no idea where I intended to go. I guess my destination was secondary to my purpose: to get the hell out of Dodge.

It had been twenty-six years since I'd last squeezed myself into the tiny space. I'd almost forgotten how damned small it was. But I remembered how it worked well enough. When I switched the bastard on, it started up instantly. Lights flickered and glowed, and the inner workings purred contentedly, like it had been waiting for me all those years.

It was nice to feel welcome but, Christ, the interior of the machine still smelled of the perfume Amy used to wear. I know I was drunk as a skunk, and when I'm sober I'm the last person to believe in all that psychic crap, but right there and then I couldn't shake the feeling that she was reaching out to me somehow.

The idea was kind of a buzzkill. So, I did the smartest thing I could think of. I tapped out some random numbers. Years. In the future. And then I hit the go button.

I sat hunched over and watched as the desert outside started to swirl. Sand puffed up and blew in through the doorway, all over my pants. I began to brush it off until it suddenly dawned on me that the goddam door shouldn't have been open.

I panicked. I didn't know what knob to turn or what switch to flick. I could propel the blasted machine into any decade, any century, but I had no idea how to shut the door!

The whole thing started to shake like it was going to tear itself apart, and the desert became blurrier. I was hurled around the tiny compartment as though I was in a tumble dryer, striking my head, shoulders and knees against pretty much every control button—except the one that closed the fucking door.

Clearly Mackay's horse was unhappy with its new jockey. So unhappy that it threw me (and my half-empty bottle of Jack) out into the desert. But it turned out that Mr Daniels wasn't my only company that night.

When I looked up into the darkening desert sky, looming over me was a man in a black suit wearing shades.

He pointed a gun at me and swore. A lot.

I had just enough energy to look around and see that the time machine was gone before I passed out, laughing uncontrollably.

*

It's been over ten years since Amy's death. I no longer see the men in black peeking out at me from behind crumpled street maps, trying hard to blend in with the tourists, like they used to. I guess they closed the case after that night. I hope the poor guy that followed me kept his job.

I guess I've made Vegas my home. I've seen a lot of the big-name hotels and casinos that I marveled at that day in 1975 disappear: the Dunes, the Hacienda, the Sands. All gone. I've watched the fanfare and fireworks as, one by one, they came down. Some have made way for new luxury palaces such as the Bellagio and the Mirage. Others, like the old Desert Inn, simply vanished without trace, to be replaced by a vacant lot. The New Frontier, where Elvis first took to the stage in Vegas in '56, where Amy shot Mackay, was torn down in 2007. Time has no sentiment. It moves on, relentless.

I don't know where or, more accurately *when*, I sent the time machine that night in the desert. I can't tell you if the changes to history I've been witnessing are down to me losing Mackay's stupid contraption, or if some future regime has built their own machine and is having a hoot of a time making changes, tweaking events, steering the planet onto a different timeline.

What I do know is that time travel is like that shit Amy used to push into her arm: it fucks things up.

Despite it all, Vegas is still Vegas. The Hilton is still standing tall and proud, just off the Strip on Paradise Road. I've never been back there but I catch sight of it in the distance sometimes and, when I do, I always think back to the night I saw the King. Then I get to wondering how everything would've panned out if I hadn't taken that trip with Mackay. But life's too short for regrets, right?

It's funny, but I've never stayed at any of the hotels or ventured inside a single casino or chapel in Vegas. I've spent the best part of my life in this town and I never so much as played the slots. Or got married. How about that?

Been working the Strip these past forty years now. If you've ever been to Vegas, you've probably seen me handing out flyers, dressed up to the nines in my white jump suit and black wig. Cheap eats, timeshare; that kind of thing. Folks come along and get their picture taken. The kids love it. It doesn't pay much but it keeps my head above water, so to speak. Sure, it's been tough but I'm still here; still marking time. If you're ever in town, why don't you take a stroll along the Strip and look out for me? Buy me a beer and I'll fill you in on a few things you won't read on the internet. It'll blow your tiny 21st-century mind.

You can find me here any day. Just ask around. Everyone on the Strip knows me.

They call me the oldest Elvis in Vegas.

III. FLESH CRAWLERS

Bad Brains

How do you sleep? Well? Badly? Me, I'm not much of a sleeper. Too much sleep is no good for you. My nan taught me that.

When I was a kid, she lived alone above a row of shops on a busy street in southwest London. I spent many enjoyable weekends there. Nan was easy to be with and my overnighters there became a welcome respite from the arguments at home.

Her little maisonette smelled different to home: biscuits, lavender water and boil-in-the-bag fish. But that was OK. On balance I preferred it to the suffocating fug of cigarette smoke, exhaled alcohol fumes and fried eggs that filled my parents' flat.

Saturdays, after an early breakfast of porridge with a blob of jam, we would watch the horseracing on TV. We picked our favourite horse, chosen by the bizarreness of their name or the pattern of their rider's shirt, and cheered them on while munching ham sandwiches. This was years ago, of course, and she only had a black and white set, but trying to visualise the dazzling colours described by the commentator was part of the fun.

On Sundays, while the religious shows were on, I'd play with an ancient train set left behind by her late brother, or gawp through a grey plastic View-Master, mesmerised by the transparent photographs of world capitals populated by little people bright with '60s fashion.

Once in a while, Nan would settle beside me on her two-seater sofa and look through a stiff photograph album depicting her at various stages in her life: a Victorian baby, a tousle-haired teen in a smock dress, a shy bride in white lace. The album fascinated me, although I found it unsettling that the vivacious girl depicted in the photos had, at some point, been transformed into the wrinkled old woman before me.

Invariably she would eventually turn her hand to some knitting. The occasion would always be accompanied by the same stern warning: "Now don't let me fall asleep, Jimbo. Too much sleep gives you bad brains."

As a rule, she would nod off after ten minutes. When she did, I would turn the volume down on the telly and listen to the soft sigh of her breath while I did something really quiet, like colouring.

Upon waking she would be grumpy and confused for a while, at least until she had made afternoon tea, which somehow seemed to restore her brains to full working order.

In the afternoons we would go to the park. Before we set off, and before exchanging it for a stiff gabardine mac, Nan would invariably disgorge a white paper bag of sweets from the front pocket of her flowery apron. Then she would cocoon her wispy violet hair in a scarf constructed from the same gaudy material as the discarded apron. It was a uniform she paraded in regardless of the weather.

When we set off, she would usually say, "Hold my arm and call me Charlie." I have no idea what she meant but it always made me giggle. Her odd little catchphrases were comforting. "Rotten swizz" was a favourite. She used it whenever she felt someone had been cheated or short-changed in some way. I would make sure to tell her some tale of childhood woe, often involving confiscated penny chews, just to hear her say it.

She never swore, but when she was angry or upset, which was rare, she had her own vocabulary of not-quite-swearwords. Once, she opened a tin of tomato soup and boiled it up for my lunch. I stared at the steaming orange liquid she set before me until it became tepid. Under interrogation, I belatedly confessed that I didn't much care for tomato soup, out of a tin or otherwise. She scowled and said I was a pernickety little cuss and I could blessed well go hungry. It was different in her day, she said. Her own grandmother, a shrivelled sepia woman in a bonnet according to Nan's old photographs, would have taken a stick to her backside if she had had the temerity to turn her nose up at perfectly good food. When she was a child, she said, she would have walked on hot coals for tomato soup. Instead, she had to make do with bread and scrape. I didn't ask what scrape was but it didn't sound very appetising. Then she sighed and heated up some chicken soup instead, with buttered soldiers to dip in, which I found most agreeable.

Nan gained access to her modest home via a stairway to one side of a fusty little office that was always closed. At least, it was always bereft of staff and customers whenever I visited. That was due to the fact that Alan Churchman, Funeral Director, wasn't open for business at weekends. In the afternoons, restored to apron order, she would pad through Mr Churchman's office and lead me out to the garden at the rear of the premises.

Garden is probably too strong a word. Sky-high walls effectively cloistered the tight, paved area in permanent shadow. The sickly plants, starved of sunlight, cowered forlornly in shallow brick borders that ran the length of a lichen-stained patio. Nan would spend an hour or so plucking handfuls of scraggly weeds from the lumpy soil and deadheading faded mauve hydrangeas that stank of cat piss. When she was done, the grimy paving would be strewn with brown petals that resembled droplets of dried blood.

And cigarette butts.

"Mr Churchman won't allow smoking inside," explained Nan. "He makes them come out here."

"Makes who?"

"His customers, sweetheart. The bereaved."

"Who are the bereaved?"

Nan smiled. "The families of the deceased."

I paused, a tiny light of realisation winking in my subconscious. "You mean like *Randall and Hopkirk (Deceased)*?" I drew the brackets in the air with my fingertips.

"Yes," she chuckled, "exactly like *Randall and Hopkirk (Deceased)*." She did the brackets too.

It was one of my favourite TV programmes. The eponymous duo were private detectives whose missions always seemed to revolve around the supernatural. That turned out to be quite convenient because, while Randall was a bleary-eyed sceptic, his best friend and partner—the somewhat prissy Marty Hopkirk—was a ghost. Marty wore a neat white suit and could appear and disappear with a wrinkle of his nose, walk through walls and suchlike. All very useful skills for a gumshoe. I liked Marty. He was funny.

*

My job in the concrete garden was to scoop up the deceased flowers, weed carcasses and fag ends, and put them in a plastic carrier bag while Nan shuffled along the borders, pruning as she went. One afternoon, I pricked my thumb on a thorn or a desiccated twig. We had only just begun the work, so Nan was reluctant to go back upstairs to tend to me. She tutted and jangled a bunch of keys out of her flowery apron pocket. She earned what she called 'pin money' to supplement her meagre pension by cleaning Mr Churchman's office twice a week and had access to the entire building.

"Mr Churchman has a little room with a sink," she said. "I suppose he wouldn't mind if you ran your pesky thumb under the tap." She pointed with a trowel towards a frosted window adjacent to the door we had just exited. Flanking the door on the opposite side was a second window; one which was blacked out entirely. My innate childhood sense of curiosity was generally sated by Nan's continuous monologues about the Blitz and her blood pressure, so I had never previously given the unmatched windows much thought. Now, for the first time, it occurred to me that they must belong to two extra downstairs rooms that I was hitherto unaware of.

Nan led me back indoors. Inside, through an arch to the left was a room with a white door.

"Why does Mr Churchman lock up his kitchen?" I asked.

Nan opened her mouth to reply but bit back her answer and mulled the question over for a good few seconds. At length she said carefully, "Because he keeps it so spick and span, Jimbo. I hardly ever need to clean up after him in here." Then she added quietly, to herself, "Thank God." She opened the door a fraction and peered through the gap. I cradled my dripping thumb and waited, although I wasn't sure what I was waiting for. Satisfied by what she saw—or didn't see—she let us both in.

The undertaker's kitchen was a sparse affair of stark white ceramic tiles. It was dominated by a long steel table at its centre. Beside it, there was a bulbous copper cylinder, rather like the boiler in our airing cupboard at home, and there were pink rubber hosepipes curled on the floor beside it like sleeping worms. It was nothing like Nan's cosy kitchen upstairs.

Nan rinsed the blood from my hand at the sink and then rummaged in a glass-fronted cabinet. I asked her what she was looking for.

"A plaster, of course. I know he keeps some in here. In case he cuts himself while he's working."

And sure enough, there were plasters. Nan deftly applied one to my thumb and ushered me back out to the garden.

It never occurred to me that, while the undertaker's garden might not have been much of a garden, his kitchen really wasn't a kitchen at all.

*

The last time I ever visited Nan, my parents had had a row. I was nine. I never understood their arguments and this time was no exception. This particular fight culminated in Dad saying, "Oh, for Christ's sake calm down, woman, your sodding mother's going to live forever." The 'sodding mother' in question, of course, was Nan. Bar the swearing, I thought that Dad's comment sounded like a good thing; was maybe even a compliment. But Mum didn't seem to like it. She started to cry.

It got me thinking. I had never questioned Nan's mortality before. I asked how old she was.

"She runs with the century," my mother sniffed. My blank expression forced further elaboration. "She was born in 1900."

A vague understanding was dawning but I offered up a semi-quizzical look that begged a fuller explanation.

Mum sighed. "So, in 1909 she was nine years old, like you are now. And in 1935 she was 35, like me. D'you see now, Jimmy?"

I did see but I tested a further example, just to be sure. "So now she must be 72 because it's 1972?"

"Well, she's 71 at the moment," said Mum a little ruefully, as though she had been caught lying. "But she *will* be 72 this year—please, God—when it's her birthday."

That weekend, which was shortly after the bleeding thumb incident, I made a point of examining my surroundings as Nan took me through the gloomy rooms leading to the garden. Through an archway, I recognized the white kitchen door off to one side where Mr Churchman kept his plasters (it was the room with the frosted glass window that looked out onto the patio). I remembered that there had been a second window, on the other side of the patio door. And, sure enough, there was another archway, this one draped with a dark velvet curtain. I knew there must be a second room behind that, too. A room I had never been in. The room with the blacked-out window.

I asked Nan what lay beyond the curtain.

"That's the chapel of rest, Jim," she said quietly.

I had never heard the phrase before but its meaning seemed obvious. "Do people sleep in there?" I asked.

Nan laughed, her bright blue eyes twinkling mischievously behind her pebble glasses. "Yes, dear. I suppose they do. So, best be quiet, eh?" She put her finger to her lips and I copied her, smiling at the thought of poor old Mr Churchman (I assumed he was old, I had never seen him) snoozing the weekend away in his curtained bedchamber, occasionally venturing out to make himself some tea and plaster his fingers in his pristine little kitchen opposite.

Thanks to the high walls, the garden was shrouded in gloom all year round. That day, although the heat intensified as the summer day progressed, the cloistered enclave seemed even darker than usual. And quiet. Usually, I could hear the traffic from the nearby main road. As morning gave way to afternoon, I became increasingly unnerved by the silence, which was broken only by the shuffling of Nan's feet and the snip of her secateurs.

My initial amusement at the idea of someone being asleep behind the blackened glass gave way to mounting unease. I took special care when collecting the dead flowers not to make any noise—and not to prick my thumb. I had a sickening feeling that if I cut myself Nan would plop her keys into my hand and send me indoors alone, where the mysterious Mr Churchman would be creeping about in the dark. I dreaded the prospect of seeing him lurking there in the shadows, all dressed up in antiquated nightwear. I couldn't shake the feeling that he would somehow be sepia-tinted and as wrinkly as a tortoise, like Nan's grandmother.

I stayed beside Nan for the whole hour, prompting her to snap more than once that I was getting under her blessed feet. I kept picturing Mr Churchman standing at the back door in a stripy nightshirt and pointy hat, a Scrooge-like sneer on his crinkled jowls, trapping us in that bleak oblong strip of brick and concrete and stinking hydrangeas. Even his absence from the doorway was no comfort, for I suspected that he was watching us through the blackened glass of his bedroom—his chapel of rest.

Nan kept swiping her brow and complaining that "it was close." She only meant that the weather was hot and muggy, but the phrase unsettled me nonetheless. I followed her gaze up the dank walls, all the way to the rumbling grey sky.

"We'll call it a day soon," she said. "Looks like it's coming on to rain."

I hoped the distant thunder wouldn't wake Mr Churchman.

So preoccupied was I with my dread of the legendary proprietor that I barely noticed when Nan took off her flowery apron and began wafting it about her face.

"Jim," she said. "Oh, Jim, it's so cussed hot. There's just no air today."

My first, selfish, thought was that she was going to ask me to go indoors and fetch her a glass of water. I began to formulate my excuses: I didn't know which key to use, I didn't know where Mr Churchman kept his drinking glasses.

Then, suddenly, she stumbled to her knees. She reached out a hand and it fell heavily upon my shoulder, pushing me down with her. Our faces drew level. Hers was the concrete grey of the paving slabs beneath us, and it glistened with a sheen of perspiration. She looked like a waxwork from Madame Tussauds, lifelike but not alive. We stayed like that for a few seconds, frozen in time, and then she said, "Oh, Jim," and fell sideways to the ground.

I knelt there, not knowing what to do or where to go. I briefly wondered if I should touch her body to find out if it would rise and fall with her breath (something else I had learned from Randall and Hopkirk), but I was afraid I would find it cold and still, so I kept my hands to myself. I half expected to see her spirit rise up like smoke, all clad in white like Marty.

As I dithered, heavy spots of rain started to smack down onto the parched patio.

I needed to do something.

I needed a grown-up.

Dad had said that Nan would live for ever. I held tight to that thought as I picked up the keys that had fallen from her apron pocket.

It was dark and cool indoors and the rain on my face and down my back quickly turned to ice water. To my left was the kitchen. It was too late to fetch Nan a drink so I turned to the right and pushed through the heavy velvet curtain. Behind it was a dark wood door bearing a plaque that said 'Chapel of Rest.'

No one answered my frantic knocking and my anxiety rose to fever pitch, heart throbbing the way it did when I ran pell-mell down Moreland Hill on the way home from school.

I needed Mr Churchman to wake up, to do whatever grown-ups do in situations like this. I craned my neck to try to see if Nan was moving, but there was no clear line of sight to the garden. I couldn't wait any longer. I hated Mr Churchman for his laziness and his deafness to my plight. I tried the brass handle. It rattled noisily but the door refused to budge so I spread out Nan's keys on the floor. I was a smart cookie as a kid. Amid the silver and rust-coloured keys, there was a single gold-coloured one that seemed a good match for the handle. I jumped up and used it.

The room was humid and airless. When my eyes adjusted to the smothering darkness, I could make out two matching white vases on mahogany stands on opposite sides of the furthest corners of the room. They were the only bright objects in there and they seemed to radiate an almost lunar glow. The drooping hydrangeas they contained were on their last legs; faded mauve-brown petals littered the carpet all around them. Their bitter stench instantly tightened my throat.

But the flowers were not the only smell.

Once, my friends and I had found a dead cat in an abandoned factory we sometimes played in. It had a thin rope pulled tight around its neck. Someone had murdered it. A colony of white maggots had set up home in its squashed, eyeless skull. When we nudged the body gingerly with our toes, an incredible stench wafted up and made us retch. Mr Churchman's dingy little bedroom bore the same underlying reek of rottenness that the sharp tang of dying flowers couldn't quite conceal.

The only window was the one that looked onto the patio and it was covered by a brief velvet curtain with gold tassels matching the one that had concealed the door. From what I could make out in the shadows, Mr Churchman's bed seemed to be incongruously planted in the very centre of the small room.

I thought about fumbling along the walls for a switch, but then remembered how frightening it can be when someone bursts into your bedroom and slaps on the light while you are sleeping. The thought of a toothless old man leaping out of bed, shrieking with terror, horrified me.

I whispered, "Mr Churchman?"

The quiet was appalling. I could hear my ankles crack as I shifted my weight from one foot to the other. And could I also hear a soft whimpering cry from outside? I held my breath and listened. Nothing.

"Mr Churchman," I said out loud. "Mr Churchman, something's wrong with my nan."

Silence.

Venturing further into the room, and into a fug of rotting-cat smell, I could see that the bed was raised on some sort of frame, like a cot. Except, instead of bars, this cot had solid, raised sides.

It puzzled me why a grown-up would sleep in a bed designed for babies. It disturbed me too. I had visions of a crippled, skeletal man, his torso wrapped in a stained nappy, burbling incoherently like I had once seen in a TV documentary about senility. That programme had given me nightmares for weeks afterwards. Suddenly, I didn't want Mr Churchman to wake up at all.

Maybe I could fix Nan myself, after all. Maybe all she needed was that glass of water that I hadn't wanted to get her.

I turned my back on the stinking room and padded across the hallway, making a conscious effort to avoid looking out into the garden on the way.

Gaining entry to the kitchen was more difficult than getting into the chapel of rest. I had to try three different bright silver keys before the door finally popped open. It smelled vaguely antiseptic in there, not like any other kitchen I knew. It was, I decided, more like the smell of the dentist's surgery. In fact, with its stark white décor, it looked a bit like the dentist's too. Even so, beneath it all there was that underlying smell of decay, just like the other room.

To get to the sink I had to navigate my way around the long steel table. This time, it was covered with a lumpy white tablecloth. At the far end of the sheet, a pair of bare feet were sticking out. My breath caught in my throat. Who on earth would sleep on a kitchen table?

The answer quickly bubbled up inside my head: someone with really bad brains.

I didn't know what such a person would look like or what they might do to me but I knew I didn't want to be in that room any more than I had wanted to be in the chapel of rest.

Just as I reached the sink, bright light flashed through the frosted window, and a glass cabinet full of white enamel trays and glistening chrome instruments rattled as the sky boomed overhead.

The last thing I wanted was for Mr Churchman to wake up now and come stumbling, bleary-eyed out of his darkened chamber like an ogre yelling fee-fi-fo-fum. Then, as the thunder subsided, a gurgling, gasping sound erupted from the hallway beyond the door.

Mr Churchman's stinking bedroom was a matter of feet away and it would take him no time at all to reach me, no matter how tired he was or how bad his brains were. Unless I acted quickly, I would be trapped in the too-white kitchen with both him and the barefoot sleeper under the sheet.

All thoughts of fetching a drink for my nan were banished by the rush of terror that was coursing through my veins. My only goal now was to get out of the place altogether and beg for help from the nearest grown-up passer-by, preferably one with good brains.

My legs wobbled like they were made of rubber. In my panic to escape I crashed into the metal table. It went gliding across the tiled floor towards the glass cabinet like a rogue supermarket trolley. Mr Churchman might already be angry with me for waking him up but how much angrier would he be if he knew I had broken things in his kitchen? And what would the person sleeping on the table-on-wheels do?

I snatched at it to try to halt its progress but I failed miserably and it went smashing into the cabinet. Shards of glass cascaded noisily onto the linoleum floor.

I had, however, succeeded in ripping the sheet away from the body it had concealed. It was a woman. She was naked and had a big, ugly zipper running from her private parts all the way up to the centre of her chest. Her eyes were closed and she was a bruised yellow colour.

I was only nine but *Randall and Hopkirk (Deceased)* had taught me a few things about the adult world. There were, I knew, some very scary people out there; people who killed other people, people who stole children and 'did things' to them. It was all right for Marty; he was a ghost so nothing much bad could happen to him. But for the rest of us, the world could be a perilous place.

Only someone very scary indeed would keep a dead body in their kitchen, I decided.

In addition to the splinters of glass, the table had spilled a chrome tray full of knives and saws out of the cabinet. They looked like the kind of weapons I had seen in a display at the Imperial War Museum about the trenches in World War One. I scooped up the largest blade I could see. It had a wicked-looking zigzag edge.

The heavens thundered again and a large, misshapen shadow twitched across the kitchen doorway. Then a pale hand slapped clumsily against the wall. It was followed by a face. But the face didn't belong to the mysterious Mr Churchman. It was Nan's. Except, her features looked different now, wrong. Her cheery, kindly appearance was contorted, hanging low on one side, like my Action Man after I had left him too close to the electric fire.

She came towards me, staggering, one leg not wanting to move in time with the other; one hand swaying freely at her side like it wasn't connected to her anymore. I squeezed the knife in my fist, as though it were a talisman that could somehow make all the scary things go away if only I wished hard enough.

"Nan?" I said. "Nan! Stop it, you're frightening me!"

My pleas were met with an inhuman gibbering from a toothless maw that dripped a thick string of saliva onto the floor. The lack of teeth made her face look caved in, like a crumpled paper bag. This couldn't be Nan, of course. Nan had a perfect set of pearly-white gnashers. I grabbed at the table, using it—and the naked corpse lying upon it—as a shield.

But the lopsided shape wobbled into the room and wrenched the barrier aside with its good hand, gurgling madly as it advanced upon me.

My fist was locked so tightly around the sawblade by then that I couldn't have dropped it even if I had wanted to. But if the creature had said something at that point, spoken in a voice I recognized, I would have known it was truly Nan and not some oozing plastic puppet-monster. I would have stayed my hand; of that, I'm sure. But all that came out of her sagging collapsed mouth was a dribbled, inhuman moan as she reached for me, and I knew that I had no choice.

Bad brains, I thought. *Very bad brains*. And, in a way, I was right.

The Voice of the Fly

He didn't need a piss, a shit or a wank, so there was only one thing for Charlie Fry to do. He squatted, pressed his right nostril and snorted.

Some of the housemates missed life's simple, private pleasures like sleeping late, watching football or gorging on junk food. Most missed their family and friends. All of them found it hard to cope without their mobile phones. Charlie could survive without all that. But he had been anticipating this reunion with his Colombian mistress since the morning of day one, twenty-four long months ago.

Someone had burned the seat with a cigarette. *Filthy habit*, he thought. He rallied the coke into shape with a fingertip and inhaled the dregs. "Waste not, want not," he said and closed his eyes, shutting out the image of himself hunched over a toilet in the nether regions of a disused army barracks somewhere in Eastern Europe.

The outer door swished open, letting in some loud music he didn't recognise; something that had been a hit with all the hepcats in Stalingrad (or wherever he was) while he had been incarcerated in a spartan, faux apartment through two long hot summers.

He sat for a moment, relishing the sensation of the coke burning its bright path of unholy goodness through his senses. The door swished shut, blotting out all but the thumping bassline. Alone again.

His brain was effervescing inside his skull. Suddenly, everything seemed more vibrant, tangible, as though life without coke was but a pale imitation of the real thing. He sniffed, rubbed his nose and lurched to his feet.

The cubicle shrivelled around him. It was quickly becoming so impossibly small that it seemed to press the air from his lungs. Gasping, he burst out of the shrinking trap and was suddenly confronted by his own reflection. He stared back at himself. He could feel the coke coursing through every inch of his body as though it were a fizzing trail of gunpowder lighting up a darkened cellar just before the barrel blows. "Shit," he groaned. "This is the good stuff, Ivan!"

The mirror above the row of sinks was vast. It made the bleak, narrow washroom seem ten times wider. As he gazed into it, he fancied he could almost hear the chirpy Scouse tones that he had come to know as the Voice of the Fly.

Buzz, buzz, Charlie. The Fly saw you sniffing happy powder in the shitter, you naughty little champ, you.

Charlie laughed aloud and tried out a couple of winning smiles. "Ready for my close-up, Mr De Mille?" His voice echoed loudly off the cracked white tiles. He added to the hellish noise by chuckling. It sounded like a gaggle of geese was following him as he swaggered to the door.

There was no handle.

Buzz, buzz. Oh dear, what can the matter be? Charlie pushed at the door. It didn't budge. *Charlie Fry got stuck in the lavat'ry.* He observed the door swimming insolently in front of him. It was ocean-blue. And burnished gold. And ruby red. The colours changed as he squinted at it from various angles. *He was there from Monday to Saturday.* Charlie strained for greater lucidity, and then for less lucidity, but the handle steadfastly refused to appear. *Nobody knew he was there.*

"You cheeky bastards," he hissed.

*

It was a UK record, Miffy had spluttered repeatedly throughout his interview. God alone knew how she kept her plum job at the helm of TV's biggest show. Perhaps it was because the programme effectively ran itself; round-the-clock footage, streamed live over the internet, of eleven wannabes making

313

complete asses of themselves in a bid to win TV's most sought-after title: The World's Longest-running Reality Show.

Speculation among the housemates about their exact location was necessarily restricted by their general ignorance about geography.

"I reckon it's Transylvania," Davey Cremona had once said. "That's where vampires come from." The other housemates agreed that Transylvania would be kind of cool but some doubted it was a real place.

Miffy had tried to set Charlie right as they prepared for the post-show wash-up broadcast. Sorry, but it definitely wasn't anywhere as interesting as Transylvania. After a couple of false starts she gave up trying to pronounce the name of the nearest town but, she said, it began with a K and ended in 'itchy'. They had a McDonald's, she added with wide-eyed astonishment.

Charlie's blank look was met with a terse intervention from a locally-bred girl who was pummelling his face with orange gloop. Charlie thought she looked like she'd have been more comfortable toting a Kalashnikov than a powder puff.

"Is between Donetsk and Pinsk," she said.

To Charlie, they sounded just as made-up as Transylvania. All he knew was that it meant there was no cheering crowd to hail his triumphant exit; no live audience to ooh and aah as Miffy stammered her way through a sterile interview in an empty makeshift studio.

"This is weird," Charlie had said as he settled into the hot seat opposite Miffy. "It's kind of dead here."

Miffy assured him that the fans back home were all eagerly watching a live stream and were tweeting like canaries on speed.

"I was expecting real people," said Charlie. "Lots of them."

"Oh, they're real, all right," laughed Miffy. "And there's millions watching. Just wave at the camera. They'll love it!" She demonstrated by flapping her hands and making cooing noises towards the lens of the sole camera in the studio.

Charlie looked at the camera. And then looked away.

Miffy Vanderbilt, former children's presenter, had blotted her copybook on live TV some years earlier. Her left tit (the one with a tattoo of Elvis milking the nipple) had somehow made an unscheduled appearance while she was building Tracy Island out of egg cartons for disabled children. Incredibly, the wardrobe malfunction didn't entirely kill off her career. Shunted unceremoniously into the grown-up schedule, she had then giggled and slurred her way through the most excruciating sixty minutes in television history as the host of one of Britain's most prestigious music awards, until she was eventually dragged screaming from the podium to sleep it off in the green room. Miffy was the reigning queen of train wreck TV and Charlie guessed that she was hired for this job as much for her own potential entertainment value as for her end-of-the-line price tag.

But, to Charlie's amazement, the unpredictable Ms Vanderbilt had retained some degree of professionalism tonight. At least, she had deftly avoided dwelling upon the reason why Charlie had been alone for the final stretch of the marathon reality show. He supposed the audience back home didn't need to be filled in. Everyone knew.

The Night Owls, those insomniac fans who watched the housemates as they snored, sobbed and screwed their way through the small hours, had been privy to a unique broadcasting experience. In the dead of night, a select demographic slice of Britain had watched as viewers' favourite, Davey Cremona, tottered unsteadily into the bathroom, fluttered his fingertips at the camera poised above the shower, and smartly drew a razor blade across his throat. The cut was deep and wide, and shown in glorious high definition (for those who had paid the appropriate subscription fee).

It was three in the morning, year two, February 15th. The skeleton crew steering the show through the watches of night were asleep at the wheel. Thousands of viewers phoned in, complaining at the poor taste of the gag. But most just sat and stared as Davey bled out onto the bathroom floor, neither knowing nor caring if it was real or fake; unable, or unwilling, to tell the difference.

It was a full six minutes before the live feed from the bathroom was cut. Or, rather, switched. The company had invested a considerable sum in pursuing its quest to become the first to stage a two-year-long hidden camera show. It wasn't about to jeopardise its shot at the title by going to black. No. The screens were suddenly filled with Charlie, still peacefully, obliviously, asleep in the bedroom he had been sharing with Davey Cremona; just the two of them since the departure of housemate number 11. At least, Charlie was asleep until the commotion of the production crew bursting into the house through a concealed panel woke him from his slumber.

The audience that had just witnessed Davey's death, could now enjoy Charlie Fry's reaction to Davey's death.

Standard procedure for intervention situations was instigated. That meant lockdown. Charlie was confined to the bedroom. The nation saw him wake up, confused and irritated by the sound of crackling radios and clumping boots, his eyes glowing night-vision green in the darkness. They watched him stagger about comically, cursing as he tangled himself in his bedding. They watched him call out and ask Davey what the fuck he was up to at this time of night.

Then Charlie was granted light. And the Voice of the Fly informed him of an 'incident'. He wasn't to worry. He was to carry on as normal. Charlie asked what normal was. The Fly didn't answer.

Nevertheless, Charlie followed the advice as best he could, his unease slightly assuaged by the knowledge that with Davey out of the equation, he was already the show's winner.

All he had to do to scoop the £1 million prize was to stay in the house for ten more months until New Year's Eve. Alone. Well, alone save for the invisible presence of an entire production crew lurking behind the walls.

*

He had envisaged being greeted by roaring crowds waving banners that proclaimed: 'WE ♥ CHARLIE FRY'; screaming admirers who would drown out the tedious post-show chitchat with their hysterical fan shrieks. And he had expected to celebrate his historic victory with a massive drug-fuelled blowout. He was itching to drink and snort his new-found freedom right up to the hilt. Perhaps a quick knee-trembler with some stray, starstruck Slavic totty was on the cards?

But it turned out that the show wasn't even broadcast in whatever snowbound Cold War relic of a country this was. He was still a nobody here. And now he was stranded in a stinking toilet, waiting for some ex-KGB mafioso to need a piss and let him out so that he could shuffle back to an aftershow gathering that had more in common with a wake than a rave.

He should have known the night would turn out shit. The modest basement function room was more like a 1950s village hall than the former officers' mess Miffy insisted it actually was. Windowless panzer-grey walls stretched narrowly all the way to an austerity-era bar that boasted a handful of unpronounceable foreign beers and dusty bottles of unfathomable spirits. The food was cold and oily, and the music reminded him of Eurovision. Charlie had rapidly reached the conclusion that wherever he was, they must still have rationing and the kids probably listened to the fucking Beatles under their bedsheets.

His erstwhile companions from the house—a.k.a. the losers—were absent from the party and Miffy was the only real celeb present. Charlie guessed the TV company had deemed it insensitive to have a full-blooded, A-list hoedown with Davey Cremona still warm in his grave. Or maybe they just wanted to save a few bob. After all, parsimony seemed to be the watchword for the whole production. It was the reason why this prime-time British TV show had been produced abroad, within striking distance of a war zone, and presumably why they had hired Squiffy Miffy to host it, instead of Davina or someone else who could read a cue card without reaching for liquid support.

The house in which the wannabe reality TV stars had languished was, they were told, an old army base. The crew were all native to the former Soviet Republic of Going-Insania (or something like that); at least, all except Miffy and the never-seen Voice of the Fly. The latter, a laconic Scouser with a dry sense of humour, delivered their daily challenges, admonished them and consoled them, and was their only link to the outside world for much of the past two years.

"You're a proper celebrity," Charlie said after he had endured thirty more agonising minutes of the so-called party. "People recognise you, don't they? In the street, I mean."

Miffy smiled. "Well, I don't know..."

"No false modesty, please, Miffy," insisted Charlie.

Miffy nodded briskly, like a hen pecking corn. "Yes, I suppose I'm fairly well known."

Charlie suppressed the urge to add, *For all the wrong reasons.*

"Right," he said. "So, d'you reckon that face of yours could get me into whatever passes for a nightclub out here?" And then, into the silence he added, "Like, now."

Miffy sighed and collapsed her bird-like shoulders. "It's 2am, Charlie."

"I didn't ask you the fucking time!" he snapped.

Miffy swallowed and brushed her hair away from her ear. She did that often, Charlie had noticed. It seemed to be more a nervous tic than vanity. Either way, it was very bloody annoying.

"Sorry," he sighed, "I didn't—" he began, and then realised he couldn't finish the sentence without lying. He had meant what he said. He was bored, she was retarded and he wanted some action; *needed* some action. "Shitting hell, it's New Year's Eve and it's the climax of the biggest fucking show in TV history. You'd think the company could have made it a bit more... well, special. A bit more exciting. A bit more—" Charlie sputtered impotently and waved his hands in the air as if sculpting something large and frilly that he couldn't quite articulate.

Miffy shrank into herself and said, "I'm sorry, Charlie. It's the budget." She looked over her shoulder to see if she could be overheard and then leaned in to him. "Between you and me, things didn't quite pan out the way we'd hoped. *Financially*."

Charlie followed her gaze. There were six tables arranged around the four sides of the room. Barrel-chested Bond villains were dourly throwing shots of clear liquid down their thick necks. He guessed they got paid whether the show bombed or not. Their compatriots, the tracksuited crew, were all sitting in silence, picking cautiously at little plates of pickled vegetables or sipping demurely from tiny green bottles of beer. Across to their left, a clutch of British TV executives hurriedly tapped their phones, each man an island of concentrated silence.

Miffy was sucking something pink up a straw.

"But we had fans, didn't we?"

Miffy wiped lipstick off the tip of the straw and shrugged. "There's a world of difference between having a fanbase and being successful, Charlie. You probably don't know this but things have really changed while—"

"While I've been gone?"

"While the show's been on air," said Miffy. "The audience just expects more."

"More *what*, for Chrissake? We all made fools of ourselves; we got drunk, we fought, we fucked. Jesus, they even watched someone die, didn't they?"

"Most of them didn't see that. They read about it next morning."

"Yeah, I bet that really put a crimp in their day: investing all that viewing time and then missing the big payoff while they slept. While *I* fucking slept!"

Miffy reached out and touched his arm. "Don't, Charlie," she said.

A cold realisation began to grow inside him, like a frozen fist trying to punch its way out of his stomach. He pulled away from her touch. "That's it, isn't it?" he said. "The show died with Davey. The rest of it was an anticlimax, a disappointment. I wasn't entertaining enough all by myself."

Miffy stirred the murky pink liquid in her glass. "The viewers loved Davey. They still love him. He's become an icon." Her eyes glistened. "There are even Davey Cremona T-shirts. You know, that goofy face he used to pull?"

Charlie stared at her. He could feel bile rising in his throat. He wanted to puke it up all over the bitch.

Miffy broke eye contact and sniffed. Her wistful smile faded and died. "You have your fans too," she said, stabbing at the dregs of ice at the bottom of her glass with the straw. "People still follow you, still want to watch you."

"Really? What bloody fans? Where is everyone?"

"You'll see, Charlie. They love you. After all, you are the winner. And everyone loves a winner, right?"

Charlie slammed down his empty beer bottle and pushed his chair back. "Fuck this, I'm getting another drink. A proper one." He felt her baffled stare drilling into him as he wove his way to the bar through the rapid pulse of another Euro hit.

It was while Charlie was peering myopically at the backwards writing on the bottles, straining to find something that looked vaguely palatable, that the barman had salvaged the night.

"Congratulations, my friend," he said with a wink. The man behind the stained counter was a stringy fellow with veiny eyes, and the simple act of winking had squirted a single yellow tear down his cheek like a rancid little waterfall.

Charlie watched its progress, sickened and mesmerised in equal measure.

"How much you win?"

"Sorry?"

"*The prize*, Charlie Fry. How much you win?"

The prize. Charlie laughed. He had almost forgotten the jackpot he stood to collect. "A million," he said. "A cool million pounds."

The barman reached out to clasp Charlie's hands and said something that sounded like a sneeze but probably meant something congratulatory. When he released his bony grip, Charlie found that he had placed a small clingfilm wrap in his palm.

He had briefly wondered if he should offer to pay the pus-eyed barman for the coke, except he had no money to give him. In any case, on reflection, he decided that a cash transaction would be crass. Charlie was pretty sure that other celebs didn't fork out for their own nose candy; it came out of the overheads or something. So he simply nodded his thanks. The barman had smiled and wiped his cheek, his interaction with Charlie Fry apparently payment enough.

So this was fame. Screw the stupid show and the grim party. He had a shitload of cash coming his way that would make his life on the outside a hell of a lot easier. Maybe things weren't so bad after all. He drifted out of the function room and along a gloomy, narrow corridor to the washrooms, wondering if they were making T-shirts with his face on.

*

When he was a kid, his mother kept a small, black pan in the kitchen. A skillet, she called it. It weighed a ton and it stank like molten metal whenever she put it on the stove. The stench used to fill his nostrils and tighten his throat, deterring Charlie from eating anything she ever cooked in it.

The night Davey Cremona died, the house had smelled like that skillet. Charlie fancied he could smell it now, right here in the washroom, underlying the mingled fragrances of cheesy dicks and bowel movements: burnt iron.

His heart was pounding out a high tempo syncopation behind his ribcage which easily outpaced the muffled disco beat from outside that was grinding away in the pit of his stomach. The discordant arrhythmia was making him feel queasy. His vision started to pixelate. He leaned on the sink and took a deep breath, sucking in the foul-smelling air. The stench of blood, rich and soupy, caught in his throat. Somewhere, something dripped, languid and viscous.

He pushed himself away from the sink. One by one, he toed open the three remaining stalls, holding on to the frames to steady himself. But inside the cubicles there was nothing except cracked porcelain spattered with dried shit, like scatological Jackson Pollocks.

As he was gazing at a bowl full of caked excrement, the white-walled room shifted on its axis, like a ship suddenly pulling hard to starboard. Charlie snatched at the doorframe to steady himself. "Shit, Ivan. What was in that fucking wrap?"

The room took a 90-degree turn at the far end, beyond the washbasins. The dripping noise convinced him there was someone lurking there in the shadows. A mountain troll shaking the drips from an unfeasibly large cock, perhaps. Keeping his balance on the suddenly undulating floor by sliding his hands along the wall, he went to take a look.

Lit by a bank of windows was a long, tarnished steel trough that occupied the final stretch of the room. A lake of piss filled it to the brim. Beneath the urinal, oily puddles shimmered under the white strip-lighting.

No troll; no monstrous penis.

Buzz, buzz, Charlie. All alone again?

"Fuck off," he hissed. His voice clanged hollowly around the room.

Legs splayed matelot-style to ward off any further change in tack, he marched back to the entrance and tried to jemmy his fingers into the slender gap between the door and the frame. He clawed furiously and watched his nails curl up and peel away from his fingertips to reveal the glistening pink flesh beneath. He knew that ripping your nails out should hurt like hell, but he could feel nothing.

"Good," he muttered. "I don't fancy pain right now. Just pleasure. Pure unadulterated fucking pleasure."

His desperate hands skidded about like big red spiders on a skating rink, but the door failed to budge. He thumped it, fists splashing in his own blood. "Hey, open up, you bastards!"

Nothing.

He took a step back from the door and kicked it. He kept on kicking, his blows becoming harder and harder, until he could no longer feel his feet and he was out of breath. Then he tumbled sideways down the wall, suddenly breathless.

He glared up at the mirror. "I know what you're playing at. You think I'm stupid or something?" In between his fevered gasps he could hear a thrumming noise, muffled and soft like a butterfly beating its powdered wings inside a jar. It was a noise he had become familiar with during his time in the house.

They thought they were oh so quiet, the cameramen and sound guys. But in those long stretches of night, Charlie could hear the whisper of stockinged feet and the whir and click of machinery as the crew tracked his every move, his every breath, from behind the walls of the house.

Charlie stared up at the mirror. The mirror stared back. During his time in the house he had developed the theory that if he watched the mirrors for long enough, the crew lurking behind them would eventually give themselves away. He decided to put the notion to the test now. He staggered to his feet and fixed the mirror with a beady eye. He had to look deep into the glass, past the reflections on the surface but, sooner or later, a light, a shadow, would reveal their presence as plainly as if they were right there in the room with him. Which, in a way, they were.

Buzz, buzz, Charlie. We can play statues, too.

"No, no you can't, you see? You have to change shifts, go home to your wives and families. You have to eat, drink. Me, I don't need anything. I can stay here watching you for ever." He leaned on the sink and watched.

The mirror, brown-speckled with age at the edges, sheeted with grease stains and a thin layer of dust, showed him the four blue cubicle doors and the water-stained ceiling. But he knew there was life beyond the reflection. He just had to look for it.

Ten minutes passed. Or maybe an hour. After a very short while, the concept of morning, noon and night had become meaningless to the housemates. No clocks or watches were permitted. It was morning whenever the Voice woke them. It was night whenever the Voice switched out the lights.

The mirror throbbed and swelled. It was almost imperceptible but Charlie could see it. And then he finally saw movement too; a shape lurking just beyond the surface—large, bulbous and emerald-black. Something was pushing from the other side. Something with multi-coloured orbs for eyes that glittered like a mosaic made from shards of broken glass. Something that wanted to come out.

Buzz, buzz, Charlie. What are you looking at?

"You! I'm looking at you!"

Slowly, so as to keep the quivering, translucent vision in focus, Charlie leaned in towards the mirror. Beyond the image of his own pallid face and the washroom behind him, held in each piece of the fragmented eyes, were the faces of the audience. In their thousands, they smiled, sneered, laughed, cried, and yawned. Miffy was right. They still wanted to watch him.

"I see you!" he said. "I see all of you!"

In reply, the giant, iridescent eyes shimmered with rapturous applause.

Buzz, buzz, Charlie. Welcome back! How will you entertain us tonight?

The smell of the skillet was becoming stronger. Melting copper; boiling mercury. The dripping sound—lazy, gelatinous splashes—was becoming louder.

His lips felt gummy and warm. That wasn't right.

Charlie's focus shifted from the Fly behind the glass to the reflection of his own face. The mirror showed him a stream of bright claret washing over his mouth and chin and down his shirt front; an oozing tide of blood.

"The coke!" he said, putting a hand to his nose. "You spiked the coke, didn't you?" He licked his fingers. He had tasted cocaine often enough to know that the bitter powder on his tongue was not the mouth-numbing residue of Medellin's most famous export. He spat at the mirror, spraying it with dozens of cherry-red droplets. "Do you want me to die, is that it? Like Davey?"

Buzz, buzz, Charlie. We gave Davey what he wanted: adulation. You like adulation, too, don't you?

"No!" shrieked Charlie, lunging at the glass with both fists. The mirror shook and the image of the Fly lurking pregnantly inside it wavered as though through a heat haze. "Fuck you! Fuck you all!" He snatched up an aluminium bin from beside the door and crashed it against the mirror. The glass shattered into thousands of dagger-like pieces and rained down into the ceramic washbasins with an ear-splitting cacophony.

Charlie stared at the grimy blank space where the mirror had been. A bare wall stared back at him. No wires, no cameras.

No Fly.

Behind him, the main door creaked on its hinges and music pulsed into the room again.

"Charlie? Jesus, Charlie, what happened?" Miffy was framed in the doorway.

"Move along," he gasped. "Nothing to see here."

"Are you all right? You look... I mean, there's blood." Miffy held the door ajar. The fuzzy baseline percolated in from the bar and muffled her voice. It sounded like she was being smothered with a pillow.

Charlie wiped a sticky red smear from his mouth, followed her gaze to the wall, then down into one of the sinks, where something skittered blackly.

Buzz, buzz, Charlie.

"So," he said breezily. "What kind of a name is Miffy, anyway?"

She shook her head, wrong-footed by his non sequitur response. "Uh, I know, ditzy isn't it? It's short for Myfanwy. Just between the two of us, I hate it."

"Just between the two of us, eh?"

"Yeah," she said. "The suits thought you'd bailed on us to go looking for a nightclub. They've been scouring the neighbourhood, silly sods. I knew better. I knew you wouldn't blow us out. Besides," she added with a wink, "I had a tip-off from the barman."

"It wanted... *They* wanted me to put on a show for them. Something unforgettable. Like Davey," said Charlie. "The audience, I mean."

"What audience, Charlie? There's no one here." She flapped her free hand at something in the air. Charlie followed her eyes. In the nearest basin, a little black blob landed on the porcelain, twitched its wings with anticipation and then picked its way gingerly through a forest of broken glass until it reached a puddle of blood.

"Look, Charlie, now we're alone there's something you ought to know."

Charlie snorted. *Yes,* he thought, *there is a hell of a lot I ought to know.* And a lot he already knew. "OK, I'll play along. Surprise me."

Miffy let the door swish closed and then put her back against it. "It's about Davey," she said. There was a shiver in her voice and she wrapped her arms around herself.

"What about Davey?"

"The show was sued over his death. It's the reason why all this is so fucking shoddy. We've gone bust."

He could see her eyes wandering over his bloodied face and hands, her expression sour and uncomprehending. "Davey killed himself," he said. "How is that the show's fault?"

"Because of what happened in the Diary Room."

Charlie hadn't liked the Diary Room; a claustrophobic velvet closet where the housemates were grilled in isolation (save for the million or so viewers) by the Voice of the Fly.

You can tell me anything, said the Fly. *I can keep a secret.*

The Fly probed their innermost feelings, encouraged them to open up, show their emotions. To Charlie, it was like undergoing surgery while fully conscious.

"We knew Davey was feeling low," said Miffy.

"He always seemed happy enough. Life and soul, and all that."

"Do you remember the night he died?"

That was a classic Miffy question; both stupid and offensive. "Of course I fucking remember."

She scooped her hair behind her ear and pressed on. "You both had sessions in the Diary Room that evening. You said something..."

"I asked for some coke."

"That's right," said Miffy.

Charlie rubbed his itchy face. "Slowest delivery ever," he said in a *Comic Book Guy* voice.

Miffy didn't crack a smile. They both knew that the jokey request for drugs wasn't all that Charlie had discussed with the Fly that night.

Charlie, the Fly had said in a quiet, sincere voice, *the Fly knows about your problems on the outside.*

"What problems?" Charlie had laughed. "Not getting enough tail; that's my problem!"

Buzz, buzz, Charlie. The Fly knows about the gambling, about the debts and the drug deal that went wrong.

"I don't know what you're talking about," snorted Charlie. The Fly did not push further, instead allowing the silence to goad Charlie into further comment.

"I play the horses now and then. A bit of a flutter. Doesn't everyone?"

More silence.

"And the coke? To be honest, that's nothing. A misunderstanding."

A pause.

"Is that it? Can I go now?"

The Fly wants you to know that you're safe in the house, Charlie. The bad men can't get you in here.

Charlie had stared silently into the camera lens until the Fly bade him goodnight.

"The Fly told Davey—told the world—that Davey's long-time partner had left him," said Miffy. "Told him the reason, too: jealousy. Seems the guy didn't like the fact that Davey was cooped up in the house, sharing a bedroom with you, getting adored by millions. So the guy goes to the tabloids, tells all about their relationship, all the gory details, and publicly dumps Davey."

The little black blob buzzed excitedly and began slurping at the shore of a scarlet lake. The way it constantly jerked its head from one side to the other made Charlie think it looked nervous, shifty.

"He killed Davey's dog, too," added Miffy. "Revenge, I suppose."

"That's fucked up," said Charlie. "And the Fly told him all this?"

Miffy nodded.

"That's harsh."

"The family thought so too. They sued us. They said that we'd provoked Davey in order to get a reaction; that we knew he was fragile and we deliberately sent him over the edge to ramp up the ratings. The press were scathing, saying we had blood on our hands, calling on people to boycott the show. The great British public duly complied. I'm surprised we haven't been lynched. Thankfully, we're beyond reach out here. To be honest, I'm kind of dreading going back to England.

"The court delivered its findings this morning. They didn't pull any punches, said we were as guilty of killing Davey as if we had reached into the house and cut his throat ourselves. They were particularly hard on Malcolm McCardle."

Charlie shook his head. "Who?"

"The Voice of the Fly—the actor who played the part. He had to return to London for the verdict." She shook her head and her hair fell over her eyes. "Nobody even recognised him until he spoke."

This was bullshit. The Voice of the Fly had had been buzzing away at him all day. Charlie looked down at the nearest basin. It was filled with smashed glass and smeared with his own blood, but there was nothing else. No sign of movement.

"The evening news interviewed Malcolm on the steps of the courtroom straight afterwards," said Miffy. "They were broadcasting live, just shoved a mic at him and asked if he felt personally responsible. So he gave them an answer. He shot himself through the head." She looked at her watch. "That was about three hours ago."

Charlie's eyes searched the rest of the debris-strewn basins but the little fly was gone.

Miffy took a deep breath. "I'm sorry, Charlie, but it means they have no prize money to pay out."

"No, that's not true! It's a lie! The Fly's not dead. I can still hear him, still see him! I can see them all!" He picked up a shard of glass and Miffy flinched as he held it to her face. "Look! Look deep!"

Miffy tried to turn away, but with her back to the door, there was nowhere for her to retreat. Cornered, she reached up with both hands to fend off the slice of broken mirror. "Stop it, Charlie! You're scaring me!"

With his free hand, Charlie gripped her left wrist and pulled it aside.

Miffy yelped.

"They're all in here," he whispered "Millions of them. They're in his eyes. You just have to look." He pushed the glass closer to her face, her right hand unequal to the task of keeping it at bay.

"Charlie, please, you're hurting me!"

"You're not... looking... deeply enough."

"But it's all right, Charlie," said Miffy, still trying to squirm out of his grasp. "English law doesn't apply here. The money might be gone but they can't shut us down, you see? Even better, the show's being bought out by a big American company. That's what the bigwigs were here for tonight. They've got a proposal for you."

Charlie relaxed his grip. "Does it involve me getting paid for wasting two years of my life?"

Miffy nodded furiously. Her hair, now drenched with sweat, fell straggling over her face. She looked like a second-hand doll. "You'll get the full amount. One million. Guaranteed."

Charlie released her hand. She shrank into a corner and scraped the wet hair from her face.

"You're full of shit," he spat.

"No, really," she said, laughing and crying at the same time. "It's going to be OK. All you have to do is go back into the house. Tonight. Two more years, that's all. Then you'll be a millionaire." She scrubbed a muddy smear of black tears from her cheek and sniffed. "How does that sound, Charlie? Two more years. What do you say?"

"What do I say?" Charlie watched her panda eyes widen, specks of eyeliner smearing across the whites, as he pushed the glass dagger into her face and drew it down her throat. She struggled for breath, choking on a foaming river of her own blood. The shard snapped off as she dropped to the ground, leaving the razor-sharp stub in Charlie's crimson-gloved fist.

Miffy coughed uncontrollably and her fingers wrestled briefly, hopelessly, with the chunk of glass sticking out of her neck. Her blood pumped rhythmically for ten seconds, then the flow ebbed and her hands fell to her sides.

On the blank space on the wall, where the mirror had been, the little black fly scurried about, leaving tiny red footprints in its wake. It paused to lick its claws, cleaning off its blood feast entrée in preparation for the main course. Charlie held his breath and slowly moved his face close to the tiny creature. In its splintered eyes he could see them all, every one of them, as clear as day. He watched their reaction to his performance: excited, horrified, bored, amused, aroused. And could he hear them now, an ever increasing crescendo of adoration, like a tide rushing up a shingle beach?

Charlie Fry! Charlie Fry!

"What do I say?" repeated Charlie. "I say, buzz, buzz, buzz..."

Flesh and Blood

A handful of scrawny women and shrivelled men gazed mutely into the open grave as though they were staring into the abyss of their own fate.

The last funeral Linda had attended had been Richard's, eight years ago. That had been harder to bear and she scarcely remembered any of it now. This one was different; a smaller, quieter affair on account of the fact that this dearly departed had precious few friends and relatives left alive.

The vicar droned monotonously like a bee buzzing against a window. "Archibald, finally relieved of his suffering, leaves a devoted wife, Hilda..."

Had Uncle Archie been ill? If her mother had been there she might have asked her.

"I'm not standing next to that bloody woman," her mother had said. "You can represent me."

Linda thought it was a churlish gesture but she held her tongue, and represented.

The bloody woman in question now stood on the opposite side of the grave, covered from head to toe in black, complete with an impenetrable veil and matching lace gloves. She could have passed for the wife of an Arab oil sheikh rather than the widow of a Welsh shopkeeper.

"Ashes to ashes, dust to dust," continued the vicar, tonelessly.

Aunt Hilda remained immobile throughout the brief ceremony. When it was over, one of the funeral men eased her gingerly into the hired limousine as though she was a crippled blackbird. She spoke to no one, receiving the whispered condolences of Archie's meagre acquaintances with an almost imperceptible nod.

With the exception of Linda.

"You'll come and visit me, Linda," Hilda had said in a thin voice.

"Yes, I will, Auntie. Some time, I promise."

"You will come tomorrow. For tea. Like you used to."

It was not one of those insincere invitations that are politely offered in the expectation, or hope, that it will never be taken up. This, Linda understood, was an order.

*

For tea. Like you used to.

But that was a long time ago. Almost a lifetime ago.

When she was small, Linda's mother would take her to visit her sister and brother-in-law most weekends.

Linda had dreaded those visits.

Hilda and Archie were pleasant enough. They fussed over her, fed her huge slices of Victoria cake and Bakewell tart while they chatted about boring grown-up matters with her mother. The problem wasn't them. It was their house.

For Uncle Archie was a talented and prolific taxidermist.

His High Street premises, above which the couple lived, was filled to the ceiling with glass tombs containing the undead husks of countless creatures. Pride of place went to a virtual aviary where humdrum garden birds roosted alongside more exotic species such as scarlet-beaked lovebirds and jungle green parakeets. Linda found the towering necropolis both stunning and ghastly.

To her great discomfort, there was no escape from the stiff, beady-eyed corpses even in the living quarters upstairs. Lurking in every room, on every table and sideboard and mantelpiece, Archie displayed his personal favourites; the oddities and curiosities that were too precious—or too disturbing—for public consumption.

Beside the front room fireplace, a giant lizard was locked in permanent combat with a glistening albino cobra. Each time she visited, she wondered if she would find that one had finally bested the other, so realistic was their struggle, so determined were their expressions.

A grinning baboon, dressed in a red soldier's tunic and clutching a rusty cutlass, stood guard in the upstairs hallway. His name was Bertie and he was at least as tall as Linda. His dusty, knowing stare seemed to threaten myriad exotic horrors, and he haunted Linda's dreams for many years after the visits had suddenly stopped around the age of twelve.

Thereafter, Linda's mother bristled at the mention of Hilda's name.

"I don't know who she thinks she is, swanning around all dolled up like the Queen of Sheba," her mother once said when she caught sight of her from a distance in Woolworths some years ago. "She plasters on that make-up with a trowel— and at her age!"

The reason her mother gave for the rift was some disagreement about inheritance, but Linda suspected that it was in fact prompted by envy, for Hilda seemed to retain her comparatively youthful looks and sense of style well into her sixties.

"Not so hot now are we, Hilda?" murmured Linda as she watched the limousine drive away from the cemetery.

*

The switch-off and lock-up routine seemed to reinforce Linda's newfound solitude. The TV unplugged, she drifted from room to room, making sure that all the windows were firmly shut. The kitchen window she could only reach with some effort and she usually left that to Amber. Tonight she stretched over the sink and closed it herself. It could stay closed until Amber returned.

Was that everything? She mentally ticked off the jobs. Front door locked, TV off, windows shut. Yes, that was it.

She was safe and sound. She put a finger to her lips and then tapped the wedding photo in the hall. "Night, Richard," she whispered.

Amber wouldn't even be thinking of bed yet. She had probably gone out; forging new friendships, exploring new places in a new city far from home. For that matter, would she still think of this as home when she came back at the end of term? Or would it have devolved into 'Mum's house'—the place where she used to live, before university, before she broke away and embarked on her own life? Linda's throat tightened and for a fleeting moment she had the certain knowledge that she would never see her daughter again. She scrubbed her face with her hand and resolved to call Amber in the morning. Not checking up, she would say, just wondering how things were going.

Her bedroom was too dark with the door closed. She looked at the phone on her bedside table, dimly lit in green neon by the clock beside it. Perhaps Amber would ring before she turned in, just to say hello. Or goodnight. Or goodbye?

Hi, Mum, just thought I'd let you know I won't be needing you anymore. Got my own place and a new life up here. A grown-up life. Ciao, you're on your own now, Mum.

Linda sighed. It was going to be a long and sleepless night.

*

The phone woke her with a start. She snatched it up and blurted out, "Hello, who's that?" before she was even awake.

"'Sonly me." Amber's chirpy voice.

"Oh, hello, love," Linda croaked, hauling herself up to look at the clock: 8.35am. The bedclothes were in a confused tangle at the foot of the bed.

"Did I wake you up or something?"

It took Linda several seconds before she could put the call into context; before it dawned on her why her daughter was calling her when she only sleeps in the next room.

University. Empty house. Bad night.

Amber began to gabble about lectures, the clubs she had joined and the new people she had met, while Linda adjusted to the disorientation of being shocked awake.

And, by the way, she had met this "great guy." Apparently, he's always had a thing for redheads.

"Isn't that sweet?"

Linda agreed it was sweet.

And he had his own car.

"He even lets me drive it. How cool is that?"

There was a long moment of silence.

"Are you OK, Mum? You're really quiet."

"Yes, no. I'm fine." *I've spent the past eight years keeping you away from boys with a thing for redheads and flashy cars*, she thought, *only for you to dive straight in as soon as you're off the leash.*

She bit her lip before the words could tumble out. Amber was a shrewd judge of character. If she thought the boy was a good 'un, he was probably OK. They're not all knife-toting rapists. Are they?

She told Amber about the funeral, and how she had rashly agreed to go and see old Auntie Hilda the next day.

"I'm not in the mood for it," she said. "But I couldn't really say no."

"I can come down if you need moral support," said Amber. "I can be there in an hour if Rob lends me the car. I'd like to see the infamous Auntie Hilda before she kicks the bucket."

Linda understood that the offer was for her benefit, not for an obscure relative Amber had never even met. It was a nice gesture, said Linda, but there was no need for her to come down. She could manage on her own.

She didn't tell Amber that she would love to see her. And to have someone to hold onto as she ran the gauntlet of monstrosities lurking beyond Archie's shopfront.

*

336

She had put off the visit until late afternoon and now wished she had got the job over with when the sun was a little higher. If Hilda started talking about the old days it would be night time before she could get away.

The white on navy sign was as simple as it was stark: A.S. Yates Taxidermist.

Hilda's instructions had been explicit: "There are no yellow lines, so you can park right outside. But the shop is all locked up now. I've no use for it. You'll have to come in the back way."

Parking outside had turned out to be impossible. Someone had taken the prime spot in front of the shop, so she had to park a block away and walk back.

Linda peered into the shop window as she passed it. The gruesome display of dead birds still dominated the place. There were a few dogs and cats scattered around too, their simpering grins frozen in time. She wondered, not for the first time, how anyone could possibly want their home decorated with stuffed corpses. She wondered, too, if Bertie the bleary-eyed baboon was still standing sentinel somewhere beyond public view, waiting for her with his rusty blade.

The back gate led her through a small patch of unkempt garden to a large, pebble-dashed structure.

"Come in through the workshop," Hilda had said. "You remember the way, don't you?"

It had been thirty years since Archie had given her the grand tour of his 'skin factory', as he called it. It wasn't an experience she was ever likely to forget.

She opened the door and was instantly assailed by the smell of turpentine and linseed oil. And there was something else; another underlying odour pervaded the place. It had smelled like this before. It was the stink of dead things.

"Hilda? Are you in here?" She propped the door ajar with a ceramic container that was filled to the brim with a greasy-looking fluid.

Once her eyes adjusted to the dim light, she saw that the room was teeming with the curious paraphernalia of the taxidermist's art. In the centre was a workbench, about seven feet long by three feet wide. Fixed at one end was a large iron vice. At the other, sunk into the table's surface, was a large square of plate glass. Along the nearest wall stood two tall, deep wardrobes. One contained the desiccated carcasses of various unidentifiable animals; grey-brown, twisted things that might have been squirrels or foxes but most closely resembled generic roadkill. Work in progress, perhaps, that would never be completed. The other cabinet carried a range of tools and equipment: steel clippers, shears, broad-bladed knives with serrated edges, pins, nails and hammers. There were bottles and boxes, tubs of white glue and a cardboard box labelled 'Mothballs (naphthalene)', adding its own uniquely awful smell to the cloying reek of decay that insinuated itself into her nostrils.

Linda wafted a hand in front of her face in a vain attempt at clearing the air.

It was getting on for dusk and little natural light made its way through the filthy panes of glass in the doors at each end of the workshop. Here and there her passage was blocked by stone and glass jars on the floor where the skins of more unidentified creatures wallowed in foul-smelling chemicals. There was so much clutter that Linda had to take care navigating her way around in the deepening gloom.

She found a switch, flipped it, and a fluorescent strip-light buzzed on and off. Deep in the shadows created by the flashing light, Linda sensed movement. "Hilda? Is that you?"

The light fluttered, buzzed some more.

"Oh, for God's sake," hissed Linda.

She toggled the switch off and on, and glared up at the offending light in the hope that she could shame it into working.

Then the twitching snapshots suddenly revealed a crouching figure on top of a tall cabinet. "Jesus!" she yelped.

Mouth agape in a snarl, revealing a tangle of broken yellow teeth, and still dressed in his moth-eaten scarlet tunic, was Bertie the baboon. He leered down from his vantage point with an expression of pure hatred, as though poised to leap on Linda and gleefully slice her apart with his wickedly curved blade.

"It's all right, Linda," said an aged voice. "Old Bertie's long dead." A twisted little silhouette at the end of the room shuffled towards her. "You never did take to him, did you?"

"Hilda? Why didn't you answer me?"

"I had to be sure it was you and not some burglar. There have been a couple of break-ins, you see. They prey on the elderly."

Linda struggled to imagine anyone wanting to steal anything from this charnel house.

The fluorescent light stuttered one last time and finally failed, pitching the room into semi-darkness. There was a torch on the workbench nearby and Linda reached for it.

"No, Linda!" said Hilda.

Too late. The sickly yellow beam from the ancient torch found Hilda's face, or rather the featureless mask she was wearing. There were blood-crusted holes for eyes, a ragged flap of skin where her nostrils should have been and a broad grinning gash for a mouth.

She stood some ten feet away, hunched over slightly, pulling a floral dressing gown tight around herself. "I need you, my dear. Will you help your old Auntie Hilda?"

Linda's mind reeled. "What... uh... what's the matter, Hilda?"

And why on earth was she wearing that hideous Halloween mask?

"I've been a silly old fool," said Hilda. She motioned to the mask. Even through it, Linda could see the old woman was cringing with agony.

"I need a keener pair of eyes than these old things of mine; a steadier pair of hands, too. I need *you*, Linda."

"I don't understand," Linda said, although some suggestion of the implied horror was seeping through. "What is the mask for, Hilda?"

"This?" she said, one knotted brown hand waving vaguely at her head. "This is not a mask," she said. With that, Hilda opened her dressing gown and let it slip to the floor.

The torch cast a dull glow that barely reached to the end of the workshop. But it showed Linda everything. The old woman's head lowered and her naked, shrivelled chest began to hitch. She was sobbing silently. Dear Lord, what had she done to herself?

The vapours from the containers made Linda feel lightheaded and Hilda's ghastly image seemed to swim before her eyes.

"The torch, please," said Hilda.

Linda tilted the beam away from her.

"Your Uncle Archie worked in taxidermy for most of his adult life. It was a hobby, a profession and, I suppose, an obsession." She pointed towards the cabinet where Bertie the baboon stood frozen in time. "As you might recall, he sometimes chose unusual subject matter."

Every slight movement the old woman made was accompanied by a curious crunching sound, and elicited a groan of agony.

"Do you know how taxidermy is performed?" she asked.

Linda shook her head.

"It's a complex process but, in brief, one has to peel the skin from the subject and soak it in certain chemicals so as to preserve it."

Linda glanced down at the tangled animal skins congealing in vats of noxious fluid that took up much of the floor space.

"While the pelt is curing, one makes a cast of the skinless body. When both parts are ready, the skin is attached to a suitably posed frame. Sounds simple enough, doesn't it?"

Linda nodded. She was staring at Hilda in the shadows, watching the old woman's mouth work almost imperceptibly behind the stiff mask.

"But one of the major challenges faced by the taxidermist is that the skin tends to dry out, to split and break apart over time. Archie was determined to make his creations last a lifetime. He pushed the boundaries of the craft. Sometimes beyond his abilities. Often beyond reason."

The old woman took a deep, shuddering breath before she continued. "Twenty years ago Archie thought he had perfected a flawless tanning process. He believed he could treat a skin in such a way that it would remain supple indefinitely."

Linda shook her head. She had a sickening feeling that she knew what was coming next.

"I've always been a vain woman, Linda. I couldn't bear the idea of losing my looks. So I asked Archie to try it out on me. I thought I could stave off the ageing process. Archie resisted the idea for a long while. But I wore him down. He saw how unhappy I had become and, eventually, he relented.

"I dosed myself up with painkillers, took countless antibiotics and downed half a bottle of gin for good measure. I was good and numb when Archie took his skinning knife and peeled away the wrinkly old hide from my body." Hilda ran her crippled fists down the shiny leather of her torso. "I passed out, of course," she said. "Whether from the pain or from the cocktail of booze and drugs, I don't know. But it was for the best. With me asleep, Archie could perform his magic without my constant cries. Unfortunately, while I was unconscious, the painkillers wore off. When I woke up on the workshop bench several hours later, I could feel *everything*!"

341

Linda was sure she was going to be sick but she didn't dare take her eyes off the monstrous sight before her. "Where... did you get the skin?"

"Ah. There's the thing. I'm afraid it's all rather unpleasant. But I had no choice, Linda. You must see that."

"Where did you get it, Hilda?"

"From the cemetery."

"The *cemetery*? Jesus, Hilda, this is mad! Worse than mad!"

"Oh, don't be so precious," hissed Hilda. "It's a waste of good flesh to let it rot in the ground. The women who provided them didn't need their hides anymore."

"Women? Plural?"

Hilda sighed. "There were a few false starts, you see? Archie had never worked with human skin before, or upon a living model. It was a while before he perfected the technique."

Linda pictured the old couple crouched over freshly dug graves, armed with the tools of Archie's disgusting trade, slicing the flesh from naked corpses. She put her hand to her mouth, afraid that she would be sick if she heard any more.

"I'll grant you, Archie and I have been a little unconventional, perhaps even a little foolish. But I can assure you that even though my body is in a state of disrepair my mind is as sharp as a new pin. And it was worth it, Linda. The results were out of this world!" said Hilda. "Suddenly, at the age of 72, I had the face and body of a twenty-year old. I was Archie's finest work!

"Once I had learned to control the pain, I revelled in my new skin. I went out. To nightclubs. Can you believe that? I flirted with all the young men. With some, I did more than just flirt, if you catch my drift. No one suspected that I was a wrinkly old pensioner wrapped in a fresh coat of skin. It was wonderful—a second lease of life."

Then Hilda sighed, a rattling, sobbing sound of despair. "After five years things started to go wrong. My new skin began to dry, to tear. I had to hide myself away until I could acquire a fresh pelt."

A fresh pelt? "You're sick! You need help!" Linda shrieked.

Hilda ignored her protestations. "By then, Archie's dementia had rendered him useless to me. He couldn't perform the operation again."

"Jesus," breathed Linda. "And you've been here all this time? Like that? Just hiding away and... rotting?"

"That's not a nice word, dear. I've been keeping myself out of public view, true enough. But I haven't wasted my time. I've been experimenting," said Hilda. "I think I understand the process now. But I need an assistant. Only you can help me replace this"—she slapped at the withered leather skin at her sides—"this monstrosity."

Linda shook her head. "I can't do that, Hilda. I don't know how."

"Your hands, my expertise. Don't worry. I'll guide you through it," said Hilda.

Linda realised that the old woman had been planning this, had convinced herself that it was as straightforward and reasonable as swapping an old overcoat for a new one. "No, Hilda. No. You need a doctor, proper medical care. You're not—"

"Not what? Not sane? Is it any wonder? I've been confined to this abattoir, slowly decaying, these past five years. And the only person who could put things right was so senile that he couldn't tell the difference between his moth-eaten old exhibits and his own wife!"

"Hilda, please. Let me call an ambulance."

"There isn't a doctor alive who could do the job I need doing, who *would* do the job."

"But this is crazy, you must see that. And where on earth are you going to get a complete human skin from? I'm certainly not going to dig one out of the bloody graveyard for you, if that's what you think."

There was silence. Linda was sure that if she could make out anything beneath the ghoulish skin-mask Hilda wore, she would see that the old woman was smiling.

"You don't need to worry about that, my dear," said Hilda as she began limping towards her. Linda could smell her; a mixture of wet leather and spoiled meat.

"Just help me get out of this filthy old shell," Hilda rasped, holding one gnarled hand out to her niece to steady herself; in the other, she clutched a long-bladed knife. Linda recoiled as she felt the cool touch of dead skin upon her arm and turned her head away so that she could suck in some air that wasn't tainted with rot.

"Here," said Hilda, sliding a grimy pair of scissors across the workbench towards Linda. "Once you get started, it's like peeling an orange. If you do my legs while I work on the top, we'll be done in half the time."

Hilda began to cut into the brittle crust that encased her torso. The hardened skin popped as the blade chopped through it. Linda thought of the crackling on a roasted joint of pork. Each stroke revealed glimpses of glistening red tissue beneath. Every incision down her arms, beneath her breasts, discharged a fresh wave of the stomach-churning odour that was filling the workshop.

"Can you imagine the feeling of raw muscle grating, chafing constantly against this dried-out rind?" asked Hilda. The fevered tone of her voice almost suggested that she relished the discomfort.

As chunks of the crispy old flesh dropped away, Linda could see sticky white sinews stretching with the old woman's exertions.

"Come on, girl," snapped Hilda. "Get busy with those scissors. If they're too blunt, I think I've got some pruning shears somewhere."

Hilda balanced herself on the bench and ripped away at her legs, pausing now and then to swipe away the pale gunk

344

squishing out from the cuts at her groin with her newly de-fleshed hand. As the skin was peeled back to reveal knotted tendons and chalky peaks of bone, the stench of decay grew stronger. Oily brown fluids from deep within Hilda's carcass mingled with the infected pus and started to dribble down her legs to spatter onto the floor. The thick smell of infection was unbearable.

It's me. I'm her new skin. She's waiting for me to pass out and then she'll flay me alive!

Hilda had almost finished stripping her torso. Linda would have to pull herself together and do the face, she told her. She didn't want to go to all this trouble only to poke her own eyes out by accident.

Linda dug her fingernails into the palms of her hand, determined to remain conscious. She took the scissors from the workbench. "Where is the new skin coming from, Hilda?"

"Don't worry, dear. It isn't from a graveyard."

Linda gripped the scissors with both hands and pointed them at the old woman's face. "Where, then?"

Hilda stopped cutting and looked up at her niece. "I'll be honest. You were my first choice."

She reached down and tugged a blue rubber sheet from a large container at her feet. The box, made of wooden slats, was filled almost to the brim with an opaque liquid the colour of dishwater. To Linda, it resembled an old-fashioned laundry tub. And soaking in it was what could have been crumpled white bedsheets.

"But then I had a spot of luck. Good sheet of buckskin, this one. When we're finished, I'll look better than ever!" Hilda laughed as she made lazy circles in the greasy fluid with a stiff, mottled finger. "Did I mention that we have a problem with house-breaking around here?" she said, kicking the tub. "I caught this little swine snooping around the workshop this morning. Poetic justice, I call it. They came here to steal from me and I end up stealing from them."

345

Linda gazed into the swirling vat of skin and pictured Hilda gleefully peeling it from her victim just before she arrived this afternoon. She slumped to the floor beside the tub, still clutching the scissors, and realised that she had gone into shock. All around her, crusty sheets of leather littered the floor, dry and shiny on the outside, slick with blood and tainted secretions on the inside.

"Now then," said Hilda, setting her blade down on the workbench. "Let's take a look at my new pelt."

But Linda had lost her mind long before Aunt Hilda reached into the tub and pulled out the dripping skin with flaming red hair.

Still Life

The doorbell rings. Martin's heart lurches so high into his throat that he is sure he will puke it up. He has told himself a hundred times that it will not be like this. They will not ring his doorbell at a reasonably civilised hour (it was just four in the afternoon) and wait patiently for him to answer. It doesn't happen like this.

He puts down his brush and creeps to the door. Despite the little yellow notice provided by the neighbourhood watch, he still endures cold callers—double glazing salesmen mostly. And, on weekends, Jehovah's Witnesses come along and ask him if he would like to discuss the Ten Commandments. The yellow notice doesn't really cater for that contingency.

In any case, it doesn't apply to the police. He has seen enough cop shows to know that they can turn up any time and kick down your door if they have reason to suspect some kind of villainy. Or even if they don't have a reason.

He looks through the spyhole. The day is slowly being blotted out by shadows, as though it is losing consciousness, but he can see that it is a woman. She seems innocuous enough. Not uniformed that he can see. And alone. No, they would not come for him like this. His pulse settles a little.

She rings again. Clearly, she isn't buying his silent routine. But what is she selling? There is no clipboard tucked under her arm, no glossy brochures, and no Bible in her hand. In fact, she isn't carrying anything except a small handbag, the strap tightly clutched to her chest. A wise precaution around here. No, she definitely hasn't come to turn the place over and throw him into a Black Maria.

It's hard to tell from a fish-eye perspective, but she seems anxious; she is biting her lip, glancing around.

It might be one of those robberies he has read about: a seemingly harmless woman rings the doorbell and, upon opening, a thug, or group of thugs, push their way in and subject the owner to all kinds of horrors in their quest for hidden treasure.

Martin turns away from the spyhole and catches his reflection in the hall mirror—hunched, furtive, with cheeks drawn. Pathetic! He wouldn't have cut such a pitiful figure thirty years ago. He looks at her again. Things have reached a sorry state if he is afraid of a scrawny woman with bleach-blonde hair. He takes a deep breath, straightens up and reaches for the doorknob.

*

He sets the brush down and pulls off the headphones. Then he twists his neck until it cracks. His arms and legs are getting stiff too. According to the clock on the mantelpiece, he's been at it for two solid hours. Time for a cuppa and a bit of a stretch.

When the weather cheers up, he can resume his long walks but, for now, he'll make do with a bit of a stroll around his small back garden, and a hot mug of tea to warm him. Come spring, he'll attack the weeds and the scraggly old rose bush with a vengeance, but right now it's too bloody cold and the ground too hard to dig over. He'll let winter enjoy its brief reign and settle for indoor pursuits instead.

A squeaking noise stops him at the door to the hallway. A curious sound; sort of outside and inside at the same time. An odd rubbing, scratching sort of noise. The postman trying to squeeze something through the letterbox? No, wrong direction. This was coming from the kitchen—the back of the house.

Martin grips the doorframe and leans his head into the hall. He peers around the doorway just far enough to see into the kitchen, across its tiled floor and between its cupboards, all the way through to the back door. On the other side of its frosted glass, there is a dark, fragmented shape.

Boards creak gently under his slippers as he shifts weight from one foot to the other and he is suddenly aware of how loudly he is breathing.

Out of the jumbled, black-grey kaleidoscope image, a sharper picture begins to crystallise: a pair of white hands. They are cutting the glass.

The door is locked. Martin always makes sure of that. But this morning, on return from taking out the rubbish, he had left the key in the lock, as he often did these days.

He clenches his fists. How could he be so stupid?

The grinding-scratching of the pebbled glass being scored fills the house. If he calls the police, the intruder is bound to hear. It might deter him. But it might just provoke him instead.

Martin feels dizzy and his legs start to tremble.

This is more than a casual housebreaker. He has all the right tools. There is even a big black sucker in the centre of the arc he is carving in the window, so that he can pluck out the section of glass, pop his arm through and unlock the door. He could be inside in a matter of seconds. The intruder will know full well that the police could take ages to arrive. Domestic robberies are a low priority nowadays. He has no need to fear being caught red-handed. He will have time to do whatever he wants to do. Besides, if Martin did succeed in frightening him off now, that wouldn't stop him from returning. In fact, it might ensure that he comes back, if only to exact revenge. And next time, he'll be more careful. Perhaps he'll come at night. With friends.

Martin tries to swallow but his mouth is as dry as old leather.

He glances at the front door and wonders if he can unlock it and make it outside before the intruder comes hurtling down the hallway to knock him down and pin him against the floor. "Nice try, old fella."

349

There is a gentle plinking sound. Martin looks back into the kitchen.

His time is up.

A thick-knuckled hand comes into sharp focus as it scrabbles in through the hole in the glass and fumbles at the keys Martin has conveniently left dangling from the kitchen door. Heart thumping fit to burst, Martin ducks back into the front room.

*

She stands on the doorstep and wrings her hands—a rather theatrical gesture, thinks Martin.

"Sorry to disturb you and that, but my husband has disappeared and I wondered if you could help me."

Her words are like an electric shock. Every day since it happened—every night—Martin has been filled with a nauseating dread that someone would know what he had done; that there would be a knock at the door, or worse, a battering ram at the door as the law home in and bring his world crashing down around him.

He can taste bile in his mouth.

"I'm sorry," she stutters, filling the silence between them. "You must think I'm mental or something."

A storm of terrors engulfs him but still no words come to his lips.

"My name's Anette. Anette Rigby," she says. She turns and points off to the distance. "I live on the Oakmead Estate?" She makes this a question, as though he might not have heard of it. But Martin is well aware of the place. It is notorious. Rat-faced youths and tattooed gang members are crammed tightly into grimy, graffiti-scarred concrete blocks; the grounds are littered with stained mattresses and burned-out cars. Most nights, the place is lit with flashing blue lights.

"Two weeks ago my fella, my Pete, left home to burgle your house. He never came back."

A cold rock of fear slides slowly down Martin's gullet. It threatens to burrow its way through his stomach and exit his body via the nearest orifice.

The fat layabout next door—Darren something-or-other—is returning from his daily trip to the off-licence, greedily ripping open a fresh pack of cigarettes. Bottles or cans jiggle and clank in a white plastic bag. He pauses on his way past, nodding to Martin and leering at the woman's Lycra-coated rear.

"Maybe you'd better come inside," Martin says. His voice comes out thin, watery-sounding. She looks puzzled. He clears his throat. "Out of the cold."

It is almost fully dark. Darren is at his own front door now, juggling his keys. He looks across and raises a knowing eyebrow as he watches Anette totter cross the threshold.

Let the idiot believe what he wants, thinks Martin.

"At first, I just assumed he'd been nicked. You know?"

Martin nods. Arrest must be a tedious occupational hazard for the likes of her Pete.

"But normally he would call," she adds. "I mean, not that he's always in trouble." She follows this with a nervous laugh that suggested Pete was, in fact, always in trouble.

"No, of course not," says Martin.

"It's been difficult, see? That's all."

"The recession," suggests Martin.

Anette frowns momentarily and then says, "Yeah." Her eyes wander around the walls, pausing to rest now and then on a painting.

Martin leads her into the front room. Alarmed as he was when she explained the purpose of her visit, Martin realises that this could be the solution to his sleepless nights. If he could convince this woman that Pete had never been here, she would start looking elsewhere. The finger of suspicion would pass him by and he could stop worrying.

She glances at the canvases on the floor, propped against the walls; sees the easel and the table laden with paints and bottles and brushes.

"They're nice," she says. "The paintings."

"Thank you."

"You do them?"

Since his retirement three months ago, Martin has spent most days mooching about the house. Apart from shopping, he has nothing much to go out for. And this, his first winter of freedom, is particularly bitter.

He kept hearing the old saying that when you retire, life begins a new chapter, but he couldn't help thinking that it is a chapter close to the end of the book. Worried he would slip into a vegetative state, he resolved to keep his mind occupied. He bought himself a smartphone and became a silver surfer, although his interest in the web has been mostly limited to *BBC News* and those sites that encourage oldies to take up hobbies. Martin had reached the conclusion that the internet was a bit like daytime TV: simultaneously addictive and boring. But one of the articles on oldies.net had prompted him to start painting again, a pastime he had enjoyed in his younger days but had drifted away from as the drudgery of real life had taken hold.

"See, we've been through a bit of a rough patch, me and my Pete. We've had some trouble with the benefits people?" She turns this into a question too, as if probing for a shared understanding.

Martin doesn't understand but he follows convention by nodding.

"I swear them stuck-up bastards do it on purpose," she says. Then, hastily, "'scuse my language."

He offers Anette a cup of tea.

She shakes her head. "I don't want to take up your time and that," she says. "It's just, I don't know what else I can do to find my Pete, see? I mean, he's disappeared before, you know, if he's gone up town with his mates. But I've asked around and no one's seen him since the morning he came to—"

"To burgle me."

Anette grimaces. "Yeah. Sorry, I know that sounds bad. Thing is, he'd been casing these places for about a week."

Nod.

"So I know he was keen, like."

*

Once he had exhausted the artistic potential of fruit, flowers and items of furniture, Martin had started digging through the detritus in his garage for possible subject matter. Old shoes were quite satisfying; lots of texture. But they didn't make for much of a picture.

The process of searching for something to paint became a pastime in itself. Entire days seemed to slide by, spent in reminiscences triggered by the discovery of things long forgotten.

One morning, he unearthed a deflated, brown leather football. They don't make footballs like that anymore, he thought. He wondered if it might make a good subject, but eventually decided that its sorry condition was slightly depressing; too symbolic of his own present state.

The cricket equipment, however, was a different proposition. It had a timeless quality to it: the still-red ball, the fuzzy off-white jumper, a pair of trusty old keeper's gloves and a battle-scarred bat. Yes, he fancied he could make a nice, summery picture with that little collection.

*

"He reckoned he could get in and out quick, like, while people was out at work and that."

"Well, I hate to disappoint you," says Martin, "but I haven't been burgled." He is tempted to add that he doesn't go out much either but decided against exposing too much of his pitiable existence to Anette.

She seems to collapse a little.

"I'm sorry," he says with a shrug.

"Oh, I knew it was a long shot," she says. She is looking down at the handbag now, a hideous plastic thing in a mock leopard print, with a gold-coloured chain for a strap. "I just wondered—hoped really, I suppose—that maybe he had come here, nicked some stuff and then gone and blown it all on a bender somewhere."

Martin almost explodes with laughter at the idea that such a dismal scenario would be considered a good outcome in Anette's world. Then he realises she is crying and covers his mouth with his hand.

"There's this old slapper he used to live with, see?" she says through jerking sobs. "That's the only option left. He's got back with her, hasn't he?"

Martin assumes the question was rhetorical and makes a tight, sympathetic smile. Relieved that he has successfully put her off the scent, all he wants now is for her to go.

She is sniffing and delving into the handbag. "Sorry," says Anette through a snotty laugh. "Run out of tissues."

"I'll get you something," says Martin. *Then you can sod off back to Planet Chav*, he thinks.

Crisis over, he tugs his phone from his pocket. As he thought, it's just about time for a mug of tea and a couple of custard creams. The battery sign is winking. He carries the phone into the kitchen, where the charger lives. Anette follows, sniffing.

Martin plugs in his phone and unreels a sheet of kitchen roll.

She thanks him. "I'll leave you in peace now. You've been ever so nice about all this. I'm really sorry to have bothered you."

"It's no bother at all," he says, thinking that, actually, it had been a blessed relief. If she were to report Pete missing now (which, judging from her current suppositions as to his whereabouts, was unlikely) she probably wouldn't even tell the police what he had been planning to do on the day he walked out of her life. Not only was it now irrelevant, but wasn't it also likely to make the authorities ill-disposed towards the couple?

Martin snaps on the kettle and opens a cupboard to find a mug while Anette blows her nose and dabs at her tears.

"You said you hadn't been burgled," she says to his back.

Gazing into the cupboard, he says, "Yes, that's right." He dons a smile and turns to face her. "I suppose I've been lucky."

Anette points to the back door, at the square of cardboard that covers a segment of the frosted glass in the bottom corner, nearest the handle. "So, what happened there?" Her tone is harsh, accusing.

That sick feeling he had felt when the doorbell rang returns with a queasy vengeance. He struggles to keep the smile in place. "Ah, that? I broke it by accident ages ago."

She pulls her own phone out of her bag and taps the screen irritably.

What the hell is she doing now?

"No you didn't," she says.

"No I didn't, what?"

Martin winces at the weakness in his voice.

"You didn't break it ages ago." She looks up, her eyes red-rimmed but dry, and shows him the screen. It is a picture of his back door—from the outside. It shows the glass intact.

"My Pete took it the day before he came to turn you over. He always takes a snap so he can plan the job, see? He's really clever like that."

Clearly a criminal mastermind, thinks Martin sourly. But the snide thought is rapidly subsumed beneath a wave of unease that roils inside him. Actually, he concedes, it is a pretty smart thing to do. *Perhaps smart enough to trip me up.*

Martin's pulse rate accelerates as he watches Anette crush the kitchen roll in her fist and stride to the back door, heels clacking on the tiled floor. Just seconds ago she was a simpering idiot, pathetically grateful that he could be bothered to listen to her miserable life story. But now, transformed from a snivelling, abandoned wife into a hard-nosed gangster's moll, she seems to have the upper hand. She is about to throw Martin's world into turmoil.

*

He rests the cricket bat on his shoulder and holds his breath. From his position behind the living room door, he can hear the rustle of the intruder's nylon windcheater. It's getting louder. He can feel his heart labouring furiously in his chest, its pulse echoing in the arteries of his throat. His vision begins to fade, a sign that his brain is threatening to shut down and drop him in a swoon unless he feeds it more oxygen. Passing out and lying on the floor at the mercy of the burglar is not an option he wants to think about.

The crackling of the nylon jacket grows louder and Martin senses rather than sees a slowly moving shadow creeping towards him at the furthest edge of his line of sight.

The cricket bat squirms in his fist as he squeezes it tighter, and a shuddering sigh escapes his lips as a greasy mop of mousy hair appears inches from his face.

When it comes, the sound is an unsatisfying clock and not the loud, skull-splitting crack he had anticipated.

In his schooldays he had been a solid enough bowler and a safe pair of hands at the wicket, but he had always failed to shine as a batsman. Too many times he had swiped away his own bails or caught the damned bat on his pads like a clown. Something to do with co-ordination. One of those things you either had or didn't have. He had never had it. Now, in this crucial test, he fails again. His grip is all wrong. Paralysed by terror and indecision, he muffs the shot, meting out a twisted blow that rips down the side of the intruder's skull and smacks into his collarbone.

"Shit!" cries Martin as pain jolts through his thumbs.

Simultaneously, the intruder yells something unintelligible and his thick-knuckled hands fly up to his head.

Martin wipes his sweaty palms on his jumper and gulps down a lungful of air as though he has just broken the surface after a long dive. He gags as he inhales the man's scent: cigarettes-and-booze breath overlaid with a meaty stink of unwashed hair and clothes.

The man, one hand furiously rubbing his collarbone, the other pressed against an ear, turns and staggers back along the hall. There are tracks on the floor where he has walked muddy footsteps in from the garden.

What happens now? If Martin lets him escape, he's bound to come back and seek revenge. He might even go to the police! They would be only too eager to nail a law-abiding citizen for defending their own home. You read about it all the time.

And what if he has a weapon of his own? The thought sends a shockwave through his limbs.

On shaking legs, Martin follows the man as he lurches into the kitchen.

The intruder stops at the back door and gingerly touches the side of his head. The blow has caused some serious damage to his left ear, which has been transformed into a string of glistening ruby red jelly that quivers above his grimy collar like a grotesque piece of jewellery. He looks down at his hand, now vermillion with blood, and hisses through gritted teeth, "You crazy old fool!"

Despite the spike of terror tearing his chest apart, the first thing that pops into Martin's head is an image of

Mr. T from the A-Team *yelling, "Crazy Fool!" in that gruff, comic voice of his.*

A look of bewildered horror washes over the lump-fisted man, and his fury seems to wilt. Martin realises that the thought of Mr. T had brought a smile to his face. He must look like some kind of grinning madman.

The second shot is still more of a muted thud than the classic willow on leather sound Martin is after, but his aim is improving. This time he is, at least, on target.

The intruder tries to say something but his words come out strangulated and unintelligible. Martin finds the garbled sounds easy to ignore.

The third blow drives the man to his knees and stops him speaking altogether.

The fourth strike is an absolute corker.

Howzat!

*

Anette places her bag on the counter. She pulls away the cardboard patch on the glass to reveal a neat cut in the corner, roughly the size and shape of a generous slice of cake.

"What are you doing?" says Martin. "Leave that alone!" He has spoken loudly and clearly, but that weakness has returned to his voice and a maniac drumroll is riffling away in his chest.

Anette peers out through the hole in the frosted glass. Dusk casts the garden into a gloomy spectrum of blues and greys, yet she is looking directly at the place where her husband is buried. Or, more accurately, places—plural.

Martin realises that the incongruous mounds in the vegetable patch look exactly like poorly buried body parts. There is one large torso mound, two longer leg mounds and two shorter arm mounds. The soil over one of the legs has been scratched away, so that the pinnacle of the earth pyramid is flattened. Is there even a bit of dirty white flesh gleaming out of the ground like the snout of a giant albino worm?

He clears his throat. "Foxes," he says.

"What?"

"Foxes," he repeats. "Little buggers."

There is a kitchen window above the sink. Anette straightens and they both lean over, like a pair of synchronised swimmers, to look through it. Martin's gaze switches between the woman's reflection and the burial mounds.

"I was right," says Anette, turning to face him. "It was this house. He was here, wasn't he? Why did you say he wasn't?"

Beyond her inverted image on the glass, the world outside seems to be blackening by the second.

"I told you. I broke it by—"

"Liar!" she shrieks. Martin flinches. Those watery brown eyes that had made her seem so childlike and vulnerable a minute ago, now shine with a furious intensity. Her sudden outburst makes the pulse in his throat flutter and he struggles to resist the urge to step away from her.

He can see how this is going to pan out. Anette will go and tell the police; the police will come and ask questions. They will see the carved-out glass and the photo on Anette's mobile, and reach the same conclusion she had: Pete had broken in. But what became of Pete after he had broken in? They will dust for prints, maybe even swab the place for DNA.

Martin looks out at the white lump protruding from the freshly dug earth. It's a knee; he can see that now. There is some flesh chewed away, exposing the patella. Thanks to the bloody foxes, the police wouldn't need forensics to solve this case.

Anette's reflection seems to solidify, become clearer. The night is gathering behind her. Suddenly, she is strong, sinewy. Threatening. "Well?" she says. She sounds like a schoolteacher admonishing a child for some minor misdemeanour. It reminds him of the day, over half a century ago, when Miss Hogarth had caught him idly scrawling a giant penis on his desk.

Well, Martin Birch? What have you got to say for yourself?

He unplugs his phone and winds the lead around his fingers.

*

The cricket bat is resting on Martin's shoulder now. Warmish blood dribbles down the length of the bat and tickles his wrist as it scurries under his shirtsleeve.

Pete is lying on his back. The red puddle under his head is very dark. His right eye follows Martin as he bends over to take a closer look. His left eye stares lifelessly up at the ceiling.

"Are you still alive?" says Martin, panting.

Pete's lips open and close, making a sticky little sound and exposing pink teeth. But no words come out. Beads of blood drip from the bat and smack his face with a gentle pit-pat sound, and he blinks. Well, his right eye blinks.

Martin loses count of the strikes. He's the same with wasps and spiders. Overkill, he reasons, is better than no kill.

But there's no denying it's a bloody mess. The cops would have his guts for garters, hang him out to dry. At what point had it stopped being a matter of self-defence? Had he, perhaps, even crossed the fuzzy line between right and wrong at the very start? Could he have just threatened the man and told him to leave? Would that have worked? Could he have avoided all this... this bloody mess?

Remarkably, he discovers, there is more than one site on the internet detailing how best to cut up a human body. People variously suggest a machete or a large meat cleaver, but most are agreed on sturdy rubble sacks and 'an iron constitution'.

On one site he even finds a diagram showing how to separate the limbs from the torso. Turns out you hammer your blade into the joints 'as you would a chicken'. Martin has never done that to a chicken, but he understands the principle. There is a smiley face at the end of the guide, followed by several exclamation marks, which makes him wonder if it is meant to be taken entirely seriously. Or perhaps it was written by a psychopath. These days, who can tell?

Dismemberment, advised the article, was essential for the effective removal of the evidence. The job was, it said, a little like pruning a wayward rose bush and facilitated easier disposal of the body. That, *thinks Martin*, makes perfect sense.

However, he finds that he has none of the equipment that the website recommended for the task. His largest breadknife is a poor substitute for a cleaver; it slices through the outer layer of skin well enough but hacking through muscle and sinew pushes it beyond its limits. It slips when tackling the joints and he cuts his own hands three times. He tries the hedge trimmer but that just sprays a splattery jam of flesh and blood up the cupboard doors. In the end he hacks off the arms and legs with a hammer and cold chisel, one with a wider blade meant for chasing electric cable into brickwork. Not a clean job, but an effective one.

Nor are the green garden sacks fit for purpose; the flimsy bags split too easily and spew their contents onto the kitchen floor more than once. As does his stomach. His constitution, he concludes, is more mercury than iron.

He knows (from lurid descriptions in countless novels, rather than through personal experience) that blood has a kind of metallic smell, but he had never appreciated quite how malodorous lots of it would be. While he mops up, he wonders how much worse it might have been had he exposed the internal organs.

He toys with the idea of burning but the mental image of pork-smelling, black smoke billowing up and drifting across the neighbours' back gardens puts him off the idea. He has *visions of Darren popping his head over the fence, six-pack in hand, inviting himself to the barbecue.*

Fly-tipping was another option. In theory, all he had to do was wrap up the bits and dump them piece by piece. He might even have put the arms in the dustbin, but no. Gulls or foxes would rip open the sacks of putrid flesh somewhere down the line. Even if he were to destroy the fingers to prevent the police from taking prints, the press would work themselves into a frenzy over the stray body parts. No, he decides, at least in his own garden he has some measure of control.

The frozen winter soil makes burial damned hard work. Every inch of his body aches like a bastard for days after, but despite hours of labouring under a tin-grey winter sky, he can't make the graves deep enough. He makes a mental note to revisit the job in a few months, as part of his general spring clean-up.

*

Anette falls back on her heels as he wrenches the lead around her throat and then crosses his arms behind her neck. She arches her spine, trying to stay upright, writhing and scratching at the wire as it cuts into the soft flesh. It is a relatively silent tableau. There is no sound except for his own panting breath and her shoes shuffling on the floor tiles, as though she is trying out a whacky new dance move. He goes down with her, making sure to bend sensibly at the knees, as she slides onto her backside, and they squat together on the kitchen floor.

The hole in the glass draws level with his eyes and the chill air from the garden pricks his face. He looks past Anette's slumped head, towards the mounds in the garden. They look almost pleasingly like little snow-topped mountains.

The wire has bitten deep into his hands and his fingers have gone numb but he is afraid to relax his grip in case Anette leaps back to life. He puts his lips to her cheek to test its warmth. It is cool, but is it cool enough?

Martin rests his chin on top of her head. Pete's hair had stunk of grease and there were flecks of dandruff in it. Anette's has a healthy sheen and smells pleasantly of apple shampoo.

He looks up at the clock. How long does it take to die from strangulation? He can't very well leave her to go and look it up. He has no idea when he began to kill Anette but he decides to give it another minute or so just to be on the safe side. It's a bit of a cliché but the one thing you have plenty of when you retire is time.

She is sat on his lap, like a child perched on grandpa's knee. Despite her slight build, she has given him dead legs. He shuffles around to disentangle himself from her. The movement releases another smell and he notices a wet patch on the front of his trousers. For a moment, he thinks he's pissed himself. Then he realises it must have come from her. But that's OK. Everything is going to be fine now. He smiles. He might be damp but he is home and dry.

Martin takes a deep breath, his fingers still tangled in the charger lead around Anette's throat, and gently lays her down.

Despite its coldness, her face is very red and puffy. Her lids are closed but do not quite cover her oddly bulbous eyes. He hopes that after he has fully unwound the wire, some of the discoloration and swelling will go down. Her face had been quite good—high cheekbones, pretty little nose, rosebud lips. Much nicer to look at than grimy old cricket gear.

Much nicer than Pete's face, too. His was so split apart that Martin had been tempted to bury it alongside the rest of his parts. In the end, common sense had prevailed.

Mindful of the lessons learnt from his previous foray into butchery, he resolves to acquire some professional equipment before embarking upon the task a second time. He will spend a little more money and buy some sturdy plastic sacks and a decent chopper. He will also bring the little jar of Vicks VapoRub down from the bathroom and smear some under his nose to mask the smell of the job, a tip he picked up from a video about autopsies.

He casts a critical eye over the kitchen, wrinkling his nose at the rich smell of urine, and adds floor cleaner to his mental shopping list.

The wire is buried so deep in the skin of Anette's throat that it is almost invisible and he has to dig his fingernails into her flesh to gouge it out.

Probably ruined, he thinks. The shopping list was getting longer.

He sighs. Still, everything is under control. He has plenty of time to change his trousers and get out the charcoal sticks for a quick sketch before bedtime. It will help him relax. While he winds down, he can make plans for tomorrow, which promises to be a very busy day. Which is good. There is nothing worse than having nothing to do.

A loud buzzing sound startles him from his thoughts. He looks up, thinking for a second that a bluebottle must have been drawn into the kitchen by the scent of death. And then the annoying thrum is accompanied by an equally irritating and inhuman piece of music.

His own mobile has a simple old-fashioned ringtone, like a proper phone.

He scurries his hands across Anette's crumpled body, his fingers and thumbs jostling frantically against her still ribcage and her cold, squishy breasts.

Her phone buzzes again and repeats its tinny, raucous tune.

"Come on, where are you, you little swine?" he whispers. He stands up, all his joints cracking out of time with each other like a shambolic twenty-one-gun salute.

As Anette's body flops to the ground, his eyes alight upon the leopard-print handbag sitting on the kitchen counter.

A sweet waft of make-up hits Martin's face as he pulls open the bag and reaches inside. The phone has stopped vibrating and trilling but he takes it out, anyway. Then it makes a little plinking sound. He taps the screen to reveal a text message: *u still with old gzr?*

His stomach curls in on itself. He looks at the back door. "You're dead," he whispers aloud. "Dead and buried."

As he is peering through the window, trying to make out shapes among the shadows in his garden, the phone makes that plinking sound again, like a violin string being cut.

It's cold here.

Martin feels his world shrinking to blackness. He clenches and unclenches hands still sore from throttling Anette, rushes over to the fridge and drops to his knees. "I know this is impossible," he gasps. "It can't be happening. It just can't." Hands trembling, he wrenches open the bottom freezer drawer. Pete's head is still there, nestled tightly alongside his emergency loaf of bread. He runs a finger down Pete's face—the puffy purple eyelids, the twisted shard of nose and the shredded lips. They are all as reassuringly solid as the loaf.

Plink.

We fancy KFC.

Martin sits upright and glances between Pete's frozen head and Anette's lifeless corpse, then rocks back on his heels and laughs. "I don't think either of you is in any state to enjoy a chicken dinner!"

Plink.

Mum???

When his laughter finally subsides, he wipes tears from his cheeks, eases himself gently off the floor and trots to the front door.

Through the spyhole, he can make out two children—one aged about eleven, the other no more than seven—standing in the darkness at his front gate, both gazing into a mobile that up-lights their sallow, underfed cheeks with an icy blue glow.

Martin watches them, his index finger hovering over Anette's phone. *A family portrait*, he thinks. *Now there's a charming idea.*

The Legend of Stanley Mann

The locals called it The Rabbit Hole. The nickname always made me think of surreal kingdoms populated by grinning cats and preening worms. I was convinced that if I ever plucked up the courage to walk through that stinking underpass beneath the railway line, I would end up somewhere far, far away from home.

Taking the longer route, above ground, had made me late.

Sunday afternoons we gathered at the park to kick a ball about. It was early October 1972. We were four weeks into our final year at St John's Junior. The colour had drained from the sky and it wanted to rain. Memories of sunshine were melting away like ice cream at the seaside but, reluctant to admit that summer was over, none of us had dressed for the drop in temperature.

"There's bonfire night soon," said Gary. "My dad's getting some real Chinese fireworks from the bloke at the New Moon."

Frosty silence. No one was ready to think about November yet.

I was not alone in shunning The Rabbit Hole. It was dark and smelly and, according to everyone in the know, it was haunted too. I didn't believe that, of course. My own reasons for avoiding it were more prosaic. It was where the big kids off the estate hung out, smoking illicit roll-ups and passing around old crisp packets filled with glue. I didn't want to run afoul of them, or of the men in raincoats who offered you sweets. No one I knew had ever been offered sweets by such a person, but we knew they existed because our parents kept warning us about them.

"They bum-fuck you to death," said Gary cheerily. "Then they feed you to their scabby dogs."

"Piece by piece," agreed Ralph, briskly rubbing some life back into his pink, marbled legs.

"Kiddie fiddlers are always old men," sneered George. "You can kick 'em in the goolies and run away. It ain't them you wanna be afraid of. And it ain't the glue-sniffers neither. They're too off their heads to do anything."

George was our sage, our oracle. His dad was a wrestler and his older brother was in borstal. It was common knowledge that his mum had fled the family home as soon as George had been born. We joked that she had run away when she saw how ugly he was. But we only whispered it behind his back.

George was streetwise and he knew all the grown-up stuff that the rest of us had been shielded from by our rather more mundane families. From George we learned about sex ("slip on a johnny in case they've got the clap"), drugs ("pot's for hippies; real men drink booze"), and rock 'n' roll ("Elvis is still the king, never mind all that modern queer shit"). George was 11, going on 44. He snorted, spat out a ball of phlegm and continued. "It's Stanley Mann you want to watch out for."

We had all heard the name bandied about for as long as we could remember. As far as the local kids were concerned, Stanley Mann was as much a part of Dalton town as the bird-shat war memorial outside the library and the patchy old recreation ground where we now stood shivering. Stanley Mann was, we understood, someone to avoid; someone we never even wanted to see. He lurked around the quiet backstreets of Dalton, in the shadowy corners of the park. And, naturally, in the underpass.

"Bernard Munt says that Stanley Mann goes to Wyndham Road," sniffed Gary. "I hope to hell I don't get sent there next year. My mum has written to the council saying it's too far to walk with my flat feet. She reckons Marlow Tech suits my needs better."

Ralph's mum had done the same, as had mine. Wyndham Road High School was a notorious hellhole that each of us was desperate to avoid being sent to when we finished at St John's next summer. Marlow Technical College was about the same distance to travel but it had a less menacing reputation. Odds were though that at least one of us would end up at Wyndham and have our head flushed down the toilet on day one as a prelude to four years of abject misery; all presided over by Stanley Mann.

George favoured us with a condescending smile. "He don't go to Wyndham, you lemons. Not anymore. Stanley Mann is *dead*. Been dead for thirty-odd years."

It felt like a lead weight the size of an anvil had been removed from my stomach. Every morning for the past six weeks I had been dreading that official-looking letter plopping onto our doormat, the one telling my parents that I was destined for Wyndham next summer.

Stanley Mann had been at Wyndham during World War Two, George explained.

"So he's long gone, then?" said Ralph. There was shrill whine of hope in his voice.

"Didn't say that, did I?" said George, twisting his weasel face into a cruel expression of glee. He was enjoying this.

George went on to explain that Stanley Mann had tormented teachers and pupils alike. He disrupted lessons, lashed out at anyone who came near him, extorted money from smaller kids—routine antics for maladjusted teenagers since time immemorial. But with Stanley Mann, it was different. He lived and breathed terror. There was never a waking moment when he wasn't trying to destroy, hurt or frighten.

"Shit," said Ralph. "All the kids should have ganged up on him and killed him." He was gnomishly short, as round as a beer barrel and wore pebble-thick glasses. He knew about bullying. "Is that what they did, George? Did they kill him?"

George shook his head and smiled. It all came to a head one summer's day in 1941, he said. Like most bullies, he had a favourite victim. For Stanley Mann, his chosen prey was Robin Cockerill. A small, skinny boy by all accounts, Robin lived in a world of hurt. His days were spent cringing in corners, peering over his shoulder, anticipating the next slap or kick. Even in the hours of darkness, there was no escape. Robin's dreams were poisoned by vivid tableaux in which Stanley Mann the demon, or Stanley Mann the phantom, would stalk him through the endless, silent corridors of a night-shrouded school.

Robin's father was on the other side of the world, fighting in the Far East; his mother's pleas for the headmaster to deal with the bully fell on deaf ears. There was no remission for him. No hope of reprieve. Wherever he sought sanctuary, Stanley would be there, his sneering face promising an eternity of pain and humiliation.

Then, on sports day in 1941, Stanley's campaign of terror reached its zenith. On the way to school that morning he encountered Robin alone. In The Rabbit Hole. Thirty years on, the details of exactly what happened beneath the railway line that day were long since lost. The legend merely records that Robin Cockerill eventually staggered onto the playing field in the late morning, half-naked and sheeted in scarlet.

Robin's horrific appearance shocked the whole school and shamed the headmaster into finally taking action. The bloodied boy was promptly driven to hospital by one of the teachers but, reluctant to disrupt the day's events any further, the headmaster decided to wait a few hours before doing anything more. He didn't want the most important day in the school calendar to be soured. He would deal with Stanley once and for all after the races were run and the prizes had been awarded. In the meantime, he locked the bully in a tiny storeroom to keep him out of harm's way.

Nobody would ever know exactly what punishment the headmaster had in mind.

While the kids were running and jumping and cheering out on the sport's field, the school began to burn. The fire brigade, busy dealing with the aftermath of a bombing raid north of the Thames, never arrived, so pupils and staff spent the afternoon watching impotently as their school slowly burned to the ground.

The cause of the blaze was never determined. And Stanley's body was never recovered.

George sat back, folded his arms and studied our reaction.

"My old man told me about the fire," said Gary. "Wyndham was rebuilt in the '50s on the same site. For the baby boom generation, whatever that means."

George nodded. "By then, Stanley Mann had already been sighted in town several times. His charred corpse had risen from the ashes of the old school building."

The lead weight returned to my guts pretty sharpish.

Now it was Ralph's turn to shiver. "I don't believe in ghosts," he said quietly.

We all murmured our obligatory agreement.

A football appeared and we half-heartedly played three-and-in just to keep warm before breaking apart and going our separate ways under the darkening sky. Stomach knotted, head filled with spiralling thoughts about Wyndham Road High School and what horrors might await me there, I went home. The long way round.

*

October half term crept up on us. Ordinarily this would have been cause for celebration, we would meet up and go on fishing excursions, have a kickabout. This year was different. A pall of dread as black as night hung over us all. We had been told that during the holiday those dreaded brown envelopes would be sent out and we would learn which secondary schools we would be going to next year.

To lighten our sombre mood a little, Gary came up with a nifty idea. In the '70s, penny-for-the-guy was still a thing: Kids would stuff a suit of old clothes with old newspaper and ask passers-by to reward their efforts by donating money for fireworks. We decided to go one better. One of us would dress up in some shabby old clothes and pretend we had built the best guy in the world, ever. We all agreed it sounded like fun. With any luck, we'd earn enough cash to buy some illicit fags as well as a few bangers and Roman candles.

We duly pestered our parents for any unwanted clothes and soon had a carrier bag containing a moth-eaten tweed jacket, shiny-kneed gardening trousers, a pair of grubby red football socks and a large brown hat. By common agreement, I was the one who best fitted into the misshapen adult cast-offs. Even then, I needed to be padded out with newspaper.

During a dry run of our jolly jape, I suggested that I could reach out and take the penny from their hand myself. I performed a brief demonstration.

The others recoiled.

"Oh, no!" yelped Ralph, eyeing me with disgust. "It's kind of horrible when you move about dressed like that. It's like you're not alive."

The others murmured agreement.

"Yeah," added George. "And the people we've hoodwinked might chuck you on the bonfire!"

No one laughed.

Every autumn, the television spewed out lurid warnings about playing with fireworks and out-of-control bonfires. They often accompanied the advice by showing us pictures of kids our age who had been blinded or scarred by an errant rocket or Catherine wheel.

The poor wretches featured prominently in all our nightmares.

On top of that, we all remembered what happened the previous year.

Last November, everyone on the Oakmead Estate had got together to build a massive bonfire. They spent weeks piling it high with planks of wood from broken pallets and sticks and branches plundered from the park. On bonfire night, they fixed the guy: a lumpy giant tied to an old wooden chair. He was wearing a livid red cardboard mask and he looked like a condemned man apoplectic with rage at facing execution.

When the dads stuffed flaming twists of paper inside the pyre, smoke billowed up around the guy's legs. He seemed so solid, so real, that I half expected him to struggle against his bindings and cry out, demanding to be released. The bonfire smoked and fizzled horribly. They had used too much green wood. Nobody seemed to care, though. Sparklers were handed out to the kids. The grown-ups had cans of beer. The guy began to smoulder, dark curls of smoke streamed from his empty eye sockets.

And then we heard screaming. It was a strangulated, growling kind of scream; a cry of bestial terror. We all fell silent. I was convinced it was the guy; that we were burning a real, live person up there. From the looks on the faces around me, I wasn't the only one thinking that. Then a small, dark shape came rushing out of the pyre. It was a fox. Its coat was singed back to the skin, its incinerated brush resembled the naked tail of a rat, and its muzzle was bright red with boiling blood. The mutilated creature dashed between me and my parents and shrieked away into the night, while adults and children alike howled with horror.

I'll never forget the sight of that nightmarish animal, nor the smell of burning flesh and scorched fur as it hurtled into the darkness, towards a slow and painful death.

I swallowed. "I'll keep still," I said.

*

The next day my parents received the letter. I was going to Wyndham.

In the weeks that followed I felt that my friends (all of whom had received similar letters but telling them they would be going to Marlow Tech) were beginning to distance themselves from me. We still talked whenever we bumped into each other, but conversation was stilted and I couldn't shake the impression that they might be meeting up behind my back, hanging around together without inviting me. We still gathered at the park at weekends, but the atmosphere was awkward. Nobody talked about next year. The subject seemed embarrassing, taboo, like discussing the terminal illness of a family member. In this case, the family member was me.

The final Sunday of the month, the last day of October, was the day we had earmarked for our Guy Fawkes masquerade. Gary would bring my bundle of clothes to change into; Ralph had the newspapers. All I had to do was provide the mask and to sit very, very still while the others trundled me around Dalton in George's home-made wooden go-kart. I commandeered a discarded plastic carrier bag from our kitchen, popped the mask in, and made my way to the park.

When I reached the playing field, there was no one there. Literally, no one at all. And it was starting to rain.

This was before mobile phones, of course. Half of us, including me, didn't even have a landline in the house. In those days you made arrangements face to face and then stuck to them. Except, as it turned out, on this occasion.

I stood there on the rain-flattened grass and wondered what to do. The sky had disappeared, replaced by a grey blanket of cloud that seemed low enough to touch. Despite the relentless drizzle, there was a deafening stillness on the field. Due to the threat of lightning strikes, the council had taken down the goalposts, and that seemed to open up the space endlessly. I felt exposed by the emptiness.

The shopping bag crackled noisily in my fist and a rustling of leaves in the distance sounded unnaturally close. Despite its vastness, the park suddenly felt horribly intimate.

I peeked into the bag. From inside, the lurid orange mask stared up at me. There was a little black Van Dyke beard painted on the pointy chin, and it had holes for eyes. It was a thing of ugliness, made for burning. Was there a cruel smile playing on its cardboard lips?

It dawned on me that my friends didn't need me for their little escapade. Any one of them could take my place. Gary was quite tall—he would fit into the costume with a little padding—and everyone had one of those damned masks.

It made sense that they weren't there. I was a leper, a dead man walking. Why hadn't I picked up on the unspoken hints? Why hadn't I understood what was going on? I was a fool for turning up, for bringing the stupid mask.

The sky flashed. The grubby mantle of cloud above my head roared, and a cataract of rain gushed down my neck. I shouted into the gloom, a strangled, wordless cry, but my voice was drowned by another rumble from the heavens.

My feet started splashing along the street before I had even consciously decided what to do. Only when I was standing at the entrance to The Rabbit Hole did I realise that I had instinctively taken the shortest route home. Perhaps a part of me hoped that I would be transported to an exotic wonderland.

The lee of the tunnel provided some shelter from the storm and I sidled into the entrance to take full advantage. My face was drenched with rain and I swiped it away, grateful for the relative sanctuary I had stumbled upon.

Peering cautiously inside the tunnel, I was blasted by a bitter stench of urine which provoked an instant gag reaction. The few overhead lights that were still working revealed a straight underpass that stretched for about two hundred yards. From ground to waist level, it was tiled in bottle-green; above the tiles, peeling khaki paint was almost fully obscured beneath layers of graffiti and ripped posters.

It was empty. No feral kids with glue-filled bags pressed to their faces, no dirty old men. And no ghosts.

There was an ellipse of daylight at the end. It would take no more than two minutes to walk through to the estate. I discovered that if I crouched low enough, I could even see the tower block where I lived. I was tantalisingly close to home.

"This is bollocks," I said.

I clutched the bag to my chest and entered the tunnel.

A train clattered overhead and, for a second, I was convinced that the roof would disintegrate like a rotting eggshell and I would be buried under an avalanche of mud and tiles and twisted wreckage. The lights fluttered and a squall of rainwater gushed down the curved walls but The Rabbit Hole remained resolutely intact.

All over the arched ceiling, the peeling paint was overlaid with dark scribble; some of it illegible, some of it extolling the virtues of one football team or another. Amid the babble of nonsense and profanity, two lines in swirling rainbow colours caught my eye:

CHILD OF FLAME
IN THE PYRE

"Child of flame," I whispered, rubbing some warmth into my arms. "In the pyre."

The constant rushing sound of rain outside was like the hiss of a blank cassette tape. Suddenly, my bladder felt very heavy. I didn't think I could wait until I got home. I shuffled over to the wall, checked that there really was no one else in the tunnel, and unzipped.

The gutters on either side of the tunnel were clogged with detritus, so lacking any means of escape, the yellow river I created splashed around the cylindrical wall and scurried over my shoes.

This would be a bad time to be caught by Stanley Mann, I thought. *A really bad time.* I pictured him creeping up behind me in the darkness and reaching around with a modelling knife clutched in his flame-scarred hand. The idea made me shrivel. The stream stopped and I peered over my shoulder.

No one there.

I quickly finished the job and zipped up. The sound echoed around the curved space.

It occurred to me that Stanley Mann and I had a connection. Now that I was going to his old school, perhaps he would see me as an ally, a fellow outcast. And then I wondered if thinking about him would somehow summon him from whatever hell he inhabited, so I tried to think of something else. Except, my head was filled with the horror of going to Wyndham next year, of being alone in the dark, of being abandoned. All thoughts seemed to lead back to Stanley Mann.

I was almost at the halfway point. The lights had petered out and I was shrouded in shadow. The air was icy and I was thoroughly soaked. I gripped my sides as I walked to stop myself from trembling but I couldn't stop my teeth clacking together like castanets.

A row of faded mauve posters advertised rock concerts from years gone by. Beside them, oozing down the filthy, graffiti-choked wall like melting candle wax was another multicoloured slogan:

PLAY THE GAME
LIGHT THE FIRE!

I shouted the new slogan. "Play the game. Light the fire!" The tunnel blasted my words back at me and I clapped my hands together. Once, twice. The sharp sound reverberated around my head—a disorienting sensation. The impact made my cold-numbed fingers ache but it got the blood flowing.

At that moment, the light at the end of the tunnel ahead became dappled. A small, stooped silhouette jittered across the opening. I stopped clapping.

I was still closer to the park end than the estate end. Relieved that I had an escape route, I took a step backwards.

And bumped into an old woman.

I felt like a prize fool. I had thought I was alone with my daydreams and all the while someone had been listening to me talking to myself. She had probably watched me pissing, too. I felt my cheeks flush hot.

A large, bony hand jabbed at the carrier bag which I had unconsciously clutched to my chest. "What you got in there?" she said. Her voice was crackly, like old-time radio, and rendered almost Dalek-like by the acoustics of the tunnel.

"It's a mask," I said. "You know. Guy Fawkes."

The woman nodded. "Show me," she croaked.

I wrestled the orange thing out of the bag. She grunted and pointed at my face. I thought of George's advice: *Kick 'em in the goolies and run away.* That wasn't going to help me here, but at least she wasn't a glue-sniffer. Or Stanley bloody Mann.

I pulled on the mask, glad that it would cover my reddening cheeks. "See?" I said.

"I bet you get up to all sorts of childish pranks, don't you?"

While I was thinking of a suitably non-committal reply, she pointed at the writing on the subway walls. "This your handiwork?"

I blurted out a hasty denial but, unsure if my muffled words could be heard through the mask, I shook my head to reinforce the answer.

"Trouble-making kids," she said, almost to herself. "All the same. Ruin people's lives with your foolishness."

The mask, with its two ill-placed peepholes, blotted out virtually everything from my sight. But, as she spoke, I became aware—almost by a sixth sense—of another presence. I looked behind me. It was the jittery figure I had seen at the end of the tunnel. A man, as far as I could tell; short, and with a lank streak of dark hair framing a lipless, nose-less face that was nothing but a mass of scar tissue. He bobbed up and down, peering at me. It was hard to define any human expression on his mutilated features but it felt as though he was smirking at me.

"This is another one of them, son," said the old woman. "Another troublemaker."

So they knew each other. My pulse began to race. I decided to take off the mask so that I could see what was going on, so that I could say something. But as I raised my hand, it was gripped tight. I spun round to see the woman rummaging in her shopping trolley. There was a sudden waft of something that reminded me of garage forecourts.

*

When I opened my eyes, it was more than dark; it was pitch-black. The stink of the tunnel, of burning petrol, was still in my nostrils, but it was overlaid by a clean, antiseptic smell. I struggled to say something but my voice didn't work. I thought it was the mask so I tried to take it off. My fingers, bound tightly in their own bandages, fumbled uselessly at the dressing and my face lit up with white-hot pain. A strangulated shriek erupted from my raw throat.

"The police will want to speak to you," said the nurse. "But not yet. You rest first."

Then there was a sharp scratch at the crook of my arm.

Another voice, a man's, said, "I hear he's been babbling about that urban legend the kids all talk about. Stanley something? That's no bloody good to us."

"He's very badly burned, Sergeant. After he's had some proper rest, he'll get his wits back. Then you'll get your answers," said the nurse.

I tried to speak again as consciousness began to slip away once more. "Not Stanley Mann," I said. But the rest wouldn't come out. It would be several hours before I could tell them about Robin and his mother.

The last words I heard before I lost consciousness again came from the nurse: "He's lucky to be alive."

She was wrong.

378

Heart Breaker

'I think that we're all mentally ill; those of us
outside the asylums only hide it a little better—and
maybe not all that much better, after all.'
Stephen King

Her eyes are still that bright cobalt blue he remembers. Her lips are still perfectly bowed and, from what he can see, she seems to have kept her figure.

"You look great," he says. And he means it.

"You need glasses," she says, and she smiles as she tugs on a lock of red-brown hair. "This comes out of a bottle these days."

He nods, his cheerful expression still in place.

"And don't even mention the wrinkles," she says into the silence.

He wasn't going to mention the wrinkles; hadn't even noticed them. But now she has drawn his attention to them they are hard to ignore.

She pulls her dyed hair around her face and pouts. "The years haven't been kind."

"Oh, no," he says. "You still look—" It was difficult to find the right words at the best of times. So many to choose from. Standing here in such a public place, with hot, sweaty strangers pressing in on all sides, he feels like the right words will never come.

The silence stretches.

There's a smile on her face but it is faltering, he thinks. In a spasm, he finally blurts, "*Lovely!* You still look... *lovely!*"

She turns her mouth down and shrugs. "Well, you're wrong but thank you, anyway," she says. Her eyes alight upon his pint glass.

"Oh, sorry," he says. "Can I get you a drink?"

She asks for a white wine.

The protocol for this sort of thing seems to have remained the same despite the passage of time, and it's starting to come back to him, slowly. A few drinks, light conversation.

She picks up her glass and they find a table. She's still twining a strand of hair around her finger. It's the mannerism of a younger woman, the woman she used to be.

And then, the question he was dreading.

"So, what made you get in touch after all these years?"

He has planned some responses to this obvious gambit but now they all seem stale, over-rehearsed. "I don't know," he says abjectly. Then a pause. "Curious, I suppose."

Her eyes widen.

Curious. Is that a good answer? Possibly not. It isn't even true. He's curious about a lot of things. But not about Tracy. He wants to have sex with her. Like he should have done years ago. Based on past experience, he knows he can't say that. Instead, he goes with one of the lines he has practiced. "I think about you a lot."

That isn't true either but she seems to accept it and tells him it's a sweet thing to say. He smiles. Flattery is always well received, especially by women of a certain age.

"I've thought about you, too, over the years," she says and then takes a gulp of wine. "Would never have found you, though."

He's drinking now, mouth too full to reply, so she continues. "I mean, d'you know how many Johns there are on Facebook?" She laughs and then stops when she sees that he doesn't understand. "I never knew your second name, see? You never told me. Fair enough, I suppose. I mean, we were only going out for a few weeks, weren't we?"

He dabs at his lips and clears his throat. He's on safer ground now. "Four," he says.

"For what?"

"No, we went out for *four* weeks. 28th of July to the 23rd of August." And then he adds with a broad smile, "1984, of course."

"Of course," she says. And adds, "Bloody hell, you've got a good memory."

He agrees, tells her he's on a quiz team and they've won trophies. They almost got on to *Only Connect* once but it didn't work out. Someone said something and there was some shouting and he was escorted from the studio. He doesn't tell her that part. Nor does he tell her why it's so easy for him to recall the minuscule details of such a brief relationship so many years after it ended. He keeps that to himself. The truth would make him seem pathetic. Which was a bad thing.

"Not quite four weeks, in fact," he adds.

"I thought it was longer," she says, her eyes drifting towards her glass. "It seemed longer."

"I must have made an impact on you, then," he laughs. "That's a joke, by the way."

She smiles. "Yeah."

"You certainly made one on me," he says. "An impact, that is."

"Ah, that's sweet of you, John."

"Technically, we only actually *went out* on three occasions in that time. But there were the phone calls, too."

She nods.

"Remember those? The long conversations we used to have?"

Now she can't speak because she's drinking. She flutters her eyes and murmurs agreement.

"You used to call me at all hours," he says. *Until Mother found out.*

Tracy swallows. "Yeah," she says. "You were a good listener."

This is going great. He leans forward. "Quick pop quiz," he says. "Who was number one on the day we first met?"

Her eyes widen like a doll's and her mouth opens and closes silently.

"Ding! Time's up!" he says with a grin. "It was, of course, Frankie Goes to Hollywood with *Two Tribes*."

She stares at him, those crystal blues unblinking.

"All coming back to you now, I bet," he says.

She takes a large glug of house white.

"That," he continues, "was Frankie's second number one in the UK. *Relax* being their first, of course."

"Of course," she agrees.

"Their third, and final, UK number one was *The Power of Love*." He gives her a cheeky grin.

She looks blank so he presses on.

"But that was in December of 1984. Obviously, it was after we... after I..." *Damn, it had been going so well!*

She sees him floundering and lends a hand. "After you dumped me?"

"Yes," he says. "After... that." John feels his heart beating too fast. He straightens some invisible creases from his shirt. And then quietly adds, "When we split up, George Michael was number one. *Careless Whisper*."

"Take your word for it," she says. "I was never much into music."

"No," he says. "Me neither."

The conversation grinds to a halt, like a rusty engine. He uses the lull to get more drinks in. It's fruit juice for him now. More than one pint of beer and he starts shooting his mouth off. And tonight, of all nights, he really needs to keep control of himself.

She's still on the wine.

"Ask if they do a larger glass," she calls after him.

While he's waiting at the bar, he thinks about what to say next. His plan to run down the number ones for 1984 was probably out the window given her unexpected disinterest in chart statistics. As a fallback he could offer up some suggestions on how she could have determined the number of Johns on Facebook.

But when he returns, Tracy looks sad. He thinks he knows why.

"I'm sorry about how it ended," he says, shuffling his chair closer to the table. "I really didn't want to split up, you know."

"Was it me? Something I said?" She's smiling, as though it is a matter of supreme irrelevance.

It was Mother.

"Or was there someone else?"

Mother made me end it. "Yes," he says, looking into his glass of orange juice. "That's it. Someone else." He takes a drink. "And I'm sorry."

Tracy's lips twitch. "You already said that, John."

"Well, I wish I hadn't... Wish I had..."

She groans. "Christ, John. It was thirty years ago."

"No hard feelings, then?" he asks.

She shakes her head and purses her lips. "I've kind of moved on, babe."

"Of course you have," he says. He sits back and sips at his drink. That went better than expected.

Tracy takes a few good swigs of wine and then takes a deep breath. "I know this sounds horrible, but when I met you, I thought, wow! He's gorgeous!"

John quickly rocks forward and laughs. "Gosh, that isn't horrible at all."

"I haven't finished, John."

He beams furiously and mimes zipping his mouth.

"I didn't care that you were a bit... different."

His smile quakes and falls.

Different. That's what Mother used to call him.

She is examining her fingernails now. They're chipped. "I'd just finished with Steve Bishop, you see. I still had the bruises. You must have noticed."

He recalls her talking a lot about someone called Steve. He doesn't remember any bruises; possibly because he didn't see enough of her flesh during their four-week romance. But he misses his chance to reply.

"I was drinking a lot back then. Things were spiralling out of control," she says. "I suppose what I'm saying is that I really needed someone like you at that point in my life. Someone I could just talk to. Someone harmless."

Harmless? Is that a good thing? He supposes it is. After all, the opposite would be *harmful*. And he hates it when people think that about him.

She looks very sad indeed. He needs to show empathy now. He dons a serious expression and puts his hand on hers. They're cold. Not nice to touch. "Sorry," he says again. *But Mother had been quite insistent. She didn't want me... breeding.*

"Believe me, Steve bloody Bishop was an angel compared to some of the scumbags I ended up with over the years." Her scowl deepens the lines, brings out the years. "I've never had much luck with men," she says. "I mean, look at you and me!" Then she laughs, which he finds odd. It doesn't seem like a humorous moment. But he gets that wrong sometimes. He matches her smile.

"All in the past, though, eh?" he says.

She beams at him, her eyes sparkle, and the years recede again. "I'd given up hope of finding you," she says. "Nothing to go on, see? Well, nothing except 'John from Bromley'." She finds his name funny all over again. "And then, you go and message me. Just like that! I couldn't believe it," she says.

"Wait—you really did try to find me?"

"Of course. Come on, John, we've all done it. Looked up old flames. Human nature, isn't it, raking over the ashes?"

This is excellent news. Really excellent news.

"Had no trouble finding all the others," she adds. "Plastered themselves all over the internet, like they're

384

something special with their slutty peroxide wives and little bastard brats." She spits the words.

"Why did you look them up if you didn't like them?" he asks.

"Had to. I want to draw a line under that part of my life; the part I spent getting fucked over by weirdoes and losers. I'm a different person now. Do you see?"

He doesn't see. She looks very much the same person to him, especially when she smiles.

"You actually got in touch with them?"

"Never mind them," she says. She drains the glass and slides it towards him. "Dutch courage," she adds.

He looks at the lipstick-smeared glass and wonders if she's finding the evening as difficult as he is. These situations can be a minefield.

"You know," she says, "I think you were the only decent bloke I ever went out with, all things considered. Ironic, eh?"

He doesn't think she's using irony the right way but he keeps his tongue still. Could she be telling the truth? Does she really feel something for him after all this time?

Up at the bar again, he reflects on how well this is going. Better than he ever hoped. Conversation is flowing again, even though the beer has worn off. He doesn't think he's shown himself up too much. He's stuck religiously to the fruit juice. He's in control. Yes, it's all going very well.

"So, how's things with you?" she asks when he sets the fresh round on the table. "What has John from Bromley been up to lately?"

"She died last week," he says. "My mother."

Tracy swipes a dribble of wine from her lips, smearing her lipstick. "I'm sorry, babe," she says.

"You don't need to be sorry," he replies.

"I understand," she says. "She'll always be with you."

He nods.

She taps her chest. "In here," she says.

He looks down and puts his hand on his heart. The beat is slow, faint.

The bar is filling up. The noise level is increasing by the minute, yet silence fills the space between them. *Light* conversation, he reminds himself. He clears his throat.

"So how about you, Trace? What have you been up to?"

She shakes her head and takes a drink. "Married. Divorced. Widowed." Her words echo into the glass as she guzzles. "Been there, done that. Bought the T-shirt."

They did T-shirts for that sort of thing? Well, why not? They did them for everything else.

"I really know how to pick 'em," she says.

He tells her he's sorry to hear it and wonders how he can change the subject to something *lighter*.

"And you? Married? Significant other?" she asks.

Did his mother count as a significant other? "Uh, no. Not really," he stammers. "No one at all."

"Good," she says with a smile that's almost not there. "That makes us both old, free and single!" She raises her wine glass.

He picks up on the hint and does likewise. She knocks her glass into his and winks. It feels as though something heavy and repressive has climbed off his chest. He watches her finish her drink. He has the measure of this situation now: she drinks and talks. All he has to do is listen.

For the next twenty minutes or so she offers up a jigsaw puzzle of facts about her life that he struggles to piece together. It seems to involve a lot of anger and death. And she's been ill, she says. But she's on the road to recovery now. He asks if it's catching and she laughs again. She does that a lot; more than she cries. Which is a relief. Perhaps he should have got her drunk all those years ago. Things might have worked out very differently. For them both.

Then she talks about ghosts. He says he doesn't believe in ghosts.

She gets serious for a moment, pins his hands to the table with those icy fingers, and insists that there are such things, and they need to be laid to rest.

"If you don't deal with them," she says, "they can really fuck you up." Tracy stares into his eyes as she slowly enunciates these last three words: *Fuck…you…up.*

Her gaze discomforts him. He retrieves his hands, rubs them warm, and tells her about his role at the library. She stops staring, tells him it's good that he's managed to get a job. Really good. He agrees.

They go back to his flat. As he closes the front door behind them, she asks him if he makes a habit of stalking his exes on the internet.

"No," he says.

"You're not telling me I'm the only one?"

"Yes," he says, "you are." And he means it. She is the only one.

"God, that's so sweet," she says. "I really did like you. Such a shame."

"A shame that you like me?"

She rolls her eyes. "I think you know what I mean."

He doesn't.

He starts to show her his CDs, promises to dig out Frankie Goes to Hollywood for old time's sake. He'll need a minute to go through his inventory.

"There's 4,352," he explains. "You have to have a system, see?"

But she can't wait. She needs to piss like a horse. "I can't hold it like I used to," she explains.

"Well, alcohol is a diuretic and you did have five glasses of house white," he says. "Four of which were the size of a small fishbowl."

A pause.

Then she laughs. Uncontrollably. Tears roll down her face. Her even, tanned complexion is lined with silver rivulets. Beneath the wet tracks, she is paler, older.

"You are funny, John," she gasps. "I always thought that about you. You were the funny one."

Still giggling, she hurries to the bathroom and shuts herself in before he can stop her. He should have told her to empty her bladder in the pub. She is taking aeons and the laughter has subsided. But Frankie is advising him to *Relax*. Sound advice. He thumbs through his inventory.

When Tracy emerges from the bathroom, she isn't smiling. She seems less drunk.

"Is everything OK?" he says, clutching a CD case to his chest.

She leads him to the sofa and puts her handbag down. He leans into her and forces kisses upon her. She tastes of wine and lipstick. He remembers that taste, her taste, even though they had only kissed twice before. Half a lifetime ago.

"You're full of surprises," she says, pulling away from him.

He watches as she undresses and puts her clothes in a neat pile beside the sofa. He wants to tell her he loves her, has always loved her. He wants to tell her that now they are back together, he won't ever let her go again. Maybe he'll say it during sex. He's seen that in films. Or maybe he'll wait until after, when it's all over.

He puts the CD case down, places his hands over her bare breasts – and catches sight of a photograph on the little table beside the sofa. Mother is watching him rolling his palms over Tracy's rigid pink nipples. He stops.

Tracy follows his gaze to the black and white photo. "Holding on to her like this," she says. "It's not healthy, John." She turns the photo to face the wall.

He wipes his hands on his trousers. "I found her on the doorstep last week."

"That must have been awful for you."

"She was covered in blood."

"There are some real maniacs about," she says.

He watches her breasts jiggle as she bends over and rummages in her handbag. A condom? He's never used one. He wasn't even sure he wanted to do anything with Tracy now. He turns the photo back the way it was.

"She answered the front door and they just stabbed her," he says. "Why would someone do that?"

"Isn't it obvious?" Tracy says. "She was an interfering old hag."

He feels it before he sees it. And by the time he sees it, it's inside him.

"Like I said, John, I never would have found you if you hadn't tracked me down."

They call it cold steel but it feels pretty hot to him. White hot, deep inside his chest.

"But I'm absolutely made up that you did. The pair of you have completed the set for me. Every last ghost."

He's almost pleased for her. It's always nice to have the full set of something. But the pain is awful. He can't speak. His hands wrap around the hilt but he can't get a grip. It's rock solid, and slippery with the warm blood that's gushing onto his lap and dripping onto the carpet. He's still scrabbling at the knife as the room blackens.

"No point pulling it out, babe," she says, rubbing her sticky scarlet fingers on the sofa and swiping splashes and smears of blood from her breasts and thighs. "Take it from me, broken hearts never mend."

She strolls back to the bathroom and checks herself in the mirror. The blood is already drying into a camouflage pattern of rust-coloured swirls and splotches. She rips back the shower curtain above the bath and pulls out the plug.

"Budge up, bitch," she says as the water gurgles down the drain, leaving a thin blanket of melting ice cubes covering John's mother.

Blind Man's Buff

Anton hovered in the kitchen doorway. The banging and clanking as the cover was fitted back onto the boiler signalled that the job was almost finished.

"Fucker!"

And then a crash as the cover fell to the worktop and a shower of screws cascaded to the tiled floor.

"Everything OK?" asked Anton.

"Yeah, it's nothing," said the boiler man. A scrape of metal followed as he returned to the job in hand.

It sounded like the idiot had wrecked the kitchen. Not for the first time, Anton wished he could see exactly what was going on.

He could feel the man looking back at him. Did his sightless stare seem to press for an explanation?

"Just a spider," said the workman. "Big bastard, though."

Then the sound of scattered screws being scratched up from the floor.

Just a spider.

Anton folded his arms around his chest, glad he hadn't seen the big bastard. One benefit of being blind. The only benefit. He would never again have to suffer the sight of their beady little eyes, their glistering tattooed bodies, their tiny serrated jaws. And the legs—scrabbling and scurrying.

Mention of them always triggered the same memories.

When he was a child, an ugly dirt-brown house spider, with bristly legs and eyes on stalks, had tumbled from the ceiling onto his bed as he lay there reading by lamplight. Anton had watched it somersault towards him, legs flailing in the air, and heard it land with a plop on his bedspread. He had uttered a high-pitched shriek, like a woman being throttled, and had leaped from the bed as though he had been jolted out of it by an electric shock. The spider skittered away. Each night, for the next four weeks, he had been compelled to check every inch of his room (every fold of the sheets, every crevice inside the pillows) before he could climb into bed. But the spider was never found.

A month after the incident, he awoke one morning to find his hands bound by threads of silk. Upon his cheeks were little bite marks, encrusted with congealing blood. Furious and terrified, he followed the trail of fine strands until they disappeared under his pillow. He dragged his bed away from the wall and ripped up the carpet. Sticking to the bare floorboards, he found a mushy white mass of eggs. Against his mother's pleas, Anton had stomped on the nest until the baby spiders were nothing more than a creamy goo.

"That's bad luck," his mother had said. "Terrible bad luck."

Now Anton cleared his throat. "That spider," he said. "Did you get it?"

"No mate, he's dropped behind the kitchen unit," puffed the workman, still straining to fit the cover back on the boiler. "But I reckon I scared him as much as he scared me. He won't come out again in a hurry."

Anton wanted to ask him exactly how big the bastard had been, and where it was, but before he could rustle up a suitably nonchalant voice, the workman's mobile rang.

Anton left the room and waited by the front door.

People think that when you go blind you develop superhuman hearing to compensate. It isn't true. But it didn't stop him straining to hear the man's whispered conversation:

"Almost done here... size of a kid's fist... getting out."

Had he really said that? What did he mean?

Anton pictured the last one he had ever seen. It was the last *thing* he had ever seen.

At first, he had thought that there was something on the road ahead. Something dark and twitching. But the object never came closer. And it soon dawned on him that the blurry blob obstructing his line of sight was in fact right in front of his eyes, clinging tenuously to the back of the rear-view mirror, exposing its twitching legs and polished bead torso as it conjured a thread around the glass. At that moment it lost its grip on the mirror, almost as if its nerve had failed under Anton's panicked gaze. The spider thrashed helplessly in mid-air, swinging like a wrecking ball.

Then it fell.

The image of an earth-brown bundle of limbs and eyes tumbling into his lap became etched onto Anton's retina.

Even though the accident had blinded him instantly, he knew that the spider had been there at the scene afterwards, ogling him from the wreckage with those jewelled eyes, as the emergency crew cut him free and stretchered him away to another life.

Terrible bad luck.

As soon as the front door closed behind the boiler man, Anton rushed to the cupboard under the stairs and pulled out the vacuum cleaner. He fired it up and shoved it down the back of the unit beneath the boiler at full blast. Then he ran it all around the rest of the kitchen, scraping the corners of the fitted cabinets, smashing it against the fridge, forcing it behind the radiator. When he was done, he tore out the bag, rushed outside and stuffed it deep into the rubbish bin.

Standing in the kitchen, his sightless eyes were drawn to the walls and ceiling. *Should have brushed them down first*, he thought. But, he reasoned, even if it was clinging to the coving watching him right now, it would probably be content to stay put, harvesting the little flies and breadcrumbs that find their way into its kitchen domain. Why would it venture further afield? And if he made enough noise entering the kitchen, surely the spider would hurry into a darkened corner and keep away from him? Sooner or later, it would quietly die of old age. It was a comforting thought.

For a while.

That night Anton jerked awake. Something had gently brushed his ear. He opened his eyes and saw dark shapes lurching across the pale pillow next to his face. Powder blue, just as the shop assistant had told him.

He threw back the covers and leaped out of bed, gasping for air. Standing beside the bed, he could see dozens of them crawling out from behind the bed, tentatively reaching out for him like a blind man would.

Like *he* would.

Anton raised a hand in front of his face. He could see it as a glowing, almost star-shaped object. He turned and slapped his star-hand against the wall where he knew the light switch was situated. It clicked.

All was black. No hand. No bed. No spiders.

He clicked the light again.

Black.

And again.

Black.

There was a lamp in the corner of the room. He ran over to it and slid his hand up the stand.

Click.

Black.

He stared at the bed for long minutes, straining to see what he could not see.

After his pulse had slowed to a steady canter, he returned to the headboard and smoothed his palm downwards, all the way to the pillow. Then he placed both hands on the quilt and felt every inch.

Nothing.

Anton slumped onto the bed and cupped his head in his hands.

The traps arrived next day. Express delivery. Twenty in all.

He spent the entire morning carefully feeling his way around the house, gently placing the traps along the skirting board, in the corners of all the rooms, and pushing them behind cupboards.

They were a simple construction. Triangles of card, with sticky inside surfaces guaranteed to immobilise any insect unlucky enough to stroll onto them.

That night he slept well.

Realisation dawned the next morning that, at some point, he would have to check the traps.

The following Saturday, Anton began to probe the inside of each sticky pyramid. His four fingers, he discovered, just about fit inside the traps if he tucked his thumb into his palm. But he had to take care to feel his way to the opening and slide his hand in steadily to avoid becoming stuck himself.

The downstairs traps yielded nothing but a lone woodlouse and a silky (and still fluttering) moth. He left those traps where they lay.

Upstairs, Anton crouched beside the balustrade. If his nightmare had any basis in reality, upstairs is where he would find the culprits.

As he slid his hand into the first trap, on the landing adjacent to the top step, the hairs on the back of his neck began to prickle. He would find something in here. That dream was just his subconscious telling him what he already knew: they had been roaming around up here in the night, skittering along the skirting, clambering up the walls, watching him, probing him as he slept.

He wanted to find a spider stuck to the trap, and yet he didn't want to feel the creature's pulpy little body wriggling beneath his touch. He hesitated, his fingertips gently hovering in the tiny space inside the little card pyramid.

Suddenly, there was a wet, tickling sensation inside his collar. Without a conscious thought, his free hand shot up to slap the back of his neck. In so doing, the hand inside the trap jittered and glued itself to the sides of the box. He yelped and leaped upright. His left hand found his neck sheeted with sweat. No spider. But pressed against his stuck right hand was a cold, slightly fuzzy object that squirmed clammily against his palm, and little stick-like protrusions scrabbled against his fingers.

He screamed and grabbed at the box with his free hand. As he did so, he felt a weird sensation of the world inverting around him. He twisted in the air, somersaulted backwards, crashed his head against the wall, tumbled over and over, and finally came to rest on his back at the foot of the stairs.

A cold sense of consciousness washed over Anton. His head felt like it had been struck with a hammer and his back seemed to have been trampled on by a herd of elephants. There was a dull crackling sound, like someone breaking twigs, whenever he moved.

He winced as he hauled himself up onto his elbows, opened his eyes. And saw that he was half draped up the first three steps of the staircase.

Saw.

His heart lurched into his throat.

His legs, immobile but painless, were twisted around from his waist like he was a human corkscrew—the source of the sickening crackling sound.

Anton blinked against the daylight lasering in through the front window. The pain in his skull sent burning rockets of blood-red and ice-white flashing across his vision each time he moved. He rolled his eyes to the left and saw that the dull brown carpet was worn threadbare in the hallway and the skirting was yellowed and peeling.

Something was digging uncomfortably into his right hand. Then he remembered everything.

Terrible bad luck.

He scraped the little card box against the grubby old carpet, breaking it apart. There was nothing inside.

A cloud must have passed overhead because the light beaming into the hallway through the glass front door suddenly darkened. Or was night falling? Exactly how long had he been lying there unconscious?

Out of the corner of his eyes he saw something plummet to the floor beside him, bouncing just a little as it landed.

It was the biggest spider he had ever seen.

Anton tried to pull himself away, but trying to drag his broken lower half off the stairs sent unbearable spikes of pain down his spine and dizzied his vision until he almost passed out.

The spider righted itself with the awkward dignity of a drunk trying to pass himself off as sober while dragging himself out of the gutter. It locked eyes with Anton and then, in no real hurry, began staggering towards him.

Anton raised a fist, the one that still had bits of spider-trap stuck to it, and slammed it down on the creature. "Bastard!" he gasped through clenched teeth.

His skull flared again and he closed his eyes against the pain. When he opened them, he saw that the walls were moving. Writhing. Wriggling. Black patches squirmed and twisted, jerked and tumbled.

Spiders.

Hundreds of them.

Thousands of glittering eyes seemed to be winking in the waning light.

Anton looked down again at his useless legs. Directly above him, trembling bodies threatened to fall in a shower of monstrous limbs. There was only one way out of this.

Screaming all the while, Anton raised his hands to his face and pressed his fingers deep into his eyes. When he had a good, firm hold on each one, he tore them out.

All the Rage

Nobody answers the door. Either the owner isn't home or they're peering through the net curtains, afraid to open up to a dishevelled man with blood running down his forehead.

He swipes at the itchy red trail with a sweaty palm, leaving a bright line of pain just above his brow.

The panting probably isn't helping. He must sound like a maniac. He turns away from the door and looks back down the overgrown drive towards the road. She hasn't followed him. Not yet. With any luck she hasn't even noticed this place tucked away behind the hedgerows lining the narrow country lane. He tries to steady his breathing by drawing a long, slow lungful of air. It's time to think, to plan what to do next.

He could break a window and climb in. If the owner is cowering inside, it might make them call the police—if they haven't already. Which would be a good thing. It would save him from wasting time explaining what had happened.

He picks up a moss-covered stone from a straggly rock garden bordering the drive and draws back his arm.

Wait!

The sound of shattering glass is bound to attract her attention. For the moment, he is safe. If she finds this cottage, he won't stand a chance. He drops the stone, swipes his hands down his jeans and tries his phone again. At last, a signal. Despite his predicament he almost laughs with relief—almost. He stabs out 999. The call is answered immediately. "Police," he gasps.

He knows that Ruth is dead. He saw her face evaporate in a cloud of red mist; saw her drop to the tarmac like a puppet with its strings cut. But he adds, "Ambulance."

They ask where he is calling from. His brain refuses to retrieve the information and he stares impotently towards the front gate. Standing here outside a locked door suddenly makes him feel vulnerable again. There's nothing between him and the road. The woman must be close. She might be able to hear him talking to the emergency people, might home in on his voice. Judging from the way she handles the shotgun, she could probably hit him from a distance.

"We were on our way to a party out in the sticks," he whispers. "I just followed the sat nav."

The operator tells him she can have his call traced but she can provide help more quickly if he can tell her exactly where he is.

There is a sudden burning pain inside his head, like someone is digging around behind his eyes with a kebab skewer, and he can feel warm liquid trickling down the bridge of his nose.

"Sir? Are you still there?"

He hears a gentle crackling sound coming from somewhere beyond the drive; cautious footfalls on dead leaves. The footsteps of a hunter.

"Sir? The system is telling me you're in east Surrey. I'm afraid that's quite a wide area so I really am going to need something more from you."

"Yes," he hisses, letting out the breath he had been unconsciously holding. "I'm trying to think. The party was in Molesby. We had a crash. Blind corner. You know what country lanes are like. The other driver got out. We argued and then—"

"Molesby in Surrey?"

"Yes, that's where the party is. But we weren't there yet."

The operator asks if he recalls any road signs. He puts his free hand to his throbbing, wet forehead. The daylight is hurting his eyes so he closes them and tries to remember. But all he can picture is the blinding flash from the shotgun muzzle and seeing Ruth's head spraying apart in front of him.

"Ruth is dead."

Maybe nobody's answering the door because nobody's home. They might be at work. Or out shopping. He needs a place to hide right now. And he needs to remember where he is.

"Sir? Who is Ruth?"

He finds a low wooden gate to one side of the cottage. It looks like it might creak if he opens it, so he clambers over it and into a muddy yard bordered by sky-high leylandii. Lined along the peeling rear wall of the cottage like sentries are two wheelie bins and a water butt and an ancient metal dustbin that has been converted into an incinerator. The secluded enclosure reeks of rotten food and burnt things. There is a peeling blue door. He tries the age-blackened brass handle. It rattles but the door doesn't open.

Now he hears the rapid crunching sound of someone striding confidently up the gravel drive towards the house.

"Please, you must help! My fiancée's been killed. The other driver—the woman from the Land Rover—she has a shotgun. And now she's coming for me. For God's sake send someone now!"

The door has a pebbled glass panel. He rams a fist into it and it snaps, releasing a ripe stench. He punches out the remaining shards and fishes a hand around inside until he makes contact with a catch. He flicks it and the door swings inward. Behind him, the little side gate squeals. He hurries into the house and slams the door closed without looking back.

He's in a kitchen. There must be knives. He knows he can't afford to hesitate but he dithers between looking for a weapon and simply running deeper into the house.

The operator has been quiet for too long so he pulls the phone from his ear. There is some blood on the screen but he can see through the greasy red smears that the call has disconnected. His battery is dead. The police can't help him now. It's too late. He rattles open a drawer and rummages through a thin jumble of tarnished cutlery but all the knives are small, blunt. He opens another. A tangle of tea towels.

On the stove he sees a large saucepan of bubbling liquid. Scummy white foam is spilling over the rim and running down the side of the pot to fizz and sputter in the guttering flames of the ancient gas hob. On a chopping board beside the stove is a pair of severed hands. A large meat cleaver rests between them and, he thinks, it looks as though the hands have somehow just finished separating themselves from their owner. He is transfixed by the gruesome display, half expecting the hands to come to life.

The pain in his head is almost unbearable now. He struggles to recall why he is standing in this stinking hovel staring at disembodied hands.

Something scurries down his face, tickling like a column of marching ants. He reaches up and his fingers follow a slick, warm trail from his forehead to his chin.

"My word, laddie. You're in a bit of a state, aren't you?"

Peering through the broken window is the woman with the shotgun. A wild frizz of greying hair swirls around a drawn, pallid face from which bulbous pale eyes glimmer. She slides the gun's barrel through the window.

Smashed glass…

The windscreen.

He remembers now. He went through the windscreen. And Ruth is dead.

The cleaver is out of reach. The pan on the stove is closer. He lunges for it, catches the handle and hurls the contents at the woman. Instinctively she raises both hands to protect her eyes against the boiling water. The shotgun jerks upwards and she shrieks as the scalding liquid douses her face. Twin volcanoes of orange flame erupt into the room and rip the ceiling apart, showering him in a storm of plaster and filling the small space with a choking fog of dust and cordite.

The head that was braising in the pan crashes into the back door and tumbles to the floor, its broiled flesh peeling from the bone as it rolls around the lumpy linoleum.

The woman has disappeared from the window. His ears are howling from the gunshot but he can still hear her shrieking at him from outside.

"You little bastard! You trash my lovely Landie, break into my home and now you've spoiled my supper!"

He looks from the sticky severed head on the floor to the blood-crusted hands on the worktop.

You've spoiled my supper!

He drops the empty pan and snatches up the cleaver, half expecting the amputated hands guarding it to leap up from the counter and stop him.

A telltale snicker-snack sound from outside means that she is breaking the gun and snapping it closed again, reloaded. Then he sees her boiled-meat face reappear at the window. The door swings open.

"Jesus, lad, I'm going to fuck you up!"

The urge to turn and run almost overwhelms him and he feels his feet shuffle backwards, as if they are being magnetically drawn away from the danger in the kitchen. But he knows it would be suicide to show her his back. His options have all been whittled down to just one possible course of action.

Her fingers, wet from the greasy liquid with which he has just soaked her, squirm on the gunstock but she manages to level the weapon at his stomach. He smashes it to one side with the cleaver. It slithers from her grasp and tumbles between her legs. He raises his arm above his head and then slams it down. The impact sends a jolt through his body as the thick blade bites into the top of the woman's skull. It sounds, and feels, like an axe hitting a log. She howls like a wounded animal but she is still alive, fumbling with the gun trapped between her thighs. He wrenches the cleaver out of her scalp and raises it for a second strike.

A gunshot. A section of the doorframe beside his face shatters.

He looks up. In the yard, three men in black, crouching, pointing at him.

He blinks away blood.

No, he decides. They're not really pointing.

The serene moment of silence is broken by a crackle of radio static. He feels the woman slump to her knees. Her loose, bloody head brushes the fingers of his left hand. His right arm, holding the dripping cleaver aloft, is frozen in time.

Another shot. And another.

"Got him," says one of the policemen. "Call it in."

Final Resting Place

Coral wrapped her arms tightly around herself. It was hard to believe that the desert, an unbearable furnace just two hours ago, could turn into a windswept, icy tundra at sunset.

Mimicking the blustery weather outside, the events of the last twenty-four hours were spinning haphazardly around her head in a tornado of sights, sounds and emotions: the noisy confusion of her arrival in Cairo, the nerve-shredding meeting she had stuttered through at the museum, and the bumpy flight out to this remote patch of desert. Her mind was screaming at her to go to sleep, yet her memories kept replaying over and over in a loop. The sandstorm hammering at the tent added to her disorientation and seemed destined to guarantee her a sleepless night.

Coral's discovery, she knew, would force change upon her. Anonymity, a precious state of being that Coral had embraced her whole life, was no longer an option. She would be brought to public attention. Not in a huge way (she wasn't going to replace footballers' wives on the cover of glossy magazines), but there would be articles written. Maybe even a headline for a day or two: *Bookworm Discovers Long-lost Mummy*.

Her stomach tightened.

She had been flattered when her colleagues had made a fuss about her findings; she was made to feel proud of her achievement. Her dry research work in the bowels of the British Museum rarely gave her any reason to feel that emotion. But the news of her discovery had quickly ignited an unexpected level of interest in the academic world and soon the whole business had rapidly spiralled out of her control. The museum had insisted she fly out to Egypt and join a brief reconnaissance mission. Afraid of disappointing her colleagues with a mousy little refusal, Coral had agreed.

The full significance of her findings only fully blossomed once she arrived in Cairo that afternoon. Having barely recuperated from a cramped and sweaty five-hour flight, Coral had been ushered in to a startlingly bright and airless room at the Egyptian Museum. There, she had been made to stand in front of a dozen experienced local Egyptologists and explain why she believed a white blob on a satellite map was the final resting place of one of the ancient world's most enigmatic and elusive figures. It had been the most harrowing experience of her life.

She almost wished she had kept her discoveries to herself. Right now, she would be snug in her cosy bed in her cosy flat in south London, her only disturbance the sound of her cat scratching at the door to be let in. Instead, she was camped out in the middle of the Sahara, listening to the howling wind and wondering what on earth she had let herself in for.

The tent must have been made for a child, she decided. It was so small and tight around her that it felt like she was wearing the damned thing. She could feel the coolness of the canvas radiating against her face and could smell the tarnished metal of the zip that kept her shut in.

The wind continued to shriek around her, buffeting the flimsy canvas structure as though determined to rip it up and hurl it (with Coral tangled inside) into the bleak desert wilderness. It felt so much like giant hands slapping at the walls that Coral had the unsettling feeling the incessant hammering was not all the wind's doing.

Intermittently, she could hear the voices of the other members of the expedition, unintelligible foreign phrases snatched away mid-sentence by the to-ing and fro-ing of the storm. It was possible, wasn't it, that they were playing a prank on her? Trying to put the fear of God into the arrogant English woman who was about to become famous for stumbling—almost accidentally—across such an important relic from their past.

She shuffled forward on her hands and knees, pinched the zip's tab between her fingertips and began to pull it down. Instinctively, she screwed her eyes into slits. The wind seemed relatively mild at the front of the tent, protected as it was by the rock tomb they had come here to investigate. But even so, a few grains of sand pattered against her cheeks and prickled the back of her hand as she worked at the opening; an oddly nostalgic sensation that revived memories of wrestling with recalcitrant windbreaks on blustery English beaches as a child.

She briefly wondered if she should call out, ask the Egyptians if they were all right, but quickly decided that she would rather not attract their attention. She felt uncomfortable in their company. She was an outsider. And she had been made to feel like a cuckoo in the nest right from the start.

The young archaeology student, Kamal, was enthusiastic enough about the mini expedition. His English was good and he seemed to enjoy practising his linguistic skills on Coral. He was open-minded about what to expect when they opened the tomb the next morning. His boss, Dr Mariam Nageib, was less keen. A senior archaeologist at the Egyptian Museum, Dr Nageib had already succeeded in embarrassing Coral at that awful meeting. She was highly critical of the whole escapade and took every opportunity to exercise her own excellent English by making a variety of patronising and dismissive observations about Coral's research.

There was a burst of laughter outside.

Coral drew her hand back inside the tent, tugged the zip closed and pulled the sleeping bag around herself.

*

In the harsh glare of the morning sun, the white blob looked even more like a miniature pyramid than when they had arrived the previous night.

"Good morning, Miss Fletcher," said Kamal cheerily.

"Morning, Kamal." Coral took the bottle of water he proffered. "Thanks."

"Looks very promising, doesn't it?"

Coral gave him a puzzled look.

"The pyramid. It looks untouched. Maybe today we find High Priest Penthu or his royal mistress. Or both!" he said.

Dr Nageib had overheard the exchange. "It *might* belong to High Priest Penthu," she said tersely. "And it *might* belong to Queen Kiya. The pair of them *might* have been having an affair and they *might* have been banished for it. All of which would be very romantic and, I'm sure, would garner great interest in European countries that revel in celebrity gossip and sexual scandals, Miss Fletcher. But your theory is highly speculative and we can't allow lurid conjecture to take the place of scientific investigation."

She sneered at the crude prismatic structure before them. "Our ancestors were famed for the quality and precision of their work," she said, waving a hand. "This *thing* looks like nothing more than a shelter built by clumsy European soldiers during some colonial expedition."

Kamal smiled sheepishly. "Well, if you look at Miss Fletcher's map, Dr Negeib, this location is clearly on a direct route to Syria—where Queen Kiya came from. It's not beyond the realms of possibility that she and Penthu were fleeing back across the border when one or both of them fell ill and died. Right here. That's all Miss Fletcher is saying, isn't it?"

Coral nodded.

"Coincidence and supposition are no substitute for a forensic investigation," said Dr Negeib. "True archaeology requires rather more skill and knowledge than the ability to trace a line on a map. And perhaps you were unaware, Miss Fletcher," she added, "that we have already found Penthu's tomb. It's in Amarna, far to the south of here, and it is well known to all genuine Egyptologists."

Genuine Egyptologists. Coral bit her lip, waited a beat. She knew she should let it go. But she couldn't. "Penthu had the tomb in Amarna built at the height of his power, in readiness for an elaborate funeral," blurted Coral. "That much is known. But it was a time of chaos and upheaval. We don't know when or where he died, or under what circumstances. And there is no evidence that his body was ever actually buried in Amarna."

"I agree it was a time of chaos," said Dr Negeib. "We know that plague swept through the New Kingdom during Akhenaten's reign."

It was, Coral knew, well documented that the Middle Kingdom era had suffered an explosion in the population of rats—rats that carried plague-infected fleas. The crowded cities and insanitary conditions meant that plague swept through communities like fire through a sawmill.

"It's more than likely," continued Dr Nageib, "that Penthu died of the disease, along with thousands of others. There would have been too many to bury individually. Mass graves or pits would have been the only viable solution. He probably ended up in one of those, along with hundreds of other poor wretches."

"And Queen Kiya?" said Kamal. "Why were her cartouches defaced? That suggests a fall from grace rather than an untimely death. Perhaps because she was having an affair with High Priest Penthu?"

Dr Nageib's face darkened. "Her disappearance and Penthu's death are totally unconnected," she said. "Kiya was a foreigner. If she didn't die of natural causes, she probably fell foul of the deteriorating diplomatic relations with her father's kingdom around that time. She was most likely either executed or simply sent home."

Probably? Most likely? Now who's relying on coincidence and supposition? thought Coral.

Suggesting alternative theories to Dr Nageib was like trying to fend off an attack dog with a string of sausages: she snapped at any challenge to her entrenched views. Coral held back her response this time. She didn't want an argument. Besides, Dr Mariam Nageib was a highly respected Egyptologist and she made a sound enough point. Coral could be wrong. They would only know who or what was inside the stone building once they had opened it up.

Dr Nageib strode away, head held high, towards the Cessna that had brought them out to the desert the previous evening. There, she spoke briefly to the fourth member of the party—the pilot, Mohammed. She was smiling; smugly, thought Coral. *She wants me to fall flat on my face. And there's every chance I will.*

The two of them disappeared inside the plane.

A few minutes later, the Egyptologist returned to the camp. Mohammed followed her, swinging a pickaxe in one hand and pulling a rusty, oil-stained metal contraption with the other.

"Are you sure we should be opening the tomb, Dr Nageib?" asked Kamal. "Perhaps we should wait for the full expedition?"

"And perhaps you should just do as you are told," said Dr Nageib. "This is not the final resting place of High Priest Penthu or Queen Kiya or anyone of any significance. Look at it! It's a travesty. I wouldn't even dare to call it a pyramid. The sooner we establish that this is a waste of everyone's time, the sooner we can forget this nonsense and get back to authentic research and legitimate archaeological investigation." Dr Negeib planted her hands on her hips and threw a viperous glance at Coral. "In fact, now that I have had the opportunity to inspect the building in daylight, I have called Cairo on the radio and told them that the whole thing is a false alarm. They won't be sending the rest of the expedition."

Coral felt her pulse grow thick in her throat and her face slowly redden.

"We will break into the structure just to confirm what I already know," said Dr Negeib. "We shall be able to return to Cairo before nightfall without wasting any more time." She flapped her hand, as though she was shooing away a mosquito. "And you, Miss Fletcher, can fly back to London."

Before Coral could construct a reply that didn't contain expletives, Mohammed said something to Kamal that made the two men laugh. Their amusement was immediately blasted away by an unintelligible reprimand from Dr Negeib.

"What did he say?" whispered Coral.

"Mohammed wants to know if there will be gold and jewels inside the tomb," said Kamal.

"Well, if it is the Queen, I suppose it might contain something of value, but that's not really what we're here for," said Coral.

Kamal translated and Mohammed grinned. He rubbed his fingers and clicked his tongue in a gesture Coral had quickly learned meant *baksheesh*—a tip for the most minimal service rendered.

Dr Nageib snapped something in Arabic and the good humour melted from both men's faces. "You'll turn his stupid head with promises of riches, Miss Fletcher. We are not sordid treasure hunters."

"I wasn't suggesting—"

"There will be nothing of value inside, either of historical significance or of monetary worth. So let's just get this over with, shall we?" She stalked off again.

Kamal nudged Mohammed and nodded at the lifting gear. In silence, they proceeded to fire up the engine and attach the equipment to the huge slab that barred the entrance.

While they worked, Coral sat under an awning scribbling notes. Now and then she ventured out to take snapshots of the white edifice and of Mohammed and Kamal's efforts at dislodging the stone door. Dr Nageib sat some twenty yards away, in the shade of the plane, only moving once in a while to bark orders at the two men.

By lunchtime, the slab had been moved sufficiently for Kamal to squeeze through the gap. Mohammed followed him inside. As soon as she saw them disappear, Coral stopped writing and hurried over to join them.

The ceiling of the hollow structure was low, no more than six feet at Coral's estimation. None of the three was tall enough to scrape their head but that didn't prevent each of them from instinctively stooping as they made their way to the centre of the chamber, where the apex rose slightly.

Mohammed switched on a storm lantern and placed it in one corner. It illuminated the sole object inside: a large sandstone sarcophagus.

"Oh my God, Miss Fletcher," whispered Kamal. "Oh my God."

Coral felt her eyes become thick with tears. Her vision blurred and she pressed a hand to her mouth to stifle a sob.

The daylight straining in through the narrow breach at the entrance was momentarily blotted out. Dr Nageib had arrived.

All four gathered around the stone coffin. Dr Nageib stood silently with her arms folded firmly against her chest but Coral and Kamal dropped to their knees and examined the crudely carved cartouche. The two exchanged glances and then looked up at Dr Nageib. But the chagrined look on the Egyptologist's face told them that she had already deciphered the hieroglyphic inscription for herself.

Coral said nothing. She still couldn't quite believe what she was seeing.

Kamal stood and turned to the only person present who was unable to read the cartouche—Mohammed.

"Kiya," he said aloud. "Queen of Egypt, princess of Mittanni; beloved of Penthu, keeper of the true faith."

But the pilot did not need a translation. He grinned and held out his hand to Kamal, who dug in his pockets and handed Mohammed two grubby notes.

"Uh, we had a bet," explained the student. "I said we would find Penthu inside. He said it must be Kiya because only a stupid priest could have built that bloody door."

"Maybe we should have put Mohammed in charge of the whole project," said Dr Nageib, her voice almost a whisper.

"It's nice to know someone had faith in me," said Coral, beaming at the pilot.

Mohammed kissed the notes and stuffed them into the breast pocket of his shirt.

"That fool has faith only in gold and jewels," said Dr Nageib. She traced the carving on the cartouche with her fingertips. "I suppose this means you were half right. You stumbled upon something after all."

Kamal beamed and grasped Coral's hands. "You're going to be famous now!"

"Well, let's confirm authenticity first," said Dr Nageib.

"Really?" said Kamal. "No one's been inside here for five thousand years. Did you smell the place when you came in? That smell. You can't describe it, Dr Nageib. I tell you, Mohammed and I were the first men to breathe that air since it was sealed."

"That's not very scientific, Kamal," said Coral. She aimed a smile at Dr Nageib.

"At least we can agree on that," sniffed Dr Nageib. "Besides, we don't even know if she's inside the sarcophagus."

"True," said Coral. She paused for effect. "It might be as empty as Penthu's tomb at Amarna."

Kamal translated for Mohammed whose face suddenly turned sour at the prospect of an empty coffin. He muttered something in Kamal's ear.

"I suppose we must wait for the proper expedition before we open her up?" asked Kamal. "Seems a pity. The lifting gear works perfectly well and we still have enough fuel to run the engine."

Dr Nageib shook her head. "Leave the sarcophagus alone. We'll need specialists out here before we do anything more. Today we'll just take photographs of the tomb. That's your job, Kamal."

She turned to Coral. "I suppose you'll want to join us again when we open the sarcophagus, Miss Fletcher? It might take a while to organise. I expect there will be a lot of international interest. You'll get your fame, after all. Maybe even a little fortune."

Coral felt something rise in her chest. "Look, I don't know what your problem is—" she began.

But Dr Nageib had turned away and begun issuing orders in Arabic, showing Mohammed and Kamal where to set up the lighting and what shots to take. When she was done, she stalked out of the pyramid and returned to the plane without another word.

Once they had fetched the camera gear, Mohammed and Kamal attached a canvas sheet to the front of the tomb, fixing it in place with loose rocks to keep out the creeping tide of sand that rippled around their feet.

Coral returned to the relative cool of the awning outside to write up the discovery. She tried to email a quick note to the British Museum but then remembered that she was in the middle of the desert. No signal. That was OK. The news could wait until they had returned to Cairo.

The find confirmed that Kiya, a princess from the Syrian kingdom of Mittanni and queen to the Egyptian pharaoh Akhenaten, had died in a remote desert location, far from any known town or city. Taken together with the obliteration of her cartouches from royal monuments, the logical conclusion was that she had fled or been banished. Moreover, the tomb's inscription made it clear that her disappearance from the royal household was indeed connected to her relationship with the high priest, Penthu.

Coral imagined the two of them slipping out of the palace grounds at night to rendezvous with a waiting caravan. There was no doubt that they had others with them. Penthu could not have constructed the pyramid alone. It would have taken dozens of men weeks to build. And that suggested some kind of following. But was it a personal following of family members and household staff, a religious congregation or a gathering of conspirators? Were they hoping to become the focal point for a rebellion against Akhenaten, who had sought to introduce a monotheistic faith to replace the panoply of deities traditionally worshipped and feared? His revolutionary ideas never took root and must have been regarded as heresy by many. Did Penthu and Kiya hope to set up a government in exile and rally an army to march on him?

Coral realised that her notes were becoming a frenzied, Joycean stream of consciousness. One idea tumbled into another, half-formed. She needed to take a breather, collect her thoughts. She didn't want to fire off something that gushed like a teenager tweeting about the latest boy band. She pushed wet hair from her brow and looked up from the screen as she tried to construct her next sentence.

In the mid-morning light, the pyramid looked as pristine as when she had spotted the tiny white speck on the satellite image. No wonder Dr Nageib was disgruntled, she thought. It was a particularly unconventional piece of research.

As she gazed at the pyramid, the canvas curtain across the doorway was torn aside. Suddenly, Kamal staggered out and weaved unsteadily towards Coral, making no attempt to shield his eyes from the blinding daylight that now beat down upon his upturned face.

He's staring right into the sun, she thought, *but he can't see it.*

She rushed out from behind her folding desk, her own hands instinctively flying up to protect her face from the unbearable glare.

413

Dr Nageib had also sensed something was wrong. She abandoned the shade of the Cessna and ran over. As she arrived, Kamal sank to his knees.

"What is it?" asked Coral. "What's the matter with him?"

Dr Nageib didn't reply. She spared one brief glance towards the tomb before grasping Kamal's face in her hands. She spoke to him in Arabic but his pained expression suggested that he could not even hear her voice.

And then he started to bleed. Dr Nageib snatched her hands away. Fresh, cherry-red blood scurried in little threads from his mouth, from his nose and from his eyes. At first a trickle, like the first warm raindrops of a summer squall. Then the storm broke and a scarlet torrent cascaded down his handsome young features.

Kamal fell forward, coughing, choking, drowning in his own blood. He clutched at the sand in suffocating desperation, as though it was a lifeline that could haul him to safety.

And then he was silent. A dark stain spread beneath his still body.

Dr Nageib tugged the canvas door aside and looked into the tomb.

"What happened?" said Coral. She had seen countless mummified corpses and skeletal remains but she had never seen someone die. She stared at Kamal's body. The maroon lake around his face had stopped spreading and was now soaking into the sand. His hair, once gloss black yet now so thick with dust that he appeared to be a much older man, was flickering.

A strong gust of wind cooled Coral's burning brow and spilled her own hair across her eyes. Grains of sand scuttled along Kamal's neck and under his shirt collar like tiny golden insects racing away from the sunlight.

"Pack up your things," said the Egyptian woman with a backward glance at the pyramid. "There's a sandstorm approaching. It is not safe to be here." She scraped back her hair and, with a set of long, steel hairpins clutched in her teeth, she set about fixing it tightly in a bun.

"But what about Mohammed?" asked Coral.

"Dead."

"Dead? How?" She looked down at Kamal. He was perfectly still. The wind was shooting tendrils of sand around his bloodied face, into his open eyes. The ground seemed to writhe under Coral's feet, as though the world was being ripped from under her. She felt the overwhelming urge to burst out crying. "But they can't be dead," she said. "Not just like that."

Dr Nageib's face was unreadable. Was it a frown of anguish, or a smirk? Behind her, the canvas door danced in the wind. To Coral, it looked as if something inside the tomb was trying to claw its way out; something that had become lumbering and ungainly from centuries of immobility.

"I can assure you they *are* dead, Miss Fletcher. As dead as that mummy in there." She nodded towards the tomb. "I have a little understanding of medical matters, but if your expertise exceeds mine in that field also, please feel free to examine them yourself."

The sand, lapping at Kamal's body like a swirling tide, had begun to shroud him in a fine layer of powder.

Coral pinched her eyes into slits and pulled her bandanna over her mouth. "What should we do about them? Should we move them?" she asked. "We can't just leave them like that."

"I think they are past caring, Miss Fletcher. Besides, it's their own stupid fault." A sudden gust struck and made her stagger a few steps. "I'm going back to the plane to contact Cairo on the radio. I suggest you find yourself a place to shelter from the storm."

Swirling clouds of sand were rapidly reducing visibility to an arm's length and the howling wind was drowning their voices so that both women had to shout to be heard. Apart from the Cessna, the tomb was the only possible refuge.

"What do you mean? How is this their own fault?" she shouted above the rising screech of the wind.

Dr Nageib jerked her head in the direction of the twitching canvas doorway. "The idiots tried to open the sarcophagus," she said. "They were supposed to be taking photographs and they decided to go a step too far. They broke the lid with a crowbar. Damned young fools."

Dr Nageib's icy indifference to the fate of her colleagues made Coral feel sick and she was almost overcome by the urge to shake the woman until she showed some emotion. "Two men are dead here, for God's sake!" she spat out in a shudder of tears. "To hell with the bloody sarcophagus. That hardly matters right now!"

"On the contrary," said Dr Nageib. "It is all that matters."

"You're crazy, you know that?" blurted Coral. "You can't even see the bloody plane anymore. You should stay here until the storm dies down. Make the call later."

"I'm still in charge of this expedition, Miss Fletcher," said Dr Nageib. "And I still make the decisions. Don't worry about me. I'm sure the plane is still in the same place we left it." Dr Nageib arranged her hair once more. Then, satisfied that it could withstand the mounting wind, she walked into the whirling dust.

"You blame me for this, don't you?" Coral called after her.

But Dr Nageib had already vanished from sight.

Tears welled up behind Coral's eyes and her throat tightened. She yelled, "Go to hell then, you callous bitch! I'd sooner ride out the storm with the dead than with a bitter old harpy like you!" But she knew her words would be snatched away by the wind long before they ever reached Dr Nageib.

Her outburst had drained her of energy and Coral felt jostled, bullied by the storm eddying around her. It reminded her of standing on a bustling railway platform in the rush hour.

That, in turn, made her think of the cool, quiet seclusion of her comfortably gloomy office at the British Museum.

A whip of sand slashed her face, knocking her back on her heels. Dr Nageib was right about one thing: she needed to get out of the sandstorm. Quickly.

Battling against the wind that threatened to send her reeling into the desert, Coral staggered to the tomb and pushed past the canvas door. Inside, at the base of the sarcophagus, bathed in the light of a storm lamp, lay Mohammed.

Coral leaned on the sarcophagus. "Miserable bitch," she heaved through her sobs.

Mohammed's pickaxe had shattered one corner of the stone coffin. Through a kaleidoscope of tears, Coral stared into the broken lid. Queen Kiya, disgraced and banished consort of the pharaoh Akhenaten, stared back at her.

In the three thousand years since her entombment, Kiya's skin had blackened and shrivelled. Her eyes had long since melted away and her lips had all but vanished, exposing ivory teeth clenched in a grimace. She looked as if she was in pain.

Coral cuffed away a dribbling tear. "How is any of this my fault? Tell me that." She reached into the coffin and touched Kiya's cheek. The queen's crumpled, age-stiffened skin was unexpectedly warm. Coral quickly moved her hand away. A frizz of hair showed beneath the remnants of Kiya's crown; hair that still bore the auburn tinge of henna dye.

"I bet you were a real looker, weren't you?" whispered Coral.

The crown was reminiscent of that worn by Nefertiti (another of Akhenaten's wives) in countless depictions: tall, blue and tapering slightly outward as it rose. It was adorned with a flattened band of gold. At the centre, a solid gold cobra. Around Kiya's neck, Coral could make out a wide golden necklace, decorated with precious stones of carmine red, aquamarine and azure. Mohammed's treasure.

The thick stone lid must have literally weighed a ton. No wonder it broke when Kamal and Mohammed tried to jemmy it open. She ran her hand along the fractured surface.

Her eyes followed the single band of hieroglyphs along the side of the otherwise plain stone coffin. And she noticed something. The pattern of the symbols was repeating. They had not had time to translate all of the ancient text earlier, assuming that unlike the simple dedication on the cartouche, it would be a long job for another day. She ran her fingers along the strip of pictograms, translating as she moved down the length of the sarcophagus. In contrast to the usual rambling list of exploits and exhortations found on similar coffins, this was just a single phrase, repeated over and over:

Death awaits all who disturb me.

She snatched her hand away as though she had touched a live wire.

Was it possible that they had invoked some kind of curse? Is that what had killed Mohammad and Kamal? The tabloids would lap this up, but the idea challenged everything Coral believed in. It was superstition of the very worst kind. Nevertheless, two men were dead. Of that there was no doubt. And they had died immediately after cracking open the sarcophagus. Cause and effect? Or just some hideous coincidence?

But if those who had opened Kiya's tomb were truly marked for death, then surely Dr Nageib was also cursed? As she had made clear to everyone, she was the leader of the expedition.

Coral envisaged Kiya rising from her stone grave and stalking the Egyptian as she cowered from the storm in the plane. "Good riddance!" she spat. But the mental image she had created made the hairs rise on the back of her neck. She disliked Dr Nageib, but she didn't want her dead. Besides, if Dr Nageib was a legitimate target of the curse, so was Coral.

The storm revived the cold of the desert night. Coral turned up the collar of her blouse and watched it rage from the relative safety of the tomb. The gusts of sand looked like shapeshifting creatures chasing each other back and forth across the desert, hunting down their quarry. The canvas doorway billowed noisily, just like her tent the night before. But her fright then had been nothing more than a momentary lapse of reason. Now she knew true fear; fear that gripped her insides and twisted them into a knot; fear that turned the sweat on her brow to ice water.

She sat down with her back to the sarcophagus and closed her eyes.

*

The makeshift door had been snatched away in the night while she slept. Coral shielded her face against the glare and stepped out into the furnace. The rising sun shone like polished brass over the eastern rim of the desert and illuminated a whole new landscape. To the west, a set of dunes the size of two-storey houses rose and fell like vast golden waves. They had not been there the day before.

And the plane was gone.

Coral was overcome with nausea as it dawned on her that Dr Nageib must have flown off without her. Then she caught sight of something behind the pyramid; something out of place, something surreal. A white column reached out of the sand and into the blazing sky like an icy finger defying the sun. It was the Cessna.

During the storm the plane had been thrown from its original location and had tumbled, nose over tail, until it was finally swallowed by the sand. The wings had been sheared away and its rear end was buried deep in a newly created dune. All that remained visible was the plane's stubby nose and the cockpit.

Coral could see Dr Nageib slumped against a cracked window. Her lifeless eyes, caked with dust and dried blood, gazed into the rising sun. "Oh Jesus," moaned Coral.

She looked around her. Of the tents, tables, lifting gear and other paraphernalia they had brought with them, there was no trace. Kamal's body was gone. Everything except the crippled plane had been sucked down into the Sahara's fathomless depths. All evidence of their presence, of their very existence, had been erased, as though they had been nothing more than chalk marks on a blackboard.

Coral stood motionless and gazed at the dead world that surrounded her. Nothing stirred. There was no breeze.

She heard a faint buzzing sound. For a second Coral wondered if it was the radio in the plane. She tilted her head. No, not the radio. It was coming from the tomb. She peered inside.

The flies had found Mohammed.

The temperature was rising by the minute, as though someone was steadily turning up the grill, and Coral could feel her hands and face starting to burn. A wave of dizziness washed over her. She was dehydrating. Her water bottle had given up its last drop during the night. Without a fresh supply she would join Mohammed, Kamal and Dr Nageib within a few hours.

Sweat dribbled down her face and she felt a tickle under the back of her collar. She swiped at it, expecting to find that the Sahara had wheedled its way inside her clothes. But when she brought her hand away she saw a tiny black dot stuck to her palm. The speck struggled to right itself and then leaped away from her, like a rat jumping ship.

Coral fancied she saw movement inside the dark interior of the tomb. A glint of pink gold. She seemed to be viewing the world through a twinkling crimson prism. Tears raced down her cheeks and she watched them drip onto the baking ground; hot, red tears that blackened to coal dust as they soaked into the sand.

Red tears?

Blood, thought Coral. *I'm crying blood*.

She laughed. She had been right, she realised. Penthu had fled the royal household, taking his mistress, Queen Kiya, with him. They were almost certainly accompanied by a band of accomplices; slaves, rebels or fellow worshippers of the old gods.

It all made sense now. Each segment of the narrative puzzle fell into place. The escape party was heading away from Amarna; a city fast imploding under the onslaught of bubonic plague. They had fled north towards the Mitanni kingdom. Along the way, Kiya had succumbed to disease and died. Penthu supervised the burial, the construction of this makeshift memorial to his queen, his lover.

Coral understood now that her idea of a romantic elopement and Dr Nageib's more prosaic hypothesis, firmly rooted in the grim reality of an epidemic, were not mutually exclusive theories after all. They were, in fact, entwined—symbiotic.

The infection-bearing fleas had been carried in Kiya's belongings all the way from Amarna, just waiting for someone to open the right crate, shake out the right garment; one of the queen's dresses perhaps, or a blanket.

For this was the mummy's curse: plague.

The sarcophagus lid was heavy but not hermetically sealed. Some of the fleas within must have made their way out of the tomb in search of fresh blood to sustain them in their new barren world. The escape bid of the deserters was doomed to failure. In the absence of succulent new hosts, they simply perished. In contrast, those loyal disease-carriers who remained nested inside the stone coffin with their queen would have fallen into a deep sleep, sustained by the relative humidity of their grim environment and by feeding sporadically on Kiya's slowly decaying carcass; sentinels, patiently awaiting due reward for their centuries of devotion, waiting for a warm, living creature to open the lid so that they could finally slake their thirst for fresh blood and pass on their legacy: infection. After aeons of abstinence, desperately eking out a meagre existence on the slim pickings of a tepid, fleshless corpse, how voracious their appetite must have become.

Coral thought of the inscription: *Death awaits all who disturb me.* "You weren't threatening us, were you, Kiya?" she whispered. "You were warning us."

As she felt her throat constrict, something else occurred to her. Penthu and his acolytes journeyed onward after the entombment of Kiya. They must have died, one by one, lost and forgotten in the vast expanse of the desert.

This time it would be different.

Coral and the rest of the expedition wouldn't be forgotten. The rescue plane might not arrive for another day. Maybe two days. But it would come. It was bound to come.

Coral knew that, by then, she would be dead. She had found the long-lost high queen, if not the priest she eloped with. She had even pieced together their story. But it was a story Coral would never live to tell. There would be no more excruciating meetings to endure and no microscope of publicity to cringe beneath.

Her skin itched. Whether it was sweat or sand or plague-bearing fleas, she didn't know. It didn't matter now. She coughed and spat more of her blood into the dust.

As she felt consciousness slip away, Coral wondered, *Along with the dead bodies, what else would the rescue party take back to civilisation?*

www.ingramcontent.com/pod-product-compliance
Lightning Source LLC
Chambersburg PA
CBHW022240020726
47496CB00004B/990